MURDER IN HAWAII

Books by Steve Allen

Bop Fables
Fourteen for Tonight
The Funny Men
Wry on the Rocks
The Girls on the Tenth Floor
The Question Man
Mark It and Strike It
Not All of Your Laughter, Not All of Your Tears
Letter to a Conservative
The Ground Is Our Table
Bigger Than a Breadbox
A Flash of Swallows
The Wake
Princess Snip-Snip and the Puppykittens
Curses!
What to Say When It Rains
Schmock!-Schmock!
Meeting of Minds
Chopped-Up Chinese
Ripoff: The Corruption that Plagues America
Meeting of Minds (Second Series)
Explaining China
Funny People
The Talk Show Murders
Beloved Son: A Story of the Jesus Cults
More Funny People
How to Make a Speech
How to Be Funny
Murder on the Glitter Box
The Passionate Nonsmoker's Bill of Rights (with Bill Adler, Jr.)
Dumbth, and 81 Ways to Make Americans Smarter
Meeting of Minds, Seasons I–IV in Four-Volume Set
The Public Hating: A Collection of Short Stories
Murder in Manhattan
Steve Allen on the Bible, Religion & Morality
Murder in Vegas
Hi-Ho, Steverino!
The Murder Game
More Steve Allen on the Bible, Religion & Morality
Make 'Em Laugh
Reflections
Murder on the Atlantic
The Man Who Turned Back the Clock and Other Short Stories
But Seriously . . .
Wake Up to Murder
Die Laughing
Dumbth: The Lost Art of Thinking
Where the Womblies Are
Murder in Hawaii

STEVE ALLEN

MURDER IN HAWAII

KENSINGTON BOOKS

http://www.kensingtonbooks.com

KENSINGTON BOOKS are published by

Kensington Publishing Corp.
850 Third Avenue
New York, NY 10022

Library of Congress Card Catalog Number: 98-066231
ISBN 1-57566-375-9

First Printing: January, 1999
10 9 8 7 6 5 4 3 2 1

Printed in the United States of America

chapter 1

"If you know what's good for you," I shouted at my wife, "you'll shut your mouth right now!"

"You don't frighten me!" she snapped back.

"I'm not trying to frighten you, dammit. I'm *warning* you."

"Warning me of *what*?"

"Well," I said, "about several things, although apparently the only one we agree on is a divorce."

"No," she shouted, "we probably agree about more than that. For example, I'm getting out of this house today. I can't take this insanity anymore."

"There's no reason you should," I rasped back. "There's no reason either of us should, and I'll be glad to get out, if that would make you any happier!"

"Hah," she said, "when did my happiness ever mean anything to you?"

At that point, hearing the sound of a footstep behind me, I whirled to see Martine Duchamps, a French foreign exchange student living with us for a few months, standing at the other end of the den, her face white in shock.

"Did you want something, Martine?" Jayne asked. Her voice was now lower in volume, but she was still breathing heavily.

"I'm sorry," Martine said. "I thought you'd want to know that a car is just coming into the driveway."

"Yes," I said. "I'm expecting Darryl from the office. Let him in, please, and tell him we'll be with him in a couple of minutes, as soon as we finish rehearsing."

Martine's jaw literally dropped open like that of a puppet. "Oh," she said. "I thought—I mean—"

Jayne burst out laughing. "Oh, my God," she said. "Didn't you know we were running over lines for a TV show?"

The three of us dissolved into hysterical laughter, and after a moment Martine retreated into the kitchen in profound embarrassment.

"Good Lord," I said, "the poor girl must have thought we'd gone crazy."

I opened the front door myself to admit Darryl Tanikawa, a member of my office staff who attends to activities connected with video and audio recording, keeps track of the details connected with my comedy and/or music concerts and the songs I write, and makes himself useful in numerous other ways as well.

He handed me a brown legal folder full of papers from the office, saying, "Gioia wanted me to remind you that the *Hawaiian Wave* show is on this evening. She also said to be sure to check the folder right away. Somebody tried to send a fax to your house, but your machine must be out of paper, so they sent it to the office."

"Okay, thanks," I said. "Make yourself comfortable for a few minutes while I sign the letters so you can take them back and get them mailed out."

"Hi, Darryl," Jayne said, approaching from the other end of the living room. "You won't believe what just happened. Steve and I were rehearsing lines from a script that's just been sent in to us. Martine overheard us and didn't realize it was a rehearsal."

That evening, promptly at eight o'clock, we seated ourselves in front of a TV screen in our living room and prepared to watch the new import from our fiftieth state.

The words *Hawaiian Wave* flashed across the screen over a moving aerial view of the island of Oahu. A classic Gabby Pahinui tune, one of my favorites, combining rock and island effects, accompanied the three-minute music video that followed. A visual montage of Hawaii served as the backdrop for the opening credits. It captured the feeling of life on Oahu, cutting from an office worker in a Honolulu high-rise to a *kau-kau* cart serving plate lunches from an empty lot near the beach. There were shots of a day care center with children of every color of the rainbow singing the chorus to Gabby's song. But my favorite clip was one of an old woman performing the hula, in slow, stately grace, for her family. They were gathered in the carport of their tract home, watching appreciatively from old sofas and lawn chairs pulled into a semicircle.

The opening credits of *Hawaiian Wave,* done MTV style, were part of what had distinguished the series from other detective shows and made it the smash hit of the fall TV season. I'd read that all the music used in the show was Hawaiian, and I was curious to hear how they'd integrated it. Just as this week's episode began, with a zoom into a little palm-shaded shack near the beach, the phone rang.

"Let the machine take it," Jayne prompted. "We can call back the minute the program ends."

I nodded in agreement, but couldn't resist wandering over to the telephone table to listen to the machine taking the call.

"Mr. Allen, Mrs. Allen, this is Billy . . . Billy Markham, remember me?" His voice sounded almost hysterical. "God, Mr. Allen, I hope you're there. Please pick up if you are. It's urgent."

I glanced in Jayne's direction as I reached for the receiver. We'd known Billy Markham since he was a child. He was now the star of *Hawaiian Wave,* and in fact was the main reason we had decided to watch tonight. Jayne smiled at me encouragingly, while making it clear that she was going to see the show, star or no star on the telephone. The sound went up a notch as she turned back toward the screen.

"Steve here, Billy. What a coincidence. We're just watching your show. Congratulations. From what I've read, you have a winner."

"Thank you, Mr. Allen. I'm just so glad you're there. I called because I'm in a real bind."

"Call me Steve, Billy, please. And fill me in. Is something wrong?"

"Everything, Mr. Allen, it couldn't be worse." Billy sounded even more distraught than he had on the answering machine. "Mom and Dad were supposed to be coming over this weekend to do a guest spot on the series. But Mom's come down with the killer flu and her doctor's afraid of complications. I wouldn't want her to do anything that might jeopardize her health. Dad doesn't want to leave her and, believe me, I understand. But we were really counting on them. So Dad suggested I call to see if you and Mrs. Allen could possibly come over and do the guest spot in their place. He thought you might enjoy the trip. It's a two-part episode, and I think you'll like your parts. And, honestly, Mr. Allen, it would really save my life. I've already spoken with the producer, suggesting you two, and he's really hyped on the idea. He's going to phone your agent tomorrow, but I wanted to call you myself first."

I should perhaps explain at this point that Billy Markham is the much-adored and somewhat overprotected youngest son of our dear friend Raymond Markham, star of stage, screen, and television. Raymond and his lovely wife, Bea, herself an actress in her youth, were two of our first and closest friends on the West Coast. Jayne and I have been so busy these last few years that we haven't seen as much of the Markhams as we used to; show business is like that. But we certainly noticed, and with pleasure, when their son rose to meteoric fame as the star of *Hawaiian Wave*. In fact, we had especially arranged to stay at home and catch the show in order to phone Raymond and Bea as soon as it was over, to talk about the program and congratulate them on Billy's success.

On the TV screen Billy's character, Jonathan MacCauley, better known as Mack, had just wandered into a tough-looking seamen's bar, where he was being attacked by two thugs with tattoos. His now-famous crooked grin, which had appeared on the cover of *People* magazine just that week, wasn't getting him very far at the moment with his assailants.

"Jayne and I appreciate the fact that you thought of us, Billy. I'm sure it's a wonderful opportunity, and we would enjoy appearing on your show another time. But, to tell you the truth, we've done a lot of traveling lately and—"

Billy interrupted in a tone of breathless urgency, in total contrast to the cool, unruffled Mack on my living room screen. "It's not just the show. I was really counting on someone coming over who could help me."

"Help you in what way, Billy?" On the screen help had come

for Mack in the shape of a muscular blond hunk who resembled Brad Pitt playing a lifeguard. Right behind him came a young Hawaiian, whose beach-boy good looks were enhanced by a slightly Asian cast to his features and a delicacy of movement. The bar scene turned into a free-for-all, fists flying and glass breaking, all to the ironic tune of a Hawaiian love song playing in the background.

". . . kill me."

"I'm sorry, Billy, I wasn't paying attention. What is killing you?"

"Someone is trying to kill me, Mr. Allen. I know it must sound crazy and melodramatic but, you know, it happens all the time. When you get to be a celebrity, all the nut cases come out of the closet and go after you. They obsess on you. Look at John Lennon, look at . . ."

At the moment I was looking at a commercial for Air Oahu. Why is it that my airplane never has that much legroom?

"All right, Billy. I hear you. Why don't you just slow down and tell me exactly what's happening. What makes you think someone is out to kill you?"

"Well, in the first place, I'm being stalked. Someone is follow-ing me wherever I go. I keep seeing the same redhead, with a crew cut. He's usually dressed in those elephant pants, you know, the kind skateboarders wear? And a huge, oversized shirt. I see him everywhere. I've tried to go after him, but he always slips away. He's short and that makes it hard. He even tails my car—he drives a green Volvo, four-door, old, you know, like early eight-ies. And two days ago, when I was leaving my new house, someone shot at me."

At that exact moment, shots rang out on the TV screen and a chase ensued through Waikiki. This time, instead of a car chase, it was a pedicab chase, just as exciting and much less dangerous to innocent bystanders.

"Did you call the police, Billy? It sounds like the sort of thing they need to know about. If this stalker is making himself so obvious, they ought to be able to apprehend him."

"Well, you know, Mr. Allen, the police here, they're different than the ones on the mainland, they, uh . . ."

"Go on, Billy. What did they say?"

"Well, I didn't call them this time because the *last* time they said they didn't want to hear from me again unless I had some real proof. I mean, what do they need, a body? I looked for the bullet shells, you know, like Mack does on the show, but there's a lot of grass in Waimanalo and . . ."

At the moment Mack was not in the grass, he was at sea, with his Hawaiian pal from the bar scene at the tiller of a beautiful little catamaran. I could almost feel the ocean spray, the scene was shot so vividly. I thought for a moment before replying to Billy's last piece of information.

"Don't you think it's possible that you're making too much of this? I'm all for reasonable caution. After all, you have become instantly recognizable and that can bring problems. But couldn't it have been a car backfiring that you heard? They can sound an awful lot like a gunshot. Is there a friend you can confide in, someone already on the spot who can help keep an eye out for this supposed stalker?"

Billy's voice came apart. "I understand, Mr. Allen, I really do. Dad suggested I call, but I know how busy you and Mrs. Allen are. I guess we aren't as close as we once were, when I used to pretend you were my uncle. I know I wasn't very good at letter-writing. . . ."

He knew how to pull out all the stops. And the truth of the matter is, he had written more regularly over the years than many of our young friends. On the TV screen, there was yet another commercial—Air Oahu was demonstrating how quickly and easily you could claim your luggage if you just traveled their airline. I didn't want to go anywhere, on any airline, at the moment. For months I'd been looking forward to a few quiet days at home. But I couldn't quite figure out how to say no to Billy. I was trying to think of which of our mutual friends I could suggest in our place, when Jayne left her cushioned throne to walk over and stand next to me.

"Tell Billy thank you," she stage-whispered. "I'd love a Hawaiian vacation. I can get my Christmas shopping done before Thanksgiving and we can see all our old friends. It's been ages since we were over for just a visit."

Jayne and I have, of course, visited the islands often over the years. In one instance, back when Jack Lord's *Hawaii Five-O* show was very popular, he invited her to play a role that required her to spend two weeks in the Honolulu area and, after completing some assignments of my own, I joined her for the second week. Jack and his wife, Marie, were gracious hosts. As his fans may recall, Jack was more than an actor, he also was a designer of jewelry. One evening he took us to one of the island's greatest restaurants. We had a meal that was unforgettable (except that I now of course forget it, so many years having passed) but what does remain clearly in the memory file is that as we were preparing to leave, Marie removed all the jewelry she was wearing—the necklace, the earrings, the bracelet—and handed them to Jack, who slipped them into a small bag he removed from his jacket pocket. Seeing the look of surprise on Jayne's face, Lord said, "It's a precaution we take against being robbed."

On that same trip Jack had put us up at a delightful condo/hotel. Kathryn and Arthur Murray, the famous dance teachers, were next-door neighbors, who took us to dinner another evening, at another superb restaurant. The food was so good that the next evening I dined there myself, alone, an occasion I recall largely because of a poem I wrote while sitting at the table overlooking the sea.

Another time Jayne and I were entertaining aboard a cruise liner, and when the ship stopped for a day at a Maui port we got off to soak up a bit of the local color and perhaps do a bit of shopping. Since no two people on earth share precisely the same interests, we quickly became separated, drifting in and out of local stores but keeping within a block of each other. On such jaunts I sometimes inspect the wares in women's shops so that I can direct Jayne to anything I've seen that she might enjoy wearing. I had spent about five minutes in one particular shop, some forty feet off the main street, and had seen some attractive shirts, blouses, and jackets. A few minutes later, when I found Jayne coming out of an art gallery, I said, "Don't miss the shop around the corner, the one with some Pucci-like jackets in the window." Seeing that she was following my advice, I seated myself on a nearby ledge, turned my brain to idle, and enjoyed the passing pedestrian parade. About two minutes later I heard a sound that shocked me into instant alertness, that of two women shrieking. Jumping up, I looked around to see from which direction the horrifying screams were coming and at once moved toward the source of the sound, which turned out to be the doorway of the shop in question. With so little evidence to go on, it was impossible to tell whether the women were being attacked, had made a grisly discovery, or were in some other sort of danger. Fortunately there was little time for speculation because the two women staggered out into the street, embracing each other, laughing and whooping like savages, if indeed savages do whoop any more loudly than the rest of us. The two were, I discovered, Jayne and a member of our extended family named Robin Rutherford. A dear girl, Robin is the daughter of my first wife, Dorothy. Our meeting was entirely by chance.

"But this won't be just a visit," I whispered back, putting my hand over the receiver as the memories faded away.

Jayne gently extricated the phone from my grip. "Hi, Billy," she said in her most warm and motherly tone. "Why don't you reserve us one of those lovely oceanview rooms at the Royal Hawaiian, in the historic wing. You can tell your producer to phone our agent and we'll work out all the details."

"Oh, Mrs. Allen, I can't tell you how relieved I am. Thank you!"

"My pleasure, dear. But do call me Jayne. We're both adults now. And tell me a bit about our role. Who are we going to play?"

"You'll be playing the owners of a string of polo ponies. They're the . . . uh, bad guys."

"We're the villains, Steve," Jayne whispered in my direction.

"Great!" I replied sarcastically. On the TV screen, the villains in this week's episode were being fished out of Honolulu harbor. I hated to think what might be in store for us!

The part about playing heavies, as they're called in the trade, was actually a plus rather than a minus. Almost any actor or actress has more fun playing a despicable character than a straight arrow.

chapter 2

Honolulu International Airport was in pandemonium. Hawaii used to have an off season, but with the influx of tourists and businesspeople from Japan, Australia, Southeast Asia, and all parts of Europe, that is no longer the case. There seemed to be at least three greeters for every passenger stepping through the debarkation tunnel into the waiting area. Their arms dripping with flower leis, they waved signs with hastily scribbled names in every language imaginable and descended on their guests, crying "Aloha" at the first sign of recognition. There was a large and well-dressed group who had a horsy look—one of the women was actually carrying a bridle. They seemed to be meeting a team of some sort, perhaps a polo team. The smell of orchids permeated the air, along with the distinctive odor of teriyaki chicken and barbecue beef.

As Jayne and I looked around for Billy, I noticed a group of Hawaiians in flowered shirts and flowing muumuus having what looked like a full-fledged luau on the plastic chairs in the next waiting area. A hand suddenly appeared over the tops of their heads and a familiar voice shouted, "Mrs. Allen, Mr. Allen, over here!"

It was Billy Markham, emerging from a pack of adoring fans. He looked older than I remembered him, of course, but younger than he had on the TV screen. He really was handsome, in a boy-next-door sort of way that had proved appealing to viewers of all ages. I could see why one reviewer had called him "the son or grandson everyone wishes they had." He rushed over now to deliver a hurried hug to each of us. Then he lifted two rather wilted-looking specimens of plumeria lei from around his neck and "leied" each of us in turn, accompanying the gesture with a kiss on the cheek.

"I made them myself," he announced proudly. "I have plumeria trees in the yard at my new house. It's traditional, you know, to make the lei yourself for the person you want to honor. I had to make them last night, though, and I'm afraid they wilted a little."

"They're just lovely, dear," Jayne said as she made appreciative sniffing gestures toward her flower necklace. Actually, they did smell wonderful despite their appearance. More than anything I can think of, the scent of plumeria means Hawaii to me.

I noticed that the group Billy had just left was still keeping tabs on him. There were a couple of dozen in the party, men, women, and children. They were talking, eating, and laughing, but with an air of expectation. One or two of the younger men had begun to serenade the group with soft, melodic tunes strummed on battered ukuleles. Billy guided us in their general direction.

"I hope you don't mind if we go back to have just one more picture together. They've been so helpful, keeping everyone away and plying me with food and drink. I get very nervous in airports, even when I'm not the one flying. And I left Bertrand, my new bodyguard, at home to prepare for your arrival. He's more than a bodyguard, actually, he does everything. I was very lucky to get him."

As we joined Billy's newfound friends, greeted by a chorus of smiles and "alohas" and a few more flower leis, I realized that the group was clustered around a very old and very large woman occupying three waiting room chairs, if you counted her voluminous muumuu. She was so bedecked in flower leis that the only features visible were two alert, amused eyes and a crown of wavy black hair. Billy made the introductions.

"This is Ma Kapihalua. She's taking her first trip off the island, to Cleveland, to visit her great-granddaughter. Ma, I'd like you to meet Steve Allen and Mrs. Allen, better known as Jayne Meadows."

"I'm very pleased to meet you," came a muffled response from under the mountain of flowers.

We had several pictures taken all together, after which I asked to see the Kamaka ukulele one of the young men had been playing. The Kamaka is the Stradivarius of ukuleles, and I was hoping to have time to visit the factory where the sons and grandsons of the original Mr. Kamaka still turn out the beautiful koa-wood instruments in the tradition of the founder. The young man seemed to enjoy my interest and played us a particularly haunting melody as we said our good-byes and headed toward the main terminal.

Billy immediately slipped between Jayne and me, being careful to keep in step with our progress.

"I hope you don't mind, but people recognize me. I still forget that, you know, it's all so recent. Two months ago, if I'd walked through this concourse, I'd have been as anonymous as that man over there." Billy waved his hand in the general direction of a party making its way slowly toward the exit, led by a distinguished-looking man in his sixties. It was the horsy set I'd noticed when we first left the plane.

Jayne and I tried to do our part, camouflaging Billy as best we could. People still tried to stop us with the ubiquitous "Aren't you . . ." but we shook our heads in a stern, businesslike manner and kept moving.

"Let me carry your bag for you, Mrs. Allen," Billy offered gallantly when he noticed the heavy load hanging off Jayne's right shoulder. I smiled as she replied with a straight face, "It's very kind of you to offer, dear, but that's my purse."

Despite our delays in the terminal, the baggage claim area for our flight had yet to come to life. Billy was beginning to look cautiously relaxed.

"I'm so glad you're here, I can't begin to tell you," he said with a sigh. "I mean, I don't want to scare you, but your airline just laid off five hundred employees in maintenance. The next time you want to go somewhere, check with me first. I can get you the latest update on which airline has the best safety record."

I let out an involuntary groan, wondering to myself whether I was too late for the turnaround flight back to Burbank. Jayne shot me an accusing glance; I think she reads my mind. She responded to Billy with a sympathetic smile.

"I guess I'm terrified of flying," he admitted. "My God, there are so many things to worry about on an airplane—bombs, the wings icing up, sea gulls getting sucked into the engines."

"Then it must be hard for you to do all the traveling required for the show," Jayne said. "I presume you do some of the interiors back in Hollywood?"

"Actually, Aunt Jayne, that's one of the great things about *Hawaiian Wave.* There's a real commitment to employing local talent, at all levels of production. Everything is done right here on Oahu. And when I do have to fly, I take these magic pills the doctor gave me."

Wondering how my wife had managed to make it from "Mrs. Allen" to "Aunt Jayne," I started paying more attention. It was Aunt Jayne who had won me over to this trip in the first place. For some reason I had never entirely understood, Billy had always looked up to us, from the time he was a toddler, and Jayne thought we might be able to help him through this crucial adjustment period. She agreed with me that he was probably imagining things and in no real danger. Perhaps we could help him to see that and to come to terms with the stresses of instant stardom. Billy had done a bit of acting in college, and later worked in summer stock and community theater, but nothing had prepared him for the notoriety conferred on the star of a hit TV series.

A crowd had collected around us by this time. Jayne was managing to keep the fans at bay with a nonstop torrent of conversation directed toward Billy and an occasional scowl in the general direction of anyone who looked as though he might be about to interrupt. The conveyor belt finally started moving and the first bags began to spit out of the center of the carousel. The people around us drifted away to look for their luggage. Personally, I can travel with one suitcase when I have to, but Jayne's idea of traveling light is keeping the overweight charges down to less than our yearly income. As I began pulling our luggage off the belt, I noticed Billy eyeing it with increasing alarm.

"Uh, is that really all yours?" he finally ventured.

Jayne laughed reassuringly. "Don't worry. Only the first five are full. The rest are for the Christmas presents I'm going to take back. It'll be such fun to give people something a little different this year. Can you still get those wonderful—"

"Aunt Jayne? I hate to tell you this, but I have kind of a small car. I think we're going to need a taxi to take the luggage. You stay here with the bags. I'll go arrange the cab and get a skycap to help us carry everything."

"I'll come with you," I said quickly. I couldn't wait to stretch my legs and get my first real whiff of Hawaiian air. We stepped through the automatic doors into the moist, tropical aroma that even car exhaust couldn't entirely dominate. We have palm trees in Southern California, of course, but somehow they aren't the same as Hawaiian palm trees. L.A. palms are made for spotlights. Hawaiian palms are made for luaus, ocean breezes, and music.

Suddenly Billy grabbed my arm in a viselike grip. "There, Steve, there! Did you see him? It's the red-haired guy I told you about!"

I looked quickly in every direction, scrutinizing the crowd for any sign of a redhead with a crew cut. There was no one who fit the description of Billy's supposed stalker.

"I'm sorry, Billy, I don't see him."

"He was there, Steve, I swear he was, over in the parking garage. But he's gone now. I wish you could see him, just once. I know it's hard for you to believe until you've actually seen him."

Not hard at all, I wanted to say. We can manufacture all kinds of terrors for ourselves when we need to. Why, I once knew a woman who was phobic about . . .

But my train of thought was interrupted by an unusual darting movement near the elevator in the parking area directly across from us. A slim figure in baggy pants and huge T-shirt slipped into the elevator just as the door was closing. The hair was cut very short and you couldn't mistake the color: carrot-top red.

chapter 3

"This is it," Billy announced with obvious satisfaction, his left arm outstretched toward his car. "Isn't she a beauty? I've wanted one of these ever since I was a kid and our gardener had one."

We stood facing a 1967 pale pink Karmann-Ghia convertible. The body work was in perfect condition. Not exactly *my* sort of car, but I could understand its allure—as long as I didn't have to try to get into it.

"I can see why you sent the luggage ahead in a cab," I told him.

"I think it's cute," Jayne said valiantly. "I've always loved convertibles." Liar, I thought.

"Who wants to ride in front?" Billy asked, walking around to the passenger side of the car and opening the door. "Actually, it should probably be you, Aunt Jayne. The backseat passenger gets pretty windblown."

"Right," I said a little too loudly. I opened the driver's door, squeezed through the opening, and somehow managed to pretzel myself into the cramped space they call a backseat in these cars. Maybe human beings were smaller in 1967. Jayne settled into the front with admirable grace, considering that her purse took up most of the leg room.

"Seat belt," I hissed in her ear.

"You all want the top up?" Billy asked as he slid his lanky frame behind the steering wheel.

"I think down is fine, don't you, Jayne?" Windblown, it seemed to me, was preferable to riding with my nose on my chest.

"Fine, dear," Jayne replied, wrapping a Givenchy scarf around her hair and smiling bravely.

It wasn't until we pulled out of the airport and headed toward the Lunalilo Freeway instead of the Nimitz Highway that I began to suspect we weren't headed toward the Royal Hawaiian Hotel.

"Where are we going, Billy?" I shouted into the wind.

"I thought we'd stop off at my house first. I can't wait to show it to you. It's the first house I've ever really had to myself. It's not very fancy, just your standard three bedroom, two bath. But it's close to the beach, you can see the ocean from the front porch, what they call a lanai here. And there's a real garage, with an apartment over it, where Bertrand lives."

Billy was yelling in my direction, half turned around in his seat. In the open car it was still difficult to catch every word. "Bertrand's a great guy, but, to tell you the truth, he intimidates me a little. I mean . . . well, you'll see for yourself. The house came with a state-of-the-art security system already installed. Wait till you see it. Even my parents never had protection anything like what I got."

I was tempted to say there's a reason for that; they're not paranoid. But then I remembered my glimpse of the phantom redhead at the airport. I'd chosen not to say anything to either Billy or Jayne about it, but I could no longer completely discount Billy's fears.

"Car feel OK?" I asked Billy a few minutes later. He seemed to be driving very erratically, speeding up, then slowing down, passing everything in sight, then just sitting back behind a slow-moving semitrailer truck. I couldn't tell if the problem was with the car or the driver, but I suspected the latter.

"The car's fine, Steve," Billy shouted back at me. "I just want to make sure we're not being followed. Evasive action, you know."

It didn't take long for my squinched legs to go completely to sleep, kneecaps closer to my chin than they should ever be outside a yoga class. But I forgot my discomfort when we turned off the freeway and headed *mauka* on the Pali Highway or was it *pali* on the Mauka Highway? No one on Oahu uses the designations north, south, east, and west. North is *mauka,* "toward the mountains," south is *makai,* "toward the sea." "Diamond Head" means east, toward that famous landmark, and *ewa* is west, toward the suburb of the same name. Even more confusing, on the Pali Highway one is actually traveling east, toward the windward side of the island. But the locals refer to it as going *mauka,* since you're heading toward the magnificent range of jungle mountains known as the Koolaus.

"Oh, look, Steve!" Jayne cried as we passed a fantastic structure on our right. It combined several eastern architectural styles into something that looked as if it had stepped straight out of *The Arabian Nights.*

"That's a Buddhist temple built in 1918," Billy shouted in her direction.

"Shin sect, built to commemorate the seven hundredth anniversary of their founding," I mumbled into the wind. Jayne had been reading Hawaiian guidebooks out loud to me for the last three days.

"Could we take the Nuuanu Pali Drive, since we're up here?" she asked Billy, who nodded with delight. She looked back at me sympathetically as I tried in vain to move to a new position. I grimaced politely and said I'd love a little detour. And actually, it was worth the pain, almost. We wound through a tropical rain forest, under spreading banyan trees and past groves of giant bamboo. The road passed beautiful old estates built by the first haole, or non-Hawaiian residents, called *kamaaina.* It rejoined the highway on the far side of the Nuuanu Reservoir. We continued to climb until Billy pulled off, again at my wife's request, to view the island from the Nuuanu Pali Lookout.

"Ohhhhh! Ahhhhhh!" These were not screams of panic, not even exclamations of wonder at the magnificent site in front of us. They were expressions of relief to be standing upright. I toyed vaguely with the idea of walking the rest of the way to Billy's house.

Billy pulled a jacket out of the trunk and put it over Jayne's shoulders. It was cold up here and very windy, but I was so relieved to be out of the car, I didn't mind. When Billy offered me a second windbreaker, I declined.

"Don't go too close to the edge," he warned Jayne, taking

hold of her arm nervously. Looking down myself, I was reminded of the one time in Billy's childhood when he was in real danger. He had fallen off a cliff while climbing a fairly challenging rock face with friends at a summer camp in Flagstaff, Arizona. He was no more than eleven or twelve as I remember, and it took the rescuers quite a while to reach him and get him down to medical attention. He had seriously injured his knee, and the doctors later told his parents that he must have been in a great deal of pain. But he hadn't made a sound except to let the rescuers know where he was. He didn't cry even when he knew he was safe. He was laid up for weeks and on crutches for weeks after that, but he hadn't once complained. Odd, and yet somehow typical of human nature.

Jayne came over and slipped her arm through mine. "Isn't this magnificent, dear? Look at that!" I had to agree that the view was breathtaking—the steep walls of the Koolau mountains falling away on either side, the emerald-green Haiku Valley stretching out toward Kaneohe Bay. It was a clear afternoon and we could see Mokapu peninsula and the towns of Kaneohe and Kailua that it separates.

"Waimanalo is over there," Billy called to us, pointing past Kailua to the south. "They say that King Kamehameha drove his enemies over these thousand-foot cliffs to gain control of the island."

"In 1795," Jayne and I said together, laughing. Billy came over next to us and Jayne put her free arm around him. "When I told our friends we were coming to Hawaii," she continued, "some of them said they hoped we'd skip Oahu all together and go straight to Maui, or Kauai, or even the Big Island. Those are all wonderful islands, of course, but Oahu is still my favorite."

We hated to tear ourselves from the view, but finally Billy said, "I guess we'd better be going before it gets to be the rush hour. The traffic can really be murder on this island."

As we turned toward the car I noticed a green Volvo drive past the parking lot. It fit the description, early eighties model, four-door, somewhat battered. Just a coincidence, I thought. There are probably a lot of green Volvos on an island this size.

Jayne headed straight for the driver's side of the car and resolutely wriggled and squirmed her way into the backseat.

"It's my turn," she said. "If you could just pass me my purse, I'll be set." I considered offering to keep it up front, but decided, on second thought, that it might function as a windbreak for her. Jayne tightened her scarf and gave me her best trooper smile.

"You sure you're going to be all right back there, Aunt Jayne?" Billy asked with a slightly disapproving look in my direction.

"Yes, dear. And just plain Jayne would be fine. I've lost the habit of hearing Aunt Jayne."

Nicely done, I thought.

We were soon under way again, headed back out to the highway for the trip down the far side of the mountains. I kept a vague eye on the side mirror, just to make sure the green Volvo wasn't behind us, while I tried to make conversation with Billy. It wasn't quite as difficult to talk over the wind now that I was in the front. But we still had to shout.

"So tell me more about this double episode of *Hawaiian Wave* we're about to appear in. You mentioned that shooting starts Tuesday morning. Do we have many lines to memorize by then?" I asked. Generally, of course, neither Jayne nor I would consider doing a show where we had not had a chance to read the script in advance—we had agreed in this instance only because Billy, whom we had known since he was in diapers, had been in such dire need. Nevertheless, I was not happy with the situation. Scripts were supposed to have been sent to our L.A. home by yesterday, but a production assistant had phoned to say the writer was making last-minute revisions and pages would be waiting for us in Hawaii. I have sometimes been called the King of Ad Lib, but frankly this was a little stressful and inconvenient; the only thing I knew about our two-part episode was that it concerned polo and Jayne and I were the bad guys. "I trust the scripts have been delivered to our hotel room so we can look them over this evening," I said to Billy in the most severe tone I could muster.

"Oh, don't worry, I've got it all taken care of. This part will be a breeze for pros like you two. Actually, I have your scripts at my house. We can go over everything together, after we've had something to eat."

"That sounds fine. But I wouldn't mind a little synopsis of the plot right now, if you know it yourself."

"Sure, Steve. Like I said, the story is set in the world of polo. It's technically an amateur sport, you know, but here in Hawaii it has some passionate followers. There are people who live for polo and spend almost every cent they have on their horses. There's also quite a bit of gambling on the outcome of the matches, which figures in our story. The script was written by a local haole, Dick Schiller. It's a real break for him, you know, a chance to get a big commercial screenwriting credit. He's a pretty strange guy though. Someone on the show recommended him. *Hawaiian Wave* is like that. There are a lot of creative people on this island who would never have gotten a chance at the big time if it weren't for—"

"This is all very interesting, Billy, but back to the plot of our double episode. Where do we fit into the polo theme?"

"Oh, you play the Brents. You're very rich owners of a string of polo ponies. The ponies are just beautiful, Steve, have you ever seen them? They're a mix of Thoroughbred and—"

"Billy?"

"Sorry. Anyway, the show opens with a polo match, lots of action, music, atmosphere, Edgar likes all that. You've heard of Edgar, I'm sure. Edgar Min? A lot of people credit him with the success of the show. He's a real genius. Anyway, one of their horses falls during the match, the Brents' horse, that is. The rider is injured and they lose the match. They call in Mack to investigate. They tell him they suspect their horse was doped and they want Mack to find out who did it. They imply that it might have been someone settling an old grudge. But that's just to put him on a false trail. Because actually, you see, it will turn out that they're the ones who are doping their horses. They hired Mack only to throw suspicion off themselves."

"Sounds like a nice couple we're playing. Why are we involved in this perfidious activity?"

"The brakes, oh, my God, the brakes!" Billy screamed through clenched teeth.

"What?" I was trying to figure out what the brakes had to do with my character. Maybe he thought he never got the breaks he deserved? And then I noticed that we seemed to be accelerating into the approaching hairpin turn.

"The brakes, Steve! I don't have any brakes!" Billy screamed again. I could see from the frantic pumping of his right leg that he was no longer talking about the script. We were careening down the steep slope of the Pali Highway in a toy car with no brakes.

chapter 4

"**F**asten your seat belt!" I called to Jayne in the backseat.

"There *is* no seat belt in the backseat," Jayne reminded me in what seemed an astonishingly calm voice, given the circumstances. "In fact, darling, there's hardly even a backseat in the backseat."

"Swell . . . try downshifting!" I cried at Billy.

His eyes were glazed. "We're going to die, Steve, I just know it."

I reached down with my left hand to make sure that Billy wasn't pumping the gas pedal in his panic. He was on the brake pedal all right, but he was steering us off the road, so I leaned over and started driving the car from the passenger side. It was the first time all day I'd been grateful to be six feet three.

"Let go of the steering wheel, Billy!" I ordered, prying his fingers loose one by one. He seemed to be paralyzed with fear. With judicious use of the emergency brake, which thankfully did work, and a zigzagging trajectory, I managed to keep us more or less on the road and gradually slow the car down. I got off the highway at the first pullout and brought the car to a complete stop by driving into a field of high weeds next to a roadside rest room.

"Perfect timing, dear," Jayne said as she squirmed her way out of the backseat and made a beeline for the door marked WOMEN. I straightened up and turned to see how Billy was doing.

"Well, that woke me up. Doesn't look like we did the car much damage, at least. When was the last time you had your brakes checked, Billy?'' There was no sound or movement from the driver's side. I got out to stretch and take a look under the car. Jayne returned, flashed me a grateful smile, and went over to check on Billy.

"It's over now," she said softly, peering into his glazed eyes. "We're fine, everything is OK. It was a near miss, but near misses happen all the time. They count as misses. Talk to me, Billy."

"You saved my life," he finally managed to say, in an awestruck voice, looking over Jayne's shoulder at me. "You saved all our lives. We could all be dead right now."

"We were lucky, that's all. There was very little traffic coming the other way this time of day." I didn't want Billy to start thinking of me as indispensable.

A battered pickup truck drove into the pullout and stopped next to us. The cab was stuffed with young men, and surfboards were sticking out of the back. I stepped over to the open passenger window.

"Could you give me a ride to the nearest telephone, so I can call a towtruck?" I asked, dubiously eyeing the various limbs hanging out the window and noting a rather herbal smell emanating from the ashtray.

"Hey, no need, brah," said a voice from somewhere in the tangle as a cellular phone appeared out the window.

"What's your Triple A number, Billy?" I called back at him.

"What, Steve, what do you need?"

"Never mind," I grumbled to myself as I pulled my card out of my wallet. "I was driving anyway." After making my call, I thanked the young men and passed their phone back through the open window.

"That your car, man?" a voice from out of the depths of the pickup asked. "Cherry. What's it doing over in the weeds?" Another voice, closer to the window, added, "That your son over there? He looks like that dude on *Hawaiian Wave*. Bet people tell him that all the time, huh?"

"All the time," I replied. "He hates it."

The tow truck arrived twenty minutes later, followed by the cab I'd asked Triple A to call for us. Billy suggested a garage in Kailua he'd heard about. We stood and watched while the Karmann-Ghia was trussed up and hauled off, then we got into the waiting taxi. Billy offered to ride in front with the driver and immediately twisted around to tell us, for the twentieth time, how much he owed us.

"I still can't believe it, you know, I just can't believe it. If it wasn't for you, I'd be dead. At least now you know what I've been living with. Someone is out to kill me." His voice began to rise dangerously. "I don't know who, I don't know why, I—"

"Billy, you need to get hold of yourself, dear," Jayne interrupted, speaking very calmly. "Why don't we wait and see what the mechanic has to say about the car tomorrow. Brakes do fail sometimes, for all sorts of reasons. Let's not assume the worst until we have more information."

Billy nodded and slumped down in his seat, facing the road. Jayne and I exchanged uncomfortable glances in the back. It was hard to know what else to say. Even the cabbie couldn't quite bring himself to come out with "Enjoying your visit to Hawaii?"

"Let's get back to the story line," I suggested finally, hoping to put Billy's mind on something other than death. "You were telling us about the show."

"The show?" He seemed to come back from a great distance. "OK . . . where was I?"

"We—the Brents, that is—had just called in Mack to throw suspicion off ourselves for doping our own horses before a polo match. I don't ride in these matches myself, do I?"

"What? Uh, no, you don't ride. You tell Mack that you used to ride, but now you hire jockeys, the best you can get here on the islands. They're from Maui, you know, the best jockeys . . . where was I? Well, anyway, you have a reputation for going to any length to see to it that your team wins. That's why it looks like someone is out to get you and no one suspects you of doping your own horses in order to lose."

"And why do we want to lose?" Jayne asked.

"I'm getting there, honestly." Billy was relaxing just a little. He even smiled at himself. "So, toward the end of the first part of the episode, a groom turns up dead. The Brents act like they're really worried. They call in Mack again and ask him to find the killer. But it will turn out that they killed the groom themselves.

He was blackmailing them, see, trying to extort money for keeping quiet about the fact that he'd been instructed to dope their horses." Billy turned around in his seat to face Jayne. "They've been rigging the matches so they can bet against themselves in private, very high-stakes gambling pools. The betting odds are on their own team, which has always been the best on the island, so they can make a lot of money betting against themselves on the matches that they fix."

"I see," said Jayne as if she didn't see at all. "But why do they need to win a lot of money. I thought they were rich?"

"They are, but they've been spending above their means. It'll come out that one reason their living expenses are so high is that they've always insisted on the best of everything for their nineteen-year-old deaf daughter. We're using a real deaf actress for the part. I mean, she's not a professional actress, but she's done some amateur plays at her school. She teaches at the local school for the deaf. Her name's Susan Harrington and she's gorgeous. We've already shot some of our scenes together and she's great to work with too. She's started to teach me sign language. I thought of asking her out, but I don't think she's interested in me that way. I didn't realize, before the show took off like it did, what it would do to my personal life. The kind of girl that goes after a big star, you know, the groupies, don't really appeal to me. And the girls— women, I should say—who are more my type, like Susan, are intimidated by the idea of going out with a celebrity. Although, in Susan's case, that may not be all of it. I think she has a crush on Keoni."

"Who is Keoni again?" I asked. "I don't recall your mentioning that name."

"You remember, Steve," Jayne joined in. "He's the actor who plays Buddy Kahiluani, Mack's friend, the one with the catamaran mai tai cruise. Didn't I read somewhere that Keoni is involved in Hawaiian music?"

"Yeah, he's really into the music thing, and he's a nice enough guy. But you wouldn't believe the way the women just hang off him. He's an ethnic Hawaiian, of course, and has all that island charm and good looks to the max."

"Back to the script," I persisted. "I want to know how my deaf daughter figures in this whole thing?"

"Sure, Steve, but we're getting near the house now." While we were talking, the taxi had carried us past Kailua and through Waimanalo.

"Turn here," Billy directed the driver, pointing down an inconspicuous dirt road. We bumped along in first gear toward the beach, past huge ironwood trees on one side of the road and a grove of coconut palms on the other.

"There it is!" Billy announced as we came out into a grassy clearing that faced the beach. "Isn't it a beauty?"

The setting was certainly beautiful. A white sand beach, nearly deserted, stretched as far as the eye could see in both directions. Lush tropical vegetation framed the house and yard. Behind us, the Koolau mountains, crowned by cumulus clouds just beginning to catch the first colors of sunset, formed a spectacular backdrop. But Billy was pointing to the one part of this idyllic picture that didn't fit: a ten-foot-high fence that looked electrified and sported razor wire rolling across the top like a wave. The fence enclosed a house, a yard, and a very unfriendly-looking German shepherd. The house itself was quite pretty and old-fashioned, a kind of island version of Victorian. There was a modest entrance *mauka,* or mountain side, and *makai,* toward the sea, sliding glass doors opened onto a long lanai, with steps down to a path that led to the front gate. It was a frame house, painted white, not exactly my own island fantasy, but it would have been pleasant enough if it weren't for the spotlights and security cameras mounted all along the eaves. There were more spotlights scattered around the yard and warning signs everywhere. BEWARE OF VICIOUS DOG. BEWARE, SECURITY SYSTEM ACTIVATED, BEWARE! Billy seemed oblivious of our dismay.

"Incredible, isn't it, Steve? It came this way; I didn't have to do a thing to it. I'm thinking of planting some flowers, you know, might even put in a swimming pool one of these days. But swimming pools always make me think of William Holden floating facedown, in *Sunset Boulevard,* you know?"

"Mmm. It must be hard to take a shower as well, without Janet Leigh popping up."

"What?"

"Nothing. Who built this place, Billy, a drug lord, or Ferdinand and Imelda?"

"Oh, the Marcos's home was ten times this size, Steve, and it was in Makiki Heights, outside Honolulu. You're not so far off on your other guess though. The original owner of my house is in prison at the moment. He was growing marijuana in the mountains and shipping it out to the mainland from here. Occasionally somebody still comes by, who hasn't heard, you know, asking if they can bum a little leaf. That's one reason I decided to keep Bertrand on."

"Bertrand. What a nice name," Jayne managed to say, making an attempt at a smile. She looked even more dismayed than I was at the sight of the concentration camp Billy so fondly called home.

"Yeah, Bertrand comes very highly recommended by his former employer, but . . . well, here he is. You can see for yourself."

The glass door slid open and a young Samoan stepped out onto the lanai and started down the stairs to greet us. He was barefoot and barechested and must have weighed at least three hundred pounds. The only clothing he wore was a piece of material wrapped around his waist that hung down to his ankles like a long, print skirt. There was a huge unsheathed machete hanging from the belt that kept his skirt in place; even from a distance, I could sense the cold sharpness of the blade.

"Better smile at him, Steve," Billy urged quietly. "Bertrand gets upset when people aren't friendly."

Jayne and I both smiled like crazy. Who says Californians aren't friendly?

chapter 5

Our cabdriver did a serious double take when he saw Bertrand and clearly wanted to make a hasty exit almost as badly as I did.

"How's about I drop you off here, that all right with you?" he asked, stopping the taxi at the gate.

"This will be fine, we need the exercise," I answered for Billy. I was already halfway out of the car. Who knew what would be involved in getting our car through the Brandenburg Gate? Besides, I was eager to begin making friends with the German shepherd who was eyeing us through the fence as if he'd just spotted dinner. Billy paid the driver as Bertrand came down the path to open a small side gate for us with one of the keys on a huge chain clipped to his skirt. He brought the dog to heel.

"Welcome Mr. Allen, Mrs. Allen. I'm honored to make your acquaintance," he said with a small bow and an unexpectedly cultivated voice. "I've read your books with such pleasure, Mr. Allen. I hope we'll have the opportunity while you're here to discuss some of the issues you've raised."

"In *Die Laughing*, you mean?" I was trying to think of any issues I might have raised in this latest in a series of books I've written, based on real-life mysteries I've found myself involved in over the years.

"Oh, no, Mr. Allen. I'm sure that was a fascinating book, but I don't read mysteries, not even true-life ones. I was referring to *Rip-off: The Corruption That Plagues America.* That was one of my favorites," Bertrand said as we made our way slowly toward the house.

Literary conversation was fine and dandy, but meanwhile it was hard to keep my gaze from the lethal-looking machete in his belt. "Is that a letter opener, or do you use it to trim the lawn?" I asked.

His smile was subtle. "Occasionally problems arise, even here in paradise." He turned toward Billy. "Did you have engine trouble, Mr. Markham?"

"We'll tell you all about it," Billy answered, bounding up the steps onto the lanai. "But first , we're starving—do you think you could take the pickup truck and get us a couple of platters of takeaway sushi with plenty of wasabi?"

"Right away, sir." Bertrand turned on his bare heel and headed toward the garage at the back end of the house, the dog at his side.

Jayne wanted a tour of the house, of course, which I left her and Billy to do on their own. I stayed in the living room, studying the pictures on the walls. Most of them were of the Markham family growing up: Billy's two older sisters posed possessively with their baby brother. Raymond and Bea looking the way they had when we first met them. And one that was really cute of Billy, aged six, with a shaggy dog named Einstein that the family used to have. The photos reminded me that the Markhams were old friends and that I should be patient with Billy. But it wasn't easy. I was starting to hope that none of my other old friends had children who had grown up to become TV stars.

I settled into an armchair facing the beach and watched the sky over the water turn salmon-pink and gold. I wondered if Billy had picked out the furniture himself or if it had come with the house. It was rattan, but the most comfortable rattan I've ever seen. My armchair was big, solid, and amply cushioned. Even the sofa looked sturdy and large enough to hold three people comfortably. I was just imagining to myself what life with the previous tenant, the drug lord, might have been like, when Billy and Jayne came back into the living room. Billy was carrying a huge frosted glass in each hand. Jayne was holding a third, which she was already sipping from.

"Mmmm, mango and papaya with just a hint of orange. It's perfect." She smiled as she settled herself into the chair next to mine.

I nodded my agreement as I turned toward Billy. "Before I forget, what is the name of the dog?"

"Oh, that's Killer. He adores Bertrand and always whines when he leaves the grounds."

"Is he safe around people he doesn't know? Like us, for example?"

"Oh, I think so. He's attack-trained, of course, that's why I have him. But as long as Bertrand is around, you don't have anything to worry about." I refrained from mentioning that Bertrand wasn't around at the moment. Hopefully, we would have no call to exit the house suddenly.

"The biggest problem I have with Killer is his habit of lying down right under your feet, in the middle of the doorway, anywhere you're sure to trip over him. That's why he's outside now. I figured we'd had enough problems for one day."

Just then the dog's whining turned to a snarl, then a bark, then a growl. Billy stood up, walked nonchalantly over to the wall near the sliding doors, and flipped a row of switches. There was a sudden blaze of light, a siren began to wail, and Killer joined the deafening racket with a barking frenzy of his own. Jayne jumped up from her chair.

"Good heavens, Billy, what in the world is going on?"

"Don't worry, it's probably nothing. I've activated the cameras. I'll just go check the monitor. Back in a flash."

"I don't know whether to laugh or cry," Jayne admitted after Billy had gone. She sat back down into her chair again. "Somehow I suspect it isn't World War Three, despite appearances to the contrary. You should see the back rooms. One of the bedrooms is completely given over to the security system. Billy's room is nice, but bare, hardly any of the personal things that make a bedroom inviting. The spare room looks rather like a detention cell. But the kitchen is lovely. I'll bet that's Bertrand's domain. There's a stack of books piled on the end of one counter and a very comfortable chair next to the back door."

Billy returned to the room, turning off the lights and sirens as he passed by the row of switches.

"It was nothing to worry about. A coconut fell and hit the fence. But I'd rather be safe than sorry."

"Your neighbors must love you," I couldn't resist commenting. Billy took me literally.

"Yeah, my house acts as protection for the whole neighborhood. I'm glad to be able to help, you know?"

Bertrand arrived back momentarily, balancing two huge platters of *nigiri* and *maki* sushi, artfully arranged into flower patterns. There was plenty of pickled ginger, wasabi, and soy sauce, and Bertrand poured us all refills of the tropical juice cocktail. Billy brought out our scripts.

"Here you go—this is the entire two-part episode," he said between bites of cucumber roll. He was avoiding the fishy ones, I noticed, which left more for Jayne and me. "Do you want me to continue with my synopsis, or would you rather read it for yourselves?"

"Go on with the synopsis," I told him. "I like to get an overview."

"Well, in part one, after the daughter meets Mack at her parents' house, she invites him to her beach birthday party. She's fallen for him at first sight. That's the scene you'll be shooting on Tuesday morning, the beach party. I have your call sheets here, by the way." A call sheet details the scenes to be shot on any given day, the cast and crew requirements, prop and transportation needs.

"The Brents are very protective of Samantha, their daughter. Anyway, they're at the beach party, looking on. We're going to film it at Hanauma Bay, with lots of great underwater shots. They've agreed to close the beach to the public for a while in the morning for the filming. That wasn't easy to arrange. It's such a popular place. But the show has actually been good for the tourist trade and the Hawaiian music business so . . ."

Actually I've never cared much for Hawaiian music itself, but it makes perfect sense when encountered in its natural setting.

And, of course, the phrase *Hawaiian music itself* is almost as meaningless as *American music itself* or *European music itself.* To start with, there is the basic distinction between the kind of music that was indigenous to the islands, the art as it flourished before the invasion of whitey, who did what he has always done, which is to impose his culture and order on those who had never invited him to their shores in the first place. Hawaiian music is as harmonically insipid as it is because it was so strongly influenced by Protestant church music of the eighteenth and nineteenth centuries. The cultural wars between European Catholics and Protestants also have their relevance, for it was the Protestant artistic ethic, with its emphasis on simplicity, that was most influential in the islands of the Pacific.

But all such background notwithstanding, island music in its natural setting is perfectly okay by me.

The same goes for those brightly colored Hawaiian shirts. We all wear them in the islands, but they don't look too hip on the streets of Cleveland.

"Back to the scene, Billy. What happens?"

"Sorry. So Mack brings his two pals, Buddy and Pete, to the party with him. He doesn't want Samantha to get too serious about him, doesn't want to mix work with his personal life, you know. One of the kids at the party almost drowns, and Mack begins to suspect that most of the guests are high on something other than just snorkeling. This gives him a chance to say something about substance abuse."

"I think I lost track of the murder mystery somewhere, Billy. How does this fit in with the polo rigging and dead groom we talked about in the car?"

"Well, it doesn't exactly, Steve. But, you know, that's the way these shows are these days. They're kind of like soap operas with a little mystery thrown in. The viewers like to follow the personal lives of the characters, know what they think, how they live. The mystery is just something to hang it all on.

"Personally, Steve, I'm glad to have a chance to say something about substance abuse. I think it's a real problem today."

"You're right, of course, Billy," I replied, taking the last bite of a *tamago-yaki*. For the first time all day, he reminded me of his father. Raymond has always used his position as a celebrity to advocate social responsibility. I was beginning to like Billy again. I hoped that didn't have too much to do with a full stomach and a comfortable place to sit. Jayne encouraged him to go on.

"Part two, that's on page seventy-six of your script, starts with some of the highrollers involved in the Brents' gambling pool catching on to what they've been doing. They're furious, of course, but they agree to let it go if the Brents will rig another match so they can recoup their losses by betting with people who aren't in the know. The Brents agree. The climactic scene is back on the polo field, lots of action stuff. We're using real polo players, you know, the best from the Diamond Head Polo Club and some Maui club as well. Anyway, one of the Brents' jockeys gets stomach cramps from the shellfish he just ate. . . ." I glanced at the pile of shrimp tails on my plate.

"So, without any warning, Samantha, who grew up around polo and has played all her life, takes over for the jockey. She wants to impress Mack, see?"

"Do they allow women to ride in polo matches?" Jayne asked. "Or does she have to pretend to be a man?"

"Oh, no, women are allowed to play. There are more and more of them all the time. So, there she is, playing for all she's worth, and her parents are looking on horrified, knowing that her horse has been drugged, but unable to stop what's going to happen next. Her horse collapses, she barely escapes being trampled to death, and Mack, Pete, and Buddy rush onto the playing field, followed by her parents."

"Do Buddy and Pete do anything in this series but accompany Mack to social events?" I couldn't resist asking.

"Oh, sure, Steve. There's all kinds of filler with them and Mack, great photography, the ongoing story of Buddy's cruise business, and Pete's love life. I was just telling you about the scenes the Brents are in. We've filmed the rest of the episode already. We were trying to squeeze the scenes with the Brents into just a few days, to accommodate my parents' schedule."

"I get the picture. So tell me, how does Mack discover that we're the bad guys?"

"Well, actually, Samantha, your daughter, figures it out. She realizes that her horse must have been drugged and puts it all together. She's so upset, she comes out with her suspicions right there on the playing field and Mrs. Brent admits to everything. Mack and his pals stay with Samantha as she watches her parents being led away in handcuffs. It's pretty dramatic. The very last scene has been left kind of ambiguous, on purpose, so that Samantha can come back in a future episode, maybe even as a girlfriend for Mack. But Danny . . ." Billy looked at us questioningly. "You know Danny, don't you? Danny Siderman, our producer? He did *East Side Story*, that nitty-gritty cop show in the sixties? My parents remembered it."

"It doesn't ring a bell," Jayne said, shaking her head. I thought I might have seen the show once. If it was the one I was thinking of, it had been pretty good.

"Anyway, Danny thinks it might hurt Mack's popularity to have a steady girl in the series, just yet anyway."

"It all sounds very interesting, dear," Jayne said politely. "I can't wait to actually read the script and find out how I'm accused of murder in sign language, by my own daughter no less."

That was my cue. "Yes, I think it's time we got to our hotel room and started unpacking. I want to glance through the script tonight, so we can begin work in earnest first thing in the morning. Will Bertrand take us or should we call a taxi?"

Billy sat forward on the couch, looking first at Jayne, then at me, in apparent surprise.

"Gee, I'm sorry. I just assumed you'd be staying here tonight, after what happened to the car and all. I mean, I don't know how any of us will be *able* to sleep. I'm sure the minute I close my eyes I'll relive the terror of stepping on the brake and feeling . . . nothing. I don't think I could stand to be alone tonight."

I saw our lovely suite at the Royal Hawaiian slipping out of my grasp. I tried to grab it back.

"But you're not alone, Billy. You have Bertrand and Killer. And I'll bet the entire Oahu police force is programmed to descend on Waimanalo if anyone trips one of those wires I've noticed on all the windows and doors.''

It was no good. Jayne got up and went over to give Billy a sympathetic hug. "We'll stay with you, just this once. But you'll have to lend us a few toilet articles. Our bags are all at the hotel.''

Billy brightened immediately. That one's worked for him before, I couldn't help thinking as I got up to follow Jayne and Billy into the guest room.

"I'd better call the hotel to tell them we won't be checking in until tomorrow morning," I suggested, putting the stress on the word *morning*.

"Don't worry, Steve, I already called." Billy turned his attention back to Jayne. "I'll have Bertrand get everything together for you. Thank you so much for staying tonight. I can't tell you how much it means to me.''

"Is this what they mean by *Aloha spirit?*" I asked my wife when we were finally alone in the overly soft guest room bed. "It was nice of Billy to lend us pajamas, but I don't think they're quite me." My pajamas had giant mai tai glasses on them, with little umbrellas sticking out the top of each one. Jayne eyed me appraisingly.

"All you need is a swizzle stick," she said with a grin. Then she looked down at her own borrowed flannel nightshirt. "Of course, I'm not sure purple pineapples dancing across a chartreuse beach show me off to best advantage either. But he is trying.''

"I agree, Billy's *very* trying.''

Jayne passed over my copy of the script. We read in silence for a while, then began feeding each other lines in the most villainous voices we could muster. Pretty soon we were laughing and rehashing the day's true-life dramas.

"Do you think he's really in danger?" Jayne asked as we finally turned out the lights to go to sleep.

"Definitely," I replied. "I was ready to kill him myself today, several times. Sleep tight.''

chapter 6

There's nothing like a Polynesian dawn to soothe the savage beast. The world is born anew in pastel light, the scent of flowers, and birdsong. There is a translucence in the air that defies description.

"What time is it?" Jayne asked sleepily.

"Early," I told her as I extricated myself from the mountains and valleys of the bed. I closed the door behind me and made my way quietly down the hall, keeping an ear out for Killer. The smell of fresh-roasted Kona coffee greeted me at the doorway to the living room. I walked over to the glass doors and looked out to sea, where a lone fisherman was just casting his line into the pastel surf. I wanted to step out onto the lanai, but didn't know if the alarm system had been deactivated. I hated to think what might happen if it hadn't. Land mines? Bullets automatically spraying the doorway? So I turned away from the view and followed my nose to the kitchen. Bertrand was seated at a butcher-block table in the middle of the room, dressed in a fresh skirt. He was studying a dog-eared copy of Hegel and taking an occasional sip from a coffee mug that read PHILOSOPHERS MAKE BETTER LOVERS. I didn't see any sign of the machete.

"Good morning, Bertrand."

He jumped at the sound of my voice. The expression on his face was so menacing, I stepped back involuntarily.

"I didn't mean to startle you. Looks like a nice day."

He tried to smile. "Good morning, Mr. Allen. I wasn't expecting to see anyone so early. Mr. Markham generally sleeps in on the days he's not filming. Can I get you a cup of coffee? We have tea, if you'd prefer."

"Stay where you are," I said. "Tea sounds wonderful, but I can make it myself."

"I wouldn't think of it," he replied, rising with unexpected agility and going over to the stove to put the kettle on. "I was just taking the opportunity to do a little research on my master's thesis. I'm sure you understand how it is; one has to take advantage of every spare minute."

"I couldn't agree more," I replied, glancing around the kitchen. It was then I spotted the machete. Bertrand had used it to prop open the back door, which looked out onto coconut palms and plumeria trees. The trees were pretty, but they didn't quite succeed in camouflaging the electric fence in the distance.

"I assume you're getting your master's in philosophy? You share the first name of a great philosopher, as I'm sure you realize."

"Of course, Mr. Allen. That's no accident. My mother was particularly inspired by Russell and wished me to be aware of him at an early age. Sugar? Honey?"

"No, that will be fine, thank you. Do you mind my asking what you're doing here, Bertrand? I'm sure you're an excellent bodyguard and butler, but couldn't you have found work more in line with your interests?"

Bertrand sat down across from me at the kitchen table. He possessed the corpulent dignity of bearing I've always imagined in early Polynesian royalty. When he spoke, there was a hint of bitterness in his voice.

"Unfortunately, Mr. Allen, there isn't much call these days for someone with a bachelor's degree in philosophy from the University of Hawaii. Mr. Markham isn't a bad employer and I have plenty of time to study. He's less demanding than his predecessor in that respect, and the company he keeps is considerably more congenial."

"So you came with the house, so to speak? You worked for the drug lord who used to live here?"

Bertrand smiled again. "I wouldn't call him a lord. But, yes, I have been here since the house was built. We Samoans have a reputation on the island. It's undeserved in most cases, but where intimidation is required, it can work to our advantage. We tend to be on the large size, as I'm sure you have noticed."

I wondered just who Bertrand was there to intimidate now. I was inclined to like him but wasn't at all sure he would be my first choice for housemate. I made a mental note to try to find out more about him from Billy.

"Tell me, does Billy have any close friends here on the island, anyone he can confide in?"

"He hasn't had much time to develop friendships, Mr. Allen. He's new to the islands and the show has kept him very busy. I gather Mr. Min, the director, works them mercilessly. And recently, of course, there have been the interviews and publicity appearances. But I'd say he's as close to Lance Brady as anyone. Mr. Brady plays Pete Lambert, Mack's sidekick on the show. You'll be meeting him tonight, of course, at the party."

"Party? What party is that, Bertrand?" This was the first I'd heard of any party, and I had my own ideas for the evening.

"You mean Mr. Markham didn't mention it yesterday? He must have forgotten in all the excitement. Mr. Brady is giving a party in your honor this evening. I believe you're expected at six. He told Mr. Markham he wanted to introduce you to the cast and crew before you actually go in front of the cameras."

"That was thoughtful of him," I said, thinking to myself that it would have been even *more* thoughtful, however, if he had asked Jayne or me first.

I made two important phone calls before Billy rose for the day. The first was to the garage in Kailua where the Karmann-Ghia had been laid to rest the day before. I remembered that the place was called Sammy's, and Bertrand found the phone number for me. A young girl answered the phone on the fifth ring.

"Yeah? Who needs me?"

"May I please speak to Sammy, or the head mechanic?"

"That's me, both counts. Whaddaya want?" I could barely hear her over the racket in the background, but she sounded about fourteen.

"Have you had a chance to look at the convertible that was brought in yesterday afternoon?"

"You bet I have. It oughta be a crime to own a car like that and not take care of it. Basic maintenance, bottom line. It's a beautiful machine, classic, but you ever bother lookin' under the hood? It's a mess in there. Would you buy a show dog and not feed it?"

I didn't bother to point out that it wasn't my show dog.

"Why did the brakes go out, do you know?"

"Sure. Cable broke," she replied as if dealing with a two-year-old.

"Does it look as though it was tampered with?"

She paused, considering the implications of my question. "Hell, I dunno. It's possible, I guess. More likely it just wore out. My advice is while we got it in here, let us do a complete overhaul. Then worry about the bodywork. And for God's sake, start changing the oil. If you're not going to take care of the basic maintenance on a car like that, you're just asking for trouble."

I couldn't have agreed more. Protecting Billy from legitimate danger was one thing. Protecting him from himself, another. Jayne might be willing to take it on, but I wasn't sure I had the patience for it. I told Willie to go ahead with whatever she thought the car needed. Then I dialed my own number in Southern California.

Cass answered on the third ring. Jimmy Cassidy, otherwise known as Cass, has been with us for years, functioning as everything from chauffeur to assistant private eye. He came to Hollywood originally from a ranch in Wyoming, hoping to be a star in westerns, and if his dream were to come true, I wouldn't know how to replace him. Jayne and I call him Our Man Monday. Today was Monday.

"Morning, Cass. I hope you're enjoying your vacation."

"Steve? I didn't expect to hear from you so soon. You're not worried about anything, are you? Forget something you need me to send over for you?"

"No, nothing like that."

"Not homesick, I trust? There are some of us back here in the smog capital of the world who wouldn't mind being in Hawaii right now. Island paradise, hula dancers, luaus, mai tais. Some of us have never been to Hawaii, you know. Some of us can only watch it on television and imagine the crystal-clear water and tropical breezes while it's gray and drizzly outside *our* doors."

"I thought you were looking forward to two weeks without us," I mentioned.

"Well, I didn't want you and the Mrs. to feel bad, leaving me behind while you went off to the one place in the world I've always wanted to see. So I tried to make out that I'd be having a grand old time without you. But the truth is . . ."

"Cass, how would you like a two-week vacation in Hawaii, all expenses paid? You'll have a room of your own, right next to the beach, a butler in skirts, a dog to keep you company, and very little work to do."

"I'll be there before you can hang up. You and Jayne need a driver, then?"

"No, a baby-sitter."

"Great, I love children. How old is this one?"

"Old enough to get into trouble."

I explained to Cass what I had in mind and then did a little fox trot into the kitchen. Billy and Jayne were sitting at the kitchen table while Bertrand was making omelets at the stove. Billy looked rumpled and still half asleep, but my lovely wife was dressed and ready for action. She seemed surprised by my good spirits.

"Bertrand says he told you about the party, Steve. Billy has just been filling me in. Apparently Lance Brady's home is quite unusual and everyone will be there. It's not expected to go past nine, so we can all get a good night's sleep before the Hanauma Bay scene Tuesday morning. I was telling Billy that we'd better get over to the hotel so we can unpack and work on our lines. I also want to spend a couple of hours at the Academy of Art before the party, since we missed it on our last visit. Billy says he'd like to join us. Does three o'clock sound too late?"

I said three o'clock sounded fine. I didn't like the way Billy had taken to arranging our schedule without consulting us, and I could have lived without the cast party. I'd been hoping for a romantic evening alone, just Jayne and me and that fabled Hawaiian moon over Waikiki. But then I thought of Cass, on the freeway headed to the airport, and I knew help was on the way. The cavalry was coming.

chapter 7

Jayne's face lit up the minute our hotel came into view.

"Oh, Steve, it hasn't changed. It's just as magical as the first time I set eyes on it. Doesn't it bring back memories?"

The Royal Hawaiian, Pink Palace of the Pacific, or Pink Lady, as it is variously called, is the kind of hotel that can't help but evoke a bygone era. It has been a landmark on the Waikiki skyline since 1927, when it first opened its doors on the site of the former summer palace of King Kamehameha's favorite wife, Queen Kaahumanu. The pink stucco Spanish-Moorish baroque fantasy was built by Matson Navigation to accommodate passengers traveling to Hawaii on the company's fabled luxury liners. It was commandeered during World War II to billet submarine crews on shore leave. Enlisted men paid a quarter, officers a dollar a night, to play poker on the Persian-carpeted staircases and hang their laundry on the balconies overlooking one of the most exquisite stretches of beach anywhere in the world.

"I agree with you, Jayne, she's still the grande dame of Waikiki. I want to walk over to the Moana and take a look at what they've done with the 'First Lady' as well." The Moana is an even older hotel, a Victorian masterpiece built in 1901 that has just undergone a multimillion-dollar face-lift. Both palaces are now surrounded by high-rise hostelries and multilevel shopping malls. But stand on the ocean side of either one, looking out across the beach to the volcanic crater of Diamond Head in the distance, and you feel like you've traveled back in time on some magnificent ship.

Since our luggage had come from the airport the day before, we were free to take a turn around the tropical gardens that surround the Royal Hawaiian. The vegetation muffles the sounds of the street and the beach, isolating the stroller in a hidden world and another time. I had to remind Jayne that we were supposed to be working.

As we entered the hotel, we were immediately engulfed by plush Turkish carpets, intricately carved ceilings, colonnaded arcades, and luxurious accoutrements. The Royal Hawaiian Hotel has guarded, intact, a 1920's vision of luxury and opulence. Pink is the prevailing color, every shade imaginable. It's like looking at the world through the proverbial rose-colored glasses, though expensive ones.

When we gave our names at the main desk, the receptionist called the manager on duty, who came over to introduce himself and insisted on personally escorting us to a suite in the original part of the hotel, which he referred to as the "historic" wing.

Jayne was delighted with the accommodations. As the manager pointed out the intricacies of the refrigerator, television, and ironing board to me, Jayne checked out the bedroom, bathroom, living room, and lanai, all luxuriously furnished in a combination of period splendor and modern comfort. The color scheme reflected the shades of sea and sky. There were huge potted palms everywhere and just enough pink in the floral prints and accessories to remind you that this was the Royal Hawaiian. The manager, finally deeming me adequately instructed, left us to our own devices. I went straight to the bedroom to check out the mattresses.

"Ah, this is more like it," I said, gazing up at Jayne from a prone position on one of the beds. She threw a script on my chest.

"We have work to do, Steve. You feed me lines while I unpack."

I was just about to oblige, when the buzzer rang.

"Could you get that?" Jayne asked from the depths of the walk-in closet. "I'm in the middle of sorting."

I tore myself away from perfect repose and went out to the living room, calling, "Who's there?"

"Delivery, sir." I opened the door on a huge bouquet of flowers with two legs sticking out the bottom.

"Where would you like these, sir?" asked a muffled voice from behind the botanical garden.

"Let's try the coffee table," I suggested, taking the card the bellman proffered as he slipped through the door sideways. The card said "Welcome, folks. Glad to have you aboard. If you have any problem, give me a call. My number is 555-5050. Otherwise, I'll look forward to renewing our old acquaintance this evening. Danny Siderman."

"Who was it, dear?" came my wife's voice from the bedroom.

"Flowers, from the producer. He sounds as if he knows us. Do we know him?"

Jayne emerged from the bedroom in time to direct the delivery man out to the balcony with the flowers. "They're lovely, but they remind me a bit too much of a funeral wreath. They'll be fine on the lanai, don't you think?"

"Undoubtedly." I handed Jayne the card. "Do you remember meeting a Danny Siderman?"

"No, but I'm sure it will all come clear this evening. We'd better get busy, though, if we want to meet Billy at the museum by three."

Jayne made herself comfortable on a large, flower-print couch, looking out toward the sea. I sat down across from her, in a matching overstuffed armchair, my feet up on a hassock, and we began to work on the script in earnest. But every once in a while I caught Jayne staring dreamily out the glass doors, toward the white sand beach and the turquoise sea. Damn that party, I thought.

It was exactly three o'clock when we descended from the taxi on South Beretania Street, in front of the Honolulu Academy of Arts.

"Do you see Billy?" I asked Jayne as I paid the driver. He wasn't in front of the museum.

"There he is, Steve, across the street."

There's a lovely old park across from the art academy, and Billy was seated on a bench under a spreading banyan tree, reading. He stood up, waved, and crossed over to where we were waiting.

"Hi! I got here early so I bought a catalogue to the collection. I'm going to be your tour guide. See that car over there?" He pointed to a dark blue late-model Chevy Impala, four-door and hardtop, parked on the far side of the square. "Bertrand rented it for me this morning, to use during your visit. He thought you'd appreciate the leg room."

Score one for you, Bertrand, I thought.

"Speaking of Bertrand," I began as we climbed the stairs to the museum entrance.

"Steve, I can't believe it," Jayne interrupted. "It's still free. This is one of my favorite museums in the world." I nodded in agreement. The Honolulu Academy of Arts is housed in a beautiful old Mediterranean building constructed in the same year as the Royal Hawaiian. It continues to offer the citizens of Oahu free access to one of the best collections of Asian art anywhere in the country. But right now I wanted to return to the subject of bodyguards.

"Billy, tell me about Bertrand. I know you're concerned for your personal safety, but do you think he's the best person to watch out for it? I assume you're aware that he worked for the horticulturist and smuggler who built your house? I like Bertrand personally, but I wonder if you might not want someone around with less of a history."

"I understand your concern, Steve. But do you know how many bodyguards have drug or alcohol addictions? I know for a fact that Bertrand doesn't use either one. He's good company, you can talk to him about anything, and he never brings his personal friends around. He's even a gourmet cook—he thinks I don't eat enough. I feel lucky to have found him, just like the house, and Killer. Do you know how many people are bitten every year by their own guard dogs? Killer has bitten the mailman a few times, that's why the box is outside the fence now. But he's never come close to attacking me."

"There's a first time for everything," I reminded him. "If I were you, I'd learn how to control Killer yourself, in case you ever need to." I decided not to press the subject of Bertrand's suitability until I knew him better. But I couldn't dispel the memory of the dangerous expression on his face when I'd startled him in the kitchen.

We passed into the gallery housing James Michener's collection of Japanese *ukiyo-e* prints, and conversation came to a halt as we all focused our attention on this superb addition to the museum's collection. We had just moved on to the Tang Dynasty porcelains, when I thought I spotted Billy's phantom stalker in the next room.

"Excuse me, I'll be right back," I said, hurrying off. But I was too late. He must have seen me coming, or maybe I had only imagined a crew-cut redhead. I'm getting worse than Billy, I thought, rejoining him and Jayne in front of an eleventh-century statue of Kwan Yin, the Chinese Buddhist goddess of mercy.

As an amateur student of the world's religions, I've never been able to fully understand the degree to which the great Chinese people consciously embraced Buddhism in the manner in which fundamentalist Christians accept the religion of Jesus. According to one school of thought, Buddha is viewed as not in any sense a divine or superhuman creature but is revered as a great teacher and moral philosopher. No problem there, but if that is so, then what sense can we make of reference to various gods and goddesses of mercy or other forms of virtuous behavior? Jayne wanted to visit the museum's famous Korean cup collection, so Billy and I, seeing that time was limited, left her on her own and moved off into the western collection. Billy led the way straight to van Gogh's "Wheatfields," where we both stood in awed appreciation. Billy was the first one to speak.

"I love this painting. I always imagine myself walking through it. . . ." He paused and then added shyly, "Holding hands with someone."

"Any prospective candidates?" I asked. "Any woman you're serious about these days?"

"Not really, Steve. My parents would sure be happy if there were. But like I was telling Jayne—"

"As you were telling Jayne," I said, though silently.

"It's hard to find the kind of woman I'm looking for. I mean, physical appearance matters, I have to admit it. But I'm looking for someone who can enjoy this museum as much as I do and still put up with the celebrity thing as well. It's a tall order, I guess, trying to find a soulmate. Sex, sure . . ." Billy laughed. "But not even much of that lately, to be perfectly honest. I've been too busy. And I want to find a real relationship, like the one you have with Jayne. I don't want to settle for anything else."

"I don't think most people 'find' a relationship," I replied seriously. "You build one, and it's a never-ending process. But it is important to choose the right building material."

We said good-bye to van Gogh's wheat field and went looking for Jayne. We found her in one of the tree-shaded courtyards in the center of the museum. She was sitting on a stone bench across from a lovely old fountain, using her bag as a table, scribbling messages on huge picture postcards of the collection we'd just seen. She smiled as we sat down on either side of her and began flipping through her cards.

"I thought you'd find me eventually. This is really why I come here, you know. The collection is marvelous, but most of all I love just sitting here, listening to the birds in the trees and the sound of the water. What a civilized, peaceful place this is."

She was right. We hadn't even been bothered by the people who looked as though they recognized one or the other of us. They stared but kept their distance.

This was refreshing because some people go all to pieces in the presence of celebrities. Their powers of speech are sometimes affected, they drop fountain pens, physically tremble or grow pale. I recall a night, years ago in New York, as I was coming out of a TV studio. A well-dressed young man handed me the reverse side of an envelope plus a pen and clearly said, "Mr. Allen, I'd appreciate it if you'd sign this for the back of my wife." I suppose to this day he has no idea why I laughed as I gave him my signature.

"Closing time," one of the guards announced. Jayne had already started packing up her bag.

"What about male friends?" I asked Billy as we made our way toward the entrance to the museum. "Any special friendships, or enmities, for that matter, that have come out of the show?" I was working up to asking him if he had any idea who might be out to get him, but I hated to spoil the tranquil mood that had come over all of us in the museum.

"It's hard to know who's really your friend and who isn't when you have a hit show—but, of course, you know that, Steve. I thought Lance Brady was my friend for a while, but I'm not sure now. I think he's kind of envious of me, to tell you the truth. He thinks I don't deserve to be the star. And with Keoni, too, you know, there's some resentment that it's a haole, not a native Hawaiian, who's getting star billing. Hawaii may seem like paradise, but there's some racial uneasiness here. A lot of the natives feel like they've been taken advantage of by outsiders, and it makes it hard to develop a real friendship. And then, of course, we're all so busy."

We had emerged from the building and were heading down the stairs to the sidewalk. Billy paused to look both ways, then took Jayne's arm affectionately as they stepped off the curb together. Suddenly, out of nowhere, an old green Volvo careened around the corner, gunned its motor, and headed straight at them.

Luckily, I was a little behind Billy and Jayne. I knocked them both out of the way, pushing Billy onto Jayne in my haste. The car sped by, missing them by inches, as I ran out into the street to try to get a license number. But the back of the car was splattered with mud—no doubt by accident—completely obscuring the plate. I caught a glimpse of the driver, however, as the car sped past. I was starting to recognize him all too well—he looked short and had crew-cut red hair.

chapter 8

Our taxi wound its way up Tantalus Drive, around Punchbowl Crater and past the fabled homes of Makiki Heights, mansions of every style and period, some of which are visible from the road. Others are hidden behind imposing gates and dense foliage. I looked over at Jayne, who was sitting up straighter than usual and keeping her attention focused out the window. She'd taken quite a fall when I'd pushed her out of the way of the speeding car. We'd gone back to the hotel so she could change clothes and assess the damage, and I'd tried to persuade her to stay in bed while I went on to the party. But she wouldn't hear of it.

"You need me, darling," she insisted, "to help you find who's trying to kill Billy."

Actually, depending on the contextual meaning of the verb "to need," Jayne was right. With or without my participation she would make a very effective police or private investigator. One reason is that she is quicker at reading people than I am. Another is that she has just a sprinkling of paranoia, which in the criminal investigation business can be a plus, if not allowed to get out of control.

"Probably it's just a reckless redhead," I said to my redheaded wife. "A crazed fan who has nothing to do with the show."

But neither of us thought that was likely. Billy might be a household word at the moment, but his fame was so recent, it was hard to imagine he'd had time to drive anyone crazy, anyone who didn't know him already, that is. It seemed more likely that our phantom redhead was acting on orders, and very possibly from someone close to *Hawaiian Wave* who might be at the party tonight.

The taxi turned into a side lane where the houses were slightly less lavish than on the main road.

"This is it," the driver announced, pulling up in front of a home ablaze with lights and ringed with cars. It was long and low, part stone, part wood, with large picture windows looking out over a meticulous lawn dotted with flower beds, old shade trees, and padded wrought iron furniture. The effect was impressive but not particularly inviting; no lanai, none of the easy island charm we associate with the best Hawaiian architecture.

The front door opened as I was paying for the cab, and Billy came hurrying down the path to meet us.

"How are you, Aunt Jayne? I'm sorry . . . Jayne. I've been worried about you. I wish you hadn't tried to come. Whenever you're ready to leave, just let me know and I'll take you back to the hotel."

There's nothing Jayne hates more than someone fussing over her. She graciously but firmly removed herself from Billy's solicitous grip and started up the path, asking questions about the guests as she went. I fell in alongside Billy.

"Where in the world did Lance get the money for a house like this?" she asked. "I can't believe he pays the bills on his salary from *Hawaiian Wave.*"

"Well, you know, he was on that soap for years, *The Loves of Our Lives?* Did you ever see it?"

Jayne and I both shook our heads. We've never been big soap opera fans.

"They killed off his character a while ago, but I always figured those things paid pretty well. Maybe he got lucky with the stock market or his family has money or something. I never thought I should ask, really. He might take it the wrong way, like who do I think I am to imply that he shouldn't live this way. He's sensitive about things like that, easily offended. But if you can get past that, he's not so bad. You'll see. In fact, here he is."

Billy indicated a muscular young man framed in the open doorway, champagne glass in one hand, the other extended in greeting. As we approached and shook hands, I noticed that he was actually older and harder-looking, than he had appeared on the TV screen. He was handsome though, with regular features, eyes so startlingly blue I wondered if they were aided by tinted lenses, and bleach blond hair cut military-style.

"Hi, Steve, welcome, Jayne. I was sorry to hear about the mishap at the museum. For a while there I thought we might be having a party without the guests of honor. Come in, let me get you something to drink, introduce you around."

We followed Lance into the house and down a few steps to a sunken living room made out of lava rock. It was like walking into a volcano. The furniture was sparse, metal-frame couches and armchairs upholstered in white leather. Quite a few people, most of them young, stood around in small clusters, eating and talking. They looked up as we entered the room and made a playfully good-natured attempt at applause, a few tapping their dinner plates with their champagne glasses. Billy had obviously been telling everyone about our close call in the afternoon. Lance insisted we eat, drink, and relax before we got too involved with introductions. He led the way across the room to a long table set up in front of the fireplace and spread with food and refreshments.

"What'll you have?" he asked, pouring himself another glass of champagne. Jayne opted for mineral water, I asked for pineapple juice, and Billy, after hesitating for a moment, followed suit. As soon as we had filled our plates, Lance suggested we join Danny Siderman, the director, who was "dying" to meet us. Jayne excused herself, saying she'd join us in a minute, and went off in another direction, casting a parting conspiratorial glance my way. She had suggested, at the hotel, that we try to spread out at the party and compare notes later. In recent years, Jayne has taken to sleuthing like a duck to water, or a storyteller to a cliché.

There were people coming through the door all the time, and it was getting difficult to move around, even in a living room the size of Lance's. Billy had gone off in his own direction by the time Lance and I made it over to the group standing next to a giant-screen TV set. A short, round, balding man in late middle age seemed to be watching for our arrival. He broke away from his companions to bound toward us, hand outstretched and smiling from ear to ear.

"Steve! It's great to see you again. Aloha! Welcome to the greatest little place on the face of the earth."

The minute I saw him up close I remembered where we'd met. The name hadn't rung a bell, partly because he used to go by Daniel. He had been the producer of a terrible panel show I was talked into appearing on many years ago. Under pressure from an old friend, I had agreed to try it for a month but declined to stay on for even one week after the original contract expired. It was a call-in panel show, the calls were staged, the show was boring despite a talented cast, and it was canceled halfway through the first season. I couldn't recall hearing any mention of Daniel Siderman since. He looked older than I remembered him, of course, and had much less hair, but he was just as short, round, and gregarious.

"Man," he said, "I was bowled over when Billy told me he'd talked you and Jayne into doing the guest spot, Steve. Isn't it a great show? It renews my faith in the American viewing public." I didn't think Danny had ever had much faith to renew, but I didn't say so. Instead, I reported that I'd seen only one episode of *Hawaiian Wave* and that was while talking on the phone.

"I don't believe it! I'll have a VCR and some tapes delivered to your hotel in the morning, so you and Jayne can get an idea of what we're doing. You should at least try to watch the season opener. It blew everybody's mind, everybody in the industry, just blew them away." Danny's eyes lit up as if he were watching the blast. He took hold of my arm conspiratorially.

"I promised to take you over to say hello to the man responsible, our illustrious director. Not that your friend Billy isn't a natural; real star material there, as you know, hah-hah. And Lance, of course," Danny added as an afterthought, looking around for the man he was trying to flatter. But Lance had abandoned us for the beverage table, where he was refilling his champagne glass yet again. Danny lowered his voice to a hoarse whisper.

"To tell you the truth, Steve, Lance is probably the weakest link in the cast. Now, Keoni, on the other hand, he was a stroke of genius. But I'm getting sidetracked. Come on over and say hello to Edgar. He says he knows you and he's delighted to be working with you on the polo episode. I've been bitten by the bug myself, the polo bug, that is. Just became a sponsor of the Diamond Head Polo Club. Bought my first pony six months ago, waiting to close the deal right now on another two. I'm negotiating with a jockey in Maui, to ride for me. He's young, looks very promising.''

As Danny talked, apparently compulsively, we wound our way through the crowd toward a serious, intense-looking man evidently in his late forties, holding forth in the center of the room. It was Edgar Min, the director, and a small group of young people appeared to be hanging on his every word. Danny made the introductions, and I discovered that the young people were part of the director's technical crew. Everyone smiled warmly except Edgar himself, who glared at me through half-closed eyes. Maybe it was the fact that I was brushing off the crumbs from my last bite of spinach quiche. I prefer parties where one is not expected to eat standing up, juggling drink, plate, and conversation. Something usually falls.

Edgar, I noticed, had neither plate nor glass. He was a tall man and almost cadaverously thin, with a prominent brow that his receding hairline served to accentuate. He looked as if he had once been handsome, but his face was now deeply wrinkled, with lines of intense concentration around his mouth and across his forehead. When he spoke it was with a pronounced Eastern European accent.

"I look forward to working with you, Mr. Allen. I have admired your musical talent for many years. I used one of your songs in the soundtrack of *Johan,* as you may remember. The film was not a commercial success, but it is a personal favorite of mine and your tune worked well with the spirit of the scene. This is important, very important," Edgar emphasized, turning to the others in the group for a moment. "You must always feel the spirit of a scene. We are not looking for reality, we are not taking a photograph. It is our job to make the truth behind reality visible for the audience."

As Edgar talked, I was remembering *Johan,* which, I have to admit, I had found a bit boring. I have a prejudice against movies where a flock of sea gulls flying west against a stormy sky means trouble and the same flock heading east into the rising sun heralds the dawn of hope. But I knew Edgar's reputation had grown since

Johan and that his directorial approach in *Hawaiian Wave* was a big factor in the show's popularity. He turned his attention back to me, this time with what I took to be an attempt at a smile.

"Excuse me, I wanted to make that point very clear to my crew. I envision this project as an educational experience for us all. I have never done television before, and I never dreamed that I would, despite the precedent set by Bergman." Edgar's audience smiled at the reference to the Swedish director.

"But music is the real theme of the series, music and movement, and I want to see what I can do with these two elements in a one-hour weekly format. In my opinion, the characters, the story line, are all incidental, an excuse for the vision, the true expression."

Danny was looking nervous. "Wait a minute, Edgar. Let's not get too carried away, hah-hah. We don't want Steve here to feel he's wasting his time by appearing. I think I'd better introduce you to Dick Schiller, Steve. He wrote your episode. I'm sure he'll take exception with Edgar."

Danny was obviously uncomfortable with the impression Edgar Min was making, but I didn't mind in the least. So far *Hawaiian Wave* had been described to me as a glorified soap opera and an existential music video. I just wondered if anyone saw it as a detective show.

As I followed Danny across the room, I looked for Billy but couldn't see him anywhere. Jayne had drawn a circle of admirers, I noticed, and was holding forth near the front door, her attention focused on a handsome young Hawaiian man I assumed was Keoni. Even from a distance I could see the sex appeal that Billy had referred to, and I didn't think it had much to do with his ethnicity. Keoni was just one of those fellows whom women are drawn to.

Danny was leading me toward an adjoining room, where a crystal chandelier hung from the center of the ceiling. The dining room table underneath was covered with desserts and large urns of coffee, decaf, and hot water. I traded my plate and glass for a cup of tea and rejoined Danny in the group around a short, thin young man with wispy brown hair and tortoiseshell glasses. He seemed to be haranguing in a high-pitched, breathless voice whoever would listen .

"I tell you, it's commercial, it couldn't be more commercial. Look at all the scandals in the news, the military can't keep their peckers in their pants these days. Excuse me, ladies, but it's the truth."

Apparently this was Dick Schiller, the writer. He paused when I joined the group and Danny jumped in with introductions all around. A few people in the group looked relieved, and someone asked me about my latest book. But Dick went on with his monologue as if he hadn't noticed. He had an idea for a movie of the week, an exposé of army life, set on a base in Oahu. From what I could make out, he'd managed to get sexual harassment, homosexuality, drugs, abortion, and misappropriation of funds into the first forty-five minutes of the script and was moving on to wild parties with local members of the coast guard. There were going to be boat chases, car chases, and a helicopter chase, which he realized was tricky to film but at least if they crashed it would be over water and, hey, what an idea, maybe . . .

Deciding that listening to this movie was only marginally preferable to having to actually watch it I was plotting my escape, when suddenly everyone's attention was drawn to the sound of shouting, followed by breaking glass, scuffling, and more shouting.

chapter 9

I stepped quickly into the living room to see what was happening. A Hawaiian man in blue jeans, his hair pulled back in a long, gray ponytail, seemed to be wrestling with a less-than-sober Lance Brady. The Hawaiian was short, stocky, and much older than Lance but he looked strong. Two men close by pulled the combatants apart, and they stood glaring at each other in the hushed silence. Finally the Hawaiian turned and walked out the door. Keoni hurried over to Lance. I couldn't hear what he said, but Lance waved him away and Keoni followed after the older man.

There was a general air of discomfort in the room as people returned to their conversations. The volume had gone down a level. I approached Lance, who was directing the cleanup of the food that had spilled when someone fell against the table. I noticed that he had a fresh glass of champagne in his hand. He spoke first.

"Sorry about that, Steve. These damn locals, think they can lord it over everyone else, with *their* island and *their* music and *their* rights. I'll be damned if I'm going to play his goddamn tape just because he asks me to. It's my house and my party and he ought to be grateful he wasn't turned away at the door."

I refuse to condone racism in any form. In this case, I thought the best way to counter it was to ignore it.

"He's a musician, then. Would I know his name? Does he do the music for *Hawaiian Wave?*"

"Not yet he doesn't. His name is Lloyd Kawelo. You may have heard of him. He has a reputation here on the island, but he's never made it to the big time. He thinks *Hawaiian Wave* is going to be his ticket to success, but he's got another think coming if I have anything to do with it. I don't know why Keoni brought him here."

"What exactly do you have against him?" I asked. "I thought Hawaiian music was an integral part of the show. Personally I think deciding to feature it was a wonderful idea. It's always been a popular musical form."

Lance didn't look as though he agreed, but he saw where I stood and refrained from saying anything further. People were beginning to move toward the door. The scuffle had put a definite damper on the evening. I went in search of Jayne, whom I finally found in animated conversation around the coffee urns. It was a silent conversation, conducted with hands and fingers flying. Jayne smiled and introduced me.

"Steve, I want you to meet Susan Harrington, our daughter for the next two weeks. And this is her friend, Elisabeth Horan."

Susan shook hands formally and said, "How do you do." Each word was very slowly and carefully enunciated, in that uninflected, slightly nasal tone peculiar to those who have never had hearing. Elisabeth practically grabbed my hand out of Susan's grip and pumped it enthusiastically. She signed as she spoke.

"Susan reads lips, Mr. Allen, so all you have to do is face her while you're talking. I'm so delighted that Mrs. Allen knows sign language. I had no idea. Susan and I met in kindergarten and we've been best friends ever since. She wanted me to come along on the filming, for emotional support, really, she has no problem communicating. But your producer, Mr. Siderman, said it was fine if I came to watch. He's been awfully nice about everything."

"Glad to hear it," I replied. Susan Harrington was a tall, slender, aristocratic beauty with thick auburn hair tumbling to her shoulders and a shy but poised manner. She was small-boned, with finely chiseled features and delicate skin. Elisabeth was just the opposite. She had a large frame, with big hands and feet and a broad, jack-o'-lantern grin. Despite her outgoing manner, she seemed less at ease than her companion.

Jayne began to say her good-byes, mentioning that we wanted to have an early night so we'd be fresh for the morning cast call at Hanauma Bay. As we moved together toward the front door, a caterer came up to say there was a phone call for me.

"Are you sure? I don't think anyone knows I'm here." And then I remembered Cass.

"Excuse me, ladies. I'll be right back."

I followed the messenger to the phone, half hidden in a nook in the lava wall.

"Cass, is that you?"

"It's me all right, boss. But I've run into a little trouble."

"Are you still in Los Angeles?"

"No, no, I made it to Oahu just fine, and took a cab out to the house. It was after that I ran into problems."

"So, you're there now, at Billy's house?"

"Not exactly. I'm in jail."

After a brief pow-wow, Elisabeth insisted on taking Jayne back to the hotel and Billy and I headed for Waimanalo in Billy's rental car to see what we could do to rescue Cass. It was supposed to be the other way around, I thought ruefully. You were supposed to come to *my* rescue, Cass.

The town of Waimanalo has just recently built its own jail. Violators of the law used to be transported up the coast to Kailua. The new facility is small and inviting. Architecturally, it's a glorified Quonset hut. But there's a big Aloha sign over the main entrance and a comfortable row of benches outside, for the use of family or friends of the incarcerated or anyone else who happens to pass by and want a place to sit. I've had the misfortune to see the inside of more than one jail in my sleuthing career. It looked to me as though Cass had done pretty well this time.

They were expecting us at the front desk. There were two men in uniform, one seated and one standing by his side. Two more passed back and forth behind them, making no attempt to hide their curiosity.

I addressed the officer standing behind the desk, since he looked as though he was the one in charge. He was late middle-aged, Japanese-American, and looked as if someone had just gotten him out of bed. "We're here for James Cassidy. It appears he was mistakenly taken into custody while trying to enter the home of Mr. Markham." Billy smiled weakly at mention of his name.

The officer was grumpy. "All right, all right, I hope this doesn't happen again. Mr. Markham, I suggest you use a little more discretion in calling out the police in the future. We do have better things to do than respond to false alarms."

"I'm aware of that, Sergeant Ashimoto," Billy replied, a hint of truculence in his voice. "But the alarm system automatically alerts the station. I wasn't even there."

"Nor, it seems, was your bodyguard. But never mind. If you will just sign these forms, please, we can release Mr. Cassidy and hopefully not see any of you again for a very long time."

A door opened into the next room, and Cass appeared in the doorway, dressed to kill in a tan suit, cowboy boots and hat, and the remains of several leis.

I was about to greet him, when he headed, not toward me, but straight for an amply-endowed, bleach-blond woman who was sitting quietly on a chair against the wall, a green suitcase on rollers by her side. She was fortyish, bursting out of a flamboyant hibiscus-print sundress adorned with wilted leis, one of which she was busy picking to pieces. She looked as though she was having second thoughts about her choice of the evening's entertainment. Cass mumbled something in her ear and she perked up a bit. He led her over to where Billy and I were standing.

"Steve, I want you to meet Dottie Konich. We met on the plane. She's a travel agent from Akron, Ohio. It's her first time in Hawaii too."

I introduced Billy and we all went outside. Dottie, it turned out, had a complimentary room waiting for her at the Hilton Hawaiian Village, so we put her bag in the trunk and headed for Waikiki, Cass and Dottie in the back. I noticed that they were sitting closer together than absolutely necessary.

"I'd offer to drive, but I had a mai tai on the plane," Cass explained. Dottie coughed.

"Well, I had a few mai tais, I guess. I was so excited about finally making it to Hawaii. That's how I met Dottie. We were sitting next to each other on the plane, in C and A, and there wasn't anyone in B, so we got to talking. Turns out we have a lot in common. So when we landed I thought she might like to come out to the house with me, meet you both, see where I was going to be spending the next two weeks, that kind of thing. I thought you'd be back from the party, but I guess that's because I forgot to turn my watch back. Anyway, we got to the house and it was all lit up, so I thought someone must be there. The cab let us off at the front gate and drove away. I tried the intercom but no one answered. I thought it was broken, maybe, and yelled a few times, thinking that you'd hear me. Well, nothing happened and it was a long way back out to the road to find a phone, so I told Dottie to wait and I went through the fence."

"How?" Billy asked in a concerned voice from the front.

"Piece of cake," Cass assured him. "Fences don't mean nothin' to an old cowboy—hell, I just picked the lock on the gate. I was heading toward the house, when all these sirens go off and a dog comes out of nowhere looking like he's out for blood. I made it up the nearest tree as fast as I could. That's where I was when the cops came, sitting in a tree full of flowers, the sweetest-smelling thing you ever saw. I thought their response time was pretty good until I saw how close the station is to your house."

Billy didn't look happy that his fortress had been entered so easily, so I made a point of reminding him that the second line of defense had done its job admirably. We left Dottie at her hotel. Now that she was out of the police station, she looked sorry to say good-bye. By the time Billy dropped me at the door of the Royal Hawaiian, Cass had recovered as well and was firing enthusiastic questions about everything we passed. I told Billy that Cass would keep an eye out for his safety and drive him to the beach for the next day's shoot. Billy looked dubious but, for once, refrained from comment. Jayne was waiting up for me in our suite, ensconced on the sitting room couch. She looked relieved to see me as I sank into the armchair and put up my feet with a sigh.

"That didn't take long," Jayne began. "So how did Cass manage to land in jail his first hour in Hawaii? Usually it takes the two of you much longer than that."

I gave her a quick rundown of Cass's evening.

"Now it's my turn to ask the questions," I went on. "What

did you think of Keoni? And his friend who got into the fight with Lance? It looked as though you spent some time with them."

"Well, I can see why Billy chooses not to compete with Keoni for women. He'd lose. Keoni has real appeal, the kind you're either born with or you're not, and most people aren't. From what he says, he got into acting rather by accident. A childhood friend dared him to try out for a Hawaiian potato chip commercial and he got the part. That's where the casting director for *Hawaiian Wave* saw him. She gave him a screen test and he turned out to be a natural in front of the camera. But the show doesn't seem nearly as important to him as his music business. He's just started his own recording studio, Hawaiian Wave Records." Jayne pronounced "records" as a verb.

"What about his rowdy friend?" I asked.

"His name is Lloyd Kawelo. I gather he plays and sings five nights a week in a restaurant in Kaneohe. Oh, that reminds me. Keoni invited us to a party at his recording studio Wednesday evening. Kawelo is going to cut the tracks they'll be using as the intros to our two-part episode. They'll be the songs that go under the opening credits. Keoni plans to release a CD of Kawelo in conjunction with the exposure on the show. The party is just a kind of informal housewarming from what I could tell. The studio is brand new and they want to celebrate a little. I told Keoni we'd let him know tomorrow morning about the party."

I nodded without much enthusiasm. "There seem to be a hell of a lot of parties on this small island. How about a little quality time strolling hand in hand on a moonlit beach instead? We could get marooned together in some nice grass shack somewhere. You can be Deborah Kerr and I'll be Burt Lancaster. We'll take a midnight swim even."

Jayne ignored me. "You know who else I met?" she asked as she got up and headed into the bedroom. "A man named Jason Patterson. He looked familiar to me. I think he may have been at the airport when we arrived, with that horsy group. He's the president of the Diamond Head Polo Club, the ones who are going to play for the camera. He mentioned that they're staging a benefit match on Wednesday, to raise money for the school where Susan Harrington teaches, the Manoa School for the Deaf. I said we'd try to make it.''

"Good God, we're going to need a secretary pretty soon to keep track of our social appointments!''

Jayne smiled. "Maybe we can arrange to get marooned on the weekend.''

"That's a date?''

I closed the sitting room curtains on the lights of a distant ship and followed Jayne into the bedroom. Sleep came quickly, but the night was too short. I was dreaming of palm trees and virgin beaches, when the phone rang. It was our wake-up call. A wake-up to tragedy, as it turned out.

chapter 10

"**R**ed sky in the morning, sailor take warning," Jayne recited to herself as we rode in the company limousine east on Kalanianaole Highway in the predawn light.

"Good thing we're not sailing," I told her. "I wonder whether the overcast skies will affect our shooting schedule?"

"From what you've told me about Edgar Min, he'll probably love the moody light. The man seems to believe he's the Ingmar Bergman of the boob tube."

Jayne snuggled a little closer to me in the backseat of the limo. We were headed toward the shoot, and even after all these years, we both still feel the excitement of the first day on a new project.

Hanauma Bay is a volcanic crater with a bay inside it, formed when the side of the caldera facing the sea eroded away. Our first view was from the highway as we approached the parking lot above the beach. A wide crescent of white sand surrounds the stunning blue-green water, which changes shade to a dark aquamarine as the bay opens out toward the sea. The area is a wildlife preserve, a haven for tropical fish and coral sea life of every description, as well as some unusual shore birds. The birds generally have to fight for a place to put their feet down with the hordes of visitors, both local and tourists, who crowd the beach to scuba, snorkel, or just feed the fish. This morning, their only competition would be our film crew.

As we approached the parking lot, it was evident that the highway patrol was out in force and already had its hands full.

Traffic policemen had blocked off most of the parking area and were busy trying to discourage curious bystanders from getting too close or parking along the highway to take a look. Some of the officers seemed just as interested in the film proceedings as the bystanders, however. I noticed several of them pointing out Lance and Keoni to each other, as they emerged from their cars just ahead of us. A man in uniform stopped our car at the entrance to the parking lot. After a short conversation with the driver, he peered into the backseat, smiled, nodded, and waved us on.

The parking lot itself looked like Studio City on wheels. Equipment trucks and dressing room trailers were set up everywhere and already open for business. Young people were bustling in and out of the makeup and costume trailers, laughing and talking in the early morning chill. Coffee containers in hand, the technical crews carted lights, cameras, generators, and cables down to the far end of the beach. I spotted Edgar Min standing in front of his trailer, staring up at the sky with a look of grim satisfaction on his face. Jayne's right, I thought, this is just his kind of sky, the perfect backdrop for the melodrama he's about to stage on the beach.

Jayne and I got a ripple of recognition as we descended from our limo. But it was nothing like the reception Billy got when he and Cass pulled into the parking lot and emerged from the rented Impala. The crowd of bystanders surged around him and needed to be restrained by the police.

"Where's the Pink Pussy?" someone shouted from the crowd. Cass looked shocked but Billy smiled and called back that she'd be on the road again soon. He headed straight for Jayne and me, and with a parting wave to the crowd began walking us toward the dressing rooms.

"It's awfully early, isn't it?" Billy began, looking around dubiously. "I still haven't gotten used to that, you know, how early you have to get up when you're shooting a show like this. I sure hope you two got some rest at least."

"Of course we did," Jayne replied. "And you?"

"Well, you know, I did as well as I could under the circumstances." Billy had assumed his martyred air and looked as though he were about to elaborate. Fortunately, Danny Siderman came bounding around the corner of the costume trailer and almost ran us down. He was bubbling over with enthusiasm.

"Good morning, folks, good morning. Beautiful day, isn't it? Edgar says he couldn't ask for anything better. You can always add sunshine, he says, but you can't take it away."

Danny went on. "Don't want you folks to catch cold though. Be sure to use the robes in your dressing rooms for the walk down to the beach." Jayne assured him we would. I was hoping that he'd eventually stop calling us "folks"; it was almost as bad as being called Uncle Steve.

"Here we are, folks. Your dressing room is right over here, Jayne, right next door to Steve's. The revised call sheets are in your trailers. Makeup will be ready for you at six forty-five, Steve, and you're right after him," Danny rattled off, turning toward Jayne. "I've arranged for someone from wardrobe to help you with your bathing costume, just in case there are any last-minute alterations needed. I'll knock on your door when it's time to go to the beach. We'll probably start down around seven forty-five. Edgar likes to address everyone for a few minutes at the beginning of the day. He calls it 'impregnating the atmosphere with meaning.' "

I escorted Jayne to her dressing room and took a quick look inside, just to make sure she had everything she needed. She did, and then some. The trailer was large and well lit, with a divan in one corner and a small refrigerator stocked with mineral water and health-food snacks. There was a small but beautiful bouquet of tropical flowers on her dressing table, tastefully arranged in a pale rose blown-glass vase. Jayne picked up the card and read it out loud: " 'My compliments to an accomplished actress and a great lady. I am looking forward to working with professionals. Edgar.' "

I was turning to leave for my own dressing room, when there was a knock on the trailer door. I opened it to a very attractive young Polynesian woman who introduced herself as Carol. She said she'd been sent over to see if Jayne's bathing costume needed adjustment. That was my cue to exit. I walked next door, fantasizing the greeting that might be awaiting me in my own dressing room. But I needn't have gotten excited. It was comfortable and functional, but there were no bouquets and no nubile attendants offering to adjust *my* bathing costume.

The makeup trailer had been set up next to the honey wagon, the term used to designate the truck accommodating the men's and women's toilet facilities. I arrived at my appointed time to find a young-looking man of Japanese extraction fluttering around Keoni. His female assistant, who looked equally young, asked me to sit down and started to work. Keoni made eye contact with me in the mirror but couldn't say anything, as the makeup man was working on his lips. I could see what Jayne meant. Keoni wasn't just handsome, he was magnetic.

When Keoni was finished, he turned to me hesitantly. "I hope your wife told you about the party tomorrow night. I'd really like to see what you think of our recording studio. I'm sure it's small-time compared to what you're used to, but you might be able to make some suggestions. I could send someone to pick you up."

"No need to do that, but we will try to make it," I replied. We shook hands awkwardly and he left the trailer. I couldn't quite make him out. I wondered if he was feeling uncomfortable about the brawl at Lance's house the night before.

The head makeup artist, who introduced himself as Mighty Mo, came over to attend to me. It was clear that Keoni had impressed him more than I was about to.

"Oh, Mr. Allen, I'm so sorry. You'll just have to wait one minute while I put my heart back in my chest. Is that boy to die for, or what? He doesn't even need any eye makeup. Did you see the length of those lashes?"

Mo went on in this vein for another five minutes as he deftly took ten years off my age. Jayne and I crossed paths outside the makeup van.

Noticing Susan Harrington and her friend Elisabeth standing in front of the trailers at the far end of the parking lot, I decided to go over and say good morning. Elisabeth, in a lime-green flower-print muumuu, was still grinning from ear to ear. Susan was in a robe like mine, her makeup and hair done to perfection. She looked nervous but mustered a professional smile when she saw me approach.

"Hello, Mr. Allen, a little cold this morning, isn't it?" she said very carefully. Then she shrugged with impatience and began to sign. Elisabeth translated.

"She says we'll appreciate the cloud cover in a couple of hours, Mr. Allen." Elisabeth laughed self-consciously. "Now she's saying she should probably start calling you Dad, just to get into character."

I faced Susan so she could read my lips. "Go right ahead. I've been called worse."

We decided to run through our lines together with Elisabeth ad libbing Jayne's part. I could tell that Susan was a talented actress, but then in the middle of a line she spotted Keoni approaching and froze up entirely, staring at him with besotted fascination. I couldn't tell whether Keoni was aware of the effect he had on Susan, but if he was, he wasn't trying to take advantage of it. He asked casually if we were ready to start for the beach. Looking across the parking lot, I could see the party extras beginning to wind their way down a steep paved road, blocked off for pedestrian use only, that ran from the cliff side to the beach.

"Shall we go, ladies?" I asked, taking one on each arm. "Party time."

We picked Jayne up on the way past her trailer. She was stunning in her perfectly fitted Armani bathing costume, which she allowed us to glimpse before rewrapping her robe with a shiver. We fell in alongside a contingent of perky young extras who were obviously thrilled to be participating in the filming of a hit TV show. They were probably already planning the parties they would have the night the episode was aired. Halfway down the hill, Billy came up behind us and gave Jayne a friendly hug. The extras all turned to look at him and then pretended they hadn't.

Billy looked my way. "I have to say, Steve, I was a little dubious at first about your friend Cass. But he made friends with Killer right away this morning. He told me he used to have a dog just like him back in Wyoming."

"Did Bertrand come back last night?" I asked.

"I guess so. He lives in the room above the garage, so I don't always hear him come and go, but he was there this morning. He seemed a little suspicious of Cass, but I think they'll get along OK."

I was about to respond, when there was a scream from the cliffs above the path.

It was only a young girl who had just caught sight of Billy Markham below, but we all jumped. For a moment all the blood drained from Billy's face and he looked as if he had been shot.

"This is awful!" Billy moaned. "I'm not sure I can go through with this!"

"Yes, you can," Jayne insisted. "All our nerves are on edge, but this is show business. Right now the show is about to go on."

chapter 11

"**A**ll right, my children? We are here now? Then let us begin," Edgar announced from his position near the camera at the far end of the beach, where the strip of sand narrows and joins the ironwood forest behind it. He was speaking through a small hand-held megaphone. Elisabeth was signing for Susan, who couldn't see his lips.

"I want you to think of this scene as the wedding of the land to the sea." Here Edgar stuck the megaphone under his arm to demonstrate his point with entwined fingers. "If your scene is on the beach, you will imagine that you are underwater. If you are being filmed in the water, imagine that you are walking on the sand. We are at the conjunction of the two primal forces of the planet. This will be the underlying spiritual reality of work today."

"Is he for real?" I whispered to Jayne, who shushed me and tried to keep her attention focused on what Edgar was saying next. I looked around and spotted Lance for the first time that morning. Mighty Mo had done a good job with his makeup, but he still looked hung over. Two frogmen with underwater cameras were fiddling with their equipment, getting ready for the scenes that would be filmed above and below water simultaneously. When I turned my attention back to what Edgar was saying, I realized that he'd left the meaning of life behind and was giving specific directions for scene thirty-seven, in which Jayne and I, as Warren and Cynthia Brent, are shown doting solicitously over our daughter Samantha's birthday celebration. We are joined halfway through the scene by Mack, Pete, and Buddy, so all five of our stand-ins were being shuffled around at the moment, to determine the angle and position of the two cameras on the beach and the one mounted partway up the cliff. When Edgar and his director of photography were finally satisfied, Jayne and I took our places, there was a final sound check, and the clapper girl snapped "Scene 37, take 1" in front of the lead camera.

Cynthia Brent, aka Jayne Meadows Allen, turned to her husband: "It's hard to believe our baby is nineteen years old today. We mustn't let anything get in the way of her happiness, ever. Promise me, Warren?" We were off and running.

When stepping into a guest spot like this, the first few takes are especially important. They give you an idea of how the rest of the filming is likely to go. To my surprise, I was favorably impressed with Edgar. Once the cameras started rolling, he came down to earth, stopping only to deliver practical suggestions in a firm but respectful tone of voice. He seemed devoid of humor, which is always unfortunate but he was not bullying or demeaning. He simply took his craft seriously and expected the cast and crew to do the same. Danny Siderman supplied the comic relief by just being himself. He bounced around the sand like an aging beach ball, exhorting, cajoling, and encouraging. Jayne and I acquitted ourselves well enough in our first scene, I thought. Edgar shot it only three times and that was because the clouds weren't right in take one and I accidentally kicked sand on Jayne at the end of take two.

"I can't take you anywhere," Jayne laughed, kicking sand back at me after Edgar had called "Cut."

We had a fairly long break until the Brents' next scene, and I decided I had my lines down well enough to take a closer look at the rest of the cast. Billy was good in front of the camera, I was pleased to notice. The night he phoned I hadn't been able to watch the show carefully enough to realize how convincing he was as Mack, and how charismatic. The "gee-whiz" personality that was putting me off gave way to a sensitive yet confident on-camera persona.

Lance handled his role like a pro, much as I had expected him to, but it was Keoni who really stole the show. The presence I'd noticed in the makeup van was even more pronounced in front of the camera. He didn't fit the stereotype of an island

Lothario. His features were too soft, his eyes almost feminine. But he had an incredible animal magnetism and grace. Susan was trying her best to be professional, but this was the first time she'd had any scenes with him, and he was dressed for the water, in surfing trunks and shark-tooth necklace. Edgar finally declared a wrap of their scene after nine takes.

Jayne and I went in front of the cameras again, with Billy, as Mack explains to the Brents that he suspects some of the invited guests at the party are high on more than the sodas the Brents have supplied for refreshment. The Brents, of course, are alarmed at the thought, especially Cynthia Brent, who fears for the daughter she has always tried to shelter from harm. Our scenes went pretty well. Jayne got a little cold and I occasionally moved in front of the very background activity that Edgar wanted to make the subliminal focus of the scene. Toward the end of the morning a crew member came hustling down to the beach from the parking lot, a lifelike dummy of a young man slung over his back. It was time to film the segment of the party scene where one of the teenagers almost drowns. As Jayne and I began to drift away from the filming area, one of Edgar's intense young assistants rushed over to let us know that the director never allowed anyone to leave until filming was completely finished for the day. He might get a last-minute inspiration and need us back to shoot a revised take on a scene.

"No problem," I said. "How about you, Jayne?" I was still concerned about the fall Jayne had taken in front of the Academy of Art.

"I'm fine. I think I'll go over and keep Elisabeth company. I like that girl!"

I glanced around until my eyes rested on some enticing props for the party scene, laid out of the way for the current segment.

"Is there any reason why I couldn't borrow a mask and fins from that pile on the sand—I'd like to do a little snorkeling over there, on the other side of the bay, while they shoot the drowning episode."

"Well, I don't know." The assistant hesitated. He was obviously uncomfortable with my suggestion. I had deviated from his script. Just then the sun broke through a hole in the clouds onto the clear, calm surface of the water. It was very inviting. Even from the beach I could see schools of brilliantly colored and patterned fish swimming in the shallow pools.

"Tell you what. I'll go ahead and take a little swim, and if Edgar needs me, just come on over and signal. I'll keep an eye out for you." Before he could protest, I had picked up some snorkeling equipment that looked as if it would fit and headed down the beach, humming a new tune that had just come into my head.

I donned the fins, mask, and air tube and waddled a few yards into the delicious Hawaiian water. The ocean around the Hawaiian islands stays in the seventies year-round, a perfect temperature for swimming. As soon as the water was deep enough, I stretched out and began to float, lazily propelling myself around and through the most incredible collection of tropical fish imaginable. Schools of surgeonfish, some striped, some spotted, some brilliant yellow, some black and orange, some almost transparent, swam by. And that was just for openers. Parrot fish, Moorish idols, lion-fish, butterfly fish—I felt as if someone had dropped me into an exotic aquarium tank. The mask leaked only a little and the fish led me on until I thought I was one of them. I didn't remember to stand up and look toward shore until I was out on the far edge of the caldera, standing on the shallow reef at the mouth of the inner bay. The filming seemed to be going along swimmingly without me, so I decided to keep going myself, just a little farther out, into deep water. It's so clear in Hanauma Bay that you can see fifty feet down. The deeper coral reefs are home to a whole new variety of fish, less spectacular in color and pattern but bigger and more mysterious. A turtle swam by and an eel poked its nasty-looking head out of a hole in the coral, pointed teeth bared.

I was just thinking about heading back in, when I spotted something in the distance that looked out of place. It was brightly colored and patterned but it wasn't moving like a school of fish. It seemed to be swaying gently back and forth, and there was something attached to it that I couldn't quite make out. I swam closer. Seen through water, everything is magnified, so what I saw looked larger than life. It was a human body, very dead, caught in the coral, scuba tank and mask pulled off to one side. It looked exactly like Billy.

chapter 12

I swam back to the edge of the inner bay as fast as I could, stood up in the shallow water with the waves breaking against my legs, and began to shout.

"Help! Over here!"

"Are you all right?" It was Edgar, calling through his battery-powered megaphone from the other end of the beach. I was relieved that someone had been able to hear me.

"I'm fine, but—"

"Then would you please stop shouting, Mr. Allen. You have just spoiled the first decent take of the drowning scene." I could hear Edgar's annoyance even through the megaphone.

"You don't understand. There's a real drowning here!"

The next voice over the megaphone was Danny Siderman's. I could just make out his little round body bouncing down the beach toward me.

"Do you need help, Steve?"

"No, *I* don't need help," I called in frustration. "But someone else does. Where's Billy?"

"He's right here, Steve, don't worry. Can you make it the rest of the way in? Quietly? We're almost finished shooting."

I gave up and swam back to shore. Jayne had joined Danny down at my end of the beach. She looked relieved when I finally waddled through the surf onto dry land and sat down to take off the flippers. I was out of breath and had a few cuts from the coral, but she could see that I was all in one piece. Danny reached me first.

"What were you doing out there, Steve? Edgar's fit to be tied. We have the beach only until eleven o'clock and it's ten forty-five now. I don't know what we're going to do if he doesn't get a wrap."

I looked at Jayne, who was coming up behind Danny, and then pointed to a man in blue, who'd been stationed at the entrance to the beach.

"Jayne, tell that policeman over there to call into the station and get us some help fast. There's a dead body out in the coral. It has scuba gear on but no wet suit. I really thought it was Billy at first—same build, same coloring, the exact outfit he wears on the show. I hate to think what it's going to do to Billy when he finds out about this."

Danny was jiggling nervously in place and finally broke in. "Wait a minute, Jayne. Let's not do anything rash. Maybe it wasn't really a body, Steve. Your eyes can play tricks on you underwater, especially if you wear glasses, like we do." He removed his and wiped them on the towel around his neck, as if to make his point. "And then, of course, if you really did see a body out there that looked like Billy, the last thing in the world we want to do is upset him, right? I say we just leave well enough alone. If there's a body, it's probably just a tourist and someone else will find it soon enough. I mean, why cause a big stir unnecessarily? Time is money, you know."

"*Just* a tourist?" I repeated in outrage.

Danny shrugged sheepishly. "Well, there really is a surplus of 'em, you know, overcrowding the islands."

Jayne and I exchanged looks. Without saying a word, she turned and headed toward the policeman on duty. Danny turned to call her back, but I stopped him.

"Danny," I said, "I realize this is inconvenient, but that's too damned bad. I don't imagine the guy who drowned is too happy about it either, whether he's a tourist or not."

He sighed and looked very put out. "Damn! Well, I guess it can't be helped. Let's see if we can wind up filming and get the cast off the beach before the police show up!"

A real humanitarian, our producer. I walked with Danny

quickly back across the sand to where Edgar was standing behind a camera.

"Did you finish the scene?" Danny asked, puffing for breath.

Edgar nodded distractedly. "Just one more setup," he said.

Danny whispered something in his ear. Edgar nodded and looked like a man who'd just won the jackpot.

"We must use this!" I heard him say. "Real life is always so much more intrinsically dramatic than make-believe!"

Meanwhile, the cast and crew were beginning to sense that something was up, and even the crowds watching from the top of the cliff seemed uneasy. A moment later we heard the sound of wailing sirens approach from the south and the first wave of law enforcement flooded into the parking lot. The squad cars continued more slowly down the road to the beach, the road that the rest of us had walked down earlier in the morning. "They wouldn't give *us* permission to do that," Danny grumbled by my side. He and I went over together to explain the situation to a beefy-looking dark-haired officer who was just stepping out of his car.

"Looks like we have a drowned tourist out in the coral," Danny told him irately, as though it were the officer's fault. "Steve here found the body while he was going for a little swim. I'm sure you realize what a tight schedule we're on, so if it's all right, we'll get back to finishing our last shot. Another half an hour and like we're out of here, dude."

"No," the officer said.

"I beg your pardon?" Danny had been speaking to the officer pal to pal, almost as equals. Now he seemed shocked. "What do you mean *no?*"

"I mean no. No one continues working, no one goes anywhere, not until we sort this out. If you have any problem with this, you can complain to Lieutenant Chen, who should be arriving any moment."

Danny was outraged. He mentioned friends in high places. He even mentioned the economy of the Hawaiian Islands, which would obviously be devastated if his world-famous cast and crew decided to pick up shop and film the series next season in Mexico—a place, he said, that had *very* lovely beaches as well as cheap labor. But the officer was unmoved. Meanwhile, everyone was moving down to the edge of the water, hoping to get a glimpse of the body. Edgar Min, I noticed, had a hand-held camera and he seemed to be hoping to sneak in a few cinema verité shots of the police and the search for the body.

More sirens were heard from up above on the cliffs, where the crowd was ballooning and spreading out across the length of highway above the beach. Three men in wet suits emerged from one of the squad cars and came my way. They asked me to pinpoint where I'd seen the body and I did my best to oblige, pointing to a patch of water about fifty feet from shore. The divers adjusted their masks, tanks, and flippers and stepped into the water. Edgar tried to follow them with his hand-held camera, but the beefy-looking officer put a stop to that fast. The scene on the beach was becoming chaotic. People were milling, everyone speculating as to what had happened. I heard someone behind me say with authority that the body was a Japanese tourist who had suffered stomach cramps from eating too much sushi, and probably this was a fitting end for a guy who ate seaweed and raw fish. Someone else said with equal conviction that it wasn't a body at all, only an old inner tube.

But it was a body, alas, and twenty minutes later the frogmen were beginning to maneuver it into shore. Billy stood at the edge of the water, watching with intense interest. Jayne had tried to convince him to go to his dressing room when the police first arrived, but he wouldn't budge. He seemed mesmerized. I made sure I was standing next to him when we got our first glimpse of the body, hauled ashore and laid out on the beach in full view. The victim had a slender build, just like Billy's. The sandy hair was a few shades darker than Billy's, but the aloha-print shirt and shorts, green and blue palm trees waving serenely over little grass shacks, were identical to the outfit Billy had on. Everyone could see that the victim looked uncannily like him. After a moment, one of the cops mercifully put a plastic sheet over him.

"Dead ringer!" I heard behind me. I turned to see who had spoken. It was Lance Brady. I turned back to Billy as Jayne, who had moved up on his other side, started pointing out that the aloha outfit was commercially available and selling like hotcakes.

"Why, just yesterday, in front of the Royal Hawaiian, I saw at least ten people . . ." It was no good. Billy's eyes rolled back in his head and he fainted dead away. I caught him before he hit the sand, but he was heavier than he looked and pulled me down with him. Meanwhile, a major commotion had broken out in the crowd that was now spilling over the guardrails in earnest, all of them trying to get a better look of what was happening. I glanced up and caught sight of a surfer who had managed to climb a tree to see better. He had on baggy shorts, an oversized tank top, and yellow-rimmed sunglasses. His hair was crew cut and bright red.

Billy's weight made it hard to talk, but I managed to croak. "Jayne, right above us, on the cliff! See if you can get the police up there!"

A crowd had collected around Billy. They all looked up toward the cliffs, then back at me as if to ask what in the world I was talking about. Fortunately, Jayne understood, and she went off to see if she could detain our mysterious redheaded friend.

Just then a doctor toting a traditional black bag hurried over and squatted down next to us, checking both our vital signs. Billy had already begun to come around, but he looked dazed, as if he'd just woken up from a deep sleep. The medic, who introduced himself as Dr. Aikiko, told us both to stay where we were for a few minutes and then snapped shut his bag and followed a frantic young assistant director, who had just run up to say that Edgar Min was in need of medical attention. Billy finally sat all the way up, so I could get to my feet and scrutinize the clifftops more closely.

Uniformed police officers were mingling with the crowd along the highway. There was no sign of the redhead, but I saw another familiar face, one that took me by surprise. It was Dick Schiller, the author of our script. He was darting from spot to spot, bobbing up and down in an attempt to get a better look over the shoulders of the people in front of him. He looked like a scared rabbit.

Billy seemed as if he was going to be all right, so I decided to walk over to find out what was happening with Edgar Min. It was obvious the director had been violently sick. One of his assistants was busy kicking sand over the mess and Edgar, his face completely drained of color, was wiping his chin with a large white handkerchief.

He said an odd thing when he saw me: "You know, Mr. Allen, there is a saying in your country, truth is stranger than fiction. But sometimes truth *is* fiction and fiction is truth." I wondered if this was just more of Edgar's gibberish or if he was actually trying to tell me something. I was pondering this riddle, when Jayne joined us. She shook her head, and unfortunately I knew what she was telling me without further need of elaboration: The redheaded crew cut had gotten away one more time.

There were more sirens now coming down the highway from the direction of Honolulu. Jayne and I looked up as a cavalcade of official cars swung into the parking area. A minute later the cars headed in a stately procession down the narrow service road to the beach. Doors slammed and a phalanx of uniformed males made its way quickly across the beach with one rather portly but agile Chinese-American dressed in a business suit at its apex. He paused at the body, uncovered it briefly, and barked a few orders to the first officers on the scene. They in turn gestured to an ambulance crew, standing by with a stretcher, and the attendants began to take the body away. The man in the business suit, whom I guessed to be in his mid to late sixties, was obviously in charge. Danny Siderman, who was looking as though he might tear out what little hair he had left, stepped quickly forward to greet the new arrival. They shook hands and conferred for a few minutes. Then Danny turned triumphantly toward the cast and crew, who were still standing in clusters on the beach.

"All right, folks, we can get our last setup and then get the hell out of here. Let's do it fast before they change their minds!"

The gentleman in the business suit, meanwhile, headed toward where I was standing with Edgar and Jayne, walked straight to Jayne, offered his hand, and said in a surprisingly melodic voice: "Lieutenant Anthony Chen, chief of homicide, Miss Meadows. I've been waiting all my life to meet you!"

chapter 13

Jayne accepted the lieutenant's outstretched hand, but I could tell from the puzzled look on her face that she was trying in vain to place him. The lieutenant, for his part, was grinning from ear to ear in obvious delight at her bafflement. He seemed to think it was a great joke and wasn't at all perturbed by the fact that he was the only one who got it. Edgar mumbled something in my ear and disappeared. Lieutenant Chen, my wife's newfound admirer, was a good-looking man, physically fit and carrying his extra weight gracefully. His suit was custom made and his Italian loafers had been perfectly polished before they hit the sand.

"I'm from Wu Chang, China," he said. "It is my ancestral home." Jayne's face lit up in recognition. Wu Chang is her birthplace as well. Her parents were Episcopalian missionaries in China for fourteen years, and she and her sister, Audrey, spent their early years there, though Audrey was born in New York. Lieutenant Chen went on with obvious relish.

"I will never forget what a beautiful little girl you were, Miss Meadows! With your fair skin and red hair you seemed like something from heaven to us Chinese children, like an angel come to life. I was a very naughty little boy. I used to spy on you by the hour, oh, nothing improper, you understand, I just couldn't stop looking at you. I was so glad that my parents converted to Christianity, it gave me the opportunity to see you more often. *Laoje* were still a rarity then, as I'm sure you remember."

Jayne laughed at the Chinese word *laoje*, which is used to designate foreigners but literally means "big noses."

"My family came to Hawaii in 1949, when the political climate became unfavorable to practicing Christians. I have followed your show business career with great interest."

Lieutenant Chen went on at length about Jayne's performances and appearances over the years, mentioning two or three even I had completely forgotten. He finished by mentioning that he'd caught her in *Love Letters* when we did the play in Maui a few years earlier.

"I saw it three times, as a matter of fact," he added with the first hint of embarrassment. Then he turned to me.

"I'm sorry, but I'll have to ask you to come down to the station with me, Mr. Allen. Since you were the one who actually found the body, I need to ask you a few questions with the tape recorder going. Miss Meadows, I wouldn't want to impose on you, but I would be delighted if you were to accompany your husband. I can order lunch brought in and we can continue our conversation under more comfortable circumstances."

"Do we have a choice?" I asked. A police station is not my idea of a setting for fine dining, and frankly I wasn't thrilled at the way the guy was making eyes at my wife.

The lieutenant gazed at me blankly. "A great lady such as Miss Meadows *always* has a choice," he said grandly. "But as for you, Mr. Allen . . . I'm afraid I must insist."

The main police station in Honolulu lacks the at-home charm of the Waimanalo branch. There is no "aloha" sign to greet you, though they do have a few "Mahalo for keeping off the grass" signs in the park next to the station. The building is only four stories high, sparkling white, and, from the outside, looks more like a public library than a police station. We climbed the front steps and entered the typical echoing halls of officialdom. Lieutenant Chen led us past the main desk, and we were buzzed through to the innards of the station. Fortunately, before leaving Hanauma Bay he had allowed me to stop briefly at my dressing room trailer so I could shed my wet bathing suit and change into dry slacks and a sports shirt. I sensed the lieutenant had allowed this detour mostly to impress Jayne as to what a civilized policeman he was; had I been on my own, it might have been a very different story.

Chen gave us a quick tour of the building, introducing Jayne as an old friend from China and occasionally forgetting to introduce me at all. At least he hasn't locked me up yet, I thought. Famous last words. Tony, as he insisted on being called, even took us in to meet the chief of police, who was young, Japanese, and so good-looking, he could have come straight from central casting. We wound up in Tony's office, which was smelling pleasantly of fresh ginger and garlic. I made my official deposition, which took all of five minutes. Then the detective began to pull takeaway containers one by one out of a large brown paper bag sitting on his desk; he had ordered this feast by cell phone as we were driving in from Hanauma Bay.

"Steamed fish with ginger and onions, eggplant Szechuan style, beggar's chicken, garlic snowpeas, shrimp over toasted rice cracker," he enumerated as we unwrapped our chopsticks—for myself the square *otay*, a knife and fork—and prepared to eat. The food was delicious, which was a good thing, since while I was eating I had to listen to my wife and Lieutenant Chen reminisce endlessly about the old days in Wu Chang Province. They went on to tackle Chinese-American trade relations, human rights, and the Tibet and Taiwan questions.

I paid lengthy visits to the water cooler, the men's room, and various reception areas. After scanning a short article in a police magazine on the wisdom of keeping your badge polished, an article every officer in sight looked as though he'd taken to heart, I decided to tell Jayne I'd meet her later. But I got back to Tony's office just as the preliminary report on the drowning victim was being placed on his desk. I was dying to get a peek at it, and Jayne knew it. She turned on all her charm.

"My goodness, Tony," she fluttered. "Could all that writing be about the body Steve discovered this morning?"

"It's only what we have so far," he said modestly. "Nothing conclusive yet."

"You know, this has been an absolute nightmare for our friend Billy Markham. He's under sedation for the shock. I can't tell you how much I'd appreciate any information you could give us, anything we might be able to pass on to Billy in order to assure him that he wasn't the intended target. The body resembled him so, and it was wearing his clothing from the show. Well, I'm sure you can imagine what he's going through right now."

"I understand completely," the lieutenant said understandingly, gazing at my wife with warm eyes. It was enough to make me want to throw up. But not until I had more information.

"So who *was* the victim?" Jayne purred.

Tony Chen glanced through the papers, looked up at Jayne, and then back at the papers. "His name was Samuel Fitzgerald. He was twenty-nine years old, a white male, and he'd been in the water approximately twenty-four hours. The cause of death was drowning, or, to be more precise, water in the lungs. It appears to have been an accidental death . . . his scuba-diving gear was faulty. The equipment was fairly old and it didn't have a rental logo on it, so it was most likely owned by the victim."

"Sam Fitzgerald," Jayne said with a sad shake of her head. "What a terrible end for him!"

"You're a very sensitive woman, Miss Meadows."

"Please call me Jayne, Tony. After all, we were childhood friends."

"Jayne!" he said a bit too ardently for my taste. I rolled my eyes, but neither of them was paying attention to me at the moment.

"I gather you must have some information on the victim, if you know his name," I said loudly, deciding I was sick of being a silent husband. "Did he have any connection with *Hawaiian Wave?*"

Tony Chen hesitated, looked up at me as though he had forgotten I was in the room, and then returned his adoring eyes to Jayne. "Well, that's interesting," he told her as though she had asked the question. "The deceased is a native of Oahu. His father was a career military man, it seems, stationed at Pearl Harbor. He's retired, living in Modesto, California. Mother deceased. Mr. Fitzgerald has held a series of rather low-paying manual jobs— caddie, busboy, construction worker. He was hired a month ago by Hawaiian Wave Records as a technical trainee to one of the sound engineers. I've just sent two men to the studio to interview anyone who might be able to tell us more about his last few days."

I was interested in this. "So you think the drowning may have been intentional after all? Are we talking about murder here?" I asked.

The lieutenant sighed, and this time turned his attention fully my way. "I didn't say that, Mr. Allen. But I wouldn't rule out any possibility until we know more."

"I certainly do appreciate your sharing this with us, Tony," Jayne told him. "Unfortunately, we still don't know enough to reassure Billy that he wasn't the intended victim, or it wasn't some kind of warning meant for him. I'm sure you understand our concern. We're old and very dear family friends. I hope you'll let us know as soon as any new information turns up."

Tony Chen laughed. Jayne may have been just a little too transparent. "I'd like to oblige you, Jayne, but you'd have to promise me not to indulge in any sleuthing. I know about your husband's penchant for playing amateur detective."

I put on my best "who, me?" look and we said our good-byes. Tony Chen walked us out and hailed a cab. He handed Jayne into the backseat and then came around to my side of the car.

"By the way, Mr. Allen, your wife has a point. It's possible that Sam Fitzgerald's death was meant as a warning to your young friend, Billy Markham. It wouldn't hurt to keep an eye out and let *me* know if you see anything suspicious, would it now?"

"Naturally, Lieutenant," I told him with a smooth smile. Thinking to myself that if I found out anything, this Chinese Casanova would be the last person I'd tell.

chapter 14

I could hear the phone ringing as I fumbled with the key to our suite at the Royal Hawaiian, rushed through the door first, and dove for it.

It was *him* again. The flirt.

"Tony Chen here. Is Jayne available?"

"Just a minute, Lieutenant."

Jayne signaled that she'd take the call in the bedroom. I hung up the extension and went through the glass doors to the lanai. The faint smell of suntan lotion and coconut oil wafted up from the beach. There were squeals of delight as children splashed in the cool water below. The beach seemed less crowded than usual. I stretched out on a lounge chair, careful to place it in the shade of the overhead awning. As I was drifting in and out of dream fragments, Jayne came out and sat next to me.

I arched an eyebrow at her. "Were you resolving the Hong Kong issue this time, or just reminiscing over your performance as Gretel in second grade?"

"I have something for you, darling—not that you deserve it," Jayne replied. "The two men Tony sent out to the recording studio have just returned to the police station. They reported that no one seemed to know Sam Fitzgerald very well. The man's a blank page. They couldn't find a single person who admitted to socializing with him outside of work. Consensus was that he was an amiable, easygoing sort. But the sound man who was assigned to train him said that he didn't seem very qualified for the job, or even particularly interested. He also said Fitzgerald hadn't seemed himself on Friday, and, of course, didn't show up for work yesterday."

"What did he mean by 'not himself'?"

"The engineer described him as distracted. Other coworkers used the words *anxious, worried, depressed.* A secretary mentioned that she thought Keoni had hired Sam because they were old acquaintances, but another employee said just the opposite. So there we are."

"There we are where?"

She shrugged. "Anyway, Tony is going out to Keoni's home to question him personally. His men heard about the recording session and party scheduled for tomorrow evening. Tony suggested that if we were to attend, we might do just a bit of spying for him."

"Can't the lieutenant do his own police work?"

"Not as well as my darling husband. Naturally I said we wouldn't miss the party at Keoni's studio for the world."

"Speak for yourself. Did Charlie Chan say anything more about the scuba-diving equipment, whether there was any sign that it had been intentionally tampered with?"

"Tony only repeated that it was faulty. He said when the victim had been in the water that long and the equipment was so banged up, it would probably be impossible to prove intentional tampering, even if it had happened."

"Pity to have a death that's so annoyingly inconclusive!" I said after a moment. "Well, I guess we'd better check in with Cass. See how Billy's doing."

"Already done, dear. Billy is sleeping like a lamb chop. And meanwhile Cass has had a wonderful swim and spoken to his friend Dottie. He's beginning to think this may turn out to be a swell vacation after all."

"I'm envious. How about a sunset cruise? I think we're entitled to some vacation time ourselves."

"Sounds good to me," Jayne agreed.

The stretch of beach that runs from the Royal Hawaiian Hotel to the Moana is famous as the best place in Waikiki to catch the late afternoon light. The tide was coming in as we strolled along the shore, scrambling for land when an occasional sneaker wave threatened to wash over our ankles. The curve of Mamala Bay afforded us an excellent view of Diamond Head crater, just beginning to turn pink in the pre-sunset glow. When we turned around, we were walking toward Fort DeRussy Park, bathed in the deepening golden light toward the west. We shed our robes in front of the hotel, waded out just past the waves, stretched out on our backs in the water, and began to float lazily back and forth, watching the sunset transmutations and occasionally giving a gentle kick or arm stroke to stay on course. I was the first to come ashore, a bit farther down the beach than I had anticipated, and I was waiting for Jayne, beach robe in hand, when she finally emerged from the pastel sea.

"Ah, this is the life!" I sighed. "Maybe there's nothing to worry about after all. Maybe Billy is imagining everything. Maybe Sam Fitzgerald got a bum deal on some used scuba-diving equipment. Maybe this is the best of all possible worlds. . . ."

Jayne nodded as she dried off, but I don't think she was any more convinced than I was. Neither of us wanted to go back to our suite, so we found a table outdoors at the Surf Room and ordered two mai tais, along with a selection of pupus, the Hawaiian equivalent of snacks or appetizers. We were just thinking about dinner, when Jayne suddenly leaned toward me and said, "Darling, don't look now . . . but look over there, by the door."

"How am I supposed to look but not look?"

"I'm sure you can find a way."

I did my best. I twirled the paper umbrella in my mai tai and looked up in an abstracted manner as if I'd just had a clever thought, meanwhile glancing unobtrusively in the direction Jayne had indicated. It didn't work. I found myself staring straight into the startled face of Dick Schiller, who was glancing at me through his tortoiseshell-framed glasses. The writer nodded a curt acknowledgment of my existence and then turned back to his dinner companion, a man who looked familiar but whom I could not quite place.

"Who is that with Schiller?" I asked Jayne.

"Jason Patterson, the president of the Diamond Head Polo Club. Remember, I told you I talked to him at Lance's party. Maybe he was Dick's consultant on the polo scenes. Filling in all the ambiance, you know. The truth of life on the turf."

I glanced over at their table again. This time Jason was on

his feet and headed our way. He was a handsome, athletic-looking man, gray-haired with an aristocratic bearing. He shook Jayne's hand first.

"Miss Meadows, Mr. Allen! I'm glad I ran into you. I wanted to personally invite you to join my wife and myself tomorrow at the benefit polo match. The proceeds go to the Manoa School for the Deaf, you know. I'll be playing in the match, but my wife would love your company and could help explain the game to you. She hates being a polo widow, but she knows more about the game than anyone I know. Danny Siderman is a novice by comparison. And, to be perfectly honest, I have an ulterior motive in trying to persuade you to be my guests. You see, Danny promised us that the cast of *Hawaiian Wave* would make an appearance at the match, and we sold tickets based on that expectation. No formal advertising or anything, but the word-of-mouth publicity was great for sales. So when Danny called to tell me what happened this morning at Hanauma Bay and mentioned that Billy Markham might not be up to appearing anywhere tomorrow . . . well, you can imagine what—"

"Speaking of this morning, your dinner companion must have an interesting story to tell," I remarked. "He had a better vantage point than any of us."

"Beg pardon? You're talking about Mr. Schiller? He just heard about the drowned man from me. He was at home all day, working on his new script. But back to tomorrow's benefit. It would mean so much to my wife and me if you could just make an appearance, even if you can't stay for the whole match. We've arranged a marvelous pre-game buffet at the Turtle Bay Hilton, as I believe I mentioned to you, Miss Meadows. Do agree to join us there, at eleven-thirty, say?"

I was kicking Jayne under the table. A chi-chi society polo benefit was not quite my cup of tea.

"Unfortunately, we have lines to memorize," I began feebly.

"Of course we can come," Jayne interrupted gaily.

"Wonderful!" Jason said. "See you tomorrow, then. The brunch has been especially designed around the polo theme. Try not to eat breakfast." Jason shook hands a second time and hurried back to his seat across from Dick Schiller, who had been eyeing us nervously throughout the conversation.

"It will be fascinating to see a bit of upper-crust life in Hawaii. The polo set, and all that . . . which makes me wonder, incidentally, what Dick Schiller is doing with Jason Patterson. I wouldn't imagine they have much in common," Jayne mused.

"And I'd like to know why Dick isn't admitting that he was at Hanauma Bay this morning," I mused right back. "I tell you, for an island known for its crystal-clear seas, the water around this show is getting awfully murky."

After dinner Jayne and I decided to take a stroll through Waikiki. The sidewalks were jammed with people from every country in the world, shopping, eating, milling, hustling, and taking the air. The flashbulbs looked like a lightning storm as the activity was recorded for the folks back home. I daresay Jayne and I will show up in a few of those photos and camcorder productions. We turned in at the International Market Place, where Jayne browsed the stalls and I wandered around, remembering how sleepy it used to be here, birds singing in the banyan trees as a smattering of tourists sauntered through and the Pearl Factory girls tried to pull you in to try your luck with a fresh oyster. I remember when Honolulu's all-Hawaiian music radio station, KCCN, had its home in a tree house in one of the banyan trees. It wasn't so long ago.

Suddenly, the hair on the back of my neck stood up. I turned around and there was Dick Schiller again. This time he was several stalls away, watching me intently from behind a huge pile of T-shirts that inelegantly announced I GOT LEIED IN WAIKIKI. I had the distinct feeling that he had been following me. I smiled and waved, while he tried to look as though he hadn't seen me. He pretended to be seriously considering a purchase, then darted around the corner and into a new maze of vendors, stalls, and shops.

I took off after him, turning the corner just in time to see him take a left at the miniature dugout canoes and koa-wood bowls. I stepped up the speed and finally caught him in the clear at the "genuine 14-karat gold chain" alley.

"Dick, hold on!" I shouted, and he had to stop. I was panting when I caught up to him.

He'd had time to collect himself and was attempting to look nonchalant again.

"Steve! What a nice surprise! I didn't see you there. Amazing place, isn't it. Schlock from every corner of the South Seas. I used to love it here when I was a kid. See that restaurant over there, where all the noise is coming from? My first job, busing tables. So I come here sometimes, just to get some air, unwind a little, all work and no play makes Dick a dull boy. But I really must get back to my computer now. I hope you and your wife have a wonderful evening."

I wasn't going to let him go quite so easily. "I was surprised to see you with the president of the Diamond Head Polo Club. Old friends?"

"Oh, Jason, well . . . I just met him, actually, um, at Lance's party." It was obvious he was lying, but I couldn't imagine why. "We hit it off, you might say. We have a lot in common, both grew up here, that sort of thing." It would be hard to find two people less alike than the suave Mr. Patterson and the nervous little man squirming in front of me. But I went on to my real question.

"You know, I could have sworn I saw you this morning, at Hanauma Bay, when they brought the body out of the water. Just driving by, were you?"

"You must have been mistaken. Unfortunately, there are a lot of people in the world who look like me. That's why I have to get back to work, so I can distinguish myself from the crowd." Schiller made another attempt to leave.

"I don't think I was mistaken, Dick. You were wearing the same clothes you have on now. I don't think there's a look-alike on this island who would have been wearing that exact same plaid jacket and chinos, *with* bow tie, do you?"

The writer turned red. "All right, dammit, I *was* there. I just didn't want it to get back to anyone on the show. I'm so worried about my script, I can't stay away from any of the shoots. Edgar Min is out to destroy my story line, you know. He acts as if he has a mission from God to reduce it to irrelevance. I can't just stand by and do nothing, can I?"

"I don't understand. What could you possibly do about it from up on the highway?"

"Good question. Drop a bomb, maybe? Hah-hah. It doesn't make a lot of sense, does it? That's why I didn't say anything. Might make me look silly. You understand, don't you?"

Not really, I thought. Dick Schiller was one of the oddest people I'd ever met. His behavior just didn't add up. But his tendency to pop up in unexpected places was reminiscent of Billy's redheaded stalker. I found myself wondering briefly if Dick was the one threatening Billy. He was certainly crazy enough. Dick, of course, had wispy brown hair, not red, but a wig was always a possibility.

"I have a question, Dick. Billy is convinced that someone is out to kill him. Do *you* think he's in danger?"

To my surprise, the writer smirked at my suggestion.

"Anything is possible, Steve, that's what I always say. Especially on an island as rife with racial tension as this one. I'd keep an eye on the guy most likely to take over his job if anything *did* happen. That's what I'd do if I were you." And with that he finally slipped away, calling "see you soon" over his shoulder.

It didn't take me long to find Jayne again. She was the one so laden down with packages, she was listing to starboard. "Just stocking stuffers, dear, for the grandchildren." Taking packages from both her hands at the same time so I wouldn't throw her off balance, I told her about my encounter with Dick Schiller.

"A *very* odd man!" I said. "And I'm almost certain he followed us here."

"You mean to say we have a stalker of our very own now?"

There was a small stack of phone messages waiting for us back at the Royal Hawaiian reception desk. I flipped through them while we were waiting for the elevator.

"There's nothing here that can't wait until tomorrow. Danny called three times. I have a feeling he's afraid we're going to pack up and go home. Cass called to say everything is still quiet at

Billy's, and Keoni called to confirm that the party is still on for tomorrow night. He hopes we'll be able to make it."

When I turned on the light in the entryway to our suite, I could tell immediately that someone had been in our room.

"Stay right there," I whispered, moving slowly down the hallway to the sitting room. I glanced around quickly, then checked the bedroom and bath. It wasn't until I came back into the front room for a second look around that I noticed the VCR and stack of videotapes on top of the TV set.

"False alarm," I called to Jayne. "Danny remembered to have the *Hawaiian Wave* shows delivered, just in case we got tired of the real thing." I collected Jayne's packages while she looked through the pile of videocassettes. She waved one in my direction.

"Shall we make Danny really happy and watch the opening episode, Steve? It's called 'Wave of Death.' "

We ended our evening on the couch, watching a fantasy Hawaii on the TV screen, while the reality outside our window proceeded toward a denouement I couldn't begin to imagine.

chapter 15

Wednesday morning started out as every morning in paradise should: tea on the lanai with the rising sun. But the mood was all too soon broken by a ringing phone.

"Flip you for it," I said. "It's probably your not so secret admirer anyway."

Jayne rose obligingly and went inside. She came back much too quickly for it to have been Lieutenant Chen.

"That was Danny Siderman. He's put a limousine at our disposal for the rest of the stay. Which is very sweet. I *love* limousines at my disposal—all we have to do is ring downstairs. I told him we'd enjoyed the *Hawaiian Wave* opener we watched last night, but he hardly seemed to hear me. He's very excited about this benefit."

We started toward the North Shore early, so there would be plenty of time to enjoy the drive around Diamond Head Crater and up the Windward Coast, through the towns I think of as the "vowel villages": Kahaluu, Kaaawa, Punaluu, and Laie. We passed beautiful beach parks, where camping families were still having breakfast and early-morning surfers were already in the water, bobbing up and down beyond the swells while they waited for the right wave to come along. Our driver was an elderly Filipino who introduced himself as Carlos Medina and kept up a melodic running commentary all the way up the coast. The farther north we went, the more surfers we saw, on regulation boards and short, Styrofoam boogie boards.

"The sea looks pretty high this morning," I commented to Carlos.

"Oh, yes," he acknowledged with an appreciative smile. "This is the best time of year for the waves. We will soon have the Hawaiian Pro and the Triple Crown of Surfing here on Oahu. You should try to see some of it if you have the time. I used to surf myself. Now I am content to watch my grandson compete."

He went on to describe the old koa-wood boards, eighteen to twenty feet long and weighing 150 pounds.

"Today," he said, shaking his head sadly, "they ride on surfboards half that length, lightweight hollow shells that they are constantly redesigning. They spend more time looking for the perfect board than waiting for the perfect wave."

We passed the Kuilima coves and pulled into the Turtle Bay Hilton at eleven-thirty sharp. The resort hotel sits on the northernmost tip of Oahu, looking a lot like the broad-backed creature it is named for. It's an appropriate image for this end of the island, where the pace is slower and the focus is toward the sea.

At the moment the focus was food, however, as a steady stream of elegantly dressed older patrons, young people of all descriptions, celebrity types and social climbers made its way toward the main dining room, closed to non-ticket holders and decorated with balloons and streamers in the pink and green colors of the Diamond Head Polo Club. When I saw how formally some people were dressed I was glad Jayne had talked me into wearing a jacket and tie. She looked stunning herself in a pink and yellow print silk dress and straw hat decorated with fresh hibiscus. The crowd seemed pretty evenly divided between those who were there to party and those who wanted to support the School for the Deaf. A number of people were signing as they conversed. Live Hawaiian music drifted happily at low volume over the sounds of laughter and tinkling glasses. The gala seemed to be in full swing already.

Jason Patterson stood at the entrance to the dining room, greeting guests individually. His face lit up when he caught sight of us.

"Welcome, Steve, Jayne. How are you, dear? I can't tell you how much I appreciate your coming up. Danny's inside. He told me we're not likely to see Billy here today. I'm disappointed, of course, we all are, but we can understand, after the trauma on the beach yesterday. I gather the brakes on his car gave out as well. The poor man is probably better off in bed."

Jayne nodded noncommittally. She had phoned Billy before we left the hotel. He was still feeling disoriented from the sedatives he'd taken the evening before and thought he'd like to spend a quiet day at home. She'd spoken to Cass as well, who was disappointed at missing the buffet but thought he'd try his hand at riding the waves. Bertrand had lent him a board and was giving him pointers.

"The brunch looks like a success, in any case," Jason went on, looking around with satisfaction at the rapidly filling room. "And everyone seems to be having a good time. I told my wife, Melanie, that you'll be kind enough to join her table for lunch. But before I take you over there, I want to introduce you to Bernice Hutchins. She's the principal of the Manoa School for the Deaf." Jason indicated the short woman standing next to him, who'd been quietly but intently following our conversation between greetings. She shook both our hands enthusiastically and thanked us all over again for taking the time to come.

"We're delighted to be here," Jayne replied. "I can't tell you how fond I've become of Susan. I'm impressed at how well she's doing for her first time in a professional production. You must miss her in the classroom though."

"Oh, we do; she's a real favorite with the students and we're all looking forward to having her back. But I think it's important for the children to see firsthand that the hearing-impaired can do anything they set their minds to."

"I agree. And you're an excellent role model yourself." It wasn't until Jayne mentioned it that I realized the principal was herself hearing-impaired.

Jason Patterson walked us through the multilevel dining room to a table by the windows. The morning was clear and the view across the bay to the distant hills was spectacular.

Some of the groups of tables we passed were getting a bit boisterous, like preschoolers at a birthday party. The volume was rising in the room; Jason had almost to shout to be heard as he pointed out this TV personality, that actor, or that scion of an old missionary family.

Melanie Patterson was sitting alone at a table for six, her back to the room. As we approached, I noticed black hair elegantly styled and a white linen suit that looked couture. Jason reached her first and whispered something in her ear. As she turned around and rose to greet us, Jayne and I both did what I hope was an unobtrusive doubletake. She was Chinese, a good thirty years younger than her husband, and one of the most strikingly beautiful women I've ever seen.

"Won't you join me?" she said in an upper-class British accent. "Jason is afraid I'll be lonely. I haven't much interest, you see, in his horsy set. But I do know polo. We play it in Hong Kong as well."

We sat down as Jason excused himself and hurried back to his duties as greeter, casting what seemed an apprehensive glance over his shoulder as he went.

Melanie smiled condescendingly. "Jason does make such a fuss about these things. I do hope you won't be too bored today. The game should be watchable, but these charity luncheons are always pretty dreadful, of course. I'd be happy to ask one of the chefs to prepare something special for you if you'd like."

"Don't bother," Jayne said with a straight face. "I'm sure we'll be able to find something we can force down. In fact, I think I'll meander over to the buffet right now, to avoid the rush later."

I started to rise with Jayne, but the beautiful young Chinese woman laid a perfectly shaped hand on my arm.

"Do stay with me, Mr. Allen," she said, "or who knows who might sit in your chair if you leave it empty."

"Of course," I replied politely, sitting back down.

Melanie talked about Hong Kong and the Good Old Days before the British sun had set on the Crown Colony. "I met my husband there, you know. He came over to play in a benefit match, of all things. But let's not talk about Jason. I want to hear about you. I gather you've had a dreadful time since arriving on this island. I sympathize." Melanie was still sympathizing when I saw Jayne headed back our way.

"Can I bring you anything from the buffet?" I asked Melanie. "A glass of champagne?"

"I'd love a little more champagne, thank you. And perhaps

just a bite of the chocolate-raspberry Cointreau torte. I hear that it's quite edible. The pastry chef is Austrian, which does help."

"Lost your appetite, *Steverino?*" Jayne asked archly, setting down a plate of food that smelled delicious and looked like a floral arrangement.

"Not at all. I was just waiting for you," I assured her, rising in a very gentlemanly fashion to fetch Melanie's dessert and drink. When I dropped them off at the table, I noticed that conversation was not flowing as smoothly as it had been before my departure. Serves Jayne right, I thought. Maybe we can introduce Melanie to Lieutenant Chen.

The buffet was spread out over several locations around the dining room. To call it magnificent would be an understatement. The presentation alone was worth the price of admission, whether you actually ate or not. The pièce de résistance was a giant pony carved out of ice, sitting in a bed of lettuce and cradling fresh prawns and lobster claws in the small of its back and the curve of its reclining legs. There was a huge map of Oahu made of edible flowers, elaborately carved vegetables, and appetizers representing the diverse culinary traditions of Hawaii.

A koa-wood bowl the size of a dugout canoe was heaped with greens and surrounded with bowls of every garnish and dressing imaginable. Main courses were being individually prepared at several different locations around the room, by a bevy of chefs, male and female, costumed in traditional polo jerseys and caps bearing the insignia of the Diamond Head Polo Club. The dessert display, a fountain of Austrian pastries cascading down to a pool of fresh fruit sorbets and homemade ice creams at the bottom, was a temptation to excess.

"I deserve a medal for restraint," I muttered to no one in particular as I filled my plate with a modest selection of delicacies.

"He's not really going to do it, is he? How *awfully* amusing!" I heard at my elbow. I turned around to see a young woman in blue jeans addressing a rather inebriated companion. "That's what I heard, darling. Won't Jason have a fit!"

I looked for Jason through the crowded dining room, where an overflow crowd was beginning to play musical chairs, wandering from table to table with food and drinks in hand. I didn't see him anywhere but did spot Danny Siderman looking very horsy in jodhpurs and boots. He was talking volubly to a small circle of older, wealthy-looking guests, his plate of food sitting untouched in front of him.

Jayne suddenly appeared at my side. "Some young people have joined Melanie, people her own age," she said pointedly. "I thought I'd come over and case the room with you. I haven't seen any sign of Keoni or Lance or . . . oh, wait, there's Edgar."

It took me a minute to spot him. The director had been backed into a corner behind the salad bowl by an angry-looking elderly matron who seemed almost of a mind to attack him with her parasol. I could barely hear her over the general din in the dining room, but it sounded as though she was taking exception to some sexually explicit footage in an earlier episode. "Crude . . . vulgar . . . obscene . . ." rang out as she gestured with the sun shade. Danny spotted the danger at the same time we did and hurried over to rescue his director. He seemed to know the woman attacker and managed to persuade her to back off, though grudgingly, and go to her seat. Edgar saw us watching him and headed our way, a gleeful twinkle in his eye.

"She was marvelous, no? That is the exact response I am looking for in my work. I want my audience to live each show. Yes, get angry, I say! I encourage an emotional response. If someone were to shoot his TV set at the end of an episode, I would consider it the highest compliment to my art."

I had to laugh. "Just as long as no one shoots *you*, Edgar. She looked as though she could do some damage with that umbrella."

Three or four members of Edgar's production crew materialized out of the crowd, and he launched into a lecture on the symbolism of the parasol. Jayne and I excused ourselves, took another look around the room, and headed back to our hostess. "There's a strange feeling in the air," my wife pointed out. "It's as if some of these people are waiting for the show to start."

Melanie Patterson had been joined by several handsome young men who were hanging on her every word. Melanie turned to me and said that they had just been discussing the polo match.

"This should be a fairly interesting one," she said with a bored smile that belied her words. "Both teams are using it as a warm-up for the filmed match tomorrow. Mr. Min may have cameramen on the field today, but I understand they'll just be rehearsing for tomorrow's filming. Though I do hear that he loves to do the unexpected. I just hope Jason isn't overdoing it, playing both days. He hasn't been sleeping well lately, and he's put so much time into making this benefit a success. Poor dear!"

Jayne and I had been listening while we ate. Suddenly my wife gave me a nudge.

"Over there, Steve." Lance Brady was standing in the doorway. He surveyed the room with a professional air, spotted a table for two that was temporarily empty, and took possession. He was followed a minute later by Susan Harrington, who looked stunning in a blue cotton sundress and broad-brimmed straw hat with ribbons. She joined him at the table, set down a small notepad and pen, picked up her plate, and proceeded with Lance to the buffet.

Jayne went on eating and making polite conversation with our table mates. But I could tell she was thinking what I was thinking. If we had a daughter, Lance Brady was not the kind of man I would want her to be spending time with.

Jayne excused herself a few minutes later and went straight to the table where Susan and Lance were seated. After a brief conversation she returned, smiling.

"I've invited Susan to ride with us the rest of the way to the polo field—I suggested we might use the time to work on our lines," she said as she sat down again.

We finished lunch, making polite conversation until we saw that Susan was ready to leave.

"You *are* going to join me at the field?" Melanie asked as we prepared to get up.

"Of course, we'd love to, as long as there's room for Susan," my wife answered.

Melanie didn't look pleased. "I'm sure we can fit her in."

Just then there was a ripple of laughter and raucous catcalls in the doorway, and a vaudeville-type polo pony, decked out in pink and green streamers and ridden by an apparently tipsy young man in a tuxedo, came lurching into the dining room, headed for the bar. The young man reached down and picked up a bottle of Dom Pérignon from a startled waiter, raised the bottle in a victorious salute to the room, and then brought it to his lips. The dining room was in an uproar. Laughter mixed with outrage and two of the young people took the opportunity to throw bits of the buffet at each other.

"I think it's our cue to leave," Jayne said. We made our way toward the door while the hotel management and polo club officials tried in vain to quell the semi-riot. I finally spotted Jason Patterson, looking as though he'd aged ten years in the last ten minutes. He ran over to the polo pony and rider and led them as quickly as pandemonium would allow toward the same doorway we were headed for.

Susan was waiting for us outside the front door. Dick Schiller was with her, mumbling so fast that I couldn't imagine she could read much from his lips. He barely acknowledged our approach.

"It's disgusting, isn't it?" he grumbled. "It's typical, the idle rich with nothing better to do than throw food at each other. They care more about their animals than they do about people!" He spun around and glared at me. "I'll bet you fifty dollars Keoni Pahia doesn't show up here . . . fifty dollars!" He reached for his wallet, took a quick look, and slid it back into his pocket. "Well, make it forty dollars. They wouldn't let Keoni in, would they?— the only Hawaiians here are busboys!"

"You'd lose the bet, but not by much," I acknowledged. Dick smirked and abruptly stormed into the dining room. A second later we heard the sound of breaking glass and his unmistakable voice raised in indignation. "For God's sake, be more careful, will you?" he said angrily to someone with whom he had apparently collided.

"Let's get out of here," Jayne suggested, leading Susan toward the beach.

And that's how I found myself, a few minutes later, wandering hand in hand with two lovely women, along the sands of Kuilima Point, whose name means "to hold hands." It was a welcome interlude. But I couldn't help noticing that even in this quiet cove, the Hawaiian surf was rising.

chapter 16

The main parking lot was already full when we pulled into the polo field at Mokuleia. Horse vans and pickup trucks sat next to BMWs and Mercedes-Benzes. Elegantly clad men in linen pants and designer shirts helped ladies in high-heeled shoes step around the horse droppings in the parking lot. Carlos Medina dropped us off at the main gate and went to park the limo in an overflow lot across the road. I had invited him to join us, but he declined politely, saying he'd rather stay with the car and catch a little snooze.

The polo club had offered two types of tickets for the benefit, with and without brunch, and it was obvious that quite a few supporters had come just for the game. Lots of people were carrying folding chairs, picnic baskets, coolers, and blankets. The temporary bleachers were already full, and club members sporting name tags were busy trying to make people comfortable anywhere they could. Susan was ecstatic, first signing to Jayne and then scribbling on her notepad and handing it to me.

"Isn't it wonderful! The benefit is bound to be a success in spite of what happened at the brunch. This money is earmarked for the school's extracurricular programs. That includes my theater project. I think we may clear ten thousand dollars today! What do you think?"

I nodded my head in agreement. At $70 for a full ticket and $30 for the match alone, they were bringing in some money.

We soon spotted Melanie Patterson in one of the covered boxes set up on the far side of the bleachers. She saw us just as she was accepting a glass of champagne from a smoothly handsome young man who seemed to be making the rounds.

"Well, there you are!" She smiled at me as we approached. "Where did that sweet boy with the champagne go?"

"Not for us, thank you," Jayne said, signing to Susan, who nodded her agreement. Melanie opened a cooler full of soft drinks at her feet and offered them around. She began to discuss the game we were about to see as if nothing out of the ordinary had happened at the Hilton buffet. We all followed her lead, which wasn't hard. Polo is an exciting game even without the warm-up we had just witnessed.

Actually it's the oldest equestrian sport, with some experts arguing that it is the oldest organized sport of any kind. It originated in Persia four thousand years ago, and moved east through Arabia to the Tibetans, Chinese, and Japanese, all of whom loved it. Muslims introduced it to India in the thirteenth century, where, six centuries later, the British saw it and had to have it. The earliest games among the British in India were between mounted military units, playing with eight men to a side and almost no rules. In the game we were about to witness there would be four players to a team and lots of rules.

As the beginning of play approached, the two teams lined up in the center of the field, facing each other. The Diamond Head Polo Club sported pink and green silks, the Maui team was in orange and blue. A mounted official bowled the ball down the alley between them and play commenced with a mad scramble for the first good shot.

The polo ponies themselves are a big part of the game. They are no longer "ponies"; that name is a carryover from a time when there was a height restriction on the horses. Today they are usually "grade Thoroughbreds" (a Thoroughbred and quarter horse mix) and often trained first as cow ponies on western American ranches or the pampas of Argentina. They don't begin training for polo play until age five and are usually not fielded for another year or two after that. A polo pony can still be actively pursuing its career at twenty.

When the two teams came onto the field, wearing their numbers over their jerseys, I noticed that Jason Patterson, our host and the president of the club, was playing position three. That's unusual for an owner. It's considered the most crucial position and hence given to the best player, who is generally not the man with the money. In polo, position one scores, position two scrambles for the ball, position three feeds the ball to one and two and helps defend his goal, and position four is primarily defensive. Any player is allowed to score, though, if he finds himself in the right place at the right time.

The field is three times as long as a football field and 160 yards wide. There are lightweight goal posts at each end, placed eight yards apart, and the object of the game is to hit the elusive little ball, about the size of a baseball, through the opponent's posts. This is harder than it might seem, and scores are relatively low, but the action is nonstop for six periods, called chukkers, of seven minutes apiece, with only a short break between periods.

The Mokuleia field is primitive compared to some, but the natural surroundings are unequaled anywhere. From our vantage point near midfield, we looked out across the huge grassy meadow to a stand of ironwood trees, wind-carved sand dunes, and the sea under a crisp blue sky. Behind us rose the northernmost end of the Waianae mountains. It was a perfect setting for the spectacle of eight magnificent horses charging up and down the field, their skilled riders determined to take or maintain possession of a tiny wooden ball. Polo may not be considered a contact sport, but, believe me, there is plenty of contact, thrills galore, and a certain amount of outright danger. The first chukker came to a close without a score, but the Oahu team was holding its own against the Maui squad. Both teams would be choosing new horses for the second chukker, from the strings of ponies lined up at each end of the playing field. At one point I noticed Edgar with a hand-held camera and one of his cameramen in tow, getting impromptu shots of the action and the crowd; this was not an official shooting day, but Edgar could not resist.

As soon as the chukker came to an end, the young man with the champagne was back, followed by a steady stream of well-wishers who wanted to welcome Jayne and me to Oahu. Some were eating as they strolled the boxes, some drinking; all seemed to be having a high old time. When people began retaking their seats for the second chukker, my wife turned to Melanie, signing as she spoke so that Susan could follow the conversation.

"Jason seems to have recovered from the pranks at the buffet. He looks wonderful out there. He must have been playing since childhood."

"Yes," Melanie answered with a boredom she made no attempt to disguise. "His first wife was as fanatic about polo, as he is. I can't get too excited about it myself, but I do try to be supportive. I'm in charge of raising money and our campaign has been quite successful."

"I can imagine," Jayne replied as Melanie bestowed another one of her exclusive, caressing smiles on me.

"The Diamond Head club means so much to Jason," Melanie went on. "He'd do just about anything to keep it going. He started the club a few years before I met him, and he continues to put all his time and energy into it. Sometimes I wonder why he bothered to marry again." Melanie pouted playfully, which made her look even more attractive. "He's not just the president, he *is* the club. He started out owning all the horses himself, but now other members can buy in by sponsoring their own ponies and jockeys. Your Mr. Siderman is planning to do that. We're even looking at the possibility of corporate sponsorship, heaven forbid. Mr. Siderman would like *Hawaiian Wave* to become a regular sponsor in exchange for advertising on the field and during the breaks. I suppose it makes sense financially, but I hate to see it happen, and it's so hard on poor Jason. It would be nice to protect one sport from commercial exploitation, don't you think?" No one answered, as the next chukker had begun and we all turned our attention back to the match.

The first period had been just a warm-up. Play intensified now, with pitched battles over each shot and sweeping gallops up and down the field. One of the Diamond Head players lost his mallet. When the chukker ended, I felt as if I needed a break as much as the players did. A voice over the loudspeaker asked for volunteers to go over the field to stamp the holes in the turf back into place. I explained the request to Susan, and she said she'd love to accompany me. Out on the field, ladies in high heels seemed to be making more holes than they were repairing, and youngsters were stomping away as if their lives depended on it. There were so many volunteers that the field was soon back in shape and Susan and I moved over to the sidelines.

"Tell me," I began, making sure I had her attention first so she could read my lips, "you've filmed some scenes already with the regular stars of *Hawaiian Wave*. What do you think of them?"

Susan pulled her notepad and pen out of a deep pocket in her sundress, wrote furiously for a minute, and handed it over to me.

"Billy is awfully sweet," she had written, "but he seems a little young to me. Edgar is a wonderful director. He has been most helpful, and patient with my inexperience. I am fortunate to have the opportunity to work with someone like him. Mr. Siderman has been supportive as well."

"What about Keoni?" I asked. Susan paused, started to write, scratched out her first few words, and stood for a moment, staring out toward the sea.

"I've never met anyone quite like Keoni before," she finally wrote. "I don't know what to say about him. I think there is more to him than what you see on the surface. I don't think he is happy despite his popularity. I think he covers up a lot." She smiled wistfully and took the notepad back from me to add, "Deaf people do that too."

Danny Siderman suddenly appeared next to Susan and gave her a fatherly hug. She excused herself to rejoin Jayne and Melanie and I stayed to talk to Danny, who seemed to have forgotten our differences of the day before in his excitement over the play that had just resumed.

"This is the life, isn't it, Steve? What a game. Can you believe it? I'd barely even heard of polo a few months ago, when we moved to the island. And now I'm a part of all this. Did I tell you about my horses?"

Before I could answer that he had, the ball rolled our way, followed by a pack of thundering horsemen. We jumped back involuntarily.

"See what I mean? It's a thrill a minute. Honestly, I'd give up producing in a minute if I could figure out a way to make money at this. That Maui guy, number three, isn't he something?

Boy, would I like to get someone like that for our team. Of course, Jason might not like it. He's the only two-goaler in our club right now, and I think he likes it that way." Danny jumped again as Jason, right on cue, thundered past in pursuit of the ball.

"I can't recall how they rate polo players, Danny. Refresh my memory."

He lowered his voice. "Speaking of ratings, that little fiasco at the beach yesterday could turn out to be a blessing in disguise. It hit the tabloids like gangbusters this morning. 'Star of *Hawaiian Wave* sees his own death foreshadowed,' that kind of stuff. It can't hurt as long as we can keep our golden boy from taking it too seriously."

"Danny, someone drowned!"

Danny did his best to look compassionate. "Oh, hey, I really *feel* for the guy. Don't get me wrong. Drowning is a terrible, terrible thing. But all I'm saying, if this guy—what's his name? Peter Yardly . . ."

"Sam Fitzgerald," I corrected him.

"If poor Sam had to kick off, he might as well do it in a useful manner, you know. A manner that might benefit those of us who are left behind to struggle on . . . and, Sam, I got to say this, his death was just what the doctor ordered publicity-wise. We've been getting tons of copy. Tons!"

"I'm sure Sam is resting more easily knowing how he's helped with the ratings," I mentioned with heavy sarcasm.

"Anyway, back to horses," Danny went on, ignoring my tone. "In polo, every player is handicapped, or rated, from minus three to ten. It's based on individual skills, value to the team, sportsmanship, oh, and the quality of the ponies, of course. Some people reckon the horse is seventy-five percent of the rating. Look at Jason out there. He's the only two-goaler on our team, and it's all because he can afford a horse like that gray he's on. Most of our players are one goal or under. I'd love to mount a two-goal jockey. It's just a matter of money. But if you've got the money, there's no thrill like it."

The action on the field had just been whistled to a stop. The foul must have been against our team, because the players from Maui were lining up for a penalty shot. They made it and the intensity of play went up yet another notch. Jason began yelling at the other players on his team.

"He doesn't like losing," Danny said, shaking his head. As if to confirm his statement, a second penalty was called, this one on Jason himself. It was for a high stick—Jason had allowed his mallet to swing dangerously near an opposing player's head.

"Foul play," Danny mumbled, and excused himself as the penalty shot, which didn't go in, ended the third chukker.

chapter 17

When I got back to the box, Jayne and Susan were nowhere in sight. In their place, sprawled across two chairs and looking very pleased with himself, was Lance Brady. His beige linen suit was open to reveal a pink shirt and maroon necktie. He had Melanie Patterson's undivided attention and greeted me with obvious reluctance.

"Hello, Steve. Not coming to steal another girl away from me, I hope?" I smiled and sat down in the chair next to him.

"I would if I could. If you'll excuse us, Mrs. Patterson, I'd like to have a word with Lance before play resumes."

Melanie turned her attention toward a young man who had just come up to pay his compliments, and I motioned the actor down a chair to where we could talk more privately.

"I think you know the real reason Jayne and I are here," I began, keeping my voice low. "Billy asked us to come because he's afraid for his life. Do you think he has any reason to be?"

"You want to know the truth, Steve? I know Billy is your friend. Hell, he's my friend too. But that kid is not what he appears to be. I've been around, you know. The real truth is, I'm the only one on the set of *Hawaiian Wave* who has any idea what's going on most of the time. Danny is a jerk, Edgar's a maniac, Keoni is a beach boy, and Billy puts on a better act off camera than on. I know what you're going to say. He pretends to be the boy next door, the original 'shucks, gee-whiz' kid. But he's shrewd, Steve, take my word for it. He knows how to use that act to get what he wants out of people."

"Can you be specific?"

"Well, take the show, for example. This series could have been big for me, really big. I would never have signed on otherwise." A dreamy look of pure egotism had appeared on Lance's face; he continued with self-absorbed seriousness: "I'm not sidekick material, Steve, you can see that. I was led to believe that *Hawaiian Wave* would be different from the run-of-the-mill buddy detective shows. We would all have our day in the sun. But Billy can't handle it. He knows I can blow him off the screen if I get half a chance. So he sees to it that I don't get one. He works behind the scenes to keep my role secondary. When I do manage to get more than a few grunts in a scene, he gets in there and tries to upstage my lines with some little improvisation he's cooked up to bring viewer attention back to himself. It's not the way to make friends in this business, man. I mean, personally, I think the kid is neurotic as hell—and he may be imagining things. But he's given more than a few people reason to want to give him a scare, or maybe even worse."

"Like who, for example?" I asked, noticing that Melanie was looking our way with an amused expression on her face.

"Like Keoni, for example. Keoni may be an amateur. Hell, he's not even that. The guy couldn't act his way out of a paper bag. But he's got a big following here on the island. You think he likes playing second fiddle to Billy Markham? And then there's Edgar, of course, our 'illustrious' director. Never underestimate a Slav."

"What in the world would Edgar have against Billy?" I asked. But I didn't get an answer. The ubiquitous Dick Schiller had joined our party. Before anyone, even Dick, could say a word, Lance was out of his seat and leading the writer away, an arm draped patronizingly over his shoulders, almost as if he didn't want Dick to speak with us. Curiouser and curiouser, I thought to myself.

Melanie motioned me to come closer, and I moved down to her end of the box. "You mustn't leave me like that again, Steve," she said, patting my knee affectionately. I assured her I wouldn't and began chatting about the game, all the while looking around for Jayne and Susan. I finally spotted them at the far end of the field, heading behind the goal line on their way back to our side of the field. Perhaps, I thought, they had been taking a look at the sea, but now the fourth chukker began with a bang as eight horses and riders charged down the field toward them. They both skipped out of the way as the polo ball went whizzing through the goal posts. Jason Patterson had just scored a goal.

Jayne and Susan hadn't been back in the box long when the chukker came to an end. Out of the clear blue Hawaiian sky, pink and green parachutes dotted the air as skydivers floated down to land in the middle of the field. It was time for the entertainment break. A large uniformed Hawaiian band marched onto the field and struck up a tune. When they had finished, little Mrs. Hutchins, the director of the school for the deaf, thanked everyone for their gracious support and declared the fund-raiser a rousing success.

Crowd participation reached a frenzied pitch during the last third of the match. Jayne and Susan got into the spirit of the thing, and it was all I could do to stay out of the way of their floppy hats as they jumped up and down in excitement. The Diamond Head Polo Club won the game, two to one.

"It's been so nice getting to know you," Melanie said, cradling my hand in hers as we said our good-byes. "I'll be in the audience tomorrow, Jason insists on it. You were so brave to stick out the whole match," she added, turning to Jayne and Susan for a brief handshake.

"Don't mention it, dear," Jayne answered. "I wouldn't have missed this show for the world." Her sarcasm was not lost on Melanie, who looked nonplused for a moment and then turned her charm toward the young man of the champagne, who'd come up to kiss her hand farewell.

Susan signed to Jayne, who answered and then turned to me.

"I told Susan we'd be glad to drop her off at Elisabeth's apartment in Kaneohe. It should be a beautiful drive this time of day."

The limousine floated us back down the coast as Jayne and Susan carried on an animated conversation in sign language and I dictated a few notes into my pocket tape recorder. Lance hadn't had a good word to say about anyone except himself. Was he capable of trying to frighten Billy off in order to get the starring

role for himself? But no, I had a feeling that behind all that
bravado he knew he wouldn't get the lead even if Billy were out
of the picture. Keoni, on the other hand ... What had Lance
been about to say about Edgar Min? And was it possible that Jayne
and I had been set up? That Billy was faking the danger to himself
in order to cover the murder of Sam Fitzgerald? But what connection could he possibly have with someone like Fitzgerald? I had
plenty of questions; what I lacked were any answers.

As Susan was getting out of the car in Kaneohe, she signed
something to Jayne, said "Thank you" out loud to me, and waved
a final good-bye. Jayne translated for me.

"She thanked us for a lovely time. And then she said it would
be hard to think of us as the bad guys during the filming. But
she would try to take a professional approach and imagine evil
lurking under the appearance of good. Something to think about,
isn't it?"

The late afternoon light was at its peak as we pulled up to the
door of the Royal Hawaiian Hotel.

"I'll be up in a minute," Jayne said, heading toward the beach.
I called Billy's house from the sitting room sofa after opening the
curtains so I could enjoy the view while I talked. Bertrand
answered, but not until the fourth ring. I could hear voices and
music in the background.

"It sounds as though Billy has recovered, Bertrand. May I
speak to him?"

Bertrand laughed. I don't think I had ever heard him laugh
before. It was a deep, genuinely mirthful sound. "I'm afraid he's
indisposed at the moment, sir. He and Mr. Cassidy are taking a
hula lesson. It was Mr. Cassidy's idea. He saw lessons at the community center advertised in the local paper and called to see if the
instructor would come to the house."

I had visions of a nubile young woman gyrating her hips, with
a self-conscious Billy and an even more embarrassed Cass trying
to shake their grass skirts in imitation.

"I wouldn't want to interrupt the serious pursuit of culture,"
I assured Bertrand as laughter accompanied the sound of the

background music being turned up. "I have to admit I'm curious though. What is she like? Young? Old? Is she wearing a grass skirt?"

Bertrand laughed again. "Oh, it's not a she, sir. *He* came in street clothes and they're working on the basics this time, hand and arm movements, footwork. They'll move on to costuming later. Everyone in Waimanalo knows Papa Bear. That's what we call him, his name is Manikuuleiliko. He's a rather portly gentleman, in his late forties, drives a truck for the Oahu Bread Company. He's a wonderful dancer, by the way. You ought to see him sometime. He always brings home a first prize from the Merry Monarch Hula Festival on the Big Island."

"Sounds like fun, Bertrand. Tell Cass to pay attention so he can teach Jayne and me. And give Billy our love. I'm glad things are getting back to normal over there."

I hung up the phone, opened a cold guava drink from the refrigerator, and dialed the number Keoni Pahia had given us. The phone rang six times at Hawaiian Wave Records before a male voice answered with "Hawaiian Wave Records. What's happening?"

"My question precisely," I replied. "Is Keoni there?"

"He's here somewhere, man. Give me your number and I'll have him call you." Less than five minutes later the phone rang.

"Steve? I don't believe it. I've been trying to get you all day. It's a madhouse over here. You know that body you found in the water? Well, the guy worked for us. The cops were all over this place yesterday. A homicide detective even came out to my house. I don't know why they have to pick on me. So the guy worked here, so what? If they think they're going to sink this company, they'd better think again. You're coming tonight, aren't you? I need you, Steve. I can't talk now, but I'm counting on you."

As I started to answer, the phone went dead in my hand.

chapter 18

Two hours later our limousine was cruising up and down the dark, deserted streets of a warehouse area on the outskirts of Pearl City. We couldn't help noticing the size of the rats scurrying across the road in front of our headlights.

"I believe we have finally escaped the tourist Hawaii," Jayne mentioned.

"This can't be right—we'd better head back to the highway and find a gas station where I can phone," I finally said to the driver. He was young, new to the island, and beginning to panic. He'd just stopped for the fifth time to scrutinize his map and a scribbled sheet of directions.

"I don't know which way the highway *is,* sir," he wailed.

"That way," said Jayne emphatically, pointing. She was wrong, but we turned the corner and practically ran into a large shed lit by the glow of a neon palm tree. A neon sun rose out of neon waves, and arching over the whole scene, above a row of boxy little windows, the words *Hawaiian Wave Records* flashed on and off in salmon pink and turquoise blue. There were twenty or so cars parked at various angles in front of the building. Jayne told the driver we'd call his pager when we were ready to leave and smiled conspiratorially as she took my arm.

"Ready, Holmes?"

"Ready, Watson."

We opened a wooden door that looked as if it had seen better days and found ourselves in front of a large desk covered with half-eaten plate lunches and soda cans. Matching chairs that looked as

if they'd first seen duty in a dentist's office were scattered around
the room, and a table in the corner was strewn with music periodi-
cals, ashtrays, and more soda cans. The room reminded me of a
kid's playhouse where no parent had ever been allowed to come
in and tell the messy children to clean up. There was no one in
sight.

"Why don't you stay here," I suggested. "I'll reconnoiter."

"Of course, dear, I'll just make myself at home," she replied,
removing a chicken bone from one of the chairs and sitting down
with a copy of *Billboard*.

I followed a corridor leading from the reception area past a
row of offices that corresponded to the windows in the front of
the building. Neon light flashed off and on in the gloom. At the
end of the hall there was a double door that looked padded for
sound reduction. I opened it slowly and found myself at the rear
of a large soundstage. There were folding chairs set up on risers
to the right of me and a string of control boards down near the
stage. A couple of dozen young Polynesian men in T-shirts and
flip-flops ran back and forth, adjusting the lights onstage, the
video cameras set up around the room, and the buttons and
switches on the soundboards. A disgusting pall of cigarette smoke
hung in the air, and more soda cans and paper cups littered the
floor. Several members of the crew looked up and nodded when
I entered the room. One young man with long hair and a T-shirt
that read AMERICA, GO HOME! came bounding up the aisle, smiling
and slapping himself on the head.

"Hey, you must be Steve Allen. Sorry, man. Things have been
kind of weird around here lately. But I guess you know that. Keoni
said you were the one who found Sam's body. He should be here
any minute, Keoni, that is. Come on down, take the weight off.
Your wife couldn't make it, huh?"

"She just hasn't made it this far. Tell me something—how
did Sam seem to you on Friday?"

"Hey, man, it was really spooky—it was like he knew it was
coming. Like a premonition, ya know?"

"No, I don't know. Tell me."

"Well, you know how he was, old Sam the Man—he was
usually so goofy and, like, stoned. He just kind of grinned at

everybody and followed directions. But Friday he was tweaked. Jumpy, like you had to say everything twice to get through to him."

Just then the double doors opened behind us and Jayne entered the room with Keoni on one side and Lloyd Kawelo on the other. Keoni had on a T-shirt with his company's logo across the front. Lloyd was wearing an aloha shirt that could have been the twin of my own. Jayne had insisted that I wear it, pointing out that old rayon shirts like mine, which I had picked up on my first visit to Hawaii, were now called silkies, the latest thing in fashion and worth hundreds of dollars.

"Hey, cool shirt." Lloyd laughed as he shook my hand.

Keoni whispered "Thanks for coming, Mr. Allen" as he clapped me on the shoulder and motioned us to some chairs on the first row of risers. "I'll be right back," he added, "I need to see how the refreshments are doing. I hope you're ready to grind tonight."

"I'm not sure I'm up for dancing," I said.

Everyone laughed, Jayne included. "*Grind* is Hawaiian slang for eating, darling," she told me.

"That's right. Hey, you've got an up-to-date old lady, Steve," Keoni said.

"Young lady, please," Jayne interjected. "And why don't I come with you and help with the food."

Jayne and Keoni left together through the studio door to arrange things so that we might grind later in the evening— though frankly, the idea set my teeth on edge and music seemed much more my cup of tea. I was curious to see what these young musicians were up to, hopeful that they were good. I sat and watched Lloyd as he arranged himself on a plain wooden chair in the middle of the lights and microphones. He exchanged a few words with the technicians and they signaled for silence. He picked up a beautiful old steel guitar sitting next to the chair, tuned for a minute or two, then nodded that he was ready to begin. It was obvious from the opening bars that Lloyd was an accomplished musician. His song was up-tempo and interesting; even the lyrics were above average. And yet there was something missing, something vital. It lacked the heart I look for in all music, no matter what the style. Good music, and this is definitely true of traditional Hawaiian, makes you feel like laughing or crying, singing and dancing, just tapping your foot with pleasure. But it makes you feel something. Lloyd's performance was technically proficient but stopped there.

Keoni came back into the studio and slipped into the seat next to me. "I left Jayne making pupus with the other ladies. So what do you think of the music?" he whispered. "I know it's not fancy, but I'm not going for a highly produced sound. This isn't disco, it's real music, by real people and for real people. I want that authenticity to come through in the videos as well. That's why we're filming the recording session, so we can use it in part of the video, and film it the way it really happens."

"I like your approach, Keoni," I whispered back. "But has Lloyd ever considered having someone else sing his songs? His own delivery doesn't seem to do them justice."

"You mean sell them to some slick nightclub entertainer who makes all the money and gets all the glory," Keoni replied, his voice rising. The sound man in charge looked over at us, and he went down to a whisper again. "No way, man. This company exists to prevent that. I admit that Lloyd is a little off tonight. It might have been a bad idea to record so soon after Sam's death. But timing is important in this business, you know that. I want to get this CD in production in time to release it right after 'The Ride of Your Life' airs on *Hawaiian Wave.*"

The sound man signaled to Keoni for silence again, and Lloyd launched into a second tune, this one slower and more plaintive. I liked it better than the first song but still found Lloyd's rendition uninspired.

Keoni turned to me, making a visible effort to appear relaxed. "Thanks again for showing up tonight. It's been a bad couple of days."

"Don't mention it. On the phone this afternoon you sounded as though you had something urgent on your mind."

"Well . . ." Keoni looked uncomfortable. "To tell the truth, I was hoping you could call the cops off. That guy came to my house yesterday—Chen, I think his name was. He sounded like he knew you and Jayne personally. You know how it is. If these guys decide to get you, they'll find something to do you for. We've got a business goin' here, but it wouldn't take much to bring it down."

"Lieutenant Chen will get off your back as soon as he discovers what happened to Sam Fitzgerald, Keoni. My advice is to cooperate with him."

"Hey, I'm clueless when it comes to Sam," he replied. There was a tone of frustration in his voice, almost anger. "I have no idea how he came to drown in Hanauma Bay."

"I gather he was an old friend of yours?"

"Where'd you hear that?"

"Why did you hire him, Keoni?" I asked him in return. "Everyone says he wasn't a very good worker and that he got the job only because he knew you."

"He was just a guy who wanted a job—why shouldn't I hire him?"

For some reason, we were going around in circles. I couldn't figure out why Keoni was so defensive. I was about to ply more questions, but the sound man motioned us to be quiet and recording resumed.

At the end of the session there was a smattering of applause and Lloyd, obviously pleased with himself, left the stage to rejoin Keoni and me.

"Great stuff, Lloyd," Keoni said quickly, though I had a feeling he didn't feel as enthusiastic about the performer as he was trying to appear.

"Did *you* know Sam Fitzgerald?" I asked Lloyd as we made our way slowly back to the reception area.

"Sure I knew him. What of it? Is it a crime to know a dead man?"

Keoni winced and immediately changed the subject. "This is a birthday party, Steve. We're two months old today, the recording company, that is. We got this place cheap, I guess that shows, huh? We converted it to a studio and offices in record time." He laughed at his own pun, nervously. "We already have two CDs on the market, with cassettes and videos as well, and sales are better than we expected. California and New York are terrific, Chicago is beginning to catch on, and Texas and the Southwest have been a big surprise. But best of all, Steve, we've gotten tremendous support here on the islands. Sales have been phenomenal, considering how new we are. I think Hawaiians are finally wising up. They're still being exploited, of course. No offense intended, but we all know who the star of *Hawaiian Wave* is, and it's not a native Hawaiian. Don't get me wrong. I have nothing against Markham personally—when I was a kid I used to like Jack Lord, in *Hawaii Five-O*—but why is Mack the star of the show and Buddy just his sidekick? Why isn't Buddy the detective?"

"As far as I can tell, no one is doing much detecting in these shows," I answered honestly. "But I agree with the point you're making, Keoni. It gets back to the sponsors and who they think will buy more potato chips or tickets on their airline, but that's no reason to take it out on Billy personally. And someone, for whatever reason, does seem to be out to get him. Even Sam Fitzgerald's death could be construed as a warning to him."

"Is that what he thinks, Steve?" Keoni's face assumed a bitterly amused look. He seemed to have more to say, but one of the technicians called him away to the phone. I continued back to the reception area with Lloyd and a sound engineer who looked too young to be out of high school yet. At my age, I sometimes feel that way about my doctor.

The waiting room had been transformed. It was clean, rearranged, and hung with balloons and streamers. Food was tastefully displayed on the desktop and magazine table, and wastepaper baskets were strategically placed next to ice chests full of beer and soft drinks. I sensed my wife's touch in all this and could see that she'd managed to make a bosom buddy of the only other female in the room. I joined them as the younger woman was saying, "I really can't tell you that much about him, Jayne. He just started here and he was kind of quiet, kept to himself, you know. He seemed kind of spacey to me. I guess it's not very nice to talk about the dead that way, but I wasn't quite sure what he was doing here."

Like me, Jayne was doing her best to dig out any information about the nebulous Sam Fitzgerald. She glanced up at me and then returned her attention to her companion. "Do you remember what brought Sam here in the first place?" she asked. "Was he answering an ad in the paper? Sent by someone?"

"Well, I guess I wasn't supposed to say anything to the cops— I sure got jumped on when they left. I don't know what the big deal is. So what if he was an old friend of Keoni's? What's wrong with giving a friend a job?"

"How do you know they were old friends?" I interrupted.

"Sam said so. He said he and Keoni were old business partners. But he said it kind of strange like. Oh, gosh, I'd better pay attention to what I'm doing. The food's running low. I've got some more in the back."

"That was Kaiulani," Jayne explained. "She's in love with Keoni but she has a mind of her own. And she's the best cook in Pearl City. What else do you want to know?"

Before I could begin to enumerate a long list of unanswered questions, a very large young man came our way. In native Hawaii, girth is considered attractive. The young man had a gentle, babyish face. He must have weighed three hundred pounds but he moved with surprising grace.

"Hey, you must be Steve Allen. I'm Shroom," he said. "Good to meet you, man."

"Shroom?" I repeated, not certain I had heard correctly.

"As in mushroom. It's my nickname."

Shroom giggled; you hear that sometimes among very large Hawaiian men, a high, almost girlish laugh. "Actually, I'm a composer, like you. It's a gas, isn't it. I'd really like to get down with you sometime, talk about music."

"Sure," I said. I was starting to feel very old. I was also starting to feel like a pest, a needle stuck in the same groove on a record. Nevertheless, I managed to bring the conversation back to the dead man. "Speaking of mushrooms, Shroom—was Sam Fitzgerald into drugs?"

"Naw, not from me anyway. He was a nice enough guy, I don't want to bad-mouth the dead or anything. But he wasn't really part of the scene. He didn't take music seriously. And this is for real, man. Some of us probably seem a little flaky to you, but all of us here, we work hard at what we do."

"And Sam didn't work hard?"

"Not that I ever saw."

If that was true, I could see why Sam hadn't gone over well with this group. The young men milling around me might be dressed casually, and speak a language that was not quite the King's English, but when it came to making music, they obviously took their work seriously.

"We each pull our own weight around here," Shroom went on, patting his stomach and laughing at his own sizable load. "That's part of the gig. We're learning about every aspect of the business. Keoni says that way no one can rip off the company or become indispensable. We're a corporation and we all own stock. It's a democracy."

As Shroom went on about his music, which sounded like a kind of new age/slack key fusion, Keoni came back into the room. I couldn't help but notice the attention he got. This democracy looked more like a constitutional monarchy to me and Keoni was definitely king. I left Jayne listening to Shroom, who had launched into a vocal rendition of his latest instrumental composition, and went looking for Lloyd Kawelo. I found him next to a large ice chest, dispensing fresh beer cans.

"So I'm still curious about Sam Fitzgerald, Lloyd. It sounds like you knew him better than most people here."

He eyed me cautiously.

"Well, maybe I did. But I wasn't about to open my mouth to those cops that came around. They would take it the wrong way."

"Take what the wrong way?"

Lloyd did not look happy. He glanced to the left of me, and then to the right, as if looking for someplace to escape. But there was no escape and finally he looked me in the eye.

"Okay, I was the one that got him into scuba diving. It's not like I made him do it. He told me he was interested in learning and didn't have the ready cash for the lessons, the course you're supposed to take to get a certificate. A certificate! What a bunch of crap. We Hawaiians have been swimming in these waters for thousands of years! So I took him out, showed him a few things, got him some equipment a friend of mine wasn't using anymore. The cops are probably going to come after me when they find out, try to say it was my goddamn fault he died. But what the hell. The way I see it, you have to take responsibility for your own fate in this world. It's no good blaming other people for what happens. Me, I take care of myself and I expect other people to do the same."

"When did you first meet Sam?"

"Here at the studio. I just knew the dude a couple of weeks. It's not like we were old friends."

Keoni came up and joined us while Lloyd was talking, but when he heard us discussing Sam Fitzgerald, a strange expression came onto his face. It was starting to bug me that everyone seemed eager to avoid the subject of the dead man. Lloyd took the opportunity of Keoni's arrival to wander off, and Keoni appeared about to vanish as well. But I grabbed his arm.

"Whoa, Keoni, stop for a moment. There's simply no way you're going to avoid telling me what you know about Sam Fitzgerald. I understand you were once business partners."

Keoni looked startled. "That's a lie. Who told you that?"

"It's what Sam told people here at Hawaiian Wave."

"Then Sam was just trying to make himself important, that's all. Act like he had a connection with the boss."

"So you're saying you were *not* in business with him?" I pressed.

Keoni's face became a mask—a handsome mask, an oddly appealing half-smile on his lips, but impenetrable. "I'm an artist, Steve. Business isn't really my bag—even this record company, this is just an artist's cooperative, you might say. So, no, I was never in business with Sam Fitzgerald."

It was a curiously roundabout answer. I was about to press further, but we were joined by a loud crowd of musicians and friends, making conversation impossible.

"Let me get you another drink, man," Keoni said smoothly. And he promptly disappeared for half an hour, leaving me drinkless. I noticed Jayne making the rounds of the room and hoped she was having better luck.

Once the food was gone the party wound down pretty quickly. Lloyd was the only one in a celebratory mood, and he persuaded a couple of the young technicians to continue on with him to a nearby bar. Keoni thanked Jayne and me for coming and invited us to be his guests at the Waikiki Shell on Saturday night. Hawaiian Wave Records would be hosting a showcase of Hawaiian music, traditional and contemporary. "None of that hotel stuff," Keoni added, his enthusiasm returning. "This will be the real thing."

Jayne said we'd try to make it. "Once again, I'm so sorry about Sam Fitzgerald," she added just as we were halfway out the door. "I know how it feels to lose an old friend."

"Do you?" Keoni asked in a resigned voice as he turned to say good-bye to another departing guest.

chapter 19

It was still dark when the phone rang the next morning for our wake-up call. They do it very pleasantly at the Royal Hawaiian. Jayne took the message and passed it on to me. "Aloha, Steve. The woman at the front desk says it's going to be a beautiful morning, when the sun eventually does rise, that is." A moment later there was a knock at the door. It was room service with a large pitcher of fresh-squeezed papaya juice, a pot of English breakfast tea for Jayne, a Kona coffee for me, whole wheat toast, and the morning paper.

"I think I'll skip the paper," I told Jayne, reluctantly emerging from the bed.

"Yes, dear," my wife answered soothingly. She opened the sitting room curtains and stepped out onto the lanai. The moon was still visible, hanging low over the water. It would have been romantic if it were evening instead of morning. I tried to get my mind off death and detective work and back into what we were supposedly doing in Hawaii—shooting a two-part TV show. Today was the big day of the polo shoot, time for us to become that villainous, horsy couple, the Brents. I practiced a world-weary sneer as I sipped my coffee.

Jayne came back inside. "I don't think it was an accident," she announced out of nowhere, assuming perhaps mind-reading capacity on my part.

"What wasn't an accident?"

"Sam Fitzgerald's drowning, of course."

"I agree," I added. "Which means it was murder. And if there *is* a murderer running around, no one is safe, Billy included."

"All of us included, dear."

Now, *that* was a lovely thought with which to start the day. Fortunately the limousine was waiting for us outside the hotel, and limousines always cheer me up. This time Carlos took the freeway through the center of the island, arriving at the polo field with the sunrise. I thought of the house in Waimanalo, Billy and Cass blissfully asleep, no doubt, Bertrand at the kitchen table, finishing Hegel. They were expecting us after the morning's shoot. I was beginning to think it was time to take a closer, more objective look at Billy Markham. Was it possible that my young friend, like the Brents in our script, had called in the cavalry to take suspicion off himself?

The parking lot was just as full as it had been the day before, with the addition of the film crew vehicles massed on the side away from the bleachers. Once again the elite of the island were making their way toward the stands, this time with shawls thrown over their dresses, and jackets buttoned against the early morning chill. The crowd seemed ill at ease but excited as well, almost as excited as the extras in the crowd scene at Hanauma Bay. It's surprising how universal the desire to see yourself onscreen turns out to be.

I escorted Jayne to her dressing room and was headed next door to mine, when a familiar figure wobbled up to me on one-inch heels. It was Elisabeth, dressed in a flower-print blouse, white silk jacket and long white pleated skirt.

I smiled. "Morning, Elisabeth. It looks as though you got yourself roped into this scene."

"Susan wouldn't let me out of it. She even had that makeup guy do me over. I don't know why, I'm just going to be in the stands, along with about a million other people. But, what the heck, I never have been able to say no to Susan."

"You're looking good," I said gallantly, and I meant it. Mighty Mo, the makeup artist, had brought out her eyes, a deep liquid brown, and played down the large, expressive mouth which, at the moment, was twisted in consternation. Susan came up behind her, pointing gleefully.

"Isn't she beautiful?" she said slowly and clearly. "She's going to be the next star."

"She'll have to take my place if I don't hurry," I said, ducking into my dressing room trailer. My outfit for the day was hanging in the corner and it managed to transform me, if not into Jason Patterson, at least into a dashing playboy type. The linen suit, a creamy beige, was set off by a pale yellow shirt and faintly striped chartreuse suspenders. The suspenders were visible through the open jacket, which a note from wardrobe warned me not to button closed on pain of death. The crowning glory was a Panama hat. I tried it at various rakish angles before deciding to let Jayne adjust it before we went on camera.

Mo, alone in the makeup room, did my face in no time. I emerged from the trailer to find Susan waiting her turn by the door, dressed in a cotton shift and sandals. She seemed more relaxed than she had at Hanauma Bay. I wondered how much of that had to do with the fact that Keoni Pahia wasn't in the polo scene we were about to shoot.

Danny Siderman suddenly bounced out of nowhere, showering me with "alohas."

"Perfect day, wouldn't you say? Edgar is fit as a fiddle, completely over that little upset on Tuesday. This is going to be a great scene, probably boost the membership of the club another hundred percent. Oh, my goodness, will you look at that, folks?"

I was the only folk there, but I did look appreciative, as he was referring to my wife, who had just emerged from her dressing room in an outfit that made mine look plebeian. A luxurious jungle-print scarf adorned the lean, smoky-rose linen suit, topped by a wide-brimmed thirties-style straw hat set to one side at just that devilish tilt I'd been looking for with mine.

"Dahling, you look mahvelous," I quipped in my best Billy Crystal voice as she sauntered toward us, already in character.

"You too, dear," she replied, adjusting my hat before I had a chance to ask. "Let's go meet the cameras."

We crossed the parking lot with Danny, waving in response to greetings from the polo crowd. Suddenly Jayne stopped in her tracks.

"Steve, that's Cass over there, next to the rented Impala. That isn't Billy standing next to him, is it?"

"Be right with you," I said, changing direction.

Cass looked pleased with himself. "Hi, boss. Billy wanted to come out to see the shoot this morning. Kind of like getting right back on the horse that bucks you."

"How's he doing. Really?" I asked in a low voice, since Billy had turned away for a moment to talk to an adoring young woman.

"Well, he is spooked, Steve. He's certain someone's trying to kill him—that whoever knocked off Fitzgerald was really after him. But he's rallied a bit. In his own way, he's trying to be brave."

"Hi, Steve," Billy said, turning and joining the conversation. In his western-style suit, cowboy hat, and dark glasses, I'm not sure I would have recognized him if he hadn't been with Cass. "I was afraid I'd be even more gun-shy if I waited until tomorrow to come back on the set."

"Well, I'm glad you're making the effort, Billy."

He shrugged fatalistically. "I'm not afraid anymore, Steve, come what may. We all got to join that great roundup in the sky sometime."

It sounded as if Cass had been pumping Billy full of cowboy lingo and stories from his childhood. Over the years, Cass's version of Wyoming has come more and more to resemble a bad western on TV. I sometimes wondered what he'd think if he saw Jackson Hole today.

I was worried about Billy's new mood of fatalism, but there was nothing I could do for him at the moment. We agreed that we'd all meet at the Impala after the shoot and go back to Waimanalo together. I hurried to join the rest of the Brents near the front row box, where we would be shot watching the polo match. Edgar had just finished his opening remarks and the stand-ins were in place as the cameramen and lighting specialists made their adjustments for the first take.

"Greed," Jayne whispered to me.

"What about greed?"

"It's the theme of the day. Edgar says so."

The Diamond Head Polo Club and the Maui club teams trotted onto the field. The number one position on the Diamond Head team had been taken by a stunt man and trained stunt horse. Jayne and Susan and I stepped into our box, play began and the cameras started to roll. The three of us made small talk in character. It felt awkward at first, but in no time at all we were acting like a real family, thanks in part to the time we had spent together the day before. The polo players, self-conscious in front of the cameras, didn't play nearly as well as they had the previous day, but Edgar worked skillfully with them, goading without berating. Eventually they forgot they were being filmed and the action scenes improved. The crowd in the stands got into the game and Edgar himself looked almost pleased.

"All right," he announced through his bullhorn. "We're ready to shoot the scene where the horse and rider fall. Polo players, you are stunned and saddened. Each of you sees yourself in the fallen rider. Steve, Jayne, you are the significance of this scene."

"What the hell does that mean?" I whispered to Jayne. The director continued.

"This could be the end for you. Your horses were not supposed to be drugged to the point where they cannot stand up. You could lose valuable horseflesh and your deception could be discovered. Susan, you are innocence itself. You're completely in the dark, as you say in English. You are confused. How could this be happening? Does everyone understand?"

We all nodded. Even Danny Siderman, standing carefully out of camera range, nodded. Play resumed on the field. Edgar gave the action time to intensify, then signaled to the stuntman. His horse fell down on one knee, and a piercing scream rang out. I wondered later if the camera had caught the look of dismay on our faces. I hoped so, because it was real. The scream had not been in the script.

Edgar yelled "Cut!" and two men with black bags rushed onto the playing field. The stuntman was writhing on the ground, clutching at his ankle. I recognized one of the medics. It was Dr. Aikiko, the *Hawaiian Wave* doctor who had attended us on the beach.

"Call an ambulance, Danny," he yelled toward the producer, who was still on the sidelines, consulting with Edgar. "He's going to be fine, but he's in a lot of pain. Looks like he's broken his ankle; it's hard to tell what else."

One of the assistant producers ran toward a row of pay phones near the front gate. The polo players had moved back to the sidelines, but the stunt horse was still standing next to the fallen man, looking as if he wanted to apologize. The two doctors, one of whom turned out to be the polo club veterinarian, brought a stretcher onto the field. They lifted the injured man very gently off the ground and carried him past us on his way to the parking lot.

Suddenly, the attention of the crowd shifted to Edgar Min and Danny Siderman, who were on the edge of the field and backing away from a wildly gesticulating Jimmy Cassidy.

"I'll go see what's happening, you stay here," I said to Jayne, slipping out of the box to join the small crowd that had collected around Cass. He saw me approaching.

"Boss, maybe you can explain. I'm just trying to convince these guys to do themselves a favor and finish the filming on schedule. It's going to take them a while to locate another stunt-man and I know how to ride these horses. I've done stunt work before and I can fake the polo stuff better than that guy did. Where do they think these polo ponies get trained anyway? Wyoming, that's where. They're just glorified cow ponies."

"Mr. Allen"—Edgar turned to me with a condescending air—"perhaps you could explain to your friend here that we appreciate his offer of assistance but we cannot accept the services of a stuntman who is not a member of the union. I am sure you understand."

"Is that all you're worried about?" Cass guffawed. "See this?" He pulled out his wallet and handed Edgar his Screen Actors Guild card with a flourish. Cass had gotten the card a few years back when he had a small part playing our chauffeur in a movie Jayne and I had been in. "I always suspected the time would come when I'd need this again," he said. "Now will you give me a try? What have you got to lose? You're not going to get another stuntman up here today, not one that knows horses like I do."

Edgar looked at me as if to say "well?" I shrugged my shoulders.

"He's right. What have you got to lose?"

Edgar raised the bullhorn to his mouth. "All right, ladies and gentlemen. We are going to take a short break. Feel free to get up and walk around, as long as you return to the same seats. I want you in your places at nine-fifteen."

Danny led Cass away to be fitted for a polo club uniform. He and Cass were the same height, but whereas Danny was as round and bouncy as a beach ball, Cass was as lean and even slightly bowlegged, like a real cowpoke.

As we took our places for the second attempt at the accident scene, Susan studied our faces. "What's wrong?" she asked. Jayne looked at me and we both burst out laughing. We were petrified, and it must have showed. We were as bad as the most doting parents, afraid that Cass might not be able to live up to his own image of himself. Danny emerged from the trailer area, Cass at his side. Our cowboy looked good in the pink and green silks of the Diamond Head Polo Club. He spent a minute or two with the stunt horse, talking softly, scratching his nose, slipping him a handful of sugar cubes he must have picked up in the catering trailer. Then he swung smoothly into the saddle, nodded in Edgar's direction, one of the polo club members handed him a mallet, and the cameras began to roll.

Before anyone realized what had happened, Cass was down the field with the ball, hitting it through the goalposts for the first score of the game. Edgar called "cut," the Diamond Head club let out a cheer, and the Maui players all started yelling at once that they weren't ready. Edgar signaled for the second take, and the cameras began to roll again. This time no one took Cass for granted. Play intensified, and he still held his own, getting his mallet on the ball more than a few times. He was a natural.

When Edgar announced the accident scene, I could feel Jayne tensing next to me. It wasn't until she flashed me a reassuring smile that I realized I had done the same. "Roll it!" Edgar shouted. Play resumed, the stunt horse fell down on one leg, and Cass slid off and lay on the ground, clutching at his back. The scene was going perfectly, just the way it had been scripted. Cass was finally getting his chance to star in a horse opera.

chapter 20

Billy was out of the stands the minute Edgar called for a final wrap. It was impossible to get to Cass through the polo players from both teams who wanted to congratulate the cowboy from Wyoming. Billy tried, jumping up and down and attempting to squeeze his lanky frame through the crowd of club members. Finally he came over to share his enthusiasm with Jayne and me.

"Wasn't that something? I couldn't believe it. I had tears in my eyes, honestly. The way he just stepped in like that, cold turkey. He isn't kidding, he really is a cowboy, isn't he?"

Jayne and I were feeling pretty pleased ourselves. I hoped we hadn't lost our man Monday, but I was prepared even for that.

"I need to talk to Danny before we go," I said, leaving Billy and Jayne to crow over Cass's accomplishments. I was hoping Danny might be able to give me some background information on Keoni Pahia, especially anything that would explain his past connection with Sam Fitzgerald and why he was so reluctant to talk about it. I found Danny in front of the dressing room trailers, in heated discussion with Edgar Min and Dick Schiller.

"No!" Danny's voice rose above the others. "Absolutely not. The script is fine just the way it is. You have to learn when to leave well enough alone."

As I joined them, Edgar was saying, "I beg to differ with you here. If Dick has seen a way to improve his script, I would like to take a look at it. He says it does not involve reshooting anything we have already done. Why not let him submit his new idea? We push the schedule of tomorrow back a few hours. Actually, that may not be a bad idea anyway. The light will be better."

"Steve, help me," Danny wailed, turning to me for support. "You don't want to have to learn a whole new script, do you?"

"C'mon, Danny," Dick jumped in. "It's not a whole new script!" He looked even more wild-eyed than usual. And he had on the same clothes I'd seen him in for the last two days. "Trust me. This is important, more important than you think. Steve and Jayne are professionals. They can handle a few new lines. I'll have the revised scripts to you first thing in the morning. Plenty of time for everyone to see what's involved before the afternoon filming. Take my word for it, these new changes are going to blow some minds."

Actually, as the years roll by the once-simple process of memorization of lines does become a bit more difficult. The ability, of course, varies from one actor to another. Some performers are famous for what are called their photographic memories. Jackie Gleason was a good example. He reportedly could memorize pages after giving them just a brief period of study.

For whatever reason, I've never been that good at memorizing lines, but the failing somehow seems to be plugged into my ability to ad-lib. Back in the 1950s, for instance, when I appeared in a Broadway play *The Pink Elephant,* I had no particular difficulty memorizing the lines, but every night the show ran, my mind suggested additional new dialogue. Fortunately all the ad libs got laughs, so the playwright didn't object.

The memorization problem came up again later during the eight weeks I spent working on the film biography of the great clarinetist and band leader Benny Goodman. Part of the problem was that I was doing the *Tonight* show live at the same time and never missed a night because of the film work. But the last two weeks I was so punchy from overwork that I actually took to pasting cues and portions of lines on nearby lampshades, pianos, even in a couple of instances on the jacket fronts of actors I was talking to.

With Edgar on his side, the writer finally prevailed and Danny went off to inform the cast and crew of the change in schedule. I was getting ready to follow him, when Dick grabbed my arm to hold me back.

"Let me buy you lunch, Steve, please."

"Actually, I was just about to speak with—"

"No!"

"I beg your pardon?"

"I won't take no for an answer. Listen to me—my whole life has been leading up to this moment. I've got to talk to someone. My car's right over here. It's not much but it runs. Run, Sammy, run, hah-hah. You're going to see some running soon."

What could I do? I hated to leave Cass in his moment of glory, but I knew he'd be well taken care of, and I had a feeling that Dick Schiller might be able to shed some light on the shadowy waters surrounding *Hawaiian Wave*. So I told him I'd meet him in five minutes, at the main gate, and went back to let Jayne and Billy know what I was up to.

"All set," I said, slipping into the passenger seat of Dick's old Chevy hatchback. "Where would you like to go?"

"Don't worry, Steve, you're going to get a taste of real life with me. I'm going to treat you to lunch island-style. I grew up here, you know. Not on the North Shore, down *makai* end of the island. But I know a great place for bento, near Haleiwa."

The town of Haleiwa lies a few miles east of the Mokuleia polo field. It has been transformed, in recent years, from a sleepy little backwater to a significant tourist attraction. The people who come here looking for a remnant of old rural life have inevitably contributed to the demise of the atmosphere they seek, but there are still a few places that look like they were community staples long before the boom. Ma Liliokalani's General Store is one of them. It sits on the highway just outside of town, distinguished by a large, hand-painted banner across the front advertising the best bento on the North Shore.

I followed Dick through the front door and into the dark interior. Reading Ma's windows, I had noticed that she stocked all the necessities, from cold beer to fish bait and 'toiletries.' But from the layer of dust on most of her merchandise, it was clear that her main business was in bento. A bento is a box lunch. The concept is Japanese originally, but the Hawaiian bento has become a local tradition all its own. I chose a box of sushi rolls and one of roast pig and poi with "two scoops rice." Dick took one that featured macaroni salad and teriyaki chicken wings.

"Is beer OK with you?" Dick asked, pulling a six-pack out of the cooler.

"I'll stick to water, thanks," I replied, wondering if I would end up driving us home. We took our food down the road, to the Haleiwa Beach Park, where the tables were already full of like-minded picnickers. Oh, well, what's a little sand in your food, I thought, when you're on the trail of mayhem and possibly a murder? We sat down on the beach, near the breaking surf, and I began to eat. Dick was too excited to do more than peck at his food. He had been talking a mile a minute since we left the polo field, but much of what he said was incomprehensible. It seemed like an internal monologue spilling out of his mouth uncontrollably. On the beach I finally came out and asked him if he was on drugs.

"Me? On drugs? I'm high, all right, Steve, but it's a natural. It's the high of knowing that my dream is finally going to come true. The nightmare is going to begin for somebody else now."

"I don't understand what you're talking about, Dick. Fill me in here." But all I got was more cackling and "you'll see, Steve. It won't be long. Everybody will see." Meanwhile, Dick was making his way through the six-pack of beer on his own. It seemed to calm him down a bit, and he started talking more coherently, about scripts he had written for Hawaiian public television.

"I did one on thalidomide babies; you remember the thalidomide babies? Some of those poor bastards are still alive. Hard to imagine, huh? And then I did one on the sugar cane industry. Talk about slavery. But the one that really made my reputation was *Father Damien, Life with the Lepers*. That one got shown on public television stations all over the country. Maybe you saw it. What a hellhole that was, Kalawao, on the east coast of Molokai. That's where they dumped the lepers at first, just threw them off the ships to swim to shore if they could. He died of leprosy himself, Father Damien. Poor bastard, trying to help those people. And some of the missionaries opposed him, you know. I really let them have it in my script."

"I don't think I saw your documentary, but I'd like to, Dick. But it does seem to me I've heard it mentioned recently, in connection with *Hawaiian Wave*."

Dick's eyes bugged out and he stared at me intently. He seemed to be gulping for air, as if, in his excitement, he couldn't breathe properly.

"Lance Brady probably told you about the show, Steve. He

played Father Damien. It was his big break. Oh, I know, he had
that soap on the mainland. What was it, *The Loves of Our Lives?*
But it was my documentary that got him the role on *Hawaiian
Wave.* They wouldn't have known he existed. He doesn't want to
admit it, but that part made his career and I wrote it. The pen is
mightier than the sword, Steve. You know that as well as I do,
don't you? That's why I like being around you. We're not like
those scumbags out there." He accompanied his last remark with
a sweeping hand gesture so out of control, it knocked my sushi
out of my hand. I don't think he even noticed.

"We're different, you and I. We can tell right from wrong
and we let the world know it." He paused for a minute while he
buried his third empty beer can in the sand. This was my chance
to try to ask a few questions.

"Dick, does all of this have anything to do with the script
changes you announced today?"

He cackled again. "You'll see, Steve, you'll see soon enough."

I tried again. "The body that was found in Hanauma Bay on
Tuesday . . ."

"The body *you* found Tuesday, Steve. Give yourself credit."

"Did you know Sam Fitzgerald?"

"Of course I knew Sam Fitzgerald. How could I not know
Sam the Man? We knew each other in another lifetime, a long,
long time ago. But not long enough ago for some people. I know,
I can see it in your face. What's this all about, you're asking
yourself. But don't worry, it will be clear to you soon, sooner than
you think. Sooner than anyone thinks."

I didn't get much else out of Dick Schiller, though I tried.
He rambled, he digressed, he repeated what he'd already said, in
one form after another, while he finished off the six-pack. This
was starting to seem to me a very big waste of time. I unburied
his cans and dropped them in a garbage bin on our way back to
the car. When I insisted on driving, he didn't put up much of a
struggle. He was so quiet on the way back to Honolulu that I
thought he'd gone to sleep. But when I looked over at the passenger seat his eyes were wide open. He was staring out the window
and tears were rolling down his cheeks.

chapter 21

Dick didn't say a word all the way back to the city. I parked his car in front of a fifties-style apartment building near downtown Honolulu. There was a sign in one of the windows that said APARTMENT FOR RENT, BY THE WEEK OR MONTH. Dick thanked me politely for driving back, but I had no clear idea why he had invited me to lunch.

"Till tomorrow," he said, a little of the old gleam coming back to his eye.

I hailed a taxi and told the driver to take me to Waimanalo.

"Is that you, Mr. Allen?" Bertrand's voice echoed through the intercom speaker. "I'll be right out." He was as good as his word, emerging from the house in a fresh skirt, the machete at his side. "They had a little excitement at the beach, sir, but everyone is fine now. I just made them tea. Would you care for some?"

"Thanks, yes," I said, taking the stairs two at a time. When I stepped into the living room from the lanai, Billy was rehashing their adventure on the beach.

"Steve! You missed all the action. Jayne almost caught the stalker."

"Well, I wouldn't say that," Jayne demurred. Bertrand brought in my tea and Cass brought the story back to the beginning.

"It was this way, boss. Jayne suggested we drive back by the coast and stop off at Pat's at Punaluu for a little lunch."

"Cass ordered rattlesnake," Billy interrupted. "I hope he told the waiter, 'Easy on the venom.' "

Nobody laughed. Who cares? I silently thought.

Cass continued. "Well, there's this real nice beach park not too far past there, Kahana Bay Beach Park, right? Shady old fish ponds, no people. So we stop to take a walk, and who should show up but that redheaded character you guys have been talking about. Jayne spotted him when she went back to the car for some sunscreen."

I turned to my wife, who picked up the narrative.

"He was just getting out of the green Volvo, Steve. I recognized the car from that day at the Academy of Art. He'd parked at the other end of the lot and I tried to wander nonchalantly in his direction, pulling my scarf over my hair. I thought perhaps he wouldn't recognize me, and I don't think he did at first."

"So?"

"I glanced inside the Volvo as I went by, but I couldn't see anything that might be a clue to his identity. It's not like the old days, when you had to keep your registration visible on the steering column. So I followed him. He hid in the trees watching Billy and Cass, until I sneezed. I tried to smother it, but I must have been allergic to something. He jumped, looked around at me, and made a beeline back to the parking lot. And then, I'm afraid, it was no contest. I kicked off my shoes, but even then trying to run in soft sand is like that nightmare you used to have as a child, where you run for all your worth and stay in one place."

Billy looked embarrassed. "I still have that nightmare," he mumbled.

"The funny thing is," Jayne went on, "he ran with a very peculiar gait. I can't quite place it, but it didn't seem right somehow. It will come to me, I'm sure. Oh, and, Steve, I almost forgot, before we left the polo field Edgar Min came up to me and said that it was time we had a talk. You know how he is; he made it sound as if we were going to decide the fate of Eastern Europe. I tried to get him to tell me what it was about, but he said it was not the right time or place, he had too much on his mind. So I suggested dinner at Keo's at seven, and he jumped at it. I knew you wanted to talk to him anyway."

"Yes, I do. If I can get him to stop playing auteur long enough, I'd love to get his interpretation of everything that's been going on with this show."

"He asked if he could bring his wife, and I said of course. I must say, I'm rather curious to see what kind of woman would put up with that man. Dick Schiller isn't married, I hope?"

I assured her he wasn't and told my own lunch story, omitting the part about Dick crying all the way home. "We'll have to just wait and see what script changes he comes up with tomorrow. I'm hoping they'll explain some of the nonsense he was spouting this afternoon!"

Our limousine pulled up to Keo's, on Kapahulu Avenue, at five minutes past seven. Keo's is one of my favorite restaurants on Oahu. The nouvelle Thai menu is small, which means that each item on it is carefully prepared. The headwaiter was expecting us and took us straight to a quiet corner, where, to my surprise, Danny Siderman and a companion were sitting with the Mins. They were all sipping fresh mango daiquiris.

"Two more please," Danny said to the waiter, rising and pointing to his drink. He pumped my hand and beamed at Jayne. "I hope you folks don't mind a little extra company. I was meaning to bring you here myself, and since I had a little matter I wanted to discuss off the set, I thought this would be as good a time as any. Did you ever meet my wife?"

Louise, Danny's better half, was tall and thin, with a long Roman nose and a patrician air. Her gray-blond hair was piled on top of her head in a style reminiscent of European royalty as rendered in some old film. It made her appear to be an extra head taller than her husband. Maria, Edgar's wife, was small, dark, and vivacious. She was a good foot shorter than her husband.

Once the introductions were over, a strangely awkward silence descended on the table. Jayne struck up a conversation with Maria, sensing that she would be the easiest to get talking. She had a lovely but heavy Eastern European accent, and we all strained to follow her nervous chatter.

"My family is Romany, Gypsy to you. But I grew up with my

godparents, good stolid Germans living in the Czech Republic. They opposed Hitler's extermination of the Jews and the Gypsies. They hid my grandparents when my mother was a child and then, when Stalin decided he didn't like Gypsies either, they took me in and raised me as their own. Some day Edgar and I are going to make a film about the Gypsies, and we'll discover my roots together." She smiled self-consciously at her husband, who did not respond.

"How do you like Hawaii?" Louise asked me without the slightest interest in the answer. She fiddled with her spoon until she dropped it. Danny and I both dove to retrieve it for her, almost bumping heads under the table. Everyone was relieved when the Thai spring rolls arrived. We ate in silence. Jayne made a few more stabs at conversation, but even she couldn't get the dinner party up to speed. By the time we'd all made our way uncomfortably through the papaya salad and spicy shrimp soup with lemongrass, I was beginning to wonder if we were ever going to find out what Edgar and Danny had on their minds.

It was a strange, flat gathering. Danny seemed to have lost all his bounce, and Edgar hadn't found the essential meaning of the evening, or wasn't telling if he had. Finally, halfway through his main course and most of the way through a bottle of white wine, Danny seemed ready to tell us what was going on. He addressed his question to me.

"Been in touch with your friend Raymond lately?" he asked, taking a bite of Sa-teh Shrimp.

"Raymond Markham, you mean?" I was eating Evil Jungle Prince Chicken. "Billy's father?"

Danny nodded.

"No, I haven't. We spoke in California, of course, after Jayne and I agreed to come over and do the show. I was hoping to be able to phone him with good news shortly after we arrived, tell him we'd solved the mystery of Billy's stalker and the possible attempts on his life. Unfortunately I don't have any good news for him yet. In fact, the stalker was at work again just this afternoon."

Jayne described the episode at the beach. Danny frowned and went on.

"I'll tell you why I asked, folks." He hesitated again. "Billy dropped a bit of a bombshell on me last week. The show has been on the air for only two months. It got great advance press, thanks to my efforts, and shot straight to the top of the ratings, where it's stayed ever since. I don't want to sound like I'm bragging, but the truth is that I've been in this game a long time and I know what I'm doing. I've had something to do with the success of this show." His voice was rising. "It's my baby. I've fed it from my own—"

"Danny!" his wife broke in with alarm.

"Sorry," Danny continued. "So here I am, at the beginning of the first season of the hit show of the year, a show that saw the light of day because of me, and Billy comes out with the suggestion, casual as you please, that his father take over as producer next season."

Silence. So that's it, I thought. No wonder things have been a little tense this evening. Jayne, ever the conciliator, was the first one to speak,

"I wouldn't worry if I were you, Danny. Billy obviously dreamed up this idea when he was feeling insecure, before Steve and Cass and I came over. I doubt that Raymond even knows about it, let alone is actually interested in producing."

Louise, Danny's wife, cleared her throat nervously and finally spoke up. "I'm sure you mean well, Jayne. But it sounds as though you haven't actually put Billy's mind at ease, despite your good intentions. And Raymond Markham, as you know, is arriving next week. He's already made an appointment with the major sponsor of the show, Air Oahu."

Another pause as that one sank in. "No, we didn't know," I answered. "But I think you're doing an excellent job of producing the show, Danny, and I'd be happy to express that opinion to anyone who asks for it."

Danny jumped in ahead of Louise. "Thank you, but we were hoping"—here he looked over at his wife, who encouraged him to go on—"that you might do even more. You seem to have a lot of influence over Billy. If he could be persuaded to drop this idea, I think his father would follow suit."

"I'll think about what you've said, Danny, and I'll get back to you. Frankly, my initial reaction is to want to stay out of it."

Edgar Min, who had been so silent to this point that he seemed half asleep, suddenly straightened up. His wife put a restraining hand on his arm, which he brushed away instantly. "I am assuming from this conversation, Mr. Allen, that your young friend Mr. Markham has also failed to mention to you his plan to try his hand at directing the series?"

Maria tried to break in, but Edgar stopped her with another abrupt wave of his hand. "I understand, Mr. Allen, that these things are done differently in America than they are in my country. You have a history of allowing superstars who fancy themselves directors to make fools of themselves behind the camera. But I will not tolerate any interference with the unique vision I have created for this series. I will not tolerate it!" Edgar's accent had become more pronounced as he went on. By the last sentence, delivered in a melodramatic, menacing tone, he was almost speaking Czech. I tried to defuse the situation.

"Have you talked to Billy about this, let him know how strongly you feel? Surely he would respect your point of view if you presented it to him. Maybe you could help?" I suggested, turning to Danny. "Perhaps you could find some TV movie for Billy to direct, if he really is determined to try. But I find it hard to believe that this is an issue to be seriously concerned about. Billy hasn't said a word to me or Jayne, has he?" My wife was frowning.

"Actually, Steve, he did say something to me, just this afternoon, about wanting to take charge of his life. He said that actors were just puppets and it was time for him to become the puppet master. But it never occurred to me that he might be referring to taking over as director of *Hawaiian Wave.* I can't imagine the sponsors would go for that, especially if you both opposed it." Jayne was probably thinking what I was thinking. We'd just heard that Raymond was coming to Oahu to talk with the chief sponsor.

Danny answered for the director. "Billy Markham is the star of *Hawaiian Wave,* Jayne, and we live in a star-driven culture. You know that, I know that. What can I do if he threatens to quit the show unless he gets what he wants? The viewer out there tunes in every week to see Mack. Without Mack we don't have a show. He has us by the short hairs, Jayne."

Louise wasn't fast enough to stop the last remark. But she added, in her patrician voice, "We all feel that you and Steve, with your experience in show business and your personal relationship to the family, are the perfect people to talk sense into Billy. Please do talk to him before it's too late."

"What do you mean too late?" Jayne and I both said at once.

"Too late to turn back," Edgar answered. It didn't make me feel any better.

The dinner table conversation had put a damper on all our appetites. No one wanted dessert and the party broke up after a desultory attempt at small talk on the part of Maria, Danny, and Jayne.

"Next time, let's order room service," I suggested, taking Jayne's arm outside the restaurant. We decided to walk back to the hotel so we could clear our heads and think about what we'd just heard. It was a beautiful night, silky and fragrant. I hated to think of all the unhappiness it harbored.

"Billy has certainly made a lot of enemies in Hawaii, hasn't he? Edgar despises him, Danny is afraid of him," Jayne said. "But Billy's the goose that's laying their golden eggs at the moment. The last thing they'd want to do is harm him. Unless Edgar just wants to scare him, in the hope that he'll be too busy worrying about his personal safety to bother with trying his hand at directing. But how did Sam Fitzgerald fit into all this? Honestly, Steve, it seems as though just about everyone connected with *Hawaiian Wave* has a reason not to like Billy."

I agreed. "You know, I think it's just as well Raymond is coming over. Maybe *he* can shed some light on things. I'm surprised Billy didn't tell us he was coming though. I'm beginning to feel like that little ball on the polo field, knocked from one side to the other. I wish someone would hit me through the goalposts."

rough in those places around closing time. If it's atmosphere you're looking for, may I suggest . . ."

"We're meeting friends," Jayne had said, smiling sweetly. "They say it's the best-kept secret in Hawaii."

Cass turned east off the freeway onto Kamehameha Highway and drove straight through Haleiwa. There was a light on in Ma Liliokalani's and a lone car was parked out front. I could picture Ma making up bentos in the back room. As we neared Waimea Bay Beach Park, Jayne called, "There it is! You passed it, Cass."

We turned around and headed back to what looked like a grass shack, partly obscured by a huge old banyan tree. There were five or six motorcycles parked in front of a sign that said it was Miller time. There were no cars in front, but I could make out an old pickup truck parked next to a side door.

"I think Cass and I should go in alone," I suggested to Jayne. "You can wait in the driver's seat with the door locked and be ready for a quick getaway."

"And miss all the fun?" Jayne answered. "Cass is the driver. He can wait in the car."

We finally agreed that we'd all go in. Cass led the way, running from the car to the doorway, pushing open the door into the bar and nodding to us to follow. It was surprisingly quiet inside. The jukebox was playing Johnny Cash, and three couples shuffled around on a floor littered with cigarette butts and other waste. They were all wearing leather jackets. A heavyset woman dressed in a fringy blue cowboy shirt and jeans was starting to put chairs on the tables at the end of the room away from the jukebox. Since there was no one behind the bar, I assumed she was the proprietor.

"We're closed," she said when she looked up and saw us standing in the doorway. She was missing a front tooth. "They're just finishing up. I can sell you a six-pack to go, if you want."

"We're looking for a fellow named Dick Schiller," I said. "Do you know him?"

"Can't say as I do," she replied. "What's he ride?"

"He has a car, actually. He's a little guy, with glasses, likes to wear sports jackets and a bow tie."

"You sure you got the right place, mister?" she asked. I

wondered myself. Then suddenly her face lit up. She was actually more attractive when she smiled, but who isn't?

"I got it! You must of come for that note. He said there'd just be one o' you and you'd be here earlier. He told me not to look at the note, but hell, somebody wants to make me a postmistress, I'm going to look. I wouldn't go on that beach tonight, I'll tell you that right now. It's high tide, the surf is up, and with the rain and all . . ."

I took the note she held out. "Dick left this for us?"

"Not if he's over fourteen and haole. This kid acted like a messenger, didn't seem to know anything about the note. Got all upset when I opened it, said I was just supposed to hand it over, period. Hell, I had to make sure it wasn't to do with no drug deal, didn't I? I run a clean place here."

Just then one of the couples pretending to dance broke apart and a hairy, tattooed giant in his fifties lumbered over to see what was happening. He smelled of stale cigarettes and stale beer.

"These people botherin' you, Belle?" I'm six feet three, but this guy made me feel delicate.

"Naw, they're all right, Joe. You might go to the beach with 'em, though, if they're dumb enough to try it."

I had read the note and passed it to Jayne. It said, "You'll find Dick Schiller on Waimea Beach, riding the Hawaiian waves."

"Nice night for a treasure hunt," I said to Joe. "Ready?" He looked back at Belle as if she'd lost a few marbles, grunted once, and lumbered out the door behind Cass. As soon as we were all in the Impala, three car windows went down, rain or no rain. We drove a bit farther up the road and turned in where the sign read WAIMEA BAY BEACH PARK. We could hear the surf crashing against the shore from the main road. We parked in the empty lot and made our way toward the beach. The rain was pouring down now, driven by a furious tropical wind. Joe produced a flashlight from somewhere in his leather recesses, but it barely made a dent in the darkness. Cass had on a rain slicker he'd grabbed from Billy's house, I was wearing a trench coat, and Jayne had her umbrella, but we were all beginning to feel wet. All except Joe, he seemed impervious.

"So what we lookin' for?" he asked, shining his flashlight

randomly over the water. "A body?" The waves were huge and most of the beach was covered by the rising tide.

"I hope not," I answered. Cass and Jayne and I automatically separated, each taking a different part of the beach. I headed toward some rocks at the far end and strained to see if I could make out anything in the dark. It took a minute for my eyes to adjust, and even then I wasn't sure of what I was seeing. There seemed to be something caught on the rocks a dozen feet out in the water. I waded into the low surf, holding on to the rocks to protect myself from being knocked down by the incoming waves or pulled out by the strong undertow.

"Over here, Joe!" I yelled, but he couldn't hear me over the sound of the ocean and the rain. I pulled myself back out of the water and walked down the beach, squishing with each step.

"I think I've found him, Joe. Can I borrow that flashlight a minute?" Joe appeared to be attached to his flashlight, so I brought him back to the rocks and pointed. It was hard to make out, even with the light, but it looked to me as if a body was caught in a shallow crevice where the sea was breaking. "I weren't here, pal," Joe grunted, and took off in his lumbering gait toward the parking lot. Not a very sociable type.

Jayne and Cass had followed Joe and me to the rocks. We just stood there for a minute, engulfed by the sea and the storm.

"I can wade in and get him," Cass said finally.

"Nah, I don't think so. The surf's awfully strong tonight. We'd better leave this to the professionals." I turned to Jayne. "I think I've finally found a use for your landsman. I'm sure he wouldn't mind if you woke him up."

She gave me a wet and salty look. "I'll call," she said. "Got a quarter?"

chapter 23

Jayne called the Honolulu police station from a pay phone in the parking lot and then joined Cass and me in the car.

"The detective on duty gave me Lieutenant Chen's home number. Apparently Tony left instructions that I'm to be able to reach him night or day—isn't that sweet?"

"Adorable," I said.

"Tony answered on the second ring. He's a lighter sleeper than you are, darling—and not nearly so grouchy about being woken up. I told him we'd found a body but I didn't go into the details. He said he'd be right here—and we shouldn't go anywhere."

"Beautiful, we'll all come down with pneumonia!"

"My sentiments exactly. I told Tony we were soaking wet and not about to sit around waiting for his men to show up. He wasn't happy with me, I'm afraid. I assured him we'd be delighted to answer any questions he might have tomorrow, at the hotel, at a reasonable hour of the morning. But not now."

"Way to go," Cass crowed. "You tell 'em."

"Home, James," I added. "My desire to know whether that is indeed the body of Dick Schiller is overridden at the moment by my desire for a hot bath, dry clothes, and a comfortable bed."

We were not destined to enjoy the comforts of bed for long, however. Jayne and I were awakened around six in the morning by a loud banging on the door of our suite.

"I'll handle it, dear," Jayne said, wrapping up in a kimono-style dressing gown. I could hear her talking to Lieutenant Chen through the door and his voice going from outrage to pussycat tame. Jayne came back to the bedroom.

"It *was* Dick Schiller's body on the rocks, Steve. I invited Tony to join us for breakfast in the Surf Room in twenty minutes. I said we'd answer all his questions then, and if he still needed an official statement, I'd go down to the station and give one. He said he'll have to interview Cass as well, of course, but for the moment, the dear lieutenant seems almost satisfied with us."

"With *you*, you mean. He's probably got lunch planned for *me* in the city jail!"

It wasn't until I was dressed and headed downstairs with Jayne that Dick's death really hit me. Poor man—that crazy, incomprehensible little man with his bow tie and silent tears. At least this time we knew it wasn't an accident. And it certainly wasn't suicide. I've never seen anyone as eager awaiting a future event as Dick Schiller. He had been murdered, and someone, for reasons unknown, had wanted us to discover the body. Why? And why had we been sent to Harley's Hangout and not straight to the beach? I told Jayne to leave the bar and Joe out of our story until I could take a closer look at both of them by the light of day. Tony could find out about Harley's from the night manager, of course, but I didn't think he'd go to the trouble of grilling the hotel staff about our activities the night before. Wrong again.

"So you two decided to go slumming on the North Shore last night?" Tony greeted us as we sat down at the table he'd chosen, overlooking the beach. A stack of pancakes, two eggs over easy, bacon, and corn muffins were spread out in front of him. There was a pot of Kona coffee next to his cup.

"The same," I said to the waiter, motioning to the table full of food. Jayne ordered yogurt and fruit salad with tea.

"You caught the murderer yet?" I asked Lieutenant Chen.

"What murderer, Mr. Allen? Quite a number of people drown every year in the Hawaiian Islands without there being any question of murder. And meanwhile, you will please allow me to ask the questions. I am the police officer and you are the—"

"Not suspect, surely," Jayne broke in. "Why, we're as much

in the dark as you are, Tony. And we have even more motivation
than you do to want to solve this murder. We could be next."

Jayne proceeded to recount our middle-of-the-night adventure, leaving out only Joe's presence on the beach with us. I
had a feeling Belle wouldn't mention it either. Lieutenant Chen
listened while he plowed his way through breakfast like a snow
shovel in overdrive. He wiped his mouth and turned to me.

"I just called your producer, Mr. Siderman, a short while ago
to let him know we'd found Dick Schiller's body. It seems the
dead man was supposed to deliver a script this morning. In the
course of our conversation, Mr. Siderman mentioned that the last
time he saw Dick Schiller was yesterday around noon—leaving
the Mokuleia polo field with you, Mr. Allen. He had the impression
that the two of you were going for lunch."

"I was, Lieutenant."

"Tell me about it, please."

"All right." I flashed my best early-morning I-have-nothing-
to-hide smile, and proceeded to relate my bizarre bento luncheon
with Dick Schiller, leaving out nothing that could be of any relevance. In the middle of my tale I signaled the waiter for another
pot of coffee; I needed all the help I could get this morning.

"So let me make sure I've understood you correctly, Mr.
Allen. It seemed to you that the deceased was very excited about
an upcoming event, a revelation of some sort that was going to
make someone very unhappy. He said he knew Sam Fitzgerald
but did not specify in what context. He left you with the impression
that the answer to his behavior might be found in the script
changes he was due to deliver to Mr. Siderman this morning."

"Yes. And I suggest that you let Jayne and me have a look at
those script changes as soon as you find them. The episode is
called 'The Ride of Your Life.' We're familiar with the original
script and might be able to spot something in the revisions that
would otherwise be overlooked."

"I have to tell you, Mr. Allen, that we have gone over Mr.
Schiller's apartment already and found no sign of those script
changes, in hard copy or on his computer."

"Have you checked the print shops? He was due to deliver

multiple copies this morning so we could begin shooting from the new script this afternoon.''

"I have a man on it right now. But it takes time. There are many places where copies can be made. And we haven't ruled out the possibility of suicide, or accidental death.''

"Do you know when he died?''

"Well, that's just it, isn't it. With bodies that have been in the water for any length of time, and especially when they're as battered as his was, it's very difficult to determine time of death. Perhaps we'll have more information when the autopsy is done, but perhaps not. At the moment, all we can say is that he died of drowning, and there were contusions to the head that occurred prior to his death. That would be consistent with his falling or jumping and hitting his head on the rocks.''

"It would also be consistent with his being hit on the head with a rock and thrown off the cliff, right?''

"That is a possibility, Mr. Allen. He was in his bathing trunks, however. And you say he was drunk when you left him. Maybe he went to the beach with friends for a late swim.''

I didn't bother to tell Lieutenant Chen that I doubted Dick Schiller had any friends.

"Who knows, maybe he just had an accident and his friends panicked and fled,'' the lieutenant went on. "Anything is possible. Those particular rocks are a place people have been jumping from as long as I can remember.''

I had a feeling that Lieutenant Chen was baiting me. "This is murder, Lieutenant. You know it, and I do too. I wasn't sure about Sam Fitzgerald, but I'm sure about this one. Dick Schiller was about to let the cat out of the bag, and someone wanted to stuff it back in. Have you had time to run a background check on him?''

"Our investigation is only just getting under way, Mr. Allen,'' Chen admitted, pouring himself another cup of coffee. "We do know that he was a navy brat. His father worked at Pearl Harbor in logistics.''

"So that could be the connection with Sam Fitzgerald. His father worked at Pearl Harbor as well.''

"Yes, Mr. Allen. We'll explore that angle, especially after what you've just told me. The two deaths could be purely coincidental, but, like you, I suspect a connection. There have been a few too many coincidences for my taste—such as the fact that you have discovered two bodies in the short time you've been on Oahu!"

"Now, Tony," my wife interrupted. "It really isn't fair to blame poor Steve for finding a body or two. It could happen to anyone."

"You think so? Mrs. Allen, if it weren't for you, I'd be holding your husband right now on suspicion."

Suspicion of what? Being in his way? I thought to myself. But Jayne kept the charm turned on all the way down to headquarters, where we both made lengthy statements about the discovery of the body and I went over my last conversation with Dick Schiller one more time. I was the very model of the cooperative, helpful citizen. This time Lieutenant Chen was too busy to suggest lunch, and we actually found ourselves at liberty and on the sidewalk in front of the central police station by midday.

"Feel like taking a stroll?" I asked Jayne. "The *Hawaiian Wave* offices aren't far from here. I called the hotel for our messages while you were in with the lieutenant. Danny has been calling every few minutes all morning long, so I phoned his secretary to let her know we were in the area and would stop by. She sounded at the end of her rope. She thanked me profusely for coming and said she was afraid Danny was going to have a heart attack. She said she'd never seen him like this."

"You don't think *he* pushed Dick Schiller off the cliff, do you, dear?" Jayne asked, taking my arm.

"No, that would be more Edgar's style, don't you think? And if he did it, we should have no problem apprehending him. He'll have gotten it all on film."

The skyscraper that housed the *Hawaiian Wave* offices looked almost transparent in the noonday sun. The company was located on the fourteenth floor. We stepped off the elevator into a reception area decorated in the same salmon and turquoise aloha print that Billy wore on the show, the same one Sam Fitzgerald's body had been dressed in. There were palms of various shapes and sizes scattered around the reception area, and bougainvillea boughs were shedding their paper lantern flowers on the off-white carpet. The woman at the reception desk spoke with a British accent.

"Mr. Allen, Miss Meadows," she said. "Mr. Siderman asked me to show you in the minute you arrived. Please follow me."

She led the way past assorted secretaries and junior executives who were discussing the morning's news in low voices. Danny, dressed in a silver jogging suit, was sitting behind a large koa-wood desk, his back toward a floor-to-ceiling window that looked out toward the mountains. There was a giant TV screen in one corner and a minibar in another. He jumped up and ran around to shake my hand and give Jayne a Hollywood-style almost-kiss on the cheek.

"My God, I don't believe it. What next? Everything was going so well, the perfect show, no dissension on the set, one big happy family, the network was already talking about spinoffs, we were negotiating for a feature film—and all of a sudden bodies start washing up every morning!" He sighed and shook his head. "I knew it was a mistake to hire that writer guy. But Billy liked his screenplay because it had good parts for his parents, the parts you and Jayne are playing. And Edgar liked the underwater stuff at Hanauma Bay and the action at the polo games."

Danny paused for a second in his stunningly insensitive diatribe.

"I guess I have to take some responsibility too, Steve," he continued. "I wanted to get in good with the Diamond Head Polo Club and Jason jumped at the idea of the free publicity. Of course, that was before he saw the actual script. He's been kind of funny about the whole thing since then, running a bit hot and cold."

"How do you mean?" I asked.

"I think the story bothered him. I told him right from the start that the bad guys were polo players, but he said he didn't realize gambling was a theme as well. It isn't, really, and I don't know why that should bother him anyway. He hardly looks like the gambling type himself."

"In my experience, gamblers come in all shapes and sizes, Danny. But getting back to Dick. Do you have any idea what kind of revisions he had in mind for the script?"

"God, I don't know any more than you do. You heard him

yesterday. The guy was a nut case! . . . By the way, I'm sorry I had to drag you into it this morning, but I did see you getting into Dick's old jalopy yesterday. That lieutenant wouldn't let up until I told him and I figured it was bound to come out. I hope he treated you all right. He did, didn't he?" Danny asked, looking at Jayne. She nodded encouragingly.

"Good. Because I've got friends in high places in this town. That Chen had better watch his step."

"He means well," Jayne replied. "He's just doing his job as he sees it. Did you know Sam Fitzgerald, Danny?"

"Me? That guy at Hanauma Bay? Hell, no. I thought he was some tourist or something. But I have to tell you while I've got you here, I'm really worried about Billy. I called his house, but he won't talk to me. That guy Bertrand he's got guarding him is like a brick wall. You *seen* that guy? Talk about the Hulk! . . . Anyway, I don't want you to get the wrong impression about last night or anything. Heck, Billy is like a son to me. If he'd let me help him, you know I would."

"The police probably upset him when they went to the house to question Cass," Jayne said. "Poor Billy—he *is* rather hypersensitive."

"Cass was with us last night when we found the body and the cops needed his statement to corroborate our story," I added.

Danny's eyes widened at my last remark. "But, Steve, that's fabulous! You and Jayne found the body? I had no idea. When the police called me, they didn't say anything about who found it. Can't you just see it now? 'Steve Allen and Jayne Meadows, famous amateur detective team, come to the rescue of *Hawaiian Wave.*' That idiot Schiller could turn out to be a blessing in disguise."

"Slow down, Danny," I broke in. "This isn't a publicity stunt, it's a murder investigation. And we haven't solved any mysteries yet, just found the bodies."

"OK, Steve, OK. We'll go slow. But as soon as you have the killer, we can go to town with this! Man, and I thought this was going to be a terrible day! Nothing personal, but I was beginning to think you two had brought this production bad luck. I mean, things have gone downhill a little with your arrival. But, my God, this could turn out to be the best thing that ever happened to us!''

I leaned forward and lowered my voice. I was feeling just a bit sadistic.

"As long as the next body isn't yours, Danny."

chapter 24

We emerged from the *Hawaiian Wave* building into a perfect tropical afternoon. The rain the night before had left the air languid and rich with the scent of orchid, ginger, and plumeria.

"I'd love to just play with you, my dear," I said, turning to Jayne. "But, alas, I think we'd better find that missing script. And while we're at it, I wouldn't mind figuring out who sent us on a treasure hunt in the middle of the night, with Dick Schiller as the treasure. Someone's toying with us, and I don't like it."

"Hmm . . . a boy toy," mused my wife.

"Seriously," I said.

"Seriously, why don't we try Dick's next-door neighbor for the missing script?" Jayne suggested.

"That dirty old man? The one who talks like Popeye?"

"He seemed clean enough to me, as old men go. And personally, I always found Popeye pretty cute. Anyway, he did happen to mention that the sound carried through the wall between his apartment and Dick's. Perhaps he heard something."

"Let's go see him, then," I agreed, flagging down a passing cab. "You first, my dear," I said, handing Jayne into the backseat. "Unless you think we should stop off and buy some spinach first?"

"Be nice, Steve."

"Amn't I always nice to your boyfriends?" I know there's no such word in any English dictionary, but I use it anyway since it does make more sense than the conventional *aren't*, given that "I am" is correct and "I are" is incorrect.

The taxi made its way through heavy traffic, jerking forward

inch by inch. Sometimes one wonders if the island of Oahu is
large enough for all the automobiles that crowd the streets. We
made our way torturously out of the downtown area to the run-
down neighborhood Dick Schiller once called home. Dick's apartment building looked even worse than I remembered. There's
something uniquely squalid about decaying buildings in tropical
places, a sort of moist entropy. The paint was peeling off the
window frames and doors and the second floor balconies looked
none too sturdy. Even the palm tree near the front door looked
as if it had seen better days. Dick's apartment was on the ground
floor, close to the street. I was glad to see that the homicide squad
hadn't sealed it off or stationed a patrolman at the door. Maybe
the old-timer next door had a key. Maybe he fed Dick's cats when
he was gone, or watered his plants. It was worth a try. Jayne knocked
on his door while I assumed a nonchalant air, softly whistling a
jazzy rendition of "Popeye, the Sailor Man" until Jayne gave me
a dirty look. To be nice, I changed tunes—to the *Credo* section
of Bach's *B Minor Mass,* complete with fugal counterpoint, which
ain't an easy whistle. I was just getting going, when the old man,
complete with teeth this morning but otherwise grizzly as ever,
answered the door.

"I thought ya might be back," he cackled. "Come on in,
missy." He gave me a resigned look. "I spose ya're with her, are
ya? Well, I can't have all the luck. Come on, then."

We entered a living room that looked as though it hadn't
been cleaned since Hector was a pup. I have no idea how old that
saying is, nor, for that matter, whether Hector was an old Roman
or a canine, but the old man's quarters were—well, the word
disgusting comes to mind. There were stacks of old newspapers in
every corner and dirty dishes scattered around, some on the floor.
Two scrawny cats rubbed themselves against a matching sofa and
armchair with shredded upholstery. The crocheted afghans
thrown over the furniture were unraveling as well and looked
crusty. A TV set droned softly in one corner, balanced precariously
on a cabinet with a broken leg.

"Sit yarself down, then." We did, gingerly, moving aside cross-
word puzzle books and old *TV Guides* to make room on the couch.
Our host perched on the edge of the armchair, which I guessed

to be his regular seat from the collection of unwashed cereal bowls around it.

"I figured ya'd be back when the police come this morning. I didn't tell 'em a thing, mind ya. I'm sorry about the young feller. I spose you know he's dead? Well, it happens to us all sooner or later, heh-heh. But look at me, I'm forgettin' my manners. Name's Cap, short for Captain. Can I git ya some coffee? I allays keep a pot goin'. The young feller never took none though."

"We just had some, thank you," Jayne answered, eyeing the curdled milk around the edge of the mug the old man was sipping from. "You must have known Dick Schiller pretty well, being such close neighbors. Did he ever talk to you about the script he was working on, for the *Hawaiian Wave* TV show?"

"Oh, no, we didn't natter 'bout nothin' like that. Can't stand television myself. Fish, that's what we talked on. Tropical fish. See, I can't keep none myself, on account o' these here cats. But I like 'em right enough, and I knows my fish. So I take care of 'em fer the young feller. I done it this morning, didn't I, after them coppers left. They don't care what happens to them fish."

"Steve and I are very big on fish—aren't we, darling?" Jayne urged.

"Oh, yeah," I agreed. "Poached or broiled. Pan-fried. Even sushi."

"Don't mind my husband," Jayne purred. "Personally, I've always wanted a nice tropical tank back home. A little underwater scene with rocks and mermaids, and all that. Maybe a sunken ship . . . Do you suppose I could take a peek at how Dick has done his tank?"

The old man squinted first at Jayne, then at me. "Ya don't fool me. Ya probly couldn't tell a angelfish from a guppy. But I'll let ya in there. Why not? The coppers already been an' took what they wanted. Come on, then." He grabbed a key ring off a hook by the door and led the way to Schiller's apartment. The old man went in ahead of us to turn on some lights. All the window shades were down and he knew enough not to raise them. I decided to try to enlist him on our side.

"We were working with Dick Schiller, Cap, and we think he was murdered. The police are still treating his death as a possible suicide or even an accident. We think there might be a clue to his actual cause of death in his office, among the papers he was working on."

"Well, yar out o' luck, then, cause the coppers took all that stuff with 'em."

A glance into the spare bedroom Dick used as an office revealed the truth of the old man's assertion. It had been cleaned out. The desktop was bare, the drawers were open and empty. There were a few books on some makeshift shelves but no manuscripts. I concentrated on the rest of the apartment, but there wasn't much there either. The walls were bare with the exception of a girlie calendar in the bathroom, a Humphrey Bogart poster on the bedroom door, and a plaque in the kitchen that said MAMA'S BOY FOREVER. There was a cheap cassette player in the living room with a few score tapes neatly stacked next to it. Most of them were heavy metal, none was Hawaiian music. There were a few more books in the living room, paperback best sellers—oddly enough— and what looked like research books on thalidomide, the sugar plantations, and Father Damien. Some high school yearbooks were stacked in the middle of the coffee table, next to a picture of a very attractive young woman in a cheerleader's uniform.

"Did Dick have a girlfriend?" I asked Cap, who was talking to the fish in a huge tank that took up most of one wall of the living room.

"Not that ya'd notice. He didn't bring no female to the house that I ever saw, if that's what ya mean. And these walls is mighty thin, I'd o' heard somethin', if ya catch my drift." As one of the world's leading drift-catchers, I did, but I didn't want to dwell on the point at that moment.

Jayne chatted with the old fellow while she combed the living room and I took one last look around the rest of the apartment. The bathroom cabinet revealed nothing but over-the-counter painkillers—giant, discount bottles of aspirin, ibuprofen, and Tylenol. The kitchen shelves were bare, with the exception of a few cans of soup and boxes of Hamburger Helper. There was a six-pack of beer in the refrigerator and a half-eaten TV dinner, with more TV dinners in the freezer. It was a depressing scene.

Dick had been a better housekeeper than his neighbor, but if I had to choose, I'd pick the old geezer for a roommate.

"Thank you again. You've been very helpful," I said, returning to the living room.

"No trouble. I kinda like the odd bit of excitement. Don't get much these days." He gazed at Jayne. "And ya sure are a sight for old eyes, ma'am, if you don't mind my sayin' so."

We left the apartment ahead of Cap, who turned to lock the door behind us. "Come agin, anytime now. I don't sleep much."

We shook hands and headed down the street toward Waia-kamilo Road. It wasn't until we were out of sight of the apartment building that Jayne pulled a folded piece of paper out of her pocket.

"I don't know if this means anything, Steve, but I found it inside one of those yearbooks on the coffee table."

I stopped for a minute to read it, with Jayne peering over my shoulder.

"Great to see you again," it said. "Glad I could do you a favor. Next time you're over, give me some warning. We'll hit the town. K"

"Hmm . . ." I hummed deep in an attempt of profound analytical thought. The note was mundane, but I found the letterhead interesting. Kenny's Kopy Shop was printed across the top in printing that looked like a lava flow. "Where Your Kopy Is King. Visit us soon, just down lava from Pele's home. Kilapani, Hawaii."

"Kilapani's on the Big Island, isn't it? How would you like to get off-island for a day?" I asked Jayne, pocketing the note. "I'll bet we could catch an early flight and still be back for Keoni's concert at the Shell. We could take Billy with us. I wouldn't mind getting him off alone anyway. If he's not the killer . . ."

"Steve! You don't really think that poor child is running around drowning people?"

"It's a nasty old world out there, and I'm leaving all my options open. If Billy *isn't* the murderer, then he could be in real danger, at the very least. So it might be just as well to get him away for a day. He's hiding something and I'd like to know what it is. But right now I want to pay a return visit to Harley's Hangout. Is Grandma ready to make the scene?"

Perhaps I should explain that when I address Jayne as Grandma, there are always invisible quotation marks around the word. We do dearly love our twelve grandchildren and talk about them constantly.

Jayne was starting to answer, when she suddenly stopped short, causing me to bump into her. We had turned a corner onto a busy thoroughfare and were halted in front of a shop called Tough Leather. Next to it was a motorcycle and scooter shop, Mike's Bikes. It had a big sign in the window that read PRE-CHRIST-MAS SALE. COME IN FOR A FREE TRIAL SPIN. MUST BE 21 YEARS OF AGE OR OLDER AND POSSESS A VALID DRIVER'S LICENSE.

Jayne turned to me with a positively dangerous smile. "What do you think, Steve? We might get more information at Harley's if we make the scene on a set of wheels?"

I did my best pre-*Godfather* Brando voice as we walked in the door. "Come on, hot mama. I'll be your biker dude, and you'll be my sweet dudette. People like us, we're just born wild, I guess. . . ."

chapter 25

Two hours later, Jayne and I breezed into the parking lot at Harley's Hangout on a cloud of exhaust, straddling not the biggest motorcycle available in the store but a respectable white Honda 450. Jayne was on the back in a black leather jacket that matched mine. I had, of course, had prior experience with motorcycles; you don't just jump on one of these babies in your late middle age and take off like a stunt driver. We had decided to rent black leather jackets. While the color is irrelevant, as soon as you are introduced to the world of motorbikes you immediately learn why leather jackets are either popular or necessary. If you're driving, say, a moderate sixty miles an hour, even on a day when the air is motionless, there is the illusion that you're moving forward into a sixty-mile-an-hour wind, and if the temperature is even slightly low, it's likely to chill your chest very quickly. At the risk of being considered sissies, we were both wearing helmets, but they had skulls and crossbones painted on them. We'd taken the long way, up the *ewa,* or west coast of the island, arriving at Harley's just in time for another Hawaiian tradition, the *pau hana,* or "work over" party. Harley's was hopping. The parking lot was full of bikes and bikers and there were so many people inside the bar we could hardly get through the front door. The jukebox was blaring, which meant everyone was shouting to be heard over it. Belle's customers tended toward middle age and paunchy and there were more men than women, but it wasn't really rowdy, just noisy.

Incidentally I've never quite understood why so many middle-aged male bikers think that they look better with a ratty Gabby

Hayes–type beard and why so many apparently attractive young women seem to prefer the company of men in that category.

A few people looked our way as we strolled in, but no one questioned our authenticity. Not until we made our way to the bar, anyway, and caught Belle's eye. She snorted, mumbled "Be right with you," and dove for the other end of the bar, trying to stifle her amusement. When she returned she had two open beer cans in her hand.

"These are on me. Thanks for keepin' Joe out of it last night. He's on parole, you know how it is. The cops were waitin' for me when I came to open this morning. I told 'em just what I told you. What's this all about anyway?"

"I was hoping you'd answer that," I said. "Are you sure you've never seen or heard of Dick Schiller? The police must have had a photo."

"Yeah, they had a picture, and naw, I never seen him before. He didn't exactly look like one o' the boys, you know what I mean. I don't want nothin' to do with it, really, but just to show you I'm grateful for your not mentionin' Joe, I'll ask around, see if anybody knew him. Call me tomorrow."

"Thanks, Belle. Here's mud in your tailpipe," I said, raising my can in salute as I moved away from the bar. Jayne and I wandered around, checking out the crowd. I hadn't really noticed Harley's decor the night before. It was Confederate South—rebel flags, crossed swords, the works.

Perhaps some modern anthropologist can explain the connection between the biker lifestyle and antigovernment sentiment. Rebelmania might be understandable among guys whose great-granddaddies fought with General Lee but why the hell bikers from rural Wyoming, Wisconsin, or New Hampshire think that people who go to work in Washington, D. C., for the federal government immediately become agents of the devil is at the least puzzling.

On the wall by the door there was a double row of Little League baseball pictures, dating back more than twenty years. One of the bikers saw me looking at the photos and came over.

"Belle's a real babe, ain't she? Been sponsoring those kids since she first bought this place. Some of 'em have gone on to do big things. That kid there"—he pointed a large, greasy finger at one of the pictures—"is Johnny Guterra. He plays for the San Francisco Giants."

Jayne was studying the photos carefully. Suddenly she broke in. "Steve, take a look at this." My biker friend grinned. "Hey, your chick's got good eyes. She spotted the other celeb, Keoni Pahia, that guy on the new TV show."

I joined Jayne in front of the Little League photo. It was Keoni all right, and he was already strikingly handsome at twelve.

"Steve!" Jayne whispered excitedly. "Look over here!" She pointed to the other end of the row of boys. "Doesn't that look just like Billy did when he was twelve?"

"You're right, but we know Billy was not on a Little League team in—just a minute." I lifted the picture carefully off the wall.

"Hey, what you doin'? Hands off," my friend of a minute before bellowed. It got the attention of most of the room.

"Just looking to see if an old buddy of mine is in this picture. I'm not going anywhere with it," I said very politely. Sure enough, the names of the boys were on the back and the toothy grin that looked so much like Billy belonged to one Samuel Fitzgerald.

I was putting the photo carefully back on the wall, when Jayne, who had continued her scrutiny of the picture gallery, tugged on my sleeve and pointed to the picture dated two years later. Keoni was still there, looking not quite as stunning as he had at twelve. I couldn't see Sam in this picture; perhaps he'd lost interest in baseball. But Jayne was pointing to one of the coaches. I didn't need to check the names on the back this time. He looked pretty much the same as when I had last seen him. It was Jason Patterson.

I noticed Belle keeping close tabs on us out of the corner of her eye. I sensed that she was a lady who didn't miss much and hoped she was leveling with us. I tossed her a wave good-bye and sauntered out the door, my biker gal on my arm.

"Well, well! That's the last place I would have expected to see Jason Patterson!" Jayne exclaimed as soon as we were in the parking lot. "Teaching polo to kids, maybe, but baseball? And don't you think it's a little odd that neither Keoni nor Jason has made any mention of the fact that they knew each other before the show? Something's going on here that started long before we came to this island, Steve, and long before Billy did either."

I nodded as I started up the bike. An idea was beginning to take shape in the back of my head. We took the freeway down to Honolulu, where we returned the bike, apologizing for the length of our trial spin and slipping the salesman a little something to ignore the extra mileage. Jayne called Billy's house from the bike shop. Bertrand answered immediately.

"I'm very glad you called, Mrs. Allen," he said. "It's Billy. . . ."

"Has anything happened?"

"Not really, but he's managed to work himself up into a real state, I'm afraid. Your friend Cass has been doing his best to keep him entertained, but he's still worried about you and Mr. Allen. He was afraid the police had detained you, even though I called the Honolulu station and they assured me you weren't being held. I think it would do him a world of good to see you."

"We'll be right there," I heard Jayne say. "I want to stop by the hotel first, but expect us in an hour."

"You sure you don't want to buy that bike?" the salesman called after us as we left the showroom. "I'll give you a dynamite price!"

The night manager was already on duty when we got back to the Royal Hawaiian, even though it was still afternoon. He tried not to react to our matching leather outfits, complete with copious studs and decorative safety pins.

We showered, washed our hair, and changed all our clothes, but we still smelled faintly of cigarette smoke and beer when we stepped into the limo. Carlos Medina, our driver for the evening, pretended not to notice as he drove us through the deepening twilight to Billy's house. He talked instead about the latest news from the Big Island, a new eruption of Kilauea.

Bertrand was in the yard when the taxi pulled up to the front gate. He had on jeans and a T-shirt that read THE MO' OF ME, THE BETTA. He was cutting the grass with his machete, very efficiently, in fact.

"Out of uniform, I see," I greeted him as he came over to open the gate. He laughed.

"I know it must seem strange to you, seeing me in native dress, Mr. Allen. But like it or not, we Samoans have a reputation on the island. People think twice before they mess with us. And that's exactly what I want them to do. The machete looks wicked and it can be lethal, of course. But most of all, it means I don't have to carry a gun."

"I see what you mean, Bertrand. Are Billy and Cass inside?"

"Yes, sir. Billy's waiting for you, Mrs. Allen. You seem to have a real way with him. Did you ever consider settling here permanently?"

"Not lately," she answered, entering the house through the open kitchen door. Billy jumped up from the butcher block table and stumbled over to give Jayne a long hug. He was wearing pajamas and a robe and looked like an invalid. Or a hypochondriac.

"They didn't keep you at the station this long, did they, Jayne?" he asked, his speech slightly slurred. He opened one arm to include me in the hug. I guessed he'd been sedated again. This was getting to be a habit. Another reason to get Billy away with us the next day. Cass materialized in the doorway, rubbing his eyes.

"Just catching a few minutes of shut-eye, in case we have another midnight appointment."

"I hope not," Jayne answered, "because Steve and I have a surprise for you. Tomorrow's Saturday, we don't have to be back until evening, and we just heard from our driver that Kilauea is erupting again. They think this could be a big one. We've decided to be volcano tourists—Air Oahu has an early flight direct to Hilo, with a late afternoon return, and we're going to be on it, all of us."

Cass looked pleased, but Billy started to mumble his regrets. "Gee, a volcano going off . . . it sounds like a heck of a show, but isn't it kind of dangerous?"

"Life is dangerous," Jayne told him firmly. "Anyway, I think it will do you good, Billy, to get out of this house, see something new. Nothing like a hit of Mother Nature unleashed to put your own problems in perspective."

"But, Jayne," Billy said, "you don't know what it's like! It's not just the volcano. People recognize me. They'll all want to know about the dead bodies! Every time I close my eyes I see bodies rolling in on the waves."

"What do you mean, I don't know what it's like?" Jayne shot back. "Do you think you're the only person to be recognized when you travel? You want to be in show business, you'll just have to get used to it. You don't have to answer any questions you don't want to answer. Besides, this is Meadows, the master of disguise. Leave it to me."

As she talked, Jayne was rummaging around in the kitchen, pulling out bowls—flour, butter, and sugar—from their various hiding places.

"Bertrand, I think a little baking might be in order to get Billy's spirits up. Now, where do you keep the macadamia nuts?" she called out the door to the bodyguard, who was still in the yard.

"You win," Billy said finally. Jayne enlisted his help and a half hour later the smell of fresh baked macadamia nut cookies filled the kitchen. Bertrand joined us for the first batch and Billy devoured most of the second batch on his own, washing it down with a half-gallon of milk. My cholesterol level rose just watching him. We paged Carlos, who'd gone into Waimanalo to wait for our call and left the beach house with Bertrand busy in the kitchen and Cass and Billy in the front yard. Cass had found an old piece of rope and was showing Billy how to lasso the keep-off signs.

Jayne and I returned to our hotel, where we spent a wonderfully uneventful evening. We had a quiet dinner in the Surf Room—both ordering mahi mahi—and retired early, telling the night manager we were taking a night off, so he could hold our calls. He mentioned that Puu Oo, the new vent in Kilauea Volcano that opened up in 1983, was suddenly showing more signs of activity than it had in years.

"I just thought you'd want to know, sir, since you and Mrs. Allen like to be where the action is. My cousin and I are checking out Harley's tomorrow night, by the way."

"Good idea. Tell them Steve and Jayne sent you," I called over my shoulder. It serves him right, I thought, for blabbing to Lieutenant Chen.

"I wonder if we'll find the missing script tomorrow?" Jayne asked sleepily as we were getting ready for bed.

"I don't know, but I think we'll find something," I replied with a yawn, pulling back the covers. I was all too right.

chapter 26

Rosy-fingered dawn was already at work when Jayne shook me gently to remind me that we had to be at the airport by seven. Cass and Billy were waiting for us at the Air Oahu desk. Jayne had done a trial run with the makeup the night before, leaving Billy with exact instructions on how to apply it himself in the morning. Even I wouldn't have recognized him if he hadn't been with Cass. He had a scarf tied over his hair, huge dark glasses, deeply tanned skin that looked blotchy, as if it were peeling, and zinc oxide on his lips and nose. He was dressed in a Local Motion T-shirt, puka-shell necklaces, baggy shorts, and rubber flip-flops, with a state-of-the-art boogie board tucked under one arm. I noticed that people tended to avert their eyes when they walked past him. Perfect.

"Ready for the waves, dude?" I greeted him.

"Cruisin'," he replied with the grin he'd made famous.

"Don't smile," I cautioned, "it's a dead giveaway." I regretted the word *dead* the moment it left my mouth. But it did the trick; Billy stopped smiling.

Even Cass looked the part of a perfectly innocuous tourist, his bowed legs sticking out of a pair of Bermuda shorts that looked like a walking aquarium. His T-shirt read FRESH SUSHI and depicted a giant cat about to devour a fish.

The waiting area was packed, but first class was nearly empty. We spread out along the windows and enjoyed the view on the short flight over to Hilo. The businessmen who bothered to look our way gave Jayne and me sympathetic nods but showed no sign of recognizing Billy. As we descended toward the Hilo airport we could see smoke rising from the south end of the island. The terminal was full of interisland hoppers come to take a look at Mother Nature putting on a show, however mindlessly.

Certain theological ideas are not an insult to the intelligence, but others are. I've never understood how anyone above the age of seven could possibly accept the ancient belief that the hand of nature is the hand of God. If it is, then we must conclude— given the daily mass tragedies of earthquakes, tornadoes, volcanic eruptions, hurricanes, floods, avalanches, and forest fires—that God is a sadistic mass murderer.

We had booked our car the evening before; Billy stuffed his boogie board in the trunk and we piled into a four-door Toyota. Jayne and I made sure she got in back with Billy, while I sat up front with Cass, directing him toward the Hawaii Volcanoes National Park. I thought we'd play tourist first, before I casually mentioned a little chore I had to do in Kilapani. As I eavesdropped on the conversation behind me. Jayne went straight to the point.

"So, my dear—we heard from Danny that your father is coming over next week. I was surprised you hadn't mentioned it, Billy. Danny seems to think that Raymond is considering taking over as producer of *Hawaiian Wave* next season. He's feeling pretty insecure about it."

"Well, that's too bad," Billy mumbled, his tone studied neutral. I couldn't tell if he was being sarcastic or just insensitive. Jayne wasn't about to give up though.

"Billy, you can be honest with me. If you don't want it to go any further, it won't. Is your father coming over here to discuss the possibility of producing the show next year?"

"You mean, is that the reason for his visit? No, I wish it was. But if Danny thinks he has to work to keep his job, that might not be such a bad thing."

"I disagree, dear. There's only so much pressure anyone can take before he reaches the breaking point. Danny seems to me to be stretched about as far as he'll go at the moment."

"Well, I don't want to sound callous, but that's his problem, not mine. I have enough to worry about."

Jayne rested for a minute, changing the subject to the flower

gardens and nurseries we were passing on our way up to the park.
Then she tried again.

"Edgar is concerned as well, Billy. He seems to think you're
going to try to direct an episode of the show. With his crazy artistic
temperament, that's like asking van Gogh to hand over his brush
and let you have a try at the sunflowers. You might at least reassure
him. If you do want to direct, you could try your hand at a movie
of the week, maybe even a project with your parents. I'll bet you
could sell the idea."

"Selling it isn't the problem. And I appreciate what you're
trying to do, honestly I do. You and Steve and Cass have all been
great. But you've been here now, what?—less than a week? And
I think you get an idea of what's going on. Two people are dead
and someone is after me. Whether I do or don't try directing the
series seems irrelevant, don't you think?"

"It's not irrelevant to Edgar," Jayne pointed out. I was thinking that Billy had done a pretty good job, once again, of skirting
the issue and avoiding a direct answer to Jayne's questions. If he
ever decided to leave the acting profession, he'd make a good
politician.

While Billy and Jayne were talking in the backseat, Cass guided
the Toyota steadily up the winding road into the high country.
As we gained in altitude, the air grew cooler and the landscape
changed from tropical to semiarid. This was no longer the Hawaii
of tourist brochures but vegetation you might find in the coastal
mountains of California, complete with stands of eucalyptus trees
and dry brush.

When we arrived at the Volcanoes Park Visitor Center, it had
just opened and was already packed. People from all over the
island, as well as off-island, had come to see the latest manifestation
of the power of the goddess Pele. Many of the visitors had brought
small offerings of coins, flowers, food, and gin, said to be Pele's
favorite beverage. We were told that the Chain of Craters Road
was still open, we should just drive carefully, keeping an eye out for
lava flows and informational roadblocks. We all felt the primitive
excitement as we got back into the car and headed slowly down
the slope of the mountain once again, toward the sea. Volcanic
activity has added six hundred acres of real estate to Hawaii since

1983, when the Puu Oo vent, on the flank of Kilauea, began to flow. It's truly awesome to be so close to the birth of land out of the inner core of the earth. Billy was suitably impressed.

Cass suddenly slowed to a near stop and pulled off the road onto the shoulder. The cars behind us were doing the same. Just barely discernible in the distance and coming toward us at an angle, so that it was hard to tell whether it would reach the road or bypass it, was a thin stream of molten lava. The land was already so barren, there was nothing much for it to burn and, as a consequence, the smoke was minimal, enabling us to actually see the glowing trail.

As we looked at the liquid fire-mush before us, even at a presumably safe distance, Cass summed up our reactions in one word, a softly muttered "Wow!"

He pulled back onto the road. When we got to the end of the highway, where the park meets the sea, a huge crowd had already collected to watch several threads of molten lava that were hitting the water with a hiss, sending up billows of smoke and steam. We watched with the others until word began to pass through the crowd that the towns up the coast were in danger again.

"Listen, I have business in Kilapani," I said to Billy. "It will take just a minute and I thought we'd all have lunch afterward. Meanwhile, it sounds as though we'd better get moving."

We drove back the way we'd come, catching another look at the lava flow near the road. It was even easier to see now, and the park rangers were out in force, trying to keep the curious from getting too close.

Once out of the park, we headed back in the direction of Hilo, took a right on Highway 130, and dropped down toward the coast again. At the end of Chain of Craters Road we had actually been very close to the town of Kilapani, but there is no road along this newly formed coastline in the path of the lava flows. Highway 130 gave us an even more spectacular view of the Puu Oo vent. Cass was so busy looking at the golden glow and black smoke in the distance, he almost ran into the car in front of us, which had come to a sudden stop at a hastily erected roadblock. He rolled down his window to talk to the highway patrolman who was addressing each driver.

"Good morning, folks. We're asking anyone who doesn't have business in Kilapani, Kupaahu, or Kehena to turn around here. We may need to order a total evacuation, so we want to keep the roads clear. If you want a good view of the eruption, I suggest you . . ."

I reached over Cass and waved the note on the Kenny's Kopy Shop letterhead in front of the patrolman. "We do have business. Kenny is expecting us. We'll be in and out in no time, Officer." He looked dubious, but when Cass slowly started to pull away, at a signal from me, he didn't bother to stop him. I felt like a Roman heading to my summer home in Pompeii as Vesuvius began to erupt. Survivors from that disaster, I remembered, had been evacuated by sea.

Kilapani used to be famous for its beautiful black sand beach. Both village and beach were smothered by the lava flows of 1990 and 1991, leaving a skeleton community that has managed to survive the whims of Pele, goddess of the volcanoes.

As soon as we spotted the sign for Kenny's Kopy Shop, we noticed the bottles of gin and piles of fruit surrounding the little wood-frame building. A young Japanese man with shoulder length hair was running back and forth from his shop to an old Volkswagen van, taking an occasional swig from one of the bottles on his route. He was dressed in knee-length surfer shorts, a tattered T-shirt, and rubber sandals.

We pulled up alongside the van, got out, and waylaid the young man as he emerged from the shop with a box in his hands.

"Kenny?" I asked. He nodded.

"Can we help?"

He barely glanced my way. "Sure. I'm going to make it—the old girl's not going to take *my* shop. She's never wanted it before, and I don't blame her. I don't know if I want it myself anymore. But just to be on the safe side, I'm taking out anything I can't live without."

We all pitched in, Jayne helping Kenny choose what to take and packing it, Cass and Billy and I carrying the boxes out to the van and stacking them in the back. In no time the ancient van was filled with boxes of CDs, computer games, clothes, and mementos, as well as the lighter-weight hardware of the copy business. It wasn't until we had everything loaded that Kenny seemed to actually notice us.

"Thanks for the help," he said. "I guess you must have come for something other than the exercise though. The Xerox machine is still hooked up if you need to make copies. They're on me."

"Actually, I'm afraid I'm here with some bad news," I began, "as if you didn't have enough on your mind. Your friend Dick Schiller was found in the water off Waimea Bay Beach Park early yesterday morning. The cause of death was drowning."

Kenny shook his head and sighed. "No kidding," he said, sitting down in the open doorway of the van. He looked genuinely shaken by the news. Dick did have a friend after all, I thought.

"Wow. And here all I could think about was the volcano and what might happen to my *stuff.*"

"I'm sorry," I told him. "Was he a close friend of yours?"

Kenny eyed me with momentary suspicion. "So what's *your* connection to Dick? How'd you get my name? I'm not in his will or anything, am I?"

"That I don't know. We found this letter in Dick's apartment," I said, showing him the note we had found. "The day before he died he was due to deliver last-minute changes on a script for the *Hawaiian Wave* TV show. He seemed very excited about the changes, talked as if they were going to reveal a long-kept secret that would change someone's life. I thought he might have brought this new script to you for printing. I know it's a long way to come, all the way to the Big Island for a printing job, but to be honest, Dick was behaving strangely before his death."

"Hey, *that's* nothing new. He was one weird dude."

"How well did you know him?" I prodded.

Kenny studied me for a moment and then shrugged. "About a year ago I helped him do research on the sugar plantations here on the Big Island. That's how my mom got here; my granddad was a field hand and my grandma was his mail-order bride. Dick said he was planning to write a script about the Japanese coming to Hawaii, and we became friends, sort of."

"Did you make copies of the script he was writing for *Hawaiian Wave?*"

"Sure. It was about a month ago. He came over from Oahu with a bunch of pages and said he needed thirty copies to take back with him. He was talking kinda wild, like you said, how he was going to spring this script on everybody when the time was right and blow some people away."

"Did you read the script yourself?"

"Naw, you know how it is. I just set the machine and we went off to catch up on old times."

"Did he give you any idea what the script was about?"

"He said it was about Angela. That he finally had a chance to get even."

"Get even with what? Who is Angela?"

"She was his girlfriend in high school. He told me about her when we first met and I asked him if he had a girl. He said there was only one woman in the entire world for him, and that was Angela."

"So she left him? That's what he wanted to get even with?"

Kenny sighed and looked very uncomfortable. "She *died* on him, man. I don't know the whole story, but he said that she'd been murdered. When he was here a month ago he said her killer was finally going to pay. I asked him if the police had caught the dude and he said, 'No, *I* have. I caught him in a web he can't escape.' . . . Say, you don't think this has something to do with the way Dick died. . . ."

"Yes, I do," I told Kenny just as a siren started to go off down the road. "Did Dick ever mention Angela's last name?"

"Never. She was just Angela. His guardian angel. His one and only true love forever, all that kinda stuff."

"How about the year she died?"

Kenny shook his head. "I guess it was a while ago, back when he was in high school. But he never said exactly."

"And he never mentioned the name of the person who killed her?"

"No. And I didn't encourage him to talk about it too much. He scared me sometimes, the expression on his face when he got on the subject."

I gave him a card for the Royal Hawaiian Hotel with our extension written in. "If you think of anything else, please give me a call immediately. I don't believe that Dick's death was accidental, and I think the answer to who killed him and why could be in that script you copied for him."

An official-looking gentleman drove up to Kenny's shop, leaned out his open window, and said, "Time to leave, Kenny. You too, folks. The flow is getting close and they're going to close the road in a few minutes. I'll keep an eye out for you, Kenny."

"Thanks, Walt. I got everything out I really need, and she's going to spare the shop again anyway. Here's lookin' at you, kid." Kenny raised the gin bottle in the general direction of the volcano, took one last swig, closed up his van, and jumped in the driver's seat. Cass led the way back out of the village and up the highway. The smoke was getting thicker and flames shot up into the sky where the lava flows, coming fast now, igniting trees and brush in their path. Every once in a while there was a big ball of flame and billows of black smoke far off in the distance. Probably a house going up. I looked behind us. Kenny was no longer there. I wondered if he'd turned around to go back and take his chances with Pele.

chapter 27

It was a relief to get back to Hilo and out of the worst of the smoke. We had a late lunch and took a quick look at the town, which still retains the atmosphere of the sugar plantations it once served and has recently received a much-needed face-lift. On the flight back to Oahu the smoke billowing up from Kilauea met the afternoon sun in a spectacular light show. The passengers let out a collective "ooh"—like a sports crowd—when lava spurted up through the charcoal haze. When Jayne moved to a vacant window seat across the aisle where she could see better, Billy came and sat next to me. Even with his surfer-dude disguise I could tell something was bothering him. There was a serious pout on his handsome face.

"I understand now why you organized this little trip, Steve—and I'm glad that you're trying to find out who killed Dick, I really am. It just seems as if you've forgotten about me sometimes. I think you care more about Dick Schiller and Sam Fitzgerald than you do about me and the danger I'm in."

I took a deep breath to maintain my patience. "Not at all, Billy. But I think all these events are connected, and that the best way to protect you is to protect everyone by getting to the bottom of all this."

"You think what happened to Sam and to Dick has something to do with *me?*" Billy seemed astonished by the thought.

"I don't know for sure, but, yes, I think so," I told him.

"But they're . . . *dead!*" he said in an awed whisper.

"You got it, kid." Frankly, I was tired of babying him.

Billy sighed. Then he went back to his seat and resumed

looking out the window while I went back to mulling over what I knew and what I didn't know. It was obvious from Kenny's information that Dick had not decided at the last minute to change the script of "The Ride of Your Life" from the one originally submitted and accepted. He had planned all along to switch scripts on us. Why? Again, the obvious answer was that he wanted to throw someone off guard, surprise someone with the new script when it was too late to do anything about it. Whom had Dick wanted to surprise? And with what? My thoughts went around and around, but I couldn't come up with any answer.

Cass dropped Jayne and me at the hotel before going on to Waimanalo with Billy. I suggested that the two of them meet us at the Shell for the Hawaiian music show, but Billy said he was tired of being in disguise and couldn't face public attention just yet, appearing in Waikiki as his famous self.

"I understand," I told him. "You vant to be alone."

"What?" he said, and I realized in the instance that he had simply never heard the old line attributed to film actress Greta Garbo.

It's interesting that even now, when I'm reporting on what happened to all of us, I'm aware that some of my readers, being young, will have to be told that Ms. Garbo was a film star of major importance in the 1930s. It's easy to become impatient at the ignorance of generations that follow one's own, but what we forget is that we were, in our time, guilty of the same dumbth. Each generation has its own interests, its own celebrities. When I was ten years old I had, of course, heard about Rudolph Valentino, but he meant nothing to me, whereas to the young women of his time he was as important as, say, Elvis Presley would become half a century later.

"Steve, you really aren't being very nice to me!" Billy whined. "I vant . . . I *want* whoever is stalking me to quit it, that's all. You don't understand how terrifying it is to be in my shoes. To have crazy fans out there, and everyone wanting something from me, and no one appreciating me for myself. It's hell to be a rich, famous TV star, it really is . . . and no one is sympathetic!"

"It's a tough world," I told him heartlessly enough.

Jayne collected our phone messages at the front desk and read them to me while I turned on the TV to the local news.

"The Earles called, Steve. They're inviting us to dine with them at Michel's and go on from there to Keoni's show."

"Tell them yes, by all means. They know everyone in Hawaii. Maybe they'll be able to tell me more about Jason Patterson. I have a feeling—"

Just then Kenny's Kopy Shop appeared on the TV screen. I turned up the sound. The announcer was saying, "There are those who scoff at the ancient Hawaiian tradition of leaving offerings to the goddess Pele. But Kenny Kumitomo will tell you to look at the evidence." The picture shifted to the back of Kenny's shop, where a strand of lava had come to a stop just feet from his building. Kenny was standing next to it, grinning from ear to ear. "I think this is what it means to have God on your side," he said. "We'll be open for business at eight A.M. Monday. For the best copies in Puna, come to Kenny's, the shop favored by Pele."

"I can almost hear your teeth gritting," Jayne said.

"You're right," I said. "Why are so many people interested in superstition and so few interested in science?"

"I'll tell you what," Jayne said "When we get home you can send Kenny a copy of *Dumbth.*"

She was referring to a book of mine that's recently been reissued, partly because the problem it addresses has gotten worse, not better, since the original edition came out in 1991. The problem, alas, is that of the general erosion—sometime seemingly collapse—of intelligence itself in our country.

Jayne and I arrived at Michel's restaurant, near the Waikiki Shell, a little before six. Walter and Margaret Earle were waiting for us on the sidewalk in front of the restaurant, catching the early evening light. The Earles have been an institution on Oahu since the 1960s. Walter, as you probably remember, was the star of one of the first TV series set in Hawaii. You can still catch the show in reruns, thirty years later, on some of the cable channels and local stations around the country. The show was very successful and helped define Hawaii in the popular imagination. Walter liked Hawaii so much he and his wife, Margaret, settled on Oahu after the series ended, becoming very active in civic affairs.

Margaret gave Jayne and me a hug as we emerged from the limousine. She looked older than I remembered. Her chiseled features were framed by spiky gray hair that looked as if she habitually ran her hands through it. The expression on her face was just as intelligent and amused with the world as ever though. It was good to see her.

"I'm so glad you could make it," she said, and I could tell that she meant it. Walter was right behind her, shaking hands heartily and repeating his wife's greeting. He's a big, rugged-looking man, now in his early seventies. He looks like an out-doorsman and is, though his favorite outdoor activity is tending his extensive rose garden. He had a bunch of the flowers in his hand, which he presented to Jayne with a flourish.

"They're beautiful, Walter," she said, plucking one for her hair and handing the rest to the limousine driver with instructions to have them put in a vase in our sitting room.

The maître d' appeared and led us through the sumptuous dining room, past well-fed faces and tables set with crisp white linen and gleaming silver. Walter seemed to know half the people in the room, which made for slow progress. He introduced us to a Honolulu hotel magnate, an Arab prince, and a French film director. At last we arrived at a window table that had a grand postcard view of the ocean and Diamond Head. We scanned the huge menus and ordered quickly. The Waikiki Shell has a ten o'clock curfew, which means that their shows start early. Margaret winced when her husband ordered the French onion soup *and* the chateaubriand, but she didn't say a word. My *opakapaka*, a local snapper served very fresh, would have been dietetic without the creamy sauce it came smothered in.

The first words out of Margaret's mouth, once the waiter had left, were about the show. "So tell me, how is life on the set of *Hawaiian Wave?* We saw the news last night, of course, and read the paper this morning. How terrible! Two deaths in one week. You certainly didn't time your visit very well!" I laughed.

Jayne and I spent the next twenty minutes, all the way through the salad course, describing our adventures so far, good and bad, on and off the set of *Hawaiian Wave*. When we reached a momentary pause, Margaret and Walter could only shake their heads in amazement.

"Well, a TV series is never easy," Margaret said. "But this sounds like a show from hell! I certainly hope they pull through— you know, it's the first locally filmed show since Walter's to win the hearts of the people who live here. The music has been a particular hit—it's really made people proud of Hawaiian culture. Walter wanted to show his support for Keoni Pahia and his recording company, so we bought a box at the concert tonight."

"You know Keoni, then?" Jayne asked.

"Oh, yes. Very interesting young man. But you must already know that. He's been on the set, hasn't he? I shouldn't say this in front of Walter, but if I were thirty years younger ..."

I turned to Walter. "Speaking of thirty years younger, I wonder if you happen to know a man named Jason Patterson. He's the president of the Diamond Head Polo Club and has a lovely young wife at least thirty years his junior."

"Ah, yes, Jason and Melanie." Walter laughed. "I don't want to be accused of spreading gossip, but since you ask, I have heard rumors that all may not be what it seems at the Diamond Head Polo Club. Jason Patterson started the club and some people are saying he treats the dues and contributions as if they were his own personal assets, to do with as he pleases. I've met the man and I find it hard to believe he'd deliberately do anything to bring down the club. But sometimes people get in over their heads and ... At the moment he seems to be counting on your producer, Danny Siderman, to bail him out. If I were Siderman, I'd take a close look at where I was putting my money."

"Walter—in our episode the plot hinges around gambling on the outcome of polo matches. Is this something that actually happens?"

"That's a hard question to answer. Officially there's no gambling. It's not like horse racing in that respect. But unofficially? There are people who will bet on anything, as you know. My guess is that there probably are private gambling pools. And given the fact that polo is still a glamour sport and the people who are attracted to it tend to be wealthy, I wouldn't be surprised if a fair amount of money changes hands late on Sunday afternoons during polo season. I wouldn't even rule out the possibility of bookies and underworld connections, either Japanese or Sicilian. We're a small island, but we haven't escaped all the vices of the mainland, unfortunately."

Our main courses arrived and the talk drifted to old friends as well as books, politics, and other matters. Walter and Margaret are good conversationalists, and it was a relief to forget for a time the dramas surrounding *Hawaiian Wave.*

"Shall we walk to the Shell?" Margaret asked when we emerged from the restaurant at last. "We'll have to hurry, but it's not far." A chorus of hellos followed us down the street. Passersby who recognized Walter from the old show greeted him as if he were a personal friend. That's the way they feel about him on Oahu.

The Waikiki Shell is an open-air bandstand in Kapiolani Park that seats just over three thousand, not counting the grassy rise where a good many more can make themselves comfortable on a balmy night. It's always advisable to bring an umbrella, and Margaret had stopped off at the car to pick up two, which were sticking out of her shoulder bag. It was hard to imagine we were going to need them tonight—the sky was clear and star-studded, but weather can change fast in the tropics. We arrived at our box just as the concert was beginning. A few autograph seekers descended on us the minute we sat down, but Walter whispered to them to come back during the intermission and they left without an argument.

Keoni walked onstage to an explosion of cheers, whistles, and stomps. Arms went up all over the audience, in the traditional "hang loose" sign, thumb and little finger extended with a rotating wrist. Keoni introduced the show and then took the opportunity to talk about his recording company. "I promise you that any demo tape of authentic island music submitted to my office will be seriously considered for production and returned to the artist with a written opinion by myself or one of my producers." Wild applause. He gestured for silence and went on. "However, our ability to record and promote new talent depends on you. It's your job to support your music at the store, and encourage your families and friends to do the same." More cheers, whistles, and wiggling fingers. "Now, let's hear it for . . ."

The show that followed covered the gamut of Hawaiian music, from a Niihau church choir, which was enthusiastically cheered, to Lloyd Kawelo, who got the reception I thought he deserved, respectful but far from delirious. We were kept busy signing autographs at the beginning of the intermission, but I wanted to take the opportunity to talk to Keoni and slipped away as soon as I could, leaving Walter in conversation with another old friend. I found the stage door and was trying to convince the guard stationed there to take a note to Keoni, when Lloyd Kawelo came bursting out of the backstage area. He started yelling as soon as he spotted me.

"Mr. Steve Allen! Just the man I want to talk to!"

"How are you doing, Lloyd?" I inquired politely.

"Do you know what your little friend William Markham has done? He just screwed me royally, that's what. He knew we were going to release my new CD and music videos to tie in with the exposure on *Hawaiian Wave.* We have the package all put together, we're even calling the CD *The Ride of Your Life.* I snagged the best director on the island to do the videos. He's very commercial; in fact, that's what he does, commercials. I'm ready for commercial, goddammit. I've been counterculture all my life, and where has it gotten me?"

"Lloyd, I'd love to talk to you about this some other time—"

"I mean, I was *there!* I was *that* close to the big breakthrough, and you know what happens? That bastard goes and tells your producer he doesn't think my music is right for the episode. He has something else in mind. And they listen to him, they friggin' listen to him!"

Lloyd had succeeded in snagging my interest. "Are you sure Billy did this?"

"Of course I'm sure! And what does that spoiled kid know about Hawaiian music? What does he know about anything? You'd better talk to him, Steve—somebody better talk to him. 'Cause if I get near him, I'm going to do more than just talk, and I don't care who knows it."

Lloyd stormed past me into the crowd. The second half of

the program was beginning, so I decided to try Keoni again later and went back to my seat. Chalk up another one for Billy, I thought. He has now successfully alienated just about everyone connected with *Hawaiian Wave.* Is he merely oblivious, I wondered? Or has he set himself up as an object of hatred on purpose?

chapter 28

The second half of the show was better than the first. Near the end of the program, the sky, which none of us had noticed clouding up, let loose with a crack of thunder and a sudden downpour. Our box was covered, so Margaret kindly lent her umbrella to some young people standing nearby. The performers played on and the audience, if anything, was even more enthusiastic. By the time the final act left the stage, the rain had stopped and stars were beginning to reappear. The world smelled brand new.

I still wanted to talk to Keoni, so I told Jayne I'd meet her back at the hotel and saw her off with the Earles. This time the guard at the backstage entrance took my note to Keoni without an argument, and Keoni himself came out a minute later.

"There's a real party going on backstage, Steve. If you want to talk, we'll have better luck just taking a walk."

We headed out through the park, past the zoo, where the peacocks were screeching and showing off to their peahens, and into the bright lights of Kalakaua Avenue.

"You put on a great show," I told him. "And it looked to me like a full house."

"Yeah, I'm stoked. But the real test is whether those people will all go out and support the music at the stores. I've been so busy pulling this thing together, I almost forgot the latest news. You must have heard about Dick Schiller?"

"Yes. That's one reason I wanted to talk to you."

"I got a call from Danny yesterday. Poor guy, Schiller, I mean. He had a pretty good career going as a screenwriter, but he always seemed like a loser to me. I've never understood what makes people kill themselves though. I've been down in my life, who hasn't, but suicide? I just can't relate to it.''

"Is that what Danny told you, Keoni? That Schiller killed himself?''

"Yeah. Why?''

"Because suicide seems highly unlikely to me. Why would he do it when he'd just announced that he had made revisions to the script that would blow us all away? He was on to something— about to expose someone, I think. I can't believe he wouldn't want to stick around to see how it all came out.''

Keoni stopped in the middle of the sidewalk, eliciting a few stares from passersby. "So you think he was murdered?''

"Yes, I do. And I think Sam Fitzgerald was murdered as well. In fact, until we figure out what's going on and why, I don't think anyone is safe . . . with the exception of the murderer, of course. That's one reason you need to level with me. I know you and Sam were childhood friends, or at least that you played on the same Little League baseball team. I know Jason Patterson was a coach of one of your teams. What do you know that you're not telling, Keoni?''

"Hey, brah, I thought you were on my side. You're starting to sound like the cops.''

"I'm trying to avoid bringing the cops into this. But I can't do that if you won't talk to me.''

"All right. Yeah, I knew Sam Fitzgerald, way back when. And Patterson too. It's a small island. You look at these tons of people walking around Waikiki, you go 'Hah, what's he mean, small?' But they're all tourists. The real people who live here, who grew up here, we know each other.''

"All right. Then start with Sam—tell me about him.''

"We were friends a long time ago, playing Little League, like I said. As adults we drifted apart, so I can't tell you all that much. He was just a goofy kid, you know? The kind that makes everybody laugh. He was always telling dirty jokes—he had a filthy mind. He also had the best comic book collection on Oahu. No one took him very seriously, he was always clowning around. And that's about all I can tell you. I never went to his home or met his

parents, and most of the time I saw him, we were together with
a whole group of boys . . . girls hadn't quite entered the picture
back then. A few months ago he showed up looking for a job at
my record company and I was able to find him something, for
old time's sake."

"Did he say what he'd been doing recently?"

"Just this and that. He'd been a waiter, then a security guard
for a while at one of the big hotels. Nothing had worked out for
him too well—it didn't surprise me. There are a lot of guys like
that on the islands, Steve. Nice guys. Fun to hang out with. But
not exactly what you'd call ambitious."

"Do you know who his current friends were?"

"Everybody. That's what someone like Sam does with himself.
He makes himself friendly. He drinks beer and jokes around, and
fits in with the scene."

I was getting a picture of Sam Fitzgerald, I supposed, but it
was still fuzzy. I switched to Jason Patterson, Keoni's one-time
coach. But Keoni couldn't tell me much more than he had about
Sam.

"Jason was an adult. The coach, you know. Sort of uptight,
but he knew a lot about baseball. He was big on discipline. He
made it a rule that when one of us missed practice, we couldn't
play the next game. You missed two practices and you were off
the team."

"Did you ever go to his house?"

"Once or twice. He'd throw us a party at the end of each
season in his backyard. But we weren't allowed to actually go *inside*
the house. I remember that bugged me a little. It's like he was
doing us a big favor, sacrificing his time to coach a bunch of poor
island boys—but it was all charity, like we weren't really in his
class. Not the sort you'd invite inside your living room."

"Is there anything else you can tell me about Jason? Any
incident that stays in your mind?"

"Not really. I'm sorry to be so unhelpful, but I was just a kid
and he really didn't interest me too much. The dumb phase I
was going through, all adults were the same—like totally boring."

"Did Jason ever talk about polo?"

"Sure. Polo was like a religion to the guy. He took the entire team to games a few times. I think he was hoping maybe one of us would turn into a jockey or something." Keoni suddenly looked at his watch. "Look, man, I'm always glad to talk with you, but I left a bunch of people hanging—I really need to get back to the Shell now."

"What about Dick Schiller?" I asked, trying to stall him.

"What about him?"

"He grew up here. Did you know him before he wrote the script for 'The Ride of Your Life'?"

Keoni shook his head.

"One last question. Jayne and I came over to appear in this episode at Billy's personal request. He's been living in fear for his life for some time, and I'm beginning to think that may not be a paranoid delusion. Do you think someone is after him?"

Keoni hesitated. When he did speak, it was with a bitterness that surprised me. "I wouldn't worry about Billy, Steve. I don't think *he's* in any danger. And now I really do need to get back." With that he turned and walked back the way we'd come.

I turned in the opposite direction and strolled to the Royal Hawaiian, a twenty-minute walk along Kalakaua Avenue, pondering how little information I had managed to get from Keoni. It was all frustrating to me, and most mysterious. When I entered our suite, Jayne was ready for bed and comfortably settled on the living room couch.

I sank into the armchair next to her.

"I want you to call Tony for me, Jayne. It's not that late and he wouldn't mind being woken up by the sound of your voice anyway. I want to know if he's gotten anywhere with that missing script yet."

"I haven't been idle, dear. No, he hasn't."

"Then I suggest we take Sunday breakfast with Cap. We'll bring it with us, just to be on the safe side—his kitchen wasn't exactly what I'd call clean. I want to take another look at the photo on Dick Schiller's coffee table and the yearbooks next to it. That girl must be Angela. If we can find a last name, we can get Tony to run a check on her. I wouldn't mind a look around Cap's apartment as well, while you keep him entertained somewhere else. You could get him talking fish in front of Dick's tank."

"Okay, I'll come up with something. To tell you the truth, I rather like the old man. Do you think *he* has the script revisions?"

"It's a possibility. We know Dick had copies for everyone printed up a month ago. He didn't leave them at the print shop. They weren't in his apartment. He trusted the old man. Who else did he trust? Lance? Actually, I suppose that's a possibility. *I* don't trust Lance, but that doesn't mean Dick wouldn't. Hand me the phone, would you?"

Lance answered on the third ring. "Hey, Steve, what's up? You had enough excitement for one week?"

"Not quite. I'm looking for a little more. Dick Schiller didn't happen to talk to you about the revisions he had planned for our episode, did he? I was hoping he might have left the revised scripts with you, or a computer disk, or some idea, at least, of what he was planning."

"Nada, Steve. But if you do find those revisions, I wouldn't mind seeing them myself. We were friends once, you know. In fact, I'm glad you called, because I was going to call you. I feel remiss in my duties. With so much happening, I haven't treated you to a real insider's view of Hawaii. How about you and I have lunch at the Pearl Harbor Tavern tomorrow. Do you know it?"

"No, I don't think so."

"What do you say I pick you up at noon?"

I hesitated, wondering why Lance wanted to see me. We were different generations and we weren't friends. It didn't quite make sense to me, his sudden urge to be friendly. I had no idea what he had in mind, but I decided to take the bait. "Noon sounds good," I said. "I'll see you then."

I hung up the phone and turned to Jayne with a smile. "Breakfast with Cap, lunch with Lance. How much fun can a person have in one morning?"

When I opened my eyes on Sunday morning the stars were still out. I tiptoed over to the balcony and stepped outside. The sky was beginning to lighten and it promised to be another beautiful day. I had a momentary pang of self-pity, thinking how nice it would be if Jayne and I could just relax and enjoy it. But then I thought of Sam Fitzgerald's body, swaying on the coral in Hanauma Bay like some huge tropical fish. And Dick Schiller, on the rocks at Waimea Bay. His dream come true had turned into the ultimate nightmare. Could I have saved him? Should I have realized that he was in danger? "The pen is mightier than the sword," he had said. Was the answer to his death really in the missing version of "The Ride of Your Life," even if we never found it? Was someone taking *me* for a ride?

"Is that you, dear?" Jayne called from the bedroom. I didn't have the heart for the punch line that would normally be my response to a question like that.

"I couldn't sleep either," she went on, joining me on the lanai. "Let's go take a dip before we tackle Cap. All work and no play . . ."

" 'Makes Dick a dull boy.' That's what he said the night I caught him spying on us at the International Market Place. You've given me an idea."

"That's good. Now you can give me some help with this zipper."

Jayne was right, as usual. The swim did wonders for my spirits. We arrived at the door of Cap's apartment at eight, carrying a brown paper bag full of bagels and lox, light cream cheese, coffee, orange juice, and three different Sunday papers from the delicatessen down the block.

"Well, didn't take ya long, did it?" he said as soon as he opened the door. "Come in, come in, that bag there sure does smell good."

Jayne and I took our places on the couch, cleared a space on the coffee table, and spread out the breakfast. Cap was delighted to have the New York and L.A. papers as well as the *Honolulu Gazette*.

I began my questions while we ate. "Do you have the keys to Dick's car, Cap?" A sly smile came over his face.

"Yer smarter than them there coppers by a whole lot. They didn't even look at the car."

"Mind if I do?"

"Help yersef, man. You know where the keys is kept."

I took the key chain off the hook by the door and went out to Dick's car. I checked the trunk first, then the inside. I found a few empty beer cans, crumpled potato chip bags, two paperback novels—*Valley of the Dolls* and *Madame Bovary,* an odd assortment of literary taste—as well as paper clips, junk mail, cigarette butts, cassette tapes, and other assorted garbage. None of it was what I had been looking for.

"Nothing," I reported back, sitting down again on the tattered sofa.

"I know," Cap wheezed. "I already checked. Ya don't think yar the only ones can do a little detectin', do ya?"

I forced a polite smile. "What can you tell me about the girl in the picture on Dick's coffee table, Cap? Did Dick ever talk about her? I think she could be important."

"Well." He coughed and looked over at Jayne. "He called her his angel. An' he loved t' look at them yearbooks."

"So would I. Do you mind?"

"Nope. Be my guest."

Jayne said she'd be right back, and we left Cap engrossed in the *New York Times Magazine.* We took the key and walked next door to Dick's apartment. The place was beginning to smell musty, but it still wasn't as bad as Cap's. It's a depressing job to go through a dead man's belongings. We wandered through the living room in silence. There was weak sunlight coming through the dirty windows from the street. Even the tropical fish in the tank looked somehow dispirited as they hovered listlessly in the green water. The four volumes of Crown High School yearbooks lay where we had last seen them, on a coffee table that was marked with the rings of past drinking parties, next to a framed photograph of a pretty, young girl who seemed out of place smiling so brightly into the desolate apartment. This was Angela, apparently, the girl Dick had once loved. In the photograph she looked pouty and sexy and probably a bit wild—or maybe I was reading these qualities into her come-hither smile. Still, from this one pose I was willing to speculate that Angela was what back in my day we would call a fast girl. There was a knowing glint in her eye that was older than her fifteen or sixteen years. She was holding two pompoms, and even with her implied sinfulness she seemed wonderfully full of life, a pretty teenager experimenting with vices that were still brand new. It was hard to believe she was dead. Looking at a photo of a dead girl in a dead man's apartment was not exactly my idea of an uplifting way to spend Sunday morning, but I was determined to get to the bottom of the mystery she posed.

"There's no name on the back of the picture," I said to Jayne as she flipped through the first yearbook.

"She looks like a cheerleader," Jayne mentioned. "Maybe we'll find her name in the football section."

I looked over Jayne's shoulder as she scanned the glossy pages of bright and not-so-bright young faces. I found myself wondering what had become of all of them. Some must be parents now, solid members of the community. Others, like Dick and Angela, were dead. We located Angela in the third book, junior year. She was wearing a short skirt and jumping in the air, part of the cheerleading squad of some long-forgotten high school football game. In the photo the girl had an enormous amount of pep, and a smile that radiated a thousand watts of energy. ANGELA SCHWARTZ it said in small print beneath the picture.

"Bingo," I said. "And this is where Lieutenant Chen is going to come in handy."

We looked her up in the index of each book and found her in the class photos of freshman, sophomore, and junior year—prettier with each passing year. And then, ominously, she disappeared; her name wasn't in the index for her senior year. We looked up Schiller in the indexes while we were at it. He was on the staff of the school newspaper and the yearbook. I wouldn't have recognized him if we hadn't been able to match up the photo with the names at the bottom. He wasn't wearing glasses, he had more hair, and he wore it long and stringy. The most recognizable feature was his body language. He looked self-conscious, nervous, and alienated from his fellow journalists.

Jayne looked up from the yearbook she was studying. "Steve, didn't you say that Keoni told you he didn't know Dick Schiller before the show? Look."

She passed me over the earliest yearbook, open to a picture of the freshman baseball team. There was no mistaking Keoni. Or Sam Fitzgerald, for that matter.

"Right," I said. "I think we're getting closer. We'd better leave these books where we found them, so Lieutenant Chen can 'find' them for himself. But I think we have enough to go on, and Cap is probably missing you."

We closed up the house and went back next door. The old man was pretty much where we'd left him. He'd finished my bagel, and Jayne's as well, I noticed.

"Dick didn't happen to give you a package to keep for him, did he, Cap?" I asked. "It would have been anytime in the past month, either small and flat, a computer disk. Or bulky and heavy—thirty scripts for a TV episode, in fact."

"A month ago, ya say?" Cap answered, another crafty look coming over his wizened face. "Nope."

Oddly enough, at that very moment I realized, for the first time, why Cap had looked familiar to me; he bore a remarkable resemblance to an eccentric character named Gypsy Boots, who became nationally famous, especially in health food circles, for his frequent appearances on the comedy talk show I was doing in the early 1960s from Hollywood. As of 1998 Gypsy was still alive, though well into his eighties.

Jayne saw her cue.

"I noticed that one of Dick's fish looked a little sluggish, Cap. Could you take a look with me? We certainly don't want the dear little thing to die, do we?" Cap was reluctant at first but finally rose from his easy chair and followed Jayne out the door. I made a hurried search of his apartment. It was small, one bedroom, one bath, the kitchen open to the living room. But there were piles of junk everywhere. Even a package of thirty scripts could take hours to find in such a mess. The bedroom closet was so full of cardboard boxes, I couldn't get the door to open, and the sliding door to the entryway closet came off in my hands, revealing more floor-to-ceiling boxes. If Cap knew where those scripts were, he would have to tell us.

I could hear Jayne's voice outside the front door. The old man rushed back into his apartment and looked nervously around. He thanked us for the breakfast and made it clear that he wanted us to go now. Jayne gave him the Royal Hawaiian card.

"That script could be the clue to everything, Cap. If you find it, or anything that looks like it, give us a call. We can keep the police out of this, you know. It will be our secret. We'll be a team.''

Cap looked as if he was thinking about what Jayne said. Then he pushed us out the door and locked it behind us.

''I think he's got it, Steve'' were the first words out of Jayne's mouth.

''I do too. But you should have seen that place. He's going to have to find it for us.''

chapter 29

We got back to the Royal Hawaiian around eleven. I bought another copy of the *New York Times* and sat out on the lanai with it. There's nothing like a good strong dose of the news of the world to put your own dead bodies into perspective. I went from the starving children in North Korea to the seemingly endless violence in Bosnia, with a few horror stories from China and Africa thrown in for good measure. And that was just the international news. By the time I'd waded through the murder and mayhem in the cities and towns of my own homeland, I was feeling positively lucky. Our problems on *Hawaiian Wave* seemed minor by comparison, no dead infants or sexually abused four-year-olds or road-rage murder victims. It was in this mood that I greeted the phone when it rang.

"Lieutenant Chen! I'm glad you called. I have someone I'd like you to run through your files. Her name is . . . yes, just a minute." I put my hand over the receiver.

"Jayne, it's your lifelong admirer. Get him to run a check on Angela Schwartz." Jayne took the call in the bedroom and I could hear her laughing all the way out on the lanai. She wasn't supposed to be having that much fun. A few minutes later she came out and sat on the edge of my lounge chair.

"I'm going to have lunch in Chinatown, dear, while you're with Lance. Tony needs a little buttering up. He's not happy at the idea that we might be trying to do his job for him."

"Then he should start doing it himself," I said cuttingly. "And get him to run a check on Angela if you can. But don't tell him about Cap yet. I want to give the old guy time to think about whether he's going to give us that script. I'm sure he has it."

Jayne nodded and went back inside. When the phone rang again, it was the lobby to say that a Mr. Brady was waiting for Mr. Allen. When I went into the bedroom to say good-bye to Jayne, she was humming to herself. I suggested that I cancel my luncheon date with Lance so I could chaperon her in Chinatown.

"Don't be silly, dear. It's all in the line of duty." She smiled and I gave her a kiss, told her I expected her home right after lunch, and went off to see what I could find out from my own date.

"I'm glad you could make it," Lance said, leading me to a fire-engine-red TransAm in the parking garage next to the hotel. He was dressed to be noticed, in an Italian sport shirt unbuttoned halfway down his chest and tight-fitting slacks. He drove like an Italian as well, fast, aggressive, skillful, and with total disregard for the other cars on the road. The picture was complete when he lit an Italian cigarette and blew the truly revolting tobacco smoke in my direction as he talked.

"The Tavern is a local institution, Steve. They have great food, Japanese and American, and they don't stint on the drinks. We can eat upstairs in the bonsai garden, or have our lunch in the bar. They got this big glass cage full of live monkeys behind the bar. It's a trip to watch 'em watching you. The place started out as a serviceman's bar in the forties, but they get a pretty mixed crowd these days."

It was a relief to get out of the car. The bartender downstairs knew Lance and directed us to a table with a reserved sign on it.

"This OK?" Lance asked. "We could always go upstairs if you'd rather. I told them to save me a table up there as well. They like me in this place. I add a little glamour, you know how it is." I said the bar would be fine. It was noisy, but that can make it easier to talk in confidence, even if it is harder to hear. We ordered lunch and drinks, a mineral water with lime for me, a double gin and tonic for Lance. He gulped his down, waved to the bartender for a refill, and started talking.

"I couldn't believe it about Dick Schiller. Well, I take that back. I *could* believe it. That's the problem. I need to talk to someone and I thought, Steve, he'll understand."

"Understand what?" I purred.

"Well, I feel like I'm to blame for all this. I know I shouldn't be so hard on myself but . . . the poor guy." Lance rubbed the hair on his upper chest. "I'm the one who got Dick involved with the show in the first place. I can see now that it was a mistake. But at the time I had no idea that he wouldn't be able to handle it."

A young man in leather and chains stopped by our table to say hello to Lance. Our food came right behind him, along with another gin and tonic. I encouraged Lance to go on. Eat, drink, and be merry—but keep talking, please.

"OK, here's what happened, Steve. I met Dick Schiller when I first came to Hawaii, almost a year ago now. I was exhausted after three years on *The Loves of Our Lives.* You know how it is, you shoot five days a week on those things, you have a few hours to learn your lines, there's no such thing as a vacation or sick leave, you're tied to your work. I was furious when they decided to kill off my character. I mean, three years of my life I gave the bastards. But it was a relief too. I got over here thinking maybe it was time for a change, a real change, you know? And that's when I met Dick. He had written this docudrama for public television based on the life of Father Damien. He's the guy who went and lived with the lepers on Molokai and died of leprosy himself. You know the story?"

I nodded. "Having grown up a Catholic, I'm well familiar with it."

"Right. Well, it's dramatic stuff, and Dick's script wasn't bad, better than the one we're shooting now. He said he wanted me to star in it, and I thought, what the hell. No real money, but it was a good part and I wasn't doing anything else."

Someone had set off the monkeys in the glass cage behind the bar. They began screeching and swinging wildly from one side of their cage to the other. Lance laughed and lit a cigarette before he went on talking. "Nothing personal, Lance, but I've got a problem about cigarette smoke, so I'd appreciate it if you could blow that stuff as far away from me as possible."

"Oh," he said, "I'm sorry. Here, let me take one more drag and I'll put the damn thing out." Which he did.

"Dick was always on the set. He wanted to make sure the director got it right. He'd freak if any of us messed with even one line. Anyway, we got to be friends, like. He was lonely and I was new. He wasn't dumb, you know. Crazy, yeah, but he wasn't dumb. You could have a real conversation with him, which is something on this island. So we started hanging out together, made the scene a little. Enter *Hawaiian Wave*. I called Dick the day I got hired for the Pete Lambert part. We went out and tied one on. Came here, as a matter of fact. Those monkeys were unreal after a while. I thought I was in the jungle."

"Right," I said.

"And then I got busy. You've seen how Edgar works. He's a perfectionist. I hear he's been pretty easy on you guys this week, but when we were doing the season opener and the first few episodes, it was another story. The schmuck was a slave driver. So I didn't see Dick for a while, didn't even talk to him. And then, all of a sudden, I get a call and he says he has a script for the show, a two-part episode no less, movie length. He thinks it's dynamite, he knows I'll love it, and he wants me to give it to Danny. I told him I'd read it, but even if I loved it I couldn't guarantee him I could get it accepted. Edgar has to pass on all the scripts and Billy gets his two cents in there. It's not just Danny's decision. Anyway, I read it and it was OK. You're working with it, you know what I mean. It's not Shakespeare, but he's pretty good with dialogue, right?"

"Are you sure Dick showed you the script we're working from now?" I asked. Lance looked taken aback.

"Yeah, of course. Why do you ask?"

"Because I have reason to believe that the revisions he was due to give us the morning his body was found were actually written much earlier. They may have been the original version of the script and the one we're shooting from could be the revised product."

"I'm not sure I'm following you here, Steve. The script Dick showed me is the one we're shooting. I thought it was pretty unprofessional of him to try to change it at the last minute, myself.

And like I told you on the phone, I'd like to see this new script myself." Lance took another gulp of his drink. The monkeys had finally calmed down, but the bar scene was heating up. It was a hip, youngish crowd. The fun set, the island hedonists—though everyone seemed to be trying too hard, and beneath the noise and booze it wasn't difficult to sense low-down emptiness and despair. Several people looked our way, as if they wanted to come over and say hello. Lance glared at them and they stayed away.

"So to continue the saga, Steve, I gave the script to Danny as a favor to Dick. I like to help people out when I can. And Danny went for it. Edgar liked the water and polo stuff and Billy wanted to do it because he figured the Brents were a perfect part for his mom and dad. I think Danny liked it because it didn't offend anybody, at least not anybody who was in a position to admit they'd been offended. Well, Dick was ecstatic. He couldn't thank me enough. He said I'd made his life. He started calling me at all hours of the day and night. I had to quit answering the phone, for God's sake. I let the machine take it and listened in to see if it was him. But even that didn't work. If he couldn't get me on the phone he'd come over anyway and sit around my house spinning these wild fantasies of himself as a rich and famous screenwriter. He was going to get off the rock—that's what he called Oahu. He was going to go to Hollywood, make some *real* money. It was too much, man, I couldn't take it after a while. I finally came out and told him just how crazy I thought he was. I told him he'd never make it in the big time. The guy just didn't know how to present himself. You saw him. That wacko stuff doesn't cut it these days. Anyway, it hit him pretty hard, I guess. I probably should have nursed him along, but I didn't think he'd take it *that* hard. I mean, I knew he was crazy, but I didn't realize *how* crazy."

"So you think Dick committed suicide?"

Lance looked as if my question had surprised him. "Of course. It could have been an accident, I guess, but that doesn't make much sense. I'd feel better if it was an accident, but why would he be out there alone at night?"

"What if he wasn't alone? What if someone was with him,

someone who helped him over the edge, hit him on the head, say, and pushed him over?''

"You kidding? No way. Who would want to kill somebody like Dick Schiller? No, you've been watching too many TV shows. You've been watching *Hawaiian Wave!* Things like that don't happen in real life. What, hit him over the head with a tire jack and throw him off a cliff? Forget it."

"A rock, he would have been hit with a rock, so it would look as though he received the injury from the fall," I countered. "And I beg to differ with your opinion of real life. I've just been reading the Sunday paper. Things like that happen all too often."

Lance shook his head and looked over at the monkey cage. "I guess if it was a mugging, that would still let me off the hook. Here I've been getting all bent out of shape thinking that he killed himself and I could have prevented it."

A waiter came over to check on our table and Lance, I was glad to note, did not order another drink. I thought it was time to change the subject.

"You said at the polo match that you thought Danny Siderman was a fool. What exactly did you mean, Lance?" I had to repeat my question twice before he heard it over the din in the bar. The TV set was on now and the crowd was following a football game.

"Mr. Show Biz? He's a card, isn't he? I guess I meant the way he's gone nuts over this polo thing."

"How has he gone nuts?" I asked, trying to look innocent. I'd had Danny's own version of his polo mania and Walter Earle's warning that things might not be what they seemed at the Diamond Head club. I was curious to hear what Lance had to say. He had appeared to know Melanie Patterson pretty well at the benefit match.

"Well, he's joined a club, you know, the one that's playing for our episode. Even bought a polo pony and talks about getting a string together. He went to all the matches this summer, when we were rehearsing and shooting the first episodes of the show. It was a standing joke on the set. The rest of us were in shorts and there's Danny in jodhpurs and riding whip. I'd see him at the games and he'd tell me he was negotiating with jockeys in Argentina. That's how he put it too, 'in negotiation.' ''

"So you went to the matches too?"

"Oh, well, you know, not the way Danny did. But I like a little action and there's not a lot happening here, no major league sports or anything."

"Do you mean 'action' as in activity or 'action' as in gambling?"

"Action as in action, Steve. All of the above and then some. You saw Melanie Patterson. She's a looker, you got to admit it."

The conversation deteriorated into irrelevances from then on, and we were soon out on the sidewalk, saying our good-byes. Lance insisted on driving, so I found an excuse to call a cab and rode back to the Royal Hawaiian thinking about Lance and Dick Schiller and monkeys in glass cages.

chapter 30

I could hear the phone ringing as I unlocked the door to our suite. I got there too late. Jayne wasn't back either. This was not turning out to be one of my better days. I picked up the phone and dialed Harley's Hangout.

"Harley's Hellhole, Satan speaking."

"Is Belle there?" I asked—pleasantly, I thought, under the circumstances.

I could hear the growly male voice on the other end of the line shouting down the bar. "Hey, Belle, it's another one of your johns. Better hurry—this one sounds like he's actually got money."

"Belle here." The jukebox was blaring and people were yelling in the background. I could imagine the scene and was glad I wasn't making it.

"Steve Allen, Belle. Just wondered if you'd managed to find out anything about Dick Schiller."

"Naw, but I got something else. Don't know if it'll do you any good, but the kid I told you left me that note? Well, he come in again, tried to buy a pack o' cigarettes and I collared him. Told him I'd blow the whistle on him if he wasn't straight with me. He says he was just walkin' along the road near my place, when this scrawny haole pulls over and offers him ten bucks to deliver the note to me."

"Could he describe the driver? Or the car?"

"He said the car was pretty beat up, dark, a foreign make. And he said the guy was scrawny, like I said, and wearin' a baseball cap. But he happened to notice the guy's hair 'cause it showed on the side an' it was bright red."

"A redhead? Thanks, Belle. That's very interesting. You've been a big help."

"Yeah, well, you can do me a favor too. Don't send me any more of your slummers from the hotel, OK? I got enough problems without these guys in black plastic an' gold chains comin' around lookin' for a little weird city. I thought Joe was gonna bust a gut laughin' "

I called the house in Waimanalo and got a recorded message. Jayne still wasn't back and I felt restless. I wanted to be doing something, but there was nothing to do but wait. So I took the script, the old one we'd be shooting from the next morning, and made myself comfortable on the lanai. The windsurfers were out in force, doing their comedy act into the water. It was a spill a minute as the high surf sent them tumbling into the blue-green sea the minute they were upright. I felt better just watching them, freer than the imprisoned monkeys. When the phone rang again I was tempted not to get it. Let Jayne wonder where *I* was. But it kept ringing and I finally went inside and picked up the receiver. It was Cap.

"Hi, sonny. It's your old Captain here, and I guess you'll be glad I called. I been over that gol-darn script o' yours five times an' I can't make head or tails out of it. It don't seem t' have nothin' t' do with the young feller I knew. So I thought you and the lady might as well have a go at it. Better you than them coppers."

"Hold on! *What* gol-darn script are you talking about, Cap?"

"Heh-heh!" He laughed in a most irritating manner. "The one you been looking for high and low, I guess. The one Dick left with me 'bout a month ago . . . o' course, if you and the lady ain't interested anymore . . ."

"I'll be right there, Cap."

Carlos Medina was on limousine duty, and when I told him I was in a hurry, he made it across town in record time. I knocked on the door of Cap's apartment and sighed with relief as the sound of shuffling steps approached the door. I was beginning to fear that I'd be greeted by silence and a dead body behind the door.

"C'mon in, then. I know ya can't wait," Cap said, leading the way into the living room. It was more cluttered than ever, but Cap hopped around the debris as if each piece were an old friend. A cardboard box sat open next to the coffee table, and one of the scripts was lying in Cap's armchair with a cat curled up on top of it.

"Just out of curiosity, where were they?" I asked, stooping in front of the box, where the second cat had taken up residence. I glanced through the scripts to make sure they were all the same before taking one over to the couch.

"That's my little secret. Gotta keep a few, ya know."

"Exactly when did Dick bring you this box, Cap? And what did he say when he gave it to you?"

"Didn't know they were scripts, now, did I? He said he needed a safe place to store some personal stuff. He said it weren't valuable-like, just personal, and he wanted it close by, not in some storage locker somewhere. I said sure and forgot all about it. When you brung up the subject this morning, I thought I'd just take a little look see first, afore I said anythin', in case it was just more o' them yearbooks or somethin'."

"If I might ask, why in God's name didn't you tell us about this box the first time we came by? It would have saved a lot of trouble!"

The old man shrugged. "You didn't ask fer no *box* now, did ya? That's the problem with people these days—they don't really know what they're lookin' for. Everybody's walkin' around in circles, kind o' aimless like. It's a good thing you got a pretty wife, mister, or I'd o' sent you on your way darn fast."

I sighed. The man was hopeless. Cap eased the cat over to the side of his chair, took up the script, and leaned back. "I sure don't see what this script could have t' do with anythin' though. I can't hardly follow the story line, even, with them camera directions an' all. Ya want some coffee?"

I said yes without thinking and began to skim my copy of the new script. In this version, the second hour of the episode opens with the Brents hiring a new groom to replace the one they bumped off in the first episode because he was blackmailing them. This time they pick a young high school student for the job, a boy who comes in after school and on the weekends. As in the original version, the Brents are put under pressure by their gambling buddies to rig one more match, and they do so, asking the new stable hand to do the dirty work. They assume he will be more loyal than the last groom due to his youth, naïveté, and gratitude for all they've done for him. What they don't count on is his familiarity with horse tranquilizers. He agrees to dope their horses for them, but without their knowledge he holds out some of the drug and takes it to school, where he sells it to one of his classmates.

Cap came back into the room carrying coffee for two. My cup looked relatively clean and I took a sip. It was so strong, it was more like eating caffeine than drinking it.

"That'll put some hair on yer chest," Cap chortled.

"Rather have it on my head." He chortled again. I resumed reading. In the script the drug used to sedate the horses eventually gets back to a party attended by Samantha, the Brents' deaf daughter, who takes it and dies of an overdose. There is quite a moving death scene, where Samantha can't tell anyone what's happening to her. She communicates her fear and desperation with face and body gestures and sign language, of course, for the viewers who can interpret it. Mack bursts into the party with his two sidekicks, Pete and Buddy, just in time to watch Samantha expire.

"Strange!" I muttered.

"Speak up, son. It ain't polite to mutter."

"It's strange that Samantha dies in this version," I said more clearly. "After all, she's the love interest of the episode and it's definitely unusual to allow the heroine to die in this type of show. Mack should have saved her somehow—it's the commercial formula at least."

"Well, people do die," Cap philosophized. "Can't say I care much fer TV shows that don't show life the way it is."

"You've got a point there," I said.

I read on. Through a bit of detection work that involves intimidating the terrified partygoers, Mack traces the drug back to the Brents' groom and puts two and two together, coming up, surprisingly enough, with four. The Brents are overcome with grief at the news of their daughter's death and hardly need Mack's prompting to confess to everything. They take full responsibility for their daughter's death. The young groom stands by and watches them being led away in handcuffs.

I set the script down in my lap and looked over at Cap, who had been watching me flip through the pages while he stroked the cat in the chair with him.

"Well, what do ya make of it?" he asked.

"I'm not sure," I answered honestly. "But I think it's all there. I just need to check a few things out. I'm going to take the box of scripts with me, for your safekeeping as well as theirs. If anyone else comes looking for them, tell him I have them and to call me right away. Got that?"

The old man nodded, but he looked as though he were beginning to regret giving up his treasure.

"I know, Cap. You'd like nothing better than to help catch Dick's killer, and you have done just that. But someone out there has killed two people and might not think twice about a third. Your cats need you, and so do Dick's fish."

The old man nodded again, but I wasn't sure I'd convinced him.

"You know where to reach me," I said as I paged Carlos to let him know I was ready to be picked up. "Don't hesitate to call, any hour of the day or night. And next time I'll bring Jayne with me, it's a promise."

He cheered up visibly at the last thought and walked me to the door, closing and locking it behind me at my insistence. I put the box in the backseat of the limousine next to me.

"Christmas shopping, sir?" Carlos asked.

"No, gambling. And I think I hit the jackpot."

I knew Jayne was back the minute I opened the door to our suite. I could smell Chinese food and almost tripped over the packages in the hallway. She was in the living room, humming softly to herself while she made notes on a piece of Royal Hawaiian stationery.

"Steve! Lance didn't keep you this long, did he?" she asked, glancing up. Then she noticed the box I had just set down next to our sparklingly clean coffee table sporting a vase full of Walter Earle's prize roses. I passed a script her way.

"The script? I knew Cap would come through! Who did it, then? You probably have it all figured out and don't even need the information I got out of Tony. I don't mind, as long as the murderer isn't anyone I like."

"Villains are usually people that someone likes. And I'm afraid I can't prove anything I suspect. So first out with your news. And then I want to know what you think of this thing," I said, indicating the script in my hand. "I'm going to take a closer look myself. I just skimmed it at Cap's. Did Tony turn up anything on Angela Schwartz?"

"He did. She died thirteen years ago, under suspicious circumstances. Her body was found in an empty house, a fancy second home that looked as if it had been broken into by teenagers who wanted a place to party. The cause of death was a drug overdose, a depressant popular with the kids and easily available on the black market. Supposedly it makes a sane person entirely crazy."

"Lovely."

"Well, it appears that Angela had a preexisting medical condition that made the drug particularly dangerous for her. She was a student at Crown High School in Nanakuli, of course, and those students known to associate with her were questioned at the time. They included Sam Fitzgerald and Dick Schiller. Tony wasn't the examining officer, but the records show that Sam Fitzgerald was suspected of having brought the drug to the party, though nothing was ever proved. Sam had been pulled in for questioning on suspicion of selling drugs before, but there was never enough evidence to convict him. The files also show that Dick Schiller was questioned at the time of Angela's death and appeared to be devastated. He claimed that the dead girl was his fiancée. Other teenagers interviewed denied this, however, and implied that Dick had delusions of importance where Angela was concerned."

"Was Keoni questioned in connection with Angela's death?"

"No, he wasn't. And he has no criminal record."

Jayne kept glancing at the script as she talked. I nodded.

"Go ahead," I said. "I'm not going to say a word. I don't want to influence your first look at it. Maybe you'll see something I didn't."

Jayne began to read, stopping every minute or two to exclaim "Of course" or "Now I see" or "Why didn't I think of that before?" I finally broke down.

"What? What do you see?"

"Don't pay any attention to me, dear. I'm just talking to myself."

Jayne is an experienced script reader. It wasn't long before she turned over the last page and looked at me with a shake of her head.

"I don't see how Danny or even Edgar would have gone for this. It's really quite different from the version we're shooting at the moment. No climactic scene on the polo field. A lot of new lines for everyone to learn. A new interior, the party house. And the whole theme of the episode is shifted from corruption in the world of polo to teen drug abuse."

"And, of course, Samantha dies in this version," I pointed out. "Mack certainly wouldn't look like much of a hero if he can't rescue a damsel in distress!"

"Let's assume Dick based his ideas on Angela's true life story. Is Sam Fitzgerald the drug pusher? But he can't be the murderer, he's a murderee. Who else wouldn't want this story to come out? The Brents, or their real-life counterparts? Steve, you don't think the Brents are the Jason Pattersons, do you?"

"I'm afraid I do. Not the present Mrs. Patterson, of course, but Melanie mentioned that she was Jason's second wife. I wonder where the first Mrs. Patterson is. And how would this script have actually hurt Jason? And what could it possibly have to do with Billy and his stalker? It's obvious that the redhead who directed us to Dick's body is the same one who's been threatening Billy."

"What?" Jayne interrupted.

"Oh, I forgot to mention that I talked to Belle. Our redheaded stalker supplied the note that sent us to Waimea Bay to find Dick's body. He must have been the voice on the phone directing us to Harley's as well."

Jayne stared into space for a minute, then stabbed a finger at her copy of the script. "The answer is here somewhere, Steve, it must be."

chapter 31

Jayne and I were still mulling over the mystery of the script, when the phone rang again.

"You get it this time," I grumbled. "I'm thinking of moving us to a grass shack on the beach with no phone service."

Jayne picked up the receiver and talked for a few minutes while I tried to ignore what I could tell was coming. She hung up saying we'd be ready in an hour.

"Cass has invited us all to a luau, dear. Actually, it's his girlfriend Dottie, the travel agent, remember?"

"No. Yes, I remember Dottie . . . no, I'm not going to a luau. I have a murderer to catch before that plane takes off, a week from today."

Jayne's smile said "I'm one ahead of you." "Guess who else is going to be at this luau?"

"Jason Patterson? Or better yet, his first wife?"

"How about his arch rival? The president of the Manoa Polo Club, who told Dottie that he'd heard Jason was participating in an episode of *Hawaiian Wave* and wanted us to know just what kind of person we were getting involved with. 'I've got some stories that'll knock their socks off' is the way he put it, and I quote thirdhand."

"You've convinced me. Where's that aloha shirt that's going to make my fortune? I may as well go to this luau in costume."

Carlos pulled the limousine up to a private beach on the Windward Coast, not far from Senator Fong's Plantation and Gardens, just as the sun was setting behind the Koolau mountains. The sky toward the sea was a watercolor wash of magenta, orange, and green. Long torches were stuck here and there in the sand and already lit, illuminating a huge pit where barechested chefs tended the roasting pig. There were about fifty people milling around folding tables laden with appetizers and drinks. I spotted Billy near the roasting pit, surrounded by a small circle of admirers who were laughing at something he'd just said.

"It's about time he started enjoying himself," I said to Jayne, nodding in Billy's direction.

Dottie came hurrying over to greet us, Cass a few steps behind. She draped a mostly lavender lei over each of our necks and shook our hands warmly. "I'm so glad you could make it. There's someone here who's just dying to talk to you. Let me introduce him."

Dottie was looking well, suntanned and relaxed, and it wasn't lost on Cass. He alternated appreciative glances her way with looks at us as if to say "Isn't she something?" Dottie led us toward the water, where three lovely young girls dressed in flowered skirts, halter tops, and leis were dancing a traditional dance in the late evening light. The mele, or chants, that accompany the hula were being sung by a small orchestra of older women in Mother Hubbard dresses playing ukuleles. The ukulele is not indigenous but was brought to the islands by Portuguese immigrants in the nineteenth century and caught on, I suspect, because its plaintive, lilting sound expressed the Polynesian sensibility so well. The girls were skilled dancers, their bodies and hands telling the story in sign language being sung by the accompanists. Against the backdrop of the torchlit sky and crashing surf, it was all genuinely enchanting.

"Steve, Jayne, I'd like you to meet Mark Morris. Mark, Steve Allen and Jayne Meadows."

"Charmed," Mark answered, extending a weak hand. He was small, slight, and wispy, with an ascot at his neck and smart British-cut shirt and slacks. "Normally, I wouldn't be caught dead at one of these dreadful tourist-traps," he went on in an English public school accent, "but when I heard you might be coming I couldn't stay away."

Dottie moved discreetly on, Cass sticking close to her side, and Jayne and I led Mark away from the show.

"I'd like to know more about Jason Patterson," I began. "I gather you've known him for a while."

"Forever. May I call you Steve? Jason and I drank in polo with our mother's milk. We grew up playing together, on real ponies, to begin with. But Jason was always so macho. He just couldn't relax and enjoy the sport. Personally, I gave up riding years ago. I'm president of the Manoa club, you know, but I stick to the administrative side of things these days. Not like our boy Jason."

"Was there ever any rumor of Jason throwing a polo match?" Jayne interjected. "It might have been ten or fifteen years ago."

"Now, where in the world did you get that information? And here I thought I had news for you. There was indeed talk of hanky-panky going on a few years back. And come to think of it, it *was* about twelve years ago. The gossip was that Jason couldn't bear to be thought of as an inferior player, so he did something to his horses. That way, he could blame them for the losing streak. When I heard through the grapevine that you were doing a show with a polo theme for that new TV series, of course I hoped our club would be asked to participate. But I wouldn't want you to go away thinking that what I'm telling you is sour grapes. I just thought you might want to know that your story line, from what I've heard about it, hits awfully close to home. Jason's, that is."

"Do you know Jason's first wife?"

"Judith? Oh, my, yes. A treasure. She left him, you know, right around the time he started losing. She had the money, of course—don't they always? She took their little girl with her. I think Jason was genuinely upset by that. He looked around for a while before he found Melanie. That was a story in itself. From what I heard . . . oh, dear, I shouldn't be telling you this, but it's so typical. You see, he met her in Hong Kong and he thought she was rich, but it turned out she thought *he* was rich. A classic case of mistaken bank accounts, I'm afraid! And she's no meek little mail-order bride either, as I'm sure you've seen. Rumor is she's spending money faster than he can make it, and poor Jason, of course, needs a fair amount himself to support his polo habit. Ah, the tangled webs we weave.''

Mark had just launched in on someone else's tangled web, when Dottie came over to announce that they were going to uncover the imu. The imu is a large pit lined with lava rocks. Hours earlier, the chefs in charge of the luau would have built a fire in it to heat the rocks, then swept out the ash and laid in the whole pig, surrounded by lau-lau, little packages of meat, vegetables, and fish wrapped in taro leaves. They would then have covered the pit with damp burlap, earth, and more leaves, in layers. The food both bakes and steams for several hours until the dramatic moment, which we were about to witness, when the coverings are lifted and the roast pig sliced and handed around. We joined the rest of the guests gathered around the pit, and our chefs, their leis dangling in the smoke and steam, began stripping away the layers covering the pit. I looked away for a second to avoid the pungent steam, and out of the corner of my eye saw someone move in the trees near the road. I wasn't entirely certain, but I thought I saw a hint of red hair.

"Save me some food," I whispered to Jayne, trying to look nonchalant as I headed in the general direction of the watcher in the trees. I looked toward the cars and slapped my pockets as if I were heading back for forgotten cigarettes. When I got close to the trees I suddenly veered away from the cars with the intention of flushing him out. I thought I was clever, but the spectator, whoever he was, saw me coming. He burst free from his hiding place and made a dash toward an old green Volvo parked on the side of the road. I had a good look at the back of his head. A redhead, without a doubt.

"Stop, I just want to talk to you!" I shouted. I could swear he hesitated a fraction of a moment, which seemed strange to me. Would the stalker have hesitated, even for a second, if he was our killer? I asked myself. I doubted it. Then he picked up speed. I ran after him, huffing and puffing, but the distance between us widened. From the way he ran, I sensed he was a young man— much younger than I am, alas, so there was no way I could keep up.

"Stop!" I shouted again. But it was hopeless. I watched in

frustration as he dove into his green Volvo, fired up the engine, and sped off down the road. I tried to read his license number, but my glasses had steamed up during the chase. I thought I saw a PL. Or maybe it was a DE, with a blurry number after it. Meanwhile the Volvo turned a corner and disappeared.

I limped back to the luau, trying to catch my breath. In the excitement of the unveiling of the imu, no one had noticed my absence or even heard my shout. No one except Jayne.

"You almost had him!" she said loyally.

"But who is he?" I wondered. "And what the hell kind of game is he playing?"

When I caught my breath and the stitch in my side disappeared, we wandered over to Billy, who was eating a huge plate of food as he listened to one of the pretty young hula dancers describing a mele. She set her plate down in the sand to demonstrate, her smile never leaving Billy's face. Jayne steered us away again. "That's just what that boy needs right now," she whispered, "something to take his mind off his problems."

"Ah, but love can be the biggest problem of all," I countered.

The moon rose over the water, the ukulele orchestra began to play sad love songs, and Billy's new friend tore herself away from her audience of one to entertain us all with a few more dances. If this had been a truly traditional luau, the party would have just been getting started. But since we all had places to be early on Monday morning, it came to an end quite abruptly. Dottie thanked us for coming while Cass tore himself away regretfully and headed toward the Impala. Billy exchanged phone numbers with the young dancer before joining Jayne and me at the car. I had arranged for Cass to take us back to the Royal Hawaiian after dropping Billy at his house. As soon as the car pulled away from the beach, Billy began expounding on the importance of the hula in Hawaiian history. He pointed out the skill of the young dancer he had just met and mentioned that she had offered to give him free lessons. "She's a lot cuter than Papa Bear too," Cass chortled, referring to their first teacher.

Cass delivered Billy to the front door of his house, assuring him he'd be right back, and continued on toward Honolulu.

"You've been with Billy for almost a week now, Cass," I began, looking sideways at Jayne. "How would you cast him, as victim or victimizer?"

"Steve, how can you?" Jayne broke in. "That boy is not a murderer, and that's all there is to it."

"I agree with Jayne there, boss. I haven't got him figured out yet, but I think he slips into that little-boy role around you and Jayne the way, you know, some people do around their parents. When it's just him and me he comes across different. I get the feeling he enjoys setting everybody on their ear. I don't think he's crazy though, and you have to be crazy to murder someone."

"Has he talked about his father's visit at all?" Jayne asked.

"His dad has changed his plans a few times, but the latest is that he's coming in tomorrow night and leaving Wednesday."

"Good. It can't be too soon," I remarked. "Any sign of the stalker around the house?"

"Well, now that you mention it, I have had the feeling that the house was being watched. Strange noises at night, Killer barking until I have to go out and talk to him, footprints that aren't ours leading from the beach toward the house. But I haven't seen any crew-cut redheads or green Volvos, if that's what you mean. And I haven't said anything to Billy or Bertrand."

"Speaking of which," I added, "tell me your thoughts on Bertrand."

"I don't know what to say, boss. I wish I could be more help, but I can't figure Bert out either. He seems to disappear in the middle of the night a lot, but he's always there in the morning, smiling and reading one of his books while he waits for Billy to get up so he can cook him breakfast. I don't think he'd hurt the kid, but I wouldn't put it past him to hurt *somebody*."

"Mmmm," I acknowledged. "I've come to pretty much the same conclusions you have."

"Well, that's a relief," Jayne sighed.

We picked up our phone messages at the front desk of the hotel and Jayne glanced through them while I made sure arrangements had been made for our wake-up call and limousine in the morning.

One of the messages was written not to Steve Allen but to *Steballen* and signed *José*. The only José I know is, of course, my pal Bill Dana, who became famous on my old NBC comedy show in the character of José Jimenez. I figured he had heard we were in the area and since he spends a good deal of his time living in the islands he'd be inviting us to dinner. I knew it wouldn't be possible because of our shortness of time, but since I was going to be doing a TV special with him back on the mainland a few weeks down the line, I made a note to phone him later about our situation.

"This is interesting, dear," Jayne said, handing me a message from Danny Siderman. It read, "Change of plans. Using Patterson house for interior shots. Limo driver knows the way. Ask at desk for call sheet."

"Very interesting," I agreed. Jason Patterson's name kept coming up in this case like a leitmotif, along with drugged horses and crooked polo, and I looked forward to having a look at his lair. What was that Mark Morris had just said at the luau? Something about our script hitting close to home . . . Jason's home.

chapter 32

The aloha lady woke us before dawn, with tea and the morning paper following soon after. The "wave" of murders surrounding *Hawaiian Wave* had already been relegated to page two, where a reporter quoted Tony Chen saying that the Homicide Division was "pursuing several leads." Not as many as I am, I thought.

Carlos Medina was waiting to hold the door for us when we stepped outside into the glorious predawn glow. When I asked how his grandson was doing in the surfing competitions, he laughed. "Wipeout. Now maybe he'll listen to an old man who's been surfing longer than his own father has been breathing."

We headed east, around Diamond Head and up into the residential area on its flanks. The houses we passed ranged from ostentatious to exquisite—many were shielded from the prying eyes of passing plebeians by security walls or banks of vegetation. Carlos stopped in front of an antebellum-style mansion that looked more like *Gone With the Wind* than *Hawaiian Wave*. The front lawn was immaculate, and I could just make out the stables and a small paddock behind the house on the left. The long, curving driveway had been left clear for exterior shots, so the cars, trucks, vans, and trailers of the film crew were already lining both sides of the street.

It felt good to be getting back to work. When we emerged from the limo into the hustle and bustle of early morning on a TV set, I realized that I wasn't alone in my desire to put questions of murder aside for a few hours. There was a feeling of controlled elation in the air, not the sense of foreboding I had expected.

Danny, as upbeat as ever, bounced down the driveway to greet us.

"You're right over here, folks, prime location. Edgar is fit as a fiddle and we're going to roll through these takes in no time. I never did like the idea of a whole new script. If we move right along, we should be able to wind up the interiors in two more days, with a break on Thursday and the final polo sequence on Friday. They're still predicting a tropical storm for the end of the week, right on cue. Hope you had a relaxing weekend, not like those suckers on the Big Island. You heard about that? Smoke, lava flows. There was this one guy, the lava missed his shop by that much." Danny illustrated with thumb and forefinger and I thought of Kenny, grinning out at us from the five o'clock news.

"We had a very relaxing weekend, Danny," I replied. "No more bodies, no police stations."

Danny looked at me quizzically and decided not to ask. Instead, he maneuvered himself next to Jayne and addressed her in a confidential tone.

"Say, you haven't heard any more about Raymond's visit, have you? I don't want to bother Billy with questions right now. The kid's got enough on his mind. I spent the last three days keeping the press off him. Had to promise them shots today though. 'All's normal back on the set of *Hawaiian Wave,*' that kind of thing. You don't have to say much, just enough to keep them happy. But why am I telling you this? You're pros, you know how it is. Maybe you could help Billy a little. He can be funny where the press is concerned. Probably a leftover from his childhood, dodging all that attention as Raymond's son."

Another amateur psychologist, I thought. One was enough.

"Say," Danny went rambling on, "you want to take a look at the house before it gets too messed up with all the equipment? It's a beauty. The one we were going to use, just down the road, fell through at the last minute. I made Jason an offer, a sweet one, I might add, and he went for it."

"Jason needed the money, didn't he?" I asked, lowering my voice a little.

"Well, yes," Danny admitted almost reluctantly. "How did you guess?"

"I don't imagine he'd be letting a TV company into his house otherwise."

Danny led us up the steps to the veranda that ran across the entire front of the two-story house and in through the antique front door. The entrance hall faced a long, curving staircase, with the public rooms opening off to either side. The furniture was sparse but looked good, Southern American, nineteenth century. It was hard to believe we were still in Hawaii. I heard a rustling at the top of the stairs, and Melanie made a grand entrance down the staircase in a satin dressing gown and high-heeled slippers.

"I hope you'll excuse me. It is a bit early," she drawled in her very British accent, favoring me with a smile and Danny with a more businesslike nod. Jayne she acknowledged hardly at all. "I'll just make my tea and be right out of the way."

We found Jason in the living room, fully dressed and looking nervous.

"Just the entryway and this room, is that correct?" he was asking Edgar. "And the stable area, of course. This was rather short notice, as you know. I'm glad to be of help, but my wife doesn't want people all over the house. I'm sure you understand."

"Yes, I understand perfectly. But a work of art is a fluid thing. It sometimes takes us where we least expect, is that not so?" Edgar replied, moving away from Jason to try out an angle from another corner of the room. Jason didn't look reassured. Noticing that Danny, Jayne, and I had entered the room, he turned our way with a weak smile.

"It's so nice of you to step in with the offer of your home," Jayne said. "I hope you don't mind if I take a look around later. I love to see how other people do their homes, don't you? . . . Oh, this table is wonderful," she added, stroking a corner piece I suspect she picked at random. "Did you find it here on Oahu?"

"Ah, no, I don't think so," Jason replied absently. "My first wife bought most of these things. She was from Alabama. If you'll excuse me . . ." Jason said, catching sight of his second wife as she mounted the Scarlett O'Hara staircase with her cup of tea in hand.

As Jayne and I passed through the front doorway on our way to the makeup trailer, we met Billy on the veranda. I flinched involuntarily. He looked just like Sam Fitzgerald when I'd found him floating in the coral at Hanauma Bay. He was wearing the aloha-print shirt and shorts that are his trademark on the show, and I hadn't seen him in them since that day. Either I was fast enough to hide my reaction or he wasn't paying attention.

"It's good to be back on the job, isn't it, dear?" Jayne asked, giving him a friendly hug. He held the embrace, then broke away with a smile and continued into the house. He hadn't answered her. Jayne and I emerged from makeup and costuming a half hour later, Jayne in beige silk shirt and slacks, me in tropical Palm Beach sports jacket and tie. As we headed toward the house, we saw Susan and her friend Elisabeth sitting on the veranda in matching wooden rockers. I had a hard time imagining Jason and Melanie in those chairs, but the two young women looked right at home. Susan was wearing shorts and a halter top for the scene where she first meets Mack at her parents' house. Elisabeth was in blue jeans and sweatshirt.

"I'm trying out for stable hand, just not the one that gets bumped off," Elisabeth quipped as we joined them.

Susan signed to Jayne, a flurry of hand motions. Jayne replied, "Yes, it is. But all we can do at the moment is give his script the best we've got."

Susan nodded and rose to follow us into the house. Edgar began his thoughts for the day as soon as he saw us in the living room doorway.

"The theme today, it is obvious, no? Deceit. The many guises of deceit. Nothing is what it appears to be, no one is who he appears to be. All of this"—he waved a hand around the room—"is how do you say?—hocked to the maximum. The Brents are pretending to a lifestyle they cannot in reality afford. It is a show, an illusion." Jason came up behind me as Edgar talked. His tan face was ashen and he seemed mesmerized by Edgar's words.

"You, Warren and Cynthia Brent, you think that no one knows what you are doing, that you are safe if you can just throw suspicion on your old enemy. The groom has not yet threatened you with his blackmail. You are deceiving everyone, even this lovely daughter of yours. But you," Edgar said, giving Susan a look that made her jump, "you are deceiving your parents as well. You are playing the role you know they expect of you, the little girl who never grows up, who lives happily ever after with Mommy and Daddy in the big house on the hill. But it is not true. The urgings of sex are awakened, no? This handsome young private investigator walks in the door and Mommy and Daddy are out the window, no?"

Susan smiled sadly.

"And you"—Edgar wheeled, pointing a finger at Billy—"even you are not quite what you seem. You ride in like Mr. Galahad, to save the king and queen and their lovely princess from the evil witch who has hexed their horses. But why do you come? Out of the goodness of your heart? You come because they are going to pay you, and as you look around this house, you think, ah-hah, they will pay me well and they can afford to. That's all. Stand-ins, take your places, please."

"You know, if Edgar ever decided to give up directing, he could make a great living as a detective," I whispered to Jayne.

"Shh," she hissed back, and I saw that she was trying to overhear a conversation taking place between Jason and his wife at the rear of the room. Melanie had come back downstairs, this time dressed, and she had pulled him away from Edgar's lecture.

"You Americans!" Melanie was saying in a low but obviously irritated voice. "When will you learn to control your emotions? It will all be over soon. Come along with me now."

Jason followed her back up the stairs, a hurt puppy-dog expression on his face. *What will be over soon?* I wondered. There was no time for further consideration because the first assistant director was calling us to our places in front of the lights. The cameras rolled and Jayne and I must have succeeded in looking suitably deceitful, because Edgar had very little further instruction for us. I was impressed, once again, at Billy's professionalism and maturity in front of the camera. I had no trouble at all forgetting he was Billy and addressing my devious dialogue to Mack, low-rent private eye. Susan had a more difficult time this morning. Edgar made her repeat her entrance into the living room and first sight of Billy over and over again, until, from sheer exasperation, she gave him the adolescent pout he was looking for. "Cut," he cried exultantly, and called for a lunch break before the next scene.

Deceit is indeed the theme for the day, I thought as I tried to look as though I were casually wandering toward the back of the house. There was no one in the library and I made a quick study. The pictures on the walls were all of polo ponies, polo matches, and trophy ceremonies. Jason hadn't changed much over the years. He'd traded his blond hair for gray and added a few lines around the eyes and mouth, but polo had kept him trim and physically fit. A picture of Melanie was prominently displayed on the old oak desk facing out a large window toward the back lawn and stable area. I strolled over to the library door, closed it nonchalantly in case someone was watching, and hurried back to the desk. There was a pile of bills in the top middle drawer—department store, hairdresser, shoe stores. The cost of keeping Melanie, I imagined. Underneath the bills was an old-fashioned handwritten ledger. I glanced quickly through the figures, which were very carefully and legibly written in. The last entry was dated the day after the polo benefit for the Manoa School for the Deaf. It was a deposit of thirteen thousand dollars. I looked through the withdrawals again. They were vaguely defined as "administrative fees" and "maintenance costs." The ending balance was a negative three thousand, which would be sixteen thousand when the club cut a check to Susan's school. Unless . . . I slipped the book back underneath the bills and opened the top righthand drawer. That one held a supply of staples, paper clips, pens, and notepads, neatly organized. The next two drawers seemed to be storage of personal documents for tax purposes, and I didn't look too closely. The lefthand drawers contained more polo club records, but only for the current year. I was about to close the bottom drawer, when I noticed that the files rode a little high, making it difficult to reclose. I felt along the bottom and pulled up a photograph in a frame designed to sit on a desk, the way Melanie's was at the moment. It was a picture of Jason, posed on the steps of the veranda with a wispy-looking woman in her early forties and a gawky, goofy-looking girl of ten or twelve. The child bore so little resemblance to her handsome parents, it was hard to imagine they'd produced her except for one trait. She shared with her mother a lovely shade of red-blond hair.

The library door suddenly opened behind me and Melanie's cultivated accent rang out. "Why, Steve, whatever are you doing in here all by yourself?"

"I'm embarrassed to have to admit it, my dear, but I've been practicing my lines for the next scene," I said loudly, opening the top drawer just enough to slip the photo inside as I regaled my hostess with choice samples of the script in comic exaggeration. Melanie laughed right on cue as I maneuvered us out of the library and into the entrance hall, where the cast and crew were beginning to reassemble.

"If you need a quiet retreat again, do let me know," she whispered suggestively. "I'm sure we can work something out." She headed back up the picture-perfect staircase and I made a dash for my dressing room to change clothes for the next scene, making a mental note to ask little Mrs. Hutchins, the director of Susan's school for the deaf, just how much the school had cleared from the benefit the week before.

chapter 33

I made it back to the living room just in time for the next scene. It was a beautiful room, long and languid with many windows looking out on the rolling lawn and deep shade of lazy old trees. With its nineteenth-century furniture, this was a room, I thought, to summon a bygone era, a time when the pace of life moved more sedately. It seemed almost a sacrilege to bring in all the lights and cameras, the electric cables and the noisy TV crew dressed in shorts and T-shirts. The prop people had moved the baby grand piano, which, I noticed, was equipped with a Piano-Disc brand attachment by means of which an owner could have his choice of popular pianists, including your obedient servant, playing his own instrument, as with the ancient piano-roll technology. The instrument was now shoved against a far wall so they could get the camera dolly closer to the windows. A sofa had also been unceremoniously pushed aside to make way for some floodlights. Jason Patterson must need money pretty badly, I thought, to allow such an invasion into the castle he called home.

Speaking of Jason, I noticed him now standing in the doorway, chatting with Jayne as if they were old friends. I heard her say "We'll look forward to it" as she broke away to take her place on the divan. I was about to ask what fiendishly boring social obligation she had gotten us into, when Edgar burst into the room shouting for silence. It was time to get to work.

The filming went fairly well. We spent most of the morning in the living room doing two scenes with Susan, as well as one long scene between us—the Brents, that is—and Billy. Edgar seemed easily satisfied today, with only six takes apiece on the scenes with Susan, and a record three on the long scene with Billy. I was always amazed at Billy's transformation in front of the camera, from a fearful, pouty young man to that suave action hero, Mack, the private eye. Late in the morning we shot the Brents accompanying Mack to the stable area to view the stall where their groom had just been found trampled to death. This was where Edgar became suddenly artistic, alas; he shot the scene so many times, we were all dripping from the aerobic workout before he finally called a "cut and wrap." Just as we were finishing up, Danny appeared in the stable. He patted the rump of a horse with casual affection and then whispered something in Edgar's ear. The director nodded with obvious distaste.

"OK, folks," Danny announced aloud, "the press has been pretty good to us, and we need to give them something in return. I promised them a half hour today live on the set of *Hawaiian Wave,* and here they come." Danny had barely finished, when there was a small tidal wave of reporters, photographers, and TV news cameramen bursting into the stable. Danny fired suggestive glances my way, making it clear that he'd like either me or Jayne to take up a position near Billy. But the star of the series seemed to be doing fine on his own. His trademark grin flashed on and off rythmically as he fielded questions and posed for the TV cameras and still photographers. Jayne gathered quite a crowd herself and managed to help Susan field her questions. I was asked everything from how soon I was going to solve the mystery of the "accidental" deaths plaguing *Hawaiian Wave* to what I thought of the new surfing champion, whose name I'd never heard before, when we moved from the stables to the main house. We posed on the veranda, like Southern aristocracy, then on the Scarlett O'Hara staircase with the Jason Pattersons by our side. Jason's smile turned to a grimace the minute the flash went off—he didn't seem particularly happy to have the crass invasion of his house captured for public viewing. I'm sure it was an embarrassment for him. The half hour promised to the media stretched into an hour before Danny managed to shepherd them away. After the last reporter left the set, an assistant director approached Jayne and me with some welcome news—we were finished for the day. Edgar had decided to spend the rest of the afternoon shooting a scene that was supposed to be done tomorrow, a scene where Mack escapes the Brents and sneaks back to the stable area by himself to investigate the polo horses.

"Great!" I said to Jayne. "Let's go back to the hotel and take a swim."

But it wasn't meant to be. Just then Billy came bounding in our direction, a worried expression on his face. "My God! I forgot all about my father! He's arriving in an hour at the airport! I was planning to meet him, but suddenly Edgar says he needs me for the afternoon . . . I know I've asked you and Jayne so many favors, but do you think . . . I mean, I heard you're off for the rest of the day . . ."

"Relax, Billy," I told him. "Jayne and I will be glad to hop over to the airport and pick up your father."

As it happened, I very much wanted a word with Raymond Markham.

Carlos guided our limousine away from the Patterson mansion, through the quiet residential streets in the direction of the Honolulu airport.

"Ah, show biz! The glamour, the drama!" I waxed, holding Jayne's hand in the backseat.

"Don't complain, Steve. You'd be bored living a normal life."

"Am I complaining? . . . And I'm not so sure you're right about me being bored with a regular sort of life. I'm sorry we're not going to get our swim, but let's make certain we have a romantic dinner for two tonight. Murders or no murders, I'm ready for a candlelight intermezzo, some balmy breezes . . ."

"Steve . . ."

". . . a big tropical moon hanging like a Japanese lantern in the sky while we walk hand in hand along—"

"Darling, I'm afraid we have dinner plans already."

"We do?"

"I promised Jason Patterson we'd join him and his wife for a light supper at his house later this evening. Shall I cancel?"

I sighed. "No. We'd better see them. Just protect me from Melanie, will you?"

Just as we were getting on the freeway, I used the limousine phone to dial information for the number of the Manoa School for the Deaf, filling Jayne in on my discovery in the library as I waited to be connected. The woman who answered the phone put me through to Bernice Hutchins, reminding me that the director would in fact be reading my end of the conversation and I should allow for a pause before her responses.

"Dr. Hutchins? Steve Allen here. I met you at the Turtle Bay Hilton the day of the polo benefit."

"Of course, Mr. Allen. What can I do for you?" She sounded strained.

"I was just curious to find out how successful that event had been for your school. Jayne and I were considering trying a similar fund-raiser in Southern California for one of our favorite organizations."

"It's odd you should call at just this moment, Mr. Allen. I've been trying to write my speech to the faculty, letting them know just how sorry I am to have to let them down after all the work they put into making the benefit a success. Jason Patterson called me this morning. He said he was terribly sorry, but with all the unexpected expenses, that man riding his horse into the dining room and the mess some of the patrons made afterward, well, the long and the short of it is, we cleared only about two thousand dollars. I don't know what to do. Our parents, our board, our teachers, are all going to be so disappointed. I know Susan will be devastated. I just can't understand how it happened. Jason was awfully apologetic. He said the polo club would have paid for the damages and extra expenses if they could, but they are having what he called a 'cash flow' problem at the moment."

"Yes, I think I know what he's talking about. The cash is flowing in the wrong direction. I'll tell you what. Hold off on that speech to your faculty for another day or two. I may have some good news for you by then."

There was a pause on her end. Then: "Why, I don't know what to say."

"Don't say anything. I'll be in touch soon."

Jayne had been watching me intently. "You don't really think Jason . . . would . . . ?"

"He's up to something, no doubt about it. Whether he's also

a murderer is another question, one I hope to answer this evening, with your help.''

I told Jayne my plan while the afternoon lengthened over Honolulu and the limousine glided toward our rendezvous with Raymond Markham.

We arrived at the Honolulu International Airport just as they were announcing the arrival of Raymond's flight from Los Angeles. Carlos dropped us off at the entrance and went to park the limousine as we made our way through the throngs of tour groups and flower-clad vacationers. Jayne picked up an orchid lei for Raymond at one of the stands inside the terminal, and we found the gate before the plane did.

"It's tempting, isn't it?" Jayne murmured.

I glanced at the flight schedule above my head and looked around at the neighboring gates. "There's a plane leaving for Tokyo in forty-five minutes. We could board for New York in twenty minutes. I'll bet there's even a plane headed for Burbank around here somewhere.''

Jayne smiled and I wondered if she was thinking the same thing I was. The people involved with our episode of *Hawaiian Wave* were all intelligent, talented, and successful by the standards of most of the rest of the world. They had every advantage, not the least of which was their abode in paradise. Yet one of them was a murderer and none of the rest were much happier, unless you chose to count Edgar Min, who enjoyed being miserable.

"There he is, Steve," Jayne said, interrupting my reverie. At first I was confused. Carlos Medina was approaching our gate area from the main terminal and, for just a second, I thought I caught a glimpse of a crew-cut redhead. But Jayne was watching Raymond Markham stride toward us with the powerful gait that had made him such a convincing police chief on television.

"Jayne, Steve, how wonderful to see you again!" He had a big, booming actor's voice. He smiled at us, but Raymond's expression soon turned to alarm when he didn't spot his son. "There's nothing wrong with Billy, is there?"

"No, no . . . Billy's just fine. Or he *would* be fine if he didn't have such a fearful imagination," Jayne told him. "Edgar rearranged the schedule so Billy had to work unexpectedly. He sent us to greet you."

While Jayne hastened to reassure Raymond that his son was safe, I took a closer look at my old friend. Raymond is a big man, my height at least, and I'm six feet three, but he was thinner than I remembered him, and he'd let his hair, carefully died dark brown for years, grow out to its natural steel gray.

Jayne "leied" Raymond with her sweet-smelling necklace, and he responded with an affectionate kiss on the cheek. "It's too bad Bea couldn't have come as well," Jayne said, taking Raymond's arm.

"Yes, it is," he sighed, looking away as he asked after our children. "I didn't check any luggage, so we can go straight to the car," he announced as we neared the outside doors.

"My, you're traveling very light!" Jayne remarked.

"I'm here for only two nights," he told us. His whole visit was frankly mysterious, but I let that lie for the moment. Carlos said he'd found a parking place close to the terminal, so we decided to walk to the car. I kept my eyes peeled for our redheaded stalker, but didn't see anything suspicious. When we reached the limousine, Jayne slipped quietly into the front seat so that Raymond and I could have the back to ourselves. As soon as we were settled and headed toward the city, I got down to business.

"I can't tell you how much Jayne and I have been looking forward to seeing you, Ray. We understand you're here to be with Billy, and we don't want to interfere with that visit in any way. But I'm hoping to discuss a few things while we drive."

His gray eyes turned my way. "Is my boy in danger, Steve?"

"I'm not sure. There have been two deaths connected with the show this past week, as you must already know. I think they were both murders, but I can't tie them to any immediate danger for Billy. He wasn't imagining the stalker; we've all seen him. In fact, the stalker led us to one of the bodies. But I can't figure out why yet, and I haven't mentioned that connection to Billy."

"I understand," Raymond murmured. "I appreciate your being here, more than I can say."

"Look, Ray—there's one thing about Billy that I'm hoping you can talk to him about. He's developed—well, an ability to antagonize people unnecessarily. He can be very charming when he wants to be. His adoring fans attest to that. But he's not Mr. Popular on the set at the moment. He's resented by his costars and he has both his producer and director tied up in knots. Do you know Danny Siderman, the show's producer?" Raymond didn't look unduly concerned by what I was saying. It occurred to me that I might not be telling him anything new.

"I've met Siderman, but I've never worked with him. Billy seems to think he's a bit of a buffoon."

"He does come across that way. But from what I've seen this past week, he's competent at his job. And he may be trying too hard because Billy has given him the impression that you're interested in taking over as producer of the show next season. This is his first hit in more than twenty years. The last thing he wants to do is hand it over to someone else."

"Of course. How interesting that Billy would say that. Wishful thinking, perhaps."

"Then you'll be able to put Danny's mind at ease?"

"What's that, Steve? Sorry, my mind was wandering."

"Why are you here, Ray?"

"I can't tell you that, Steve. I wish I could. But you'll find out soon enough. Tell me about the show instead. How do you like working with Edgar Min? I know what my son thinks of him, but I was curious to hear from you and Jayne."

At the mention of her name, Jayne turned around and joined the conversation.

"Edgar's fine once you get used to him," she responded. "His bark is worse than his bite. But Billy's been dropping hints that he'd like to direct the series himself, or at least try his hand at an episode, and that has Edgar in conniptions."

"He hasn't threatened my son, has he?"

"Of course not," Jayne replied quickly, while I thought back to Edgar's speech at the dinner table at Keo's. "But it would ease tensions on the set if Billy could reassure him."

Several long seconds passed in silence. Finally Raymond commented on the tropical sunset that was just starting to glow over Waikiki, and began to spin anecdotes about his last visit to the islands. It was frustrating, but evasion seemed to run in the family.

chapter 34

Billy spotted the limousine the minute it pulled into view of the house in Waimanalo. He and Cass had brought two chairs and a floor lamp out onto the lanai and sat leaning over the top of an ice chest in what appeared to be the throes of a cowboy-style poker game. Billy jumped up and ran down to greet our car, deactivating the alarm system before he slipped through the gate. Bertrand must have had dinner under control; he was standing in the doorway, in dress shirt and slacks, holding Killer by the collar. Every light in the house was on, and the grounds were floodlit in a style reminiscent of San Quentin.

"My God!" Raymond groaned under his breath.

"As Billy's security goes, this is nothing," I remarked. "Bertrand is out of uniform tonight."

Billy almost pulled his father out of the car in his enthusiasm. Once the hugging was over, he waved a hand toward the house and yard, assuring his father proudly that "mi casa es su casa, Papa." Raymond grinned weakly in response, thanked Jayne and me once again for meeting him at the airport, and waved good-bye with a "see you tomorrow" as Billy dragged both him and his bag up the path toward the floodlit house.

Night had fallen, a moonless, star-studded night, by the time we pulled into the curving driveway in front of the Patterson home. The huge Southern mansion looked deserted, and Carlos waited to make sure someone came to the door before he left to get his own dinner and await our pickup call. Jason himself answered the door, turning on the lights in the entryway as he escorted us in. He turned them off behind him as he led us to the dining room, where places for four had been set at one end of a long mahogany table. Melanie came out of the kitchen to greet us.

"I hope you don't mind. It's servants' night out and we thought we would keep it simple. It's more intimate this way, don't you think?" The only light came from two candles in cut-glass holders on the table. I looked up where you'd expect to find a crystal chandelier. There was nothing but a light spot in the ceiling paint. I had a feeling it had been servants' night out for a while.

Melanie disappeared into the kitchen and came back with four bowls of egg drop soup on a tray. The soup was delicious and Jason was visibly relieved to see us enjoying it.

"Jayne was telling me about your newfound interest in polo," he began, peering around Melanie at me. Melanie had insisted I sit on her left, Jason was on her right with my wife on the other side of Jason, as far away from Melanie as possible under the circumstances.

"There's no sport like it, to play or to watch," Jason went on. He talked about his childhood and the early years of the Diamond Head Polo Club, when it was a one-man operation. "Polo was better in those days," he told us. "A sport for the pure of heart."

"Actually, we met an old friend of yours from those early years," I mentioned pointedly. "Remember, Jayne?"

"Fascinating man, with *so* many stories to tell. I believe Mark Morris was his name," she responded right on cue.

Melanie abruptly pushed back her chair and left the room, mumbling something about seeing to the next course. Jason shifted position and finally said, "Well, yes, Mark and I were childhood friends, but we had a falling out a few years ago. He was spreading some rather nasty rumors about me. Probably still is. His club has never drawn the best people, you know. You mustn't believe everything you hear. Oahu is like a small town in some respects, things get blown out of proportion."

"Speaking of small towns," Jayne went on lightly, "you'll

never guess who Steve and I saw you with in an old photograph. Keoni Pahia. I was so impressed that you found time for baseball as well as polo. My goodness, it must be very challenging to coach a Little League team. Was Sam Fitzgerald ever on your team? We noticed him in the pictures for the previous two years and wondered why he wasn't in *your* picture."

Jason commenced a coughing fit and Melanie came back into the room with separate rice bowls for each of us, followed by chicken and peanuts in a hot pepper sauce, braised eggplant, and sautéed greens.

We sampled the food, correctly pronounced it delicious, and Jayne went back to the kill. "So tell us about Sam and Keoni, Jason. We never met Sam—alive, that is. What was he like? Keoni was beautiful even as a child. That much we could tell from the pictures."

"Well, uh, I'd forgotten Keoni was on my baseball team, to tell you the truth. It was such a long time ago. Wherever did you find a copy of that photograph?"

"In the hottest new night spot on the North Shore. It's called Harley's Hangout. You two ought to try it sometime," I supplied. "Delicious food, Melanie, my compliments to the chef. Szechuan dishes, aren't they?"

"Yes," she replied with obvious relief. "We had a maid from Szechuan who taught me how to prepare them. Jason prefers Szechuan to Hong Kong cuisine." Jason was having difficulty swallowing anything at the moment.

I wasn't sure whether Melanie knew that Jayne was born in China and lived there for the first seven years of her life. Oddly enough, what flashed through my mind at the moment was a dumb joke I had done the first time Jayne had served me Szechuan food, which was to the effect that it was so called "because it sets-you-on your ear."

"Don't be shy," Jayne pressed, sticking to the point of the moment. "Surely you can dredge up some anecdotes for us. I understand that Keoni and Sam were good friends. Are you sure Sam wasn't on your team as well?"

"I really don't remember, Jayne, it was such a long time ago. To tell you the truth, I coached that team only because my daughter wanted to play on it. Fifi was always an incorrigible tomboy, despite her mother's best efforts at taming."

"Fifi?" Jayne raised an eyebrow.

"Yes, Fiona actually, named after her grandmother on her mother's side. But it was soon shortened to Fifi. You know how those things happen."

"Cute." Jayne smiled. "Was Fifi a friend of Keoni's, or Sam's? I'm just so interested in finding out more about this mysterious Sam Fitzgerald. And Keoni, what was he like then? Do try to remember for us."

Jason looked trapped. Finally he glanced at Melanie and said, "As a matter of fact, I do remember now that there was a bit of a problem over one of the boys. It may have been Sam Fitzgerald. He was quite a good pitcher, I believe, and Keoni played first base. But Sam came to practice one time high on marijuana, and we had to ask him to leave the team."

"What about Keoni?"

The candlelight sent shadows flickering across Jason's face, exaggerating the look of pain that had come across it. "Keoni wasn't a problem. He came from a very poor family if I remember correctly, very poor. He—"

Melanie interrupted. "God, I find baseball boring! Can't we talk about something more interesting?" She graced me with a valiant effort at her seductive smile. Jayne excused herself to go "powder her nose." That was my cue to keep Jason and Melanie occupied. It wasn't difficult. As soon as Jason returned from lighting Jayne's way to the bathroom, I began discussing my possible financial contribution to the Diamond Head Polo Club. Both Melanie and Jason were so relieved to be rid of Jayne's questions and so eager to open the floodgates of Hollywood money that the time flew by. Neither of them appeared to notice that Jayne had been gone a good twenty minutes until she came breezing back in and settled herself at the table, reaching for her water glass.

"Sorry to be so long, I hope I haven't missed anything."

"Nothing Steve can't fill you in on." Jason smiled, looking more cheerful than he had all day. "How about dessert now, darling?" This last was directed toward his wife, who could barely conceal her distaste for the role forced upon her by the lack of a servant. She returned with lychees in an iced brandy sauce, and I took over the role of interrogator.

"Dick Schiller's death must have been a terrible blow to you, Jason. You two seemed to be quite intimate when we ran into you in the Surf Room last week."

Melanie sat up straight and looked inquiringly at her husband. Jason floundered. "I don't know why you say that, Steve. I barely knew the man, actually. Odd little fellow. I . . . that is . . . he asked to see me about a project he was working on. In point of fact, I don't think he was beyond the talking stage. You've known people like that, I'm sure. Wanted to know more about the game of polo."

"Dick went to high school with Sam Fitzgerald and Keoni, Crown High School in Nanakuli. Did you know that?"

"Uh . . . no, I don't remember his mentioning that. A bit of a coincidence, isn't it?"

"Yes, it is. If I were Keoni, I'd stay away from the water."

Melanie put her napkin firmly on the table and rose. "I'm so sorry to put an end to such a lovely evening, Steve, but I find myself just exhausted by the day's activity. I hope you don't mind. We must get together again very soon. When is it that you go back to the mainland?"

Carlos arrived at the front door minutes after our call. Jayne made the appropriate good-byes while I called out to Jason that I'd consult with my financial manager and get back to him shortly. As the Pattersons waved good-bye from the doorway, I noticed Jason reaching over to put his arm around his wife. She slipped smoothly out of his grasp and disappeared inside the dark hallway of the mansion.

"All right, Sherlock. What did you come up with?" I asked as soon as we were moving. "It worked perfectly, by the way. They were so glad to trade your awkward questions for my promise of easy money, they hardly noticed how long you were gone."

Jayne answered triumphantly. "Aren't you glad now that I always carry a flashlight with me? You never know when you might need one. Melanie must not have suspected anything when she caught you in the library this afternoon. The photo was still in the top middle drawer. I put it back where you said you'd found it. I see what you mean though, poor Fifi really was a bit of a dog at ten, wasn't she? Of course, it may have been just an awkward phase—she may be a beauty today, you never can tell. Anyway, I spent most of my time looking at the financial figures for the club and Jason's personal accounts, copying down dates and numbers. It's obvious he's been siphoning off club funds to pay his credit card bills."

"Melanie's bills, most likely," I added.

"I think we have enough to convince Tony Chen to send in the fraud department with a search warrant, Steve. But I still don't see how Jason's financial problems relate to the two dead bodies."

Unfortunately, I didn't see how this connected either. We both sat thinking for several miles. Finally I put forth a possible scenario:

"Let's say Jason knew what was in the missing script, the one we found in Cap's apartment. Let's say, just for the sake of argument, that Dick Schiller told him he was going to pull the new script out of his hat and it would implicate the Brents— the Pattersons, in fact—not just in rigging polo matches but in contributing to the death of an innocent young girl. We'll assume for the moment that Sam Fitzgerald was the stable hand who drugged the horses and sold the leftover drug at his high school. Everything points to him as the pusher. Jason sees supporters fleeing from his polo club like rats from a sinking ship, sees them joining his rival's club, the Manoa Polo Club that Mark Morris runs. Maybe Melanie threatens to leave him the way his first wife did. He's already in a very precarious position. Didn't someone tell us that he's an investment counselor? If he loses his reputation, he loses everything. He panics . . ."

Jayne was looking at me skeptically. She shook her head.

"I know," I said wearily. "I don't quite see Jason as a murderer either."

"Now, Melanie . . ." we said at the same time, laughing.

"Seriously, Steve," Jayne went on, "I think we need to look at Melanie more closely . . . and don't you *dare* smile at me like that! Let's say that Melanie doesn't want to go down with a sinking ship and she decides she has to do something. Jason is going to be ruined by innuendo and rumor if that new script sees the light of day. Maybe Dick Schiller has threatened Jason with exposure— perhaps that was the dinner date we saw at the Surf Room. Melanie could have lured Sam out for an underwater romp and Dick to the edge of a cliff.''

"It's possible,'' I agreed. "But before we call in the cavalry, I'd like to see if Lieutenant Chen can find out anything about Fiona Patterson. And I want to try to talk to Keoni one more time. I doubt if your favorite lieutenant would get anything out of him, but he might be persuaded to talk to me. And he's the only one left out of those high school classmates from Nanakuli. If Keoni *does* know anything, he could be the next victim.''

chapter 35

It seemed as though my head had hardly hit the pillow, when the phone rang.

"Not another body," I mumbled toward Jayne's side of the bed.

She handed me the phone, and I was wide awake at the first sound of Cap's voice. Beneath his usual Popeye imitation, I could tell something was wrong. "Sorry ta disturb ya, sonny. But ya did say to call. Not that it ain't all under control. I ain't lost my aim yet. An' them there cats is just as good as watchdogs, ya know."

"Are you all right?"

"Fit as a fiddle. Nothin' like a little action to get the ticker up to speed, so t' speak. So ya want to hear what happened er just go on back t' sleep."

"Shoot. I mean, who did you shoot?"

"Well, I can't rightly answer that. He got away, see. Lemme start back at the beginnin'. I was snoozin' in front of the TV, when Saucer, that's the gray tabby, she starts clawin' at my leg. Blackface has her back up an' she's growlin' low in her throat, lookin' out the winder. So I go and get the gun, what I keep to spray the toms that come around, ya know, and I go to the back door and look out. There's somebody tryin' t' get into the young feller's apartment. He's broke the back window an' he's reachin' in to unlock the kitchen door. I tiptoe over an' when he looks up I give it to him right in the eye. He sure let out a yell and hightailed it out o' there. That stuff works, all righty, heh-heh."

"Let me get this straight. You sprayed him in the face with a shotgun and he was able to run away?"

"I ain't got no shotgun. I got a can full o' pepper gas. Got the varmint pretty good."

"I see. And what did this varmint look like, Cap?"

"Well, I was afeard you was going to ask that. See, my eyesight ain't so good in the dark an' he had a hat pulled down an' a scarf pulled up an' I couldn't rightly see much but the eyes, an' they looked startled, like."

"Tall, short, skinny, fat?"

"Truth is, sonny, when yer my height, everbody looks tall. About average, I'd say, weight an' height."

Then it could have been just about anyone, I thought, except Danny Siderman and perhaps Edgar Min.

"Are you sure it was a man?"

"You don't think no woman is goin' to sneak around like that in the middle of the night, do ya?"

I refrained from remarking on the sexist nature of that observation.

"What about skin color? Light, dark, tan?"

"Like I said, my night vision ain't so good. Everybody looks dark to me at night."

"Did you see a car, Cap?"

"Nope, an' I looked around the front after I went back in. I reckon he parked a ways away, whoever it was."

"Have you called the police?"

"Me? What do I want with them fellers?"

"Call them now, Cap. Don't say anything about what we've been doing. Just report the attempted break-in. Got that."

"Gotcha, pardner."

"I'll talk to you soon."

I hung up the phone, put on my robe, and went out on the lanai. The moon had just risen. I leaned against the railing and looked up and down the beach. The sounds of music wafted up from late-night clubs and a few couples wandered hand in hand by the surf. An occasional group of young men lurched along the tide line perhaps in search of their lost hotel. There was a breeze coming off the water that gave a slight nip to the tropical air. Who had tried to break into Dick Schiller's old apartment? And why? Jason had said that Oahu was like a small town. Hadn't Keoni said the same thing to me after his show at the Shell? But what about the new kid in town? Isn't he always the one who shakes up the local boys, stirs up the action? I thought of Raymond and Billy. What was it they were so hesitant to talk about? And did it have anything to do with the murders? The sound of the surf finally worked its magic, and I slipped back into bed and instantly to sleep.

Jayne put the phone receiver next to my ear as she got out of bed and began moving around the room.

"Aloha, Mr. Allen. Welcome to another perfect day in paradise. The temperature is seventy-nine degrees, the breeze is out of the east-northeast, and the sun will be rising soon."

"In the east, I presume."

"That's correct, Mr. Allen," she replied as if she were speaking to a child who needed encouragement. "And what would you like for breakfast this morning?"

"Another hour of sleep, please."

That got me a dirty look from Jayne, so I ordered fresh guava juice for two, sliced pineapple, oatmeal with raisins, and hot Kona coffee. I hung up the phone and began to shave.

"I hope you're going to find the killer for me this morning . . . while I'm busy committing a little murder myself," I called to Jayne, who was already dressed and out on the lanai.

"I have my own plans, darling," she called back. Jayne, lucky redhead, didn't have to be on the set until eleven, whereas I was due at the Diamond Head house by seven. The first scene on the schedule was the one in which Warren Brent kills the groom who is threatening to tell the Brents' gambling buddies what they've been up to.

"Tell you what," I tried again. "Cynthia Brent can kill the groom and Warren can go back to bed."

"Courage, dear," was the only response I got.

"Are you going to tell me what my favorite sleuth is up to this morning?" I asked as I prepared to leave the apartment.

"It's a woman thing," was Jayne's reply. I told her to be

careful, she assured me she always was, and I left for the Patterson house wondering just why she looked so chipper.

The antebellum mansion that the Pattersons called home looked less gloomy in the early morning light than it had the night before. The company limousine dropped me off in the circular driveway before the front door, and I spent a moment surveying the house and gardens. Even with the dozens of TV trucks and trailers lined up on the street, and grips in shorts and sweaty T-shirts stringing electric cables up the driveway, the old house cast an aristocratic spell. I could imagine Jason's daughter, Fifi, playing croquet in the front yard, her rope swing dangling from one of the shade trees. It was Jason Patterson who was dangling at the moment, by his hands, from a limb just high enough to allow him to do chin-ups. Danny Siderman stood on the grass in front of him, punctuating his conversation with wild arm gestures. He was so engrossed in what he was saying, he didn't hear me approach.

"Good morning, folks," I said. He nearly jumped out of his skin.

"My God, Steve, scare a man to death will you? I . . . we were just talking about you, weren't we, Jason?"

Jason dropped to the ground from a chin-up and nodded cordially as Danny went on.

"Jason's been telling me all about your plans to join the club. You couldn't make a better move. Look at me. It's changed my life. Next thing you know, you'll be looking to settle here," Danny went on in his usual mile-a-minute manner. "Hey, I might be able to help you out, find you a nice little bungalow, condo, you name it. I got contacts in real estate, you know. Too bad you play the bad guys in this episode. We could have written you into the series. But don't worry, we'll figure out a way to get you and Jayne back here for the polo season. Which reminds me, we'd better get this show on the road. Let me walk you to your trailer. See you later, Jason."

Talk about your Type A personality—it was exhausting just to listen to Danny Siderman. I gave Jason the thumbs-up sign and headed back toward the street with Danny. This show was beginning to demand more acting off camera than on. It was going to be a relief to play a straightforward bad guy for the cameras.

The minute we were out of Jason's earshot, Danny turned on his most earnest persona. "Billy mentioned that you and Jayne were going to the airport to pick up his father," he said. "That's the way to go, Steve. I knew you were on my side. You must have had time for a nice long chat. Everything settled?"

"Danny, I went to the airport as a favor to Billy, not to you, and I still haven't any idea why Raymond is here. I'm concerned about him, if you want to know the truth. But I don't think *you* need to be."

"Wonderful, wonderful! I mean, I'm sorry that you're concerned. Personal problem, is it?"

"Aren't they all?" I replied, ducking into my dressing room trailer to avoid further conversation. Makeup took longer than usual this morning, as Edgar had requested bags under the eyes and lines across the forehead to indicate a man strained to the breaking point. With the amount of sleep I'd been missing lately, I was surprised they needed to apply any makeup at all. One of Edgar's assistants came in just as Mighty Mo was finishing my hair. He said Edgar would meet me in the stable area as soon as I was ready. It seemed that I was to have the dubious pleasure of receiving the director's morning lecture on the meaning of life all by myself.

When I got to the stables, Edgar was holding forth to an earnest young Hawaiian I assumed to be my upcoming victim. The young man had a glazed expression on his face and he kept nodding as Edgar spoke, trying to take in all the directions and turn in, perhaps, an Emmy-winning performance as a future corpse. The director stopped in midsentence when he spotted me.

"Mr. Allen. I hope you are ready for this scene. Myself, I do not like to shoot out of sequence, but I have been told I have no choice. This particular episode has been held up too many times already, and we must, how do you say, slice corners. But we will take the time to absorb the *ambience*, no?"

"Sure thing," I told him pleasantly, trying hard not to laugh.

I was glad to have a chance to take a closer look at the stable area, while soaking up the ambience and getting into character. The first thing I noticed was how well maintained everything appeared. There were stalls for ten horses as well as a tack room and another where a groom or guard might sleep and take his meals. There were only three horses in residence at the moment, the gray I'd noticed Jason riding in the deciding chukkers of the benefit polo match, a roan gelding, and a black mare. But all the stalls were clean and in perfect condition, the tack room was meticulously organized, and the smell of saddle soap laced the air. I saw no sign of a real groom and had to assume that Jason was filling the post himself. The stables reminded me of Jason's secret ledger on the polo club's finances, maintained with scrupulous care.

The real polo ponies had been placed in stalls on the back side of the stables, as far away from the lights, cameras, and stunt horse as possible. They still didn't look thrilled by all the activity. As we were heading back toward the stall where we'd be filming, the handler for the stunt horse came up to Edgar and muttered something in his ear. Edgar nodded, gave me his excuse for a smile, and began the morning lecture.

"We know, don't we, Mr. Allen, the theme for today. It is murder, no? But we must think for a minute. What drives some people to commit this ultimate crime? Is Warren Brent a monster? I don't think so. He loves his wife, he loves his daughter, he loves his polo. But he has backed himself into a corner. He cannot flee, therefore he must fight."

I felt someone come up behind me and turned around to see Jason, one hand full of sugar cubes.

"I've just come to calm the horses if they need it," he muttered apologetically, and continued on toward the big gray. But he was still within earshot of Edgar's sonorous voice, I noticed.

"The groom thinks ah-hah, this man is rich and I help him get there by doing, what do you say, his soiled work for him. I am entitled to some compensation. But his employer does not have the money to pay the groom's blackmail even if he wished to. It is *unbearable*"—Edgar seemed to pull the word out of his mouth and roll it around—"unbearable financial pressure that has driven him to fix the polo match in the first place. If the groom makes good on his threat and tells the world what he knows, our Mr. Brent will be ruined. Without his reputation he will lose everything, including the love and respect of this lovely daughter of his. He has to act. And it is so easy, it hardly seems like murder. An accident, that is all, he almost convinces himself that it is truly an accident. Remember, Steve, every murderer feels justified. Every murderer believes that he *has* to do it, that he has no choice."

I couldn't see Jason's eyes where he stood in the shadows behind his horses, but his body was rigid and hadn't changed position throughout Edgar's speech.

"I would like you to just walk through this scene first, to get the feel of the flow, the rhythm. This scene is like a dance, the dance of death, no?"

I was glad to accommodate him. Scenes like this one, where the filming is close-up and intimate and a stuntman has to take the place of an actor in the middle of the scene, are always tricky. But Edgar's style of shooting, in which he insisted on having both the action and the witness to the action in the same frame rather than switching from one to the other, made it even more difficult to pull off. The young man playing the groom was professional and had prepared well for his part, but we still went over and over the scene before Edgar was willing to summon the crew and start the actual filming. I saw what the cast of *Hawaiian Wave* meant when they talked about how demanding the director could be. But I also saw what he was trying to achieve. Eventually, after several dry runs, the crew came into the stables, the assistant director called for silence on the set, the clapper boy called out "Scene 46, take one!" and the cameras began to roll. In the scene, the groom is relentless, he insists that he's entitled to a "reward," as he puts it, for what he's done for Brent. He crowds the older man until finally, in desperation, Brent pushes back. The groom hits his head on the corner of the stall and falls down unconscious. It's only then that Brent sees his chance. He closes the door of the stall, torments the horse inside until he rears, and then, in a frenzy of despair and relief, continues to goad the horse until the groom is mangled beyond recognition. The filming included shots with the actors, shots with a stuntman, and shots with a dummy that looked disturbingly real. The horse performed admirably, and I managed to stay in character through what turned out to be a grueling two and a half hours of takes and retakes. When we finally got to the last shot, where Warren Brent, the reality of what he's just done beginning to sink in, drags himself back to the big white house on the hill, it wasn't hard for me to look exhausted. When Edgar pronounced himself satisfied at last, I noticed Jason coming away from the far end of the stable looking as if he had just seen a ghost. I made a mental note to see if Jason had ever lost a groom under suspicious circumstances. This show was getting too close to reality for anyone's comfort, mine included.

chapter 36

I had lunch sent to my dressing room so I could go over my lines before the afternoon scenes. There was one between Jayne and me and one with our irate gambling buddies, who talk us into rigging one more match. Jayne was already in the Patterson living room, seated on the antique couch, when I entered for the beginning of the afternoon shoot. Edgar was by her side.

"I was just telling Edgar how we found Dick Schiller's body," Jayne explained. "Actually, it's quite a coincidence—he knows Harley's Hangout. His son used to go there."

Now, that was interesting. But before I could open my mouth, Edgar had unwound his long, angular frame from the couch and walked over to one of the cameramen.

"Don't worry," Jayne whispered. "I've got news for you."

"Good," I whispered back. "I've got news for you too. I want to catch this murderer and go on a real vacation. How does Burbank sound?"

The afternoon scenes were a breeze after the workout at the stables. There was no sign of Melanie and no further sign of Jason. Jayne and I had a break before our scene with the gamblers, but we used it to get to know the extras we'd be shooting the scene with. So it wasn't until late afternoon, when Edgar called a final wrap, that I was able to get Jayne off alone, on our walk back to the dressing room trailers. The sun was low in the sky, casting a nostalgic golden glow over the house and lawn.

"You tell me your morning and I'll tell you mine," I began. Jayne looked at her watch.

"Oh, dear. I will, tell you mine, but it will have to be in the car. I spoke to Raymond and he insisted we meet him and Billy at the Hilton Hawaiian Village for a drink at six-thirty. He said he'd be through with his business by then. It seems the Hawaiian Village is where he and Bea stayed the first time they came to the Islands, and he practically begged me to come. It wasn't like Raymond at all, Steve. He's never seemed the sentimental type before. Bea was always the one who—"

"Maybe he's going to clear up the mystery of his sudden visit. See you at the car in a jif."

We had a new driver this time, so I closed the window between the front seat and the back before turning to Jayne with an inquiring look. She began in a low, conspiratorial tone.

"Well, I called Tony Chen as soon as you left for the filming. You did say you wanted some information, remember? We met in Chinatown for breakfast. There's this wonderful little place on Maunakea Street that has the best dim sum . . ."

"The dim sun also rises," I said. "Go on, what's your favorite homicide detective been up to these last few days?"

"Not much until this morning. He hasn't found anyone who saw anything suspicious at Waimea Bay Beach Park the night of Dick Schiller's death, so he's assuming that Dick went into the water very late that night. Otherwise someone should have seen him. It's a popular park. He even suggested that Dick might still have been alive when we got the phone call to go to Harley's Hangout. He hasn't been able to track down where Sam got his diving gear, but we know why, of course," Jayne said.

I nodded. Lloyd Kawelo had told me during the party at Keoni's recording studio that he had given Sam the secondhand diving equipment. "Did you tell the romantic Lieutenant Chen about Lloyd?" I asked.

"I told Tony as little as possible, dear. Nothing about your conversation with Lloyd Kawelo. By the way, he has a copy of the missing script and says he can't make anything out of it."

"Wait a minute. Where'd he get that script?"

"Where do you think? The Burglary Division alerted him

when Cap's call came in last night about the attempted break-in at Dick Schiller's apartment. Tony went out to investigate. It appears that Cap kept a copy of the script for himself and couldn't resist bragging about it to Tony. Cap didn't say anything about us or the box with the rest of the scripts, but I think Tony suspects that we've seen a copy and were holding out on him. The only reason he's not making an issue of it is—"

"Your winning ways?"

"Well, I *did* bat an eyelash or two—but only in the cause of truth and justice."

"Very noble," I told her.

"Back to Tony Chen—the dear man doesn't believe the missing script really has anything to do with the 'unexplained deaths,' as he still calls them. He's not dumb though, Steve. He noticed the picture on Dick's coffee table and assumed it was the Angela Schwartz I'd asked him about. He wanted to know how we got her name. I had to do some quick thinking. I'm afraid I gave him Kenny's Kopy Shop."

"Good. That should keep him busy for a while. Maybe he'll get caught in a lava flow. What about the Pattersons?"

"Well, as Tony pointed out, the polo matches are private and the fact that people gamble on them, which he seemed to take for granted, is still illegal. But if Jason *were* rigging matches in the past, it would not necessarily have come to the attention of the police. They simply haven't paid much attention to the polo scene. Tony knew nothing about Jason's first wife and daughter, or Melanie, and seemed to consider them irrelevant. I don't think he's going to be much help there. But he was very interested in the possibility that Jason was scamming the other members of his polo club, and especially concerned about the possibility of his absconding with the proceeds from the benefit for the school for the deaf. It's not his jurisdiction, but I got the impression that the Diamond Head Polo Club would be receiving a visit from a state auditor later today."

Jayne suddenly turned around in her seat to glance out the back window.

"What?" I asked, looking after her.

"Nothing, dear. Just thought I saw an old green Volvo in the next lane."

I turned around, momentarily alarmed. "That's not a Volvo—it's a Cherokee," I observed.

"Something green," Jayne agreed. She settled back into the soft leather cocoon of the seat and stretched her legs.

"I haven't told you the real news yet, dear. I had an early lunch with Melanie Patterson and Louise Siderman."

"Did you? I'm surprised that Melanie would go for any luncheon party that didn't include at least one member of the opposite sex. Soliciting funds, was she?"

"Of course. I was counting on that when I called her. 'I just don't know if I want Steve putting his money into something like this. Can I talk to you about it?' It worked. Louise was a little more reluctant, especially when she heard that Melanie would be there. There's no love lost between those two, I can tell you. But I finally persuaded her. I took them to Orchids."

As Jayne talked on, I pictured the three women seated around a linen-clad table on the terrace of the elegant hotel dining room.

"Melanie was awfully aristocratic and charming," Jayne went on. "A bit like an aristocratic and charming snake. Louise took the opportunity to tell me, right in front of Melanie, that she wasn't at all keen on Danny's involvement with the polo club and had tried repeatedly to dissuade him from investing in ponies and jockeys. Melanie took the position that of course she agreed, but what were you to do when the 'boys' insisted on playing their silly games."

"Silly boys," I agreed. "Yet what is life but a matter of batting a ball around a field of grass, trying to score a goal or two, and not fall off our horses?"

"Yes, darling. To return to planet earth for a moment, I brought up Sam Fitzgerald and Dick Schiller again, about the time we were nibbling dessert—a divine chocolate mousse torte that we shared with three forks. I wanted to really look at Melanie's reaction. If she did send them to a watery grave, she did it without remorse. There wasn't the slightest hint on that beautiful, perfectly made-up face of hers that the two men had anything to do with her. Louise, on the other hand, looked very upset at mention of the bodies. But the *really* interesting thing—"

"Yes?"

"—was when Louise started talking about children."

"Fiona, by any chance?"

"No, Edgar's son, Gregory. I asked Melanie about Fiona, but apparently Melanie has no interest in the child from Jason's first marriage. She said she'd met Fifi only once and had found her a very unattractive little thing. That's when Louise compared her to Edgar's son. It seems they both have a penchant for motorcycles, body-piercing, and dying their hair a different color every week or so. I asked Louise if Edgar's son lived here on Oahu, and she said, 'Oh, yes, though Edgar and Maria have done everything in their power to discourage him.' "

"That could make him the stalker, possibly. But why? You don't suppose he's trying to win over Papa by doing away with that bad boy, Billy Markham, who's threatening Dad's artistic sovereignty, do you?"

"The thought did cross my mind. But it's pretty thin, don't you think?"

"Very thin," I agreed.

We had left Waikiki behind and were pulling into the parking lot at the Hilton Hawaiian Village when the sun dipped below the horizon and the sky began to turn a picture-perfect pink. Sunsets are short in the tropics, but they're usually magnificent. I told the driver we wouldn't be long, and Jayne and I headed into the twenty-acre fantasy of life in paradise. The Village sits in a choice location, between Fort DeRussy Park and the Ala Wai Yacht Harbor. It's a maze of overnight accommodations, gardens, pools, shops, restaurants, bars, and clubs. We wound through increasingly narrow pathways and tunnels of jungle foliage, every once in a while spotting another sign for our destination, the Candlenut Bar. At one point we found ourselves on a path called Hong Kong Alley. It was lined on both sides by curio shops selling everything from grass skirts to miniature grass shacks. Somehow I didn't think Melanie would approve of the name. Suddenly I realized that I'd lost Jayne. I turned around to see which shop had grabbed her attention and found myself looking into the eyes of the redheaded stalker.

I was so startled, my glasses somehow slipped off my nose and fell onto the ground. Alas, I am terribly nearsighted without my glasses, so this turned him into a redheaded blur. Nevertheless, we stared at each other in mutual astonishment for several heart-beats..

"I've got you this time," I cried as I grabbed at his baggy T-shirt. But he whipped around, pulling loose from my hold and bolted down the path. By the time I reached down to pick up my glasses, he had gotten a good head start in the escape department.

"Stop," I yelled as I headed after him. My quarry didn't pay any attention. He plowed through a group of Japanese business-men who were sporting identical yellow sun visors above their pin-striped suits and led by a tour guide with a bright yellow flag. I followed in breathless pursuit right through them as well, I'm afraid, to the sound of camcorders colliding with still cameras. I felt a bit like a kamikaze.

"It's all part of the show," I yelled over my shoulder, and their frowns turned into quizzical smiles. I couldn't see the stalker anywhere and slowed down to a fast walk as I approached an area of kiosks and small shops. I spotted him again near the conch shell booth. He seemed undecided which way to go, and I thought I had him, when a dozen muumuued matrons suddenly converged onto the main path, completely blocking my way. As I was attempting to duck around them, the woman in the lead shrieked, "Oh, look, girls, it's Steve Allen!" and grabbed hold of my arm. Then she hesitated. "You are Steve Allen, aren't you?"

"No, but I hear that all the time," I gasped, extricating myself from her grip and running around behind her. Once again the stalker was nowhere to be seen. I looked up and down each side path as I continued in the general direction of the parking lot, but I didn't hold out any great hope. And then I spotted him again, coming back my way on a parallel path almost completely obscured by the giant ferns that lined its edge. I ducked behind a huge flowering-hibiscus, waited until he'd passed me going in toward the center of the village, slipped down a connecting path, and turned to trail him, staying about thirty feet behind. Two can play this game, I thought. And it's a hell of a lot easier to follow him than it is to try to outrun him. He led me straight to the Candlenut Bar, an open air, grass-roofed platform near an artificial lagoon, with a bar in the center and tables all around the edges. Jayne had found her way there without me, and was seated next to Raymond, with Billy on his other side. They all looked concerned—about me, I presumed. Where *was* that gallant fellow Steve Allen? I was lurking, in fact, behind a convenient banyan tree.

The stalker found a wooden bench from which he could just barely see what was going on in the pavilion and slouched down onto it, pulling his backward baseball cap low over his eyes as if he were taking an evening snooze. I stayed behind my tree a few feet away. Jayne and Raymond finished their drinks. Billy, I noticed, barely touched his. Raymond paid, and they all stood looking around for a while before heading slowly back in the direction of the parking lot. The stalker slipped off his bench and followed a few yards behind, with me a few yards behind him. I'd begun to think I was going to be able to catch him in a pincher maneuver at the parking lot, where there would be fewer places to hide and I could cover the Village while Jayne and company headed him off by the cars. But suddenly he reached into his pocket and pulled out something that looked like a gun. I wasn't taking any chances.

"Drop it!" I yelled in my best imitation of a policeman. He wheeled around, glared at me, and took off again, this time heading toward the beach on our right. I ran after him, huffing and puffing, pumping my arms, keeping him in sight almost all the way to the beach. Unfortunately I didn't see the six-year-old with the shave ice cup who veered suddenly into my pathway. (Yes, *shave* ice, not *shaved* iced, is the correct island slang, if I might be allowed a brief culinary aside.) The kid dropped the snow cone concoction as he fell—cherry flavored, I noticed, which did not make for less of an accident. I slipped on the wet ground and fell down next to him. The kid let out a howl to wake the dead, and his mother did too.

Any chance I had of catching the stalker was long gone. I pacified the little boy by buying him another shave ice and the mother with the promise of an autographed copy of my latest book. The security guard who converged on us was the hardest one to deal with, but I finally convinced him that I had only been trying to protect a companion from a purse snatcher. I gave him a description of the stalker and he said he'd keep an eye out for him. By the time I made it back to the limousine, Raymond and Billy had gone on to dinner and Jayne was looking genuinely worried.

"Steve, where in the world . . . ? Good heavens, what have you been up to?" she finished, catching sight of my shirttails, torn knees, and cherry shave ice–stained pants.

"Just indulging in a little recreational activity, dear. Wanted to work up an appetite for dinner."

chapter 37

Once I'd tidied up and we were comfortably settled back in the limo, headed toward our hotel, Jayne insisted on a serious explanation of my recent disappearance.

"I'm afraid there *isn't* a serious explanation," I told her. "All I have to offer is slapstick."

"Go ahead, then. After forty years of marriage, slapstick no longer worries me."

This wasn't a very nice comment, but I told her the whole preposterous story. At the end, my wife could only sigh.

"A pity your glasses fell off. Could you see *anything* about the stalker's face?"

"Not really," I told her. "But that's about it. What did Billy and Raymond have to say?"

"Not much."

Apparently the drink with Raymond and Billy had been uneventful. Raymond avoided any mention of his appointment with the Air Oahu brass, saying only that he had decided to stay on until the end of the week.

"I told Raymond and Billy you had a toothache. That way I figured when you did show up I could ask you how your tooth was feeling."

"Were you worried about me, then?" I asked.

"Of course I was. I thought you might have taken up life as a beachcomber. Do you really think the stalker meant to shoot Billy?"

"I don't know, but I wasn't about to take any chances. After all, Billy was flanked by one of my best friends and my only wife."

As our limousine approached the corner of Kalakaua Avenue and Lewers Street, traffic slowed to a crawl. We told our driver we'd walk the rest of the way, as we were only two blocks from the hotel. Once we were on the sidewalk, it didn't take long to figure out what was holding up traffic. Kalakaua had been partially blocked off and the familiar *Hawaiian Wave* logo glowed on the sides of the trucks, vans, and trailers parked up and down Lewers. The evening sky was turning from deep blue to purple everywhere except where it was lit up by the outdoor movie lights that were focused on a pedicab stand.

"Edgar really is a maniac," I commented. "No wonder he always looks so morose. He's probably suffering from chronic exhaustion. I wonder if the meaning of this scene is how much worse you can make an already impossible traffic situation."

"Let's take a look, Steve. I haven't seen Lance since the day Sam Fitzgerald washed up on Hanauma Beach."

"You haven't been missing much, I assure you." But I agreed to go across the street and join the crowd milling around the set, hoping for a look at someone they'd seen on their TV screen.

As soon as we got close to the cameras, I was astonished to see one of Edgar's assistants rushing our way, hands waving.

"Mr. Allen, I'm so glad you're here. Lance is very eager to talk to you. He told me to take you straight to his dressing room the minute you showed up. He's been leaving messages at your hotel all afternoon."

I looked at Jayne. "What do you think?"

"You go, darling. You'll have a better chance for a man-to-man talk if I'm not there. If I'm not here when you get back, you'll know where to find me."

"In our suite, with room service and candlelight, I hope."

I followed the young assistant director over the electric cables and various hazards peculiar to a TV company on location to a small trailer halfway down the side street. He let me in and said Lance was due for a break in a few minutes, he'd be right there. Lance's trailer was about half the size of Jayne's and two-thirds the size of mine. The only place to stretch out between scenes was an armchair with a pull-out footrest. There was a paper cup of cappuccino half drunk on the makeup table, and the smell of

coffee and stale cigarette smoke permeated the stuffy air. Lance
had either been late for the shoot or he was just plain messy; his
street clothes were strewn everywhere. I peered at the snapshots
stuck along the edge of the mirror over the makeup table. Lance
on the beach, Lance in front of his house, Lance in his TransAm,
Lance as Pete Lambert on *Hawaiian Wave,* standing in front of
his pedicab. No family, no friends, just Lance. I turned around
at the sound of the door opening.

"God, Steve, I'm glad you're here. I didn't think you'd make
it. You won't believe what came in the mail today. I picked it up
on my way to the set. What do you think I should do?"

Lance handed me a computer printout, one of the old-style
ones with little holes down both sides. I grabbed it by the top and
bottom edges and read it twice.

"Don't hide your light under a bushel, Lance, or should I
say Kevin Crass? I have copies of your film debut in *Behind the
Blue Door* addressed and ready to send. I think the *National Enquirer,*
People magazine, and *20/20* will do for openers, don't you? You
still have time to save your career. I'm not asking for much, just
a little financial help with my own career. Have $20,000 in small,
unmarked bills ready by this Friday. Don't call me, I'll call you.
This is a one-time payment, I will never bother you again. But if
you involve the police, or anyone else, you'll be sorry. Take my
word for it. Your new best friend."

I laid the note carefully down on the makeup table. "It's
probably too late, but I suggest you avoid handling that paper as
much as possible, and when you have to, do it at the top and
bottom edges. Whoever sent it, if they didn't wear gloves, is likely
to have gripped it on the sides."

Lance looked confused. "I'm not going to go to the police
with this, Steve. That's why I wanted you to see it."

"Do you know who sent it?"

"Believe me, if I did, I wouldn't be here talking to you. I'd—"

"I assume that the allegation is true? You made porno films?"

Lance sat down at the makeup table and motioned me to
the armchair.

"Well, sure, it's true. I wouldn't be worried if it weren't. But
it's not as bad as it sounds. It was a long time ago, before *The*

Loves of Our Lives. I was desperate to get in front of a camera, any camera. It was soft-core porn, the kind they make for closed-circuit viewing at hotels. At least that's what I thought in the beginning. It turned out to be pretty bad, I have to admit. I dyed my hair and used an alias, of course—Kevin Crass. And then I got out of the whole thing as fast as I discovered that porno flicks are *not* a door to the big-time. To tell the truth, I haven't even thought about it for years."

Lance reached for the pack of Italian cigarettes on the makeup table, looked inquiringly at me, and pushed it away again.

"Is there anyone working on *Hawaiian Wave* who knew you back then? A cast member? One of the crew?" I asked.

"I don't think so. Anyway, if it was someone from the old days, they probably would have recognized me on *The Loves of Our Lives* and hit me up then. Besides, I look a lot different now. No, I think it's someone new who stumbled on my little secret by accident. It's my own fault, I guess."

"What makes you say that?"

"Well, a couple of weeks ago, before you and Jayne arrived, we had a kind of cast party and I really tied one on. I don't usually do that, you know. I can hold my liquor and I know when to stop. But this time something just got into me. I got stinkin' drunk, and then somebody, I don't even know who, said that it was ironic that I had been cast as the stud of the series. The implication was that I couldn't actually get it up, so I dared any of them to do it in front of a camera. I think I even made a joke about Kevin Crass."

"Who might have heard you?"

"Hell, I don't know. I wasn't seeing too well by that time."

"Was Jason Patterson there by any chance?"

"He was at the party. It was for the people in this episode, you know. But I think I may have been sitting with Keoni and that creep Kawelo at the time."

"Was Billy at this party?"

"Of course. He threw the party."

"At his house?"

"You call that a house? We call it Fort Apache. Sure, it was at Billy's place. He's so proud of that dump. And his bodyguard,

Bertrand. What kind of name is that? It was the Samoan's fault I got so drunk, actually. He kept plying me with mai tais."

Lance reached for his cigarettes again, pulled his hand away, then grabbed the pack, opened the door to the trailer, and stood in the doorway, smoking. He scowled at anyone passing by who looked inclined to stop.

"So what do you think?" he asked after a few puffs. "Damage control? I pay the money and chalk it up to experience. Or I try to catch the bastard and let him have it."

"Neither," I replied firmly. "If you really want my advice, you'll go straight to the police as soon as you get off the set. But then, you knew that's what I'd say, didn't you?" And I rose and moved toward the door.

"Hey, look, Steve, I'm not stupid. I know you don't like me much. But honestly, I'm beginning to get freaked. First that guy Sam, then Dick Schiller, now this blackmail note. If it weren't for the fact that *Hawaiian Wave* has turned into such a hit, I'd be on the first plane back to the mainland. But this could be my big break. Movie roles, spinoff show, who knows? I can't let a measly twenty thou stand between me and millions, can I? Don't tell me you wouldn't pay it if you were in my position."

I didn't tell him. Edgar's assistant came to bring him back to the set and I went out the door with them, wishing both Lance and the assistant a pleasant evening. Lance looked pathetically over his shoulder at me as he headed back toward the cameras. For a moment I actually felt sorry for him.

chapter 38

Jayne and I did get our candlelight dinner that night, complete with an after-dinner stroll in the moonlight. Even amateur sleuths need to take a break once in a while. We played what-if? as we were getting ready for bed, and came up with an array of possible murder suspects that included our limousine driver and Belle up at Harley's Hangout. I tried to throw Cass in for good measure, but Jayne said we had to draw the line somewhere. The one piece of real business I conducted was putting in a call to Keoni Pahia. I got his answering machine.

"If you're there, Keoni, pick up the phone," I said into the machine. "It's Steve Allen and I need to talk to you as soon as possible."

I tried Keoni again early in the morning and got a machine both at his house and at the recording studio. There were no messages for us at the front desk and we weren't due on the set until one.

"I'm stymied, Jayne," I admitted over breakfast on the lanai. "What do you say we take a little trip into the past, to Nanakuli, where the real story behind our episode seems to have started."

An hour later we were on the freeway, Carlos Medina back behind the wheel of the limousine, headed west toward Oahu's Waianae Coast. The *ewa*, or west side of the island is the hot, dry side, much less developed for tourism than the windward side or Waikiki, and traditionally the poorest economically. Once we left the freeway and headed north on Old Farrington Highway, traffic slowed to a snail's pace. It was midmorning before we pulled into

Nanakuli. We headed straight for the post office and I left Jayne and Carlos in the car with the air conditioning on while I went in to try my luck.

"Good morning," I began with my friendliest smile. But the postmistress didn't seem to agree.

"I wonder if you can help me," I added courteously. She looked as if I could keep wondering forever. "Does Keoni Pahia still have family here?"

I finally got a response. "Would you like to mail a letter?"

"I'd love to. To Keoni's relatives. Could you give me their address."

"Sorry," she replied, and went to take care of something in the back room. Someone else came into the office and she returned.

"You still here?"

I looked down at myself. "Apparently." She didn't crack a smile.

After she'd checked general delivery for the other patron and he'd gone out the door, she turned back to me.

"Look, mister. We're real proud of Keoni in this town. But we don't like reporters or fans or whatever you are snooping around. And his family, what's left of it, does not want to be bothered either."

I tried to explain who I was and that I was there out of concern for Keoni's welfare, but I got nowhere. I finally bought a book of stamps, just so the visit wouldn't be a total waste of time, and emerged back out into the glaring sun.

Jayne tried next, at Kristy's Korner beauty shop. She came out forty minutes later with beautiful nails and very little else. Keoni's grandmother lived on her own and didn't take to strangers at all, she'd discovered. Dick and Sam may have gone to Nanakuli High School, but they lived at Pearl Harbor, so the townspeople didn't consider them local boys and seemed unaffected by their recent demise.

For years I've marveled at how casually we humans can react to the death of others if they're far enough removed. We're all appropriately impressed emotionally if the death takes place right in front of us, with the corpse's blood splattering our shoes. But if the same sort of tragedy occurs half a mile away, it doesn't mean nearly as much to us. In the late 1970s there was a massively cata-strophic earthquake in China, near the city of Tientsin, which re-sulted in over 400,000 deaths, but I doubt if any Americans, or other foreigners for that matter, missed a social appointment as a result.

Finally we sent Carlos into the hardware store. He came out ten minutes later with a ratchet wrench.

"I've never seen a bunch of old men so disinclined to 'talk story,' " he said, shaking his head and sliding back into the driver's seat. "It makes you wonder what they're hiding."

We were about to give up, when we spotted a diner, on the road just outside of town. The sign over the door said ONO, the Hawaiian word for "good."

Carlos turned around to give us an inquiring look.

"Why not?" I answered. "I'm thirsty anyway."

We trooped inside the surprisingly cool trailer that housed the diner and sat down in a booth by the window. Hawaiian music was playing on a small transistor radio sitting on a shelf next to the coffee cups. The man behind the counter was late middle aged and huge. He barely fit between the counter and the shelves behind him. He came around to our table with four glasses of water and explained that he didn't really have a menu, then rattled off the specials of the day. We ordered one of each, to share around, and I moved over to the counter so I could chat with him while he prepared the food. I mentioned that we were working on an episode of *Hawaiian Wave.*

"I thought you looked familiar. The lady too. Like TV people. Keoni Pahia grew up just down the road. Did he send you over here?"

"Not exactly," I hedged. "But he mentioned how good the food is here."

"That's the truth! On this part of the island, we really know how to grind. Keoni's a real hometown boy made good all right. His grandma is still here, she wouldn't hear of living anywhere else. Just as eccentric as she always was. Keoni told her as soon as he got famous that she could have whatever she wanted. But she said he'd already given her what she wanted most. It's funny, isn't it? I mean, they were really poor when he was growing up. No TV, no electricity, for that matter. He was a wild one, you know, when he was a kid. He had a devil in him for sure. And look at him now, a TV celebrity, in all the magazines. Sometimes kids just straighten out all by themselves, don't they?"

"That was certainly true in Keoni's case, wasn't it," I prompted.

"Well, of course, he was never into the hard stuff. That makes a big difference. With him it was just a little pot, psychedelics, PCP, that kind of stuff. It's hard to blame them really, even when they try their hand at selling. I mean, how else are you going to make any real money? Not working in a diner." He chuckled. "Get yourself on a hit TV show, that's how," he added. And with that he brought out the food.

The lunch lived up to the name over the door. The *lomilomi*, salmon with minced onions and tomatoes, was delicious, but the *laulau*—steamed pork, butterfish, and taro tops wrapped in ti leaves—was even better. Carlos ordered seconds of the roast pig and Jayne declined the *haupia*, a dessert made from fresh coconut, in order to have a second helping of the salmon. Carlos and Jayne chatted with the proprietor while I ate in silence. The man seemed to regret having said as much as he had and steered pointedly clear of any further discussion of Keoni Pahia, past or present. But he'd given me something to think about.

The minute we were back in the car, Jayne turned to me excitedly.

"That's it, Steve, that's the drug that killed Angela Schwartz. PCP. I couldn't remember the name, I just remembered that Tony Chen said it was a depressant that was commonly available on the black market. What is it anyway?"

"It's a horse tranquilizer," I answered.

The flow of traffic was with us, and we made it back to the Patterson mansion ahead of schedule. I walked Jayne to her dressing room door. "I still think it's Melanie," she said. "See you inside."

I walked over to Keoni's dressing room trailer and knocked on the door. A faint "come in" came through the wall, and I opened the door. Keoni was sprawled out in his lounge chair, going over the script. I was struck once again by how extraordinarily good-looking he was as he glanced up at me over the pages. When he saw who it was he jumped up, offered me the chair, and

sat down on the stool next to the makeup table. I perched on the
edge of the lounge chair. Keoni's dressing room was no bigger
than Lance's, but he'd made an effort to decorate it. There was
a piece of painted bark on one wall and a fine carving of an
outrigger canoe and its crew sat on the table. There was only one
photo stuck in the edge of Keoni's mirror. It was of a very old
woman, smiling a toothless grin. His grandmother, I assumed.

"I'm sorry I didn't get back to you, Steve. I didn't check my
messages until this morning, and you'd already left the hotel.
Anything I can do for you?"

"Yes, you can level with me. Two of your classmates at Nanakuli High School are dead. My guess is that either you're next in
line or you're responsible."

The color drained out of Keoni's face and a slight twitch
appeared above his left eye. "I . . . I don't know what you mean."

"Keoni, it's either me or the police. You have to talk to
someone."

Just then there was a loud knock on the door and a voice
calling for "places." Keoni jumped up, pulled himself together
in front of the mirror, and turned back to me with an attempt at
a "what the hell" smile. He was trembling, I noticed, very slightly.

"OK, Steve. You're right. It is time to talk. But I can't do it
today. I go straight from here to the studio and who knows when
we'll get out. Tomorrow, in the afternoon. Promise me you won't
bring in the police and I'll tell you everything you want to know.
Is it a deal?"

"You may be in danger, you know."

"I can take care of myself, Steve. I have friends."

"Sometimes those are the people you have to watch out for."

He looked at me as if he thought I was a mind-reader and
walked out the door. I picked up the script that had dropped on
the floor, set it on the makeup table, took another look at
Grandma, and followed him out.

I must say I understood the old woman's pride. Of all the
things I've been lucky enough to do with my life—the comedy,
the piano playing, the movies, the Vegas appearances, Broadway,
TV, and all that—my favorite role has been that of Grandpa.

The front door of the Patterson house was open and Danny's

voice, high-pitched and hysterical, reached me as I was climbing the veranda steps.

"Stop it now, just stop it. That's enough. Time to settle down, folks. We have work to do. Where's Steve? We need to get this show on the road."

I'm not that late, I thought, checking my watch to make sure. I made it to the living room doorway just in time to see an antique needlepoint cushion flying through the air. It landed at Billy's feet. He promptly picked it up, ran around the lights and cameras set up in front of the nineteenth-century divan, and slammed Susan over the head with it. They were playing like teenagers. But that wasn't the most startling thing. It was Susan herself. She was positively radiant, vibrating with energy and grinning from ear to ear. "Truce," she said carefully, and she and Billy began picking up cushions and returning them to the sofa. Edgar had retreated to a corner, either for safety or to have a word with his cameraman, it wasn't clear which. Jayne was standing next to one of the cameras, smiling and shaking her head. Keoni was nowhere in sight.

Danny bounced over to the doorway, wiping his forehead with a plaid handkerchief. "I don't know what's gotten into her, Steve," he hissed. "And Edgar's no help at all. Jeez, they could have torn one of those pillows. They're real antiques, you know. A little loosening up for the scene, I can see it. But this is going too far."

Keoni appeared behind me at that point and Susan turned around. The energy that passed between them was so thick, you could cut it with a knife. Everyone involuntarily breathed in, and Edgar took that as his cue to begin.

"All right, ladies and gentlemen, we are ready to work now, I trust? Steve and Jayne, for your benefit I will reiterate the underlying principle of the scenes we shoot today. It is, of course, first love." He allowed himself a sardonic hint of a smile. Susan looked down at her feet, then up again, watching Edgar's lips intently.

"You all have the order of shooting for the afternoon, I presume? All right, let's get to work. . . ."

The filming went surprisingly well, considering the state everyone was in. Edgar pronounced himself, if not satisfied, at least finished and ready to call it a day by a little after five.

"Steve, I'm worried about Susan and Keoni," Jayne said when

I met her outside her dressing room door. "You notice the way she looks at him when he's around? She really has a schoolgirl crush. The only problem is, he's not a schoolboy. He's too old for her. And . . ."

"He may even be a killer," I added. "And a blackmailer, a drug pusher, and some other unpleasant things as well."

"Exactly. That's why you should have a little talk with Susan, dear."

"*Me?* You'd be much better at that. Woman-to-woman."

"No, I think you'd do better in this case. As a man of the world. A father figure."

I gave her my finest man-of-the-world leer and then went off to find Susan. I wasn't looking forward to this sort of chat, frankly, but I was willing to give it a try. There was something about Keoni I was finding more and more worrisome, and it didn't reassure my troubled mind that he had sold PCP in high school. You had to wonder if someone blessed with his good looks had ever had to develop any strength of character.

I suppose just about every young person in our increasingly goofy society would like to be either handsome or beautiful, but those who are of course have their own problems. I recall the time, in the company of philosopher Gerald Heard, I visited a number of California prisons. At one of them, as we mingled freely with some of the inmates, a young boy I'll never be able to forget attached himself to me, looking directly into my eyes the way some dogs do, obviously hungry for almost any sort of affection.

Since he looked about twelve, I was naturally shocked to see him in such an ugly setting, but one of our escorts said, "No, he's older than he looks; he's sixteen." The boy had blond hair and could accurately be described as beautiful, with a sort of an innocent, choir-boy look. There was absolutely nothing about him that seemed typical of the common young street criminal.

"Why on earth is he here?" I asked the officer who was leading us.

"He's here," the man said, "because he killed his mother with an ax." What a world we live in.

I looked in Susan's dressing room first, then the stables, then the house again. I finally knocked on Keoni's dressing room door.

No answer. I was headed toward my own dressing room, when Elisabeth caught up with me.

"Mr. Allen, I wondered if I could talk to you. I've been walking around all afternoon, trying to decide what to do."

"I think I can guess what you want to talk about. Susan and Keoni?"

"Oh, Mr. Allen, I'm so worried. I've known Susan almost all my life and I've never seen her like this. She doesn't have much experience, I'm afraid, when it comes to the opposite sex."

"It's called first love. I'm sure a lot of girls fall for Keoni."

"But she's not like the girls he's used to, Mr. Allen. She's serious. I thought maybe, man-to-man, you know, you could just talk to him, let him know how vulnerable she is. I'm scared."

This was getting a little thick, all these man-to-man and man-to-woman chats I was supposed to undertake. I am willing to do my part on behalf of virtue, but . . .

"Listen, Elisabeth. I understand your concern, but Susan is a grown woman and you can't protect her from the real world all her life. If you want to be her friend, you can warn her of danger, but you'll have to respect her right to live her own life."

Elisabeth didn't answer for a moment and I was sure I had angered her. But finally she smiled ruefully.

"I guess I deserved that, Mr. Allen. Susan has always seemed so fragile to me, by comparison, you know." She looked down at her own sturdy coverall-clad frame. "I guess I'm afraid she'll fall and break. I'll think about what you've said. But if you do find yourself with Keoni and the opportunity presents itself . . ."

"I'll tell him if he so much as looks at her, I'll get my shotgun off the wall and make him wish he was riding a mule in Molokai!"

We both laughed and exchanged hugs at my dressing room door. But I was more worried than I let on. Keoni could be in real danger, or he could be a desperate young man willing to do anything to protect his own interests. Either way, he was trouble. Trouble for an innocent young girl. And maybe for some other not-so-innocent people as well.

chapter 39

I stepped out of my dressing room door and straight into Cass. He was looking more and more the island beach bum, dressed at the moment in a gaudy blue and green Hawaiian shirt, knee-length surfer shorts, rubber sandals, and wraparound dark glasses.

"Hey, boss, Jayne sent me looking for you. We're all heading over to Billy's house."

"Why is it, Cass, that I sense you're having too much fun in Hawaii?"

"Hey, you need to relax, man!"

"Sounds lovely," I told him cuttingly. "And if it weren't for a few murders and a TV show I have to do, I bet I wouldn't feel any stress at all. But don't worry about *me* . . . at least *you're* having a swell time for both of us. Now tell me about Billy's house. Who all is going, and why?"

"I don't know, boss. Billy got a call from his dad just now and he asked Jayne if you two could come out to the house with us. He said Raymond had something he wanted to say to you in person."

"I hope he is going to tell us what's going on," I said. "I'm fed up with evasion, Cass. It's time for some real answers."

The house in Waimanalo didn't seem quite right as we approached. It was Billy, in the backseat of the Impala next to Jayne, who put his finger on it.

"That's funny. Killer isn't in the yard." He sat up straight and lowered his window. "That must mean Bertrand has gone out. He always takes him along. But he told me he'd be here all day. You don't think . . ." Suddenly Raymond appeared from the direction of the beach and headed toward the car. Billy wasn't the only one who sighed with relief.

"Hey, Dad," he called out the open window. "You haven't seen Bertrand, have you?"

"No, why? Is he missing? I've been on the beach since lunch, which was delicious, by the way. Are you sure he hasn't just gone out for more supplies?"

Billy jumped out of the car to disengage the security system at the front gate, then performed another elaborate ritual at the kitchen door and entered the house quickly, calling Bertrand's name. Raymond followed him in and we stayed in the car while Cass parked it in the garage.

"The truck's here, boss. If Bert is gone, someone picked him up."

"That doesn't sound quite right," I said, frowning.

Billy met us at the door to the kitchen. "He's not here and Killer isn't either."

"Is there a note?" Jayne asked, ever the practical one. Billy shook his head. Jayne turned and went around to the door that opened onto the lanai as Cass and I entered the kitchen.

"Ah, here it is—good old Bertrand. You see, he *did* leave a note!" she called through the glass. I hurried into the living room to open the sliding door for her, half expecting to set off atomic warheads in the front lawn. Jayne handed me the piece of paper. "Something came up. Will return ASAP. My apologies. B."

"It was stuck in the doorframe," Jayne explained. "As if it were a last-minute thought."

Billy, Raymond, and Cass joined us in the living room. It suddenly felt chilly in there.

"Has this ever happened before?" I asked Billy, handing him the note. He glanced at it and started to pass it to his father, then changed his mind and handed it to Cass first.

"Never!" he exclaimed with just a hint of rising panic. "I don't understand. Cass says the truck is there."

"Maybe he just went for a walk, dear," Jayne suggested. "Maybe he took Killer for a walk."

"He never takes Killer for a walk. Killer doesn't *like* to walk," Billy wailed, looking toward his father as if for confirmation.

"Tell you what," I decided. "Everybody just sit down and relax, enjoy the sunset. I'm going to make us all a nice cup of tea."

I started toward the kitchen, calling back over my shoulder as if it were a casual afterthought. "Billy, do you by any chance have a phone number for Bertrand's mother?"

"Yeah, sure, Steve. It should be right there on the bulletin board, by the phone. Mrs. Suuanu."

I closed the door to the kitchen, put on the kettle, and dialed. A woman answered on the third ring.

"Mrs. Suuanu?" I asked, carefully pronouncing all the Us.

"Yes?" She sounded wary.

"My name is Steve Allen. I—"

"Why, Mr. Allen!" she exclaimed, all apprehension gone from her voice. "My Bertie has told me so much about you, I feel like I know you myself. He's always been a big fan of yours, you know?"

"I'm delighted to hear that. Do you happen to know where Bertie is at the moment?"

"What's that?"

"I don't want to alarm you. He left a note that something had come up and I thought perhaps you had needed him."

"Why, no, not at all," she told me. But her voice had become wary again.

"Do you have any idea where he might have gone?" I pressed.

"No ... well, yes. Perhaps. Have you listened to the news today?"

"No," I replied, baffled. "What does the news have to do with it?"

"It's his uncle Davie Keanui. He broke out of prison today. It was quite a sensational escape, I gather. A helicopter managed to set down on the prison athletic field and carry him away. The TV is full of it."

"Tell me something, Mrs. Suuanu—would Uncle Davie be

Bertrand's former employer? The previous owner of this house?"
The drug lord, in other words.

"That's right. But Bertie's a good boy. He never had anything
to do with Davie's agricultural pursuits, I can promise you that."

"Agriculture? I'm not quite following you."

"*Pakalolo,*" she said. "Lots of the island boys grow it up in
the mountains if they can. I imagine that sounds terrible to you,
Mr. Allen, but we're all so poor here that it's very tempting.
Besides, in this climate it really does grow like a weed."

"It *is* a weed," I told her with a sigh. *Pakalolo,* of course, was
the Hawaiian word for "marijuana." While I was absorbing this
new twist, the teakettle started its soft scream. "Thank you for
your information, Mrs. Suuanu. Good-bye now."

I hung up, turned off the kettle, and made tea in a huge pot
with a Hawaiian maiden reclining around the middle. Good Lord!
A *pakalolo*-growing drug lord busting out of prison! I was wondering just how much more excitement could happen on this small
island, when an explosion rocked the house. Air raid sirens set
up a deafening wail and floodlights snapped on in every corner
of the lot. I dropped the phone and ran into the living room.
They were all on their feet, but only Cass had bolted through the
door onto the lanai. I went after him.

"My God, Steve!" he cried, pointing outside the gate to a
huge cloud of smoke that was rising from what used to be the
mailbox. "It's a bomb!"

"You sure it isn't just the security system backfiring?"

The Waimanalo police were the first on the scene. They didn't
do much beyond admiring Billy's security system until Lieutenant
Tony Chen showed up with his bomb experts.

"Not you again, Mr. Allen," he groaned when he spotted me
by the mailbox, or what used to be the mailbox.

The lieutenant gave me a sour look. Fortunately Jayne was
by my side, and after pouring on the charm for both of us had
the lieutenant purring inside of two minutes. He questioned us
together in the living room and we all insisted we hadn't the
slightest idea who might want to send Billy a letter bomb. Then

he asked where Bertrand was. As if by mutual agreement, we all played down his absence as routine and said we expected him back shortly.

"I suggest you people find another place to stay tonight," Tony said as he was getting ready to leave. "My men will be here awhile, finishing up, and we'll put a guard on the house."

While we were talking, the head of the bomb squad came our way from examining the mailbox. He whispered something in Lieutenant Chen's ear and then walked away.

Lieutenant Chen frowned. "Well, it wasn't a bomb after all," he said. "Just a bit of mischief. A firecracker of some kind— probably what the kids call a cherry bomb."

I went inside to tell Billy the news, but he had taken some Valium and was lying down in a darkened room. If someone was trying to drive Billy Markham over the edge, a king-sized fire-cracker was a job well done.

chapter 40

There were torches burning along the seawall that separated the surf from the beach bar in front of the Royal Hawaiian, giving everything a kind of ancient Polynesian glow. It was a perfect night. The stars sparkled overhead in the tropical sky, the waves lapped against the Waikiki sands, the palm trees did a gentle hula in the breeze, and soft ukulele and steel guitar music played through hidden speakers set in the foliage.

"What a night!" exclaimed Cass. "I feel like a pineapple!"

"Actually, you could stand a haircut, Cass," I agreed. "You're looking a little prickly on top."

"No, no. I mean I feel like one of those drinks that come inside a pineapple with a little paper umbrella sticking out of the top."

"Well, I feel like a mai tai," Jayne told the waiter who had just come to our table. "What do you feel like, Steve?"

"A guava juice," I said.

Jayne, Cass, and I were sitting at an outdoor table, waiting for Raymond and Billy. Everyone had moved into the hotel for the time being, forsaking Billy's house as too dangerous—Cass was in a room down the hall from Jayne and me, and Raymond and Billy were sharing a suite on the top floor. Our drinks came and we were nibbling on a bowl of macadamia nuts, when I noticed Raymond and Billy walking slowly our way. Billy was holding his father's right arm and they both had a weary, shell-shocked look, like two soldiers stumbling off a battlefield. Billy was ashen.

Jayne saw it too. "What's wrong?" she demanded as they sat down.

The waiter had appeared at the same moment. Raymond took a moment to order a double scotch on the rocks and Billy said he would have the same, please. I was getting more and more worried, wondering what new disaster had befallen the unlucky cast and crew of *Hawaiian Wave.*

"Listen, I'm getting scared here," I told them after the waiter left. "What's going on here?"

Raymond looked at me slowly. "I just told Billy about it," he said. "I couldn't keep it from him anymore."

"Told him what?"

"It's my mother," Billy said. He sighed. "She has breast cancer."

"Damn disease! Bea's been battling breast cancer for the past five years," Raymond added. "She didn't want to tell anyone. But I'm afraid she's lost the battle—the cancer's spread throughout her body and the doctors are giving her perhaps two months to live."

"Oh, no!" Jayne cried. "Not Bea! This is just too terrible!"

"Is she in much pain?" I asked.

"She's been awfully brave. You know Bea. She's on a hell of a lot of medication, but it's not pleasant for her, of course. Thank God for Bertrand—that's been some help, as I'm sure you can appreciate."

I blinked, not following this non sequitur. "Bertrand?" I asked cautiously when Raymond didn't explain. "You mean Billy's bodyguard?"

"Of course. He's been sending us packages of *pakalolo* to California. Marijuana's very helpful to cancer patients to ease the nausea and the pain—theoretically it's legal in California for medical use, but the idiots have made it so difficult to get, I just asked Bertrand instead. Billy didn't know about any of this, of course, until I told him just now. His mother didn't want him to know—she was afraid all the worry would distract him from his big chance on this series."

I could only shake my head in numb sorrow. Jayne and I have known and loved Bea Markham for years and years. She's a wonderful woman, and a real show-biz trouper. It was just like her to keep her illness to herself in an attempt to spare others pain, and not to distract Billy from his acting career.

"God, I feel so selfish!" Billy declared in a low, choked voice. "Here I've been worrying about myself, and all the time my mother's been dying! I'm flying back to Los Angeles tonight to see her."

"No, you're not," Raymond told his son firmly. "That's exactly what Bea doesn't want—to interfere with your work. You can come next week for a few days after this episode's finished—not before."

Billy only sighed and shook his head. We sat in silence for a few moments, all of us too disheartened by this news to speak. But despite my sorrow, my brain kept working. After a while I couldn't help but ask a question. "So that's why you came to Hawaii, Ray? Not to take over as producer of the series, but to tell Billy about his mother?"

Raymond nodded. "Of course. I'm not in the mood to produce anything right now, Steve—except maybe a miracle to save Bea."

"I'm so sorry about this, Raymond," I told him. "But tell me something—how did you know that Bertrand had drug connections?"

"Oh, Billy mentioned it once in passing when we were visiting last spring. I managed to get Bertrand alone one afternoon when Billy was on the set and we worked out a system. Bertrand, of course, was under instructions not to say anything about this to Billy."

I knew I should just shut up. Jayne, in fact, was giving me a loaded look from the other side of the table to let detective work go for the moment. But I couldn't quite still my curiosity.

"Did Bertrand send you the *pakalolo* in the mail, Ray?"

"Oh, no. That wouldn't do, not with drug-sniffing dogs in the post office. You're probably disapproving, Steve . . . ."

"Oh, no," I assured him. "It's totally understandable that you'd want to ease her pain in any way possible. I'm only curious how it was done."

"Well, I'm not supposed to talk about it, but we're old, old friends, so I will anyway. There's a pipeline, of course. A way that marijuana travels from Hawaii to the mainland. Mostly it goes in private yachts traveling from here to California. I don't know the exact details, and I'm not sure Bertrand does either—he has a relative, an uncle, I believe, who runs a big *pakalolo* operation from prison. Bertrand got in touch with his uncle and requested this as a personal favor. We had to wait for the next yacht that was sailing to Los Angeles, and then about two months ago someone knocked on our door with a package. It was half a pound of high-grade Hawaiian buds—much more than Bea needs, of course. I feel a little strange having it in the house—hell, I play a police chief on TV! But it's done Bea a lot of good, it really has. It's not only the effect the drug has on her pain—it seems to give her a kind of philosophical detachment so she can look upon dying as something natural that isn't to be feared."

"Yes, I understand," I told Raymond.

And I did understand too. Yet it disturbed me nonetheless, to think of my old friend Ray Markham receiving shipments of illegal drugs coming into California in the holds of pleasure yachts. It also made me wonder about Bertrand, how deeply involved he was with his uncle Davie, who had escaped from prison that morning.

This case was growing more and more complicated. We sat in gloomy silence around the table, nursing our drinks. My mind was going around and around, back and forth from crooked polo to blackmail to drug running, trying to figure out how all these things added up. I wondered if anyone connected with *Hawaiian Wave* just happened to own an oceangoing yacht. Jason Patterson perhaps? Danny Siderman? Keoni? Lance? A lot of money could be made sailing Hawaiian *pakalolo* to the mainland.

We were all lost in our own thoughts—Jayne, Cass, Billy, Raymond, and me—when a small bomb landed on our table. Literally. It landed right next to Cass's pineapple drink, a small round object with a burning fuse. It was a cherry bomb, like the one that had destroyed Billy's mailbox. We all gaped at it in astonishment, unable to move.

"Duck!" I cried.

My shout seemed to break the spell. We dove from our chairs in unison toward the ground. Just before the explosion, I saw a familiar figure running from the bar over the seawall toward the beach.

"That's not the stalker!" Jayne said, lying on the ground next to me.

"No, it's—"

BOOM! The cherry bomb exploded, destroying the languid peace of the Hawaiian night.

chapter 41

Cass and I ran after the fleeing figure on the beach. He was splashing in the edge of the surf, running for all he was worth. We followed behind him, trying to stay on the hard sand for better footing. The cherry-bomb thrower had gotten a head start on us, but fortunately he was overweight and not in much better shape than we were.

We were running in the Diamond Head direction. Suddenly the figure made a dash from the beach toward the elegant old Moana Hotel. We followed him through the dining room to the lobby and then out onto Kalakaua Avenue. We were all too tuckered out to actually run through the hotel—it was more of a fast walk. Just as well, probably, with the security guards around. But on Kalakaua, our bomb thrower seemed to catch his breath and he broke into a run again. We followed as well as we were able, bashing our way through a few startled groups of tourists. For a moment I thought we had lost our fleeing figure, but then I saw him a few dozen yards ahead, getting into a pedicab that was operated by a healthy-looking young man wearing white shorts, a T-shirt, and tennis shoes. The cab pulled away from the curb and headed in an *ewa* direction down Kalakaua.

Cass and I jumped into the back of the next cab in line.

"Follow that pedicab!" I cried, pointing at the fleeing figure of Lloyd Kawelo. "There's a twenty-dollar tip in it for you if you catch him."

Our pedicab driver turned to smile at me. She was an attractive young woman, smooth of face, long of limb.

"Make it a hundred," she said.

"A *hundred?*" I howled.

She shrugged. "I'm working my way through college in economics. I'm going to be an investment banker."

"I sense you'll be a huge success too. All right, a hundred. If you catch him. Now let's get this show on the road!"

The girl set her legs in motion and our bicycle-driven carriage lurched into the evening traffic. We hurried down Kalakaua and hung a left turn on Kapiolani Boulevard, keeping Lloyd in sight most of the time.

"Snazzy way to travel," Cass observed, glancing at our driver's legs.

"Cass! I'm ashamed of you!"

"It's the tropics, Steve. Makes me feel young again. But what I want to know is why in the world Lloyd Kawelo would throw a cherry bomb at us while we're having cocktails."

"I have a few ideas," I muttered. "But let's see what he says when we catch him. I bet he put that cherry bomb in Billy's mailbox as well!"

From Kapiolani, Lloyd's cab made a left onto South King Street and headed toward Chinatown. We managed to keep him in sight, but only barely—we certainly weren't going to catch him at this rate.

"Can't you go any faster?" I asked our girl.

"I'm an intellectual," she replied huffily, "not an athlete."

Just my luck! In Chinatown we followed Bishop to Hotel Street. The traffic was very heavy here, moving at the speed of a clogged artery. Then up ahead, past two cars and a stalled bus, I saw Lloyd jump out of his cab and run down the sidewalk. He ducked into Minnie's, a seedy-looking bar.

"We'll get out here," I told the girl. I pulled a crisp Ben Franklin from my wallet and handed it to her when we were safely on the sidewalk.

"You said a hundred-buck tip," she mentioned. "You owe me twenty-five bucks more for the ride itself."

"Sorry, but I said you'd get a hundred dollars if you caught up with him. Which you didn't, my dear. So count yourself lucky you're getting as much as you are."

She shrugged. "You can't blame a girl for trying."

"Good luck in investment banking," I told her sourly as Cass and I took off down the sidewalk toward Minnie's Bar.

The bar was dark and run-down and smelled of cheap beer and decades of stale cigarettes. A few desolate-looking souls were scattered at the Formica tables, a few more on stools at the bar itself. Some were Chinese, others haoles—but none were tourists. Hawaiian music was playing on the jukebox, and everyone at Minnie's looked as though they had been there a long, long time. I sensed it was not the sort of establishment where drinks were served with paper umbrellas.

"I don't see him," Cass said.

I didn't either. We wandered through the dim, smoky haze inspecting weary faces, but none of them belonged to Lloyd Kawelo. At last I turned toward the bartender, a wizened old Chinese woman with a wrinkled face.

"A middle-aged Hawaiian man just ran in here," I said. "Where did he go?"

She shook her head. "Didn't see no one."

"It was Lloyd Kawelo—I'm sure you know him. He's a well-known local musician."

"Don't know no Lloyd Kawelo," she insisted. "Didn't see nobody either. What are you fellas drinking?"

I studied the old woman, certain that she was not telling me the truth. "I have to tell you, I'm a good friend of Lieutenant Tony Chen's," I pressed not particularly truthfully. "I'm sure you know the lieutenant here in Chinatown, and I bet you don't want him looking into your business too closely."

Her face only became more stubborn. "I don't break no laws, so the police don't scare me. Now, either order a drink or get out."

I turned to Cass and gave it a final try. "Well, I think we're going to have to phone Tony and have him close this place down. I'm sure there must be some health code violations here. Maybe even the fire code as well . . ."

"All right! Enough!" said a low voice behind us.

Cass and I turned to face Lloyd a few inches away. He was glowering at us angrily. "This is my auntie you're trying to hassle, and I don't like that," he said. "That's right—there's a Chinese part of my family, and I'm proud of it."

"You should be," I told him. "But that still doesn't give you any right to terrorize people with cherry bombs. What's going on, Lloyd?"

He sighed. "You wouldn't understand. You're rich and famous! What do you care for a poor island musician who's trying to get a record deal?"

"Why don't you try me? Maybe I'm more understanding than you think."

"Okay, okay!" he said with resignation. "Let's grab a table and talk. Maybe I'll tell why I did it."

"You'll tell us everything," I insisted. "It's your only chance."

"Okay," he agreed. "If you're ready to listen, I'm ready to talk."

chapter 42

We sat around a dim, tired-looking table that had cigarette burns on the surface. Cass brought us three cups of coffee from the bar while I began the grilling of Lloyd Kawelo.

"You got to understand, Steve—I'm nearly fifty years old," Lloyd said, a complaining note in his voice. "I don't like to tell people that, because with music, it helps to be young. I got my first group together when I was fifteen, so I've been playing music, like, forty-five years, you dig?"

I did some basic arithmetic in my head. "Thirty-five years, Lloyd. But, yeah, that's a long time."

He shrugged. "Well, I never did too good in school. Music was everything for me. I was very poor. Me and my family, all my friends—we had nothing, you know. Music was the only way I could think of to do something with my life. And I've worked at it for a hell of a long time. Trying to get a recording contract. Trying to get a hit on the radio and make something out of my life. And that's why that little brat . . . that spoiled, whining kid from California who grew up in a big mansion and never had to do anything for himself—"

"You're talking about Billy Markham."

"You bet I'm talking about Billy Markham! You can't understand what a huge break it was for me to finally have my music on a show like *Hawaiian Wave*. I mean, national exposure. The big time, at last! No more playing crummy bars in Pearl City! I'm a guy who's paid his dues, and this was finally the payoff. And then Billy goes and ruins it for me. Like I told you the other day, he convinced Danny that my songs were no good for the show. So I guess I snapped a little, that's all."

Cass and I studied Lloyd across the table as we sipped our coffee. I should say for the record that I feel a good deal of empathy for the Lloyd Kawelos in the world—all the talented people, musicians and actors, who spend their lives trying to make it in show business and never quite succeed. It's a hard profession that's neither kind nor just, and where luck—or call it fate— often determines the roll of the dice. But still, that's no justification for committing crimes.

"Lloyd, I'm sorry Danny decided not to use your material," I told him. "It's a tough break, and maybe you'll have better luck down the line. But it doesn't give you any right to terrorize people with firecrackers. You could have done some serious damage with that cherry bomb you threw at our table this evening."

He groaned. "I'm sorry, man, I wasn't trying to hurt you or your friends. It was that little bastard Billy Markham I was after!"

"You really hate him that much?"

"Your damn right I hate him!"

"And you're trying to get revenge?"

"Do you blame me?"

"Blame isn't up to me," I said evasively. "I'm simply trying to understand you. Tell me, Lloyd, why did you kill Sam Fitzgerald?"

Lloyd blinked at me and slowly shook his head. "What are you talking about?"

"You lent Sam that defective scuba gear, Lloyd. You made certain that when he went underwater he wouldn't be coming up again anytime soon. What I want to know is why?"

He continued to shake his head. "Whoa, you got me all wrong, Steve. I didn't do anything to that scuba gear. Why should I want to kill Sam? It's Billy Markham I wouldn't mind seein' dead!"

"Once you let hatred take over your life, Lloyd, it has a way of destroying a lot of things. So let's move on to Dick Schiller . . . why did you kill him?"

Lloyd Kawelo laughed nervously. "Hold on a moment. Man, I never killed anyone, and I don't want to either. All I did was put a cherry bomb in Billy's mailbox and throw a big scare into you guys tonight at the Royal Hawaiian. That's all I'm guilty of, I swear to God.''

"You didn't kill Sam or Dick?"

"No way, José!" he assured me. There's apparently no way to get away from badly overworked clichés.

We went over and over this ground. I spent nearly a half hour working on Lloyd, trying to get him to confess, and when I ran out of breath, Cass took over, telling Lloyd how much he sympathized with a musician trying to make it—Cass even recounted his own saga in Hollywood, how he had tried to be a cowboy star in the westerns. But we got nowhere, and at the end I was starting to believe that Lloyd was telling the truth. He was a firecracker terrorist and a fool, but he was not a killer.

"This case is an awful mess," I told Lloyd. "If you didn't kill Sam or Dick, do you know who did?"

He shook his head morosely. "I don't have a clue. I wish I did."

"Tell me about Jason Patterson. Do you know him at all?"

"Not really. I know who he is, but I never traveled in that rich haole crowd. Keoni knows him pretty well, I guess. Personally, I wouldn't give Patterson the time of day. A friend of mine used to work on his yacht and had some stories to tell about how snotty the guy was. He treated people that worked for him like dirt."

"Wait a second! Jason Patterson has a yacht? I didn't know that."

"*Had* a yacht. This was maybe ten years ago, before that Melanie babe. When Jason was married to his first wife. It was a pretty nice sailboat, fifty feet, fancy cabin, slept six. A rich man's boat—but I guess old Jason had to sell it when he started having money problems."

"You seem to know a lot about Jason Patterson."

Lloyd shrugged. "Well, I got all this secondhand from Keoni. I went out on the boat once with Keoni a few months ago. We spent a day sailing around the windward side of the island."

"Hold on . . . you're saying that Keoni has this yacht now?"

"Didn't I tell you that? Yeah, Keoni bought it from Jason three or four years ago."

"Keoni had that much money? A fifty-foot sailboat sounds like an expensive toy!"

"I guess so. You know Keoni—he has a way of charming his way into everything. He and Jason had some kind of deal."

"Some kind of deal!" I repeated, wondering. "You know anything about it?"

Lloyd shook his head. "Keoni can get silent very fast when you ask him things."

"I've discovered that too," I agreed. "Well, you've given me a lot to think about, Lloyd. By the way, what's the name of this yacht?"

"*Oahu Flower,*" Lloyd said. "It's docked at the Ala Wai Yacht Harbor, pretty close to the Ilikai Hotel. A nice boat. You should take a look at it sometime."

"I will indeed," I assured Lloyd, wondering to myself exactly what kind of Oahu flower Jason and Keoni had in mind.

chapter 43

Cass and I flagged down a cab on Hotel Street to take us back to Waikiki—a real cab this time, with a gas-burning engine rather than a college girl to propel us forward. However, before we reached the Royal Hawaiian, I changed destinations. I gave the driver, an elderly Filipino, the address of the Patterson antebellum mansion near Diamond Head.

"What's up, boss? You want to play a little late-night polo?" Cass asked.

"What I want to play, Cass, is more like truth or consequences." Frankly, I was frustrated. I was tempted to beat some answers out of Jason Patterson—with a polo mallet if necessary.

The posh neighborhood around the Patterson mansion was dark and quiet. The TV crew had departed, all the trucks and cables and trailers were gone, leaving behind only the deep hush of money, and the scent of plumeria flowers wafting on the gentle evening breeze. I had the taxi let us off at the gate, paid the driver, and then Cass and I walked up the driveway to the house, our shoes clacking on the pavement. There wasn't a light on anywhere, and the house was silent as a tomb.

Cass and I walked up to the impressively large front door and I rang the doorbell. I could hear a bell chiming deep within the house. After a moment I rang again, but no one came to open up.

"The house almost feels abandoned," I said. "Let's check the stables."

We walked around to the back and found Jason's polo ponies

in their stalls. The horses neighed and stomped their hooves when they saw us.

"You know, Steve, these horses are acting like they're hungry. Maybe they haven't been fed tonight. Let me ask 'em," Cass said.

"You speak horse talk, do you?"

"Sort of. Well, I've got horse sense."

Cass, bless his soul, did a little neighing, and they seemed to answer him in return, knowing an old cowboy when they saw one.

"Nope," Cass said. "The poor things haven't eaten." He found some hay stacked in a corner and spent a few minutes throwing flakes of alfalfa into the stalls.

This was seeming more and more mysterious. Cass and I walked back toward the main house and stared into a dark downstairs window, trying to figure out what was going on.

"Shall we?" I asked.

"Commit a felony, you mean?"

"It wouldn't be the first time we've done a little B and E."

Cass found a shovel that had been left in a flower bed and used it to smash a downstairs window. It wasn't the subtle method of B and E, but it worked. He took off his gaudy Hawaiian shirt and used it as a rag to brush off the broken glass and then we climbed inside the darkened living room.

"Anyone home?" Cass called.

"Cass, if they didn't hear you breaking that window, they're not going to hear you call."

"Well, I'm just trying to be polite, Steve. Respect a person's privacy."

"Of course," I agreed.

We spent the next half hour searching the house but finding very little. The electricity had been turned off, perhaps for lack of payment, which did not help our task. In the downstairs den I found an answering machine—dormant, of course, from lack of electric power.

"Let's take this," I said to Cass. "Maybe we'll find something interesting, a message we need to hear."

It was about two hours later when we plugged the machine into an outlet in our Royal Hawaiian suite. Cass and I had had to walk halfway to Waikiki before we managed to hail a taxi, but that's neither here nor there—just part of the dedication that goes into being an amateur sleuth. But it all paid off, more or less.

Jayne, Cass, and I gathered around the machine. There were three messages on the tape. The first two were from creditors—the telephone company and American Express—both demanding payment for long-overdue bills. The third was from Wong's Travel Service, a woman's voice saying that she had succeeded in making a reservation for the Pattersons at the Hong Kong Grand Hyatt, a nice room that was only 3,850 Hong Kong dollars per night.

"Hong Kong!" Jayne exclaimed. "They're returning to Melanie's homeland apparently! But how can they afford the Grand Hyatt if they can't pay their phone bill?"

I was wondering the same thing myself, and would have asked them. But they were gone, gone, gone.

In the morning Jayne phoned Lieutenant Chen to inform him that the Pattersons had apparently taken off to Hong Kong. This wasn't a crime, of course—no one had accused the Pattersons of anything. But the lieutenant thanked Jayne and agreed it looked suspicious. He said he would check with the airport and find out exactly when they had departed. But he called back an hour later to say it was very odd, but the Pattersons had not been booked on any flight, to China or elsewhere, and that the customs bureau at the airport had no record of them leaving the country. *Ergo,* they were still most likely on Oahu.

Stranger and stranger, I thought. Then in the afternoon I got a bright idea. Maybe finding the answering machine with such convenient information on the tape had been designed to throw us off. Perhaps the Pattersons weren't heading toward Hong Kong at all, but somewhere else entirely. I phoned Wong's Travel Service. "This is Wong's—the wight way to travel," said a playfully chipper voice. She introduced herself as Shelley. She looked through her computer files for me and said that yes, Jason and Melanie Patterson had indeed made a reservation for the Hong Kong Grand Hyatt, though they had not booked a plane flight to China—at least, not with her—nor had they actually paid the necessary deposit for their expensive room.

More and more suspicious.

I decided to phone Keoni, but he wasn't at home, nor was he to be found at his recording studio. Sometimes it seems like the whole world is out to lunch. But I did get a young man at the recording studio who remembered me from the party there, and he suggested that I might find Keoni at the Ala Wai Yacht Harbor on his sailboat, *Oahu Flower.*

I left Jayne and Cass at the hotel—Jayne had an appointment with the hairdresser, and with things being the way they were, I didn't want her to be alone. I took a taxi from the hotel to the yacht basin, which was only a few minutes away. It was a bright, lovely afternoon. I made my way along the docks, glancing enviously at all the lovely boats, huge cabin cruisers and oceangoing yachts, many from distant parts of the world. There was the *Down Under* from Sydney, *Casa Mia* from Majorca, *Sir Toby Belch* from Southampton, England. A good many of the boats were from California; some had for sale signs on them; Walter Earle told me once that a lot of California couples spend years building their dream yacht, and then sail off at last into the great blue yonder— only to find that life on a sailing ship is cramped and difficult and not quite what they imagined. As a result, a lot of California marriages end in Hawaii and boats are put up for sale.

I walked toward the Ilikai, which was one of the first huge hotels to mar the Waikiki skyline in the early sixties. Lloyd had told me this was the part of the huge yacht harbor where I might find Keoni's boat. At first I didn't see anything, just more expensive yachts. Then I saw it, *Oahu Flower,* a sleek, long sailboat that was white as a dove. Unfortunately, the boat wasn't in its berth—it was motoring out of the channel, the sails furled, gas fumes rising in its wake. Keoni was on the deck, along with Jason and Melanie Patterson. The Pattersons, I noticed, were dressed very properly in white yachting clothes—broke or not, they weren't the types to be inappropriately dressed for any occasion. Keoni was more casually attired in a T-shirt and blue-jean cutoffs.

"Hey!" I cried. "Stop!"

But the wind was against me, and probably they wouldn't

have stopped anyway. I ran along the dock to the very end. It was extremely frustrating. I could see the *Oahu Flower* in mid-channel now, not yet past the buoys. Keoni was unfurling the sails, which were flapping in the stiffening breeze.

"Hey!" I cried again. But it was useless.

Then I glanced down from the end of the dock to the water below. A young man was straddling a windsurfer, the sail lying in the water. I walked down a ladder and climbed onto the back of his board.

"Hey, dude!" the young guy cried in protest. "You can't get on this—it's only meant for one person. Me."

"Too bad," I told him. "This is an emergency. I'll give you a hundred dollars to follow that yacht!"

chapter 44

I thought we'd be able to catch up with the *Oahu Flower* quickly, before it sailed out of the channel into the open ocean, but the yacht was sleek and fast—a beautiful boat, really—and when Keoni raised the mainsail and set the jib in front, the fifty-foot yacht was like a polo pony that had suddenly been given its head. The boat fairly leapt forward through the swells and out into the wild blue yonder. I watched the three figures on the deck getting smaller on the horizon.

"Can't you go any faster?" I cried.

"Hey, man, like it's astonishing we're making any speed at all."

My chauffeur was deeply tanned with long sun-bleached hair, a dumb-looking earring in his left earlobe, and a tattoo on his right arm that said JERRY GARCIA LIVES. I was dressed in tan slacks, Gucci loafers, and a blue polo shirt, all of which clothes were soggy at the moment as I straddled the end of the windsurfer board, my legs dangling in the water. At least the Hawaiian water is warm, almost blood temperature, which made my situation a little more comfortable. As we sailed out from the yacht harbor, a postcard vista of Waikiki opened up on my left—or, I should say, the portside—with the crater of Diamond Head straight ahead, and the interior mountains of Oahu rising up into its usual shroud of clouds. The great hotels lined the famous beach like a string of jewels, separated from me by a ribbon of blue water. I could even see the familiar pink shape of the Royal Hawaiian, where I longed to be. There are always lots of boats, of course, cruising and bobbing off the coast of Waikiki. Sailboats, other windsurfers, even a few floating restaurants. We sailed past several catamaran tourist boats crammed full of people with cameras—

several people waved, which was friendly of them. Unfortunately, the boat I was interested in, the *Oahu Flower,* was headed straight out into the open ocean and getting farther and farther away.

"Man, I'm open to just about anything," my chauffeur remarked, "but this is ridiculous."

I had to agree. I was about to suggest we turn around and head back to land, when I noticed a speedboat about twenty yards ahead that had stalled momentarily in the water. A large man with a potbelly was pouring gin and vermouth into a silver shaker while his wife held the boat steady; the engine was sputtering in neutral; apparently they had stopped to perform this delicate operation associated with the cocktail hour.

"Ahoy, there!" I called. Do sailors still talk like eighteenth-century pirates? "Can I bum a ride?"

The man and woman glanced my way. "Look, it's Steve Allen!" the woman cried. "Aren't you Steve Allen?" There are times to hide one's celebrity, and times to flaunt it. This, I sensed, was a flaunting moment.

"I am indeed, madam," I assured her.

"Why, we used to watch your show all the time! Never missed it for anything. Did we, honey?"

"I'm your biggest fan," the man assured me. "Used to laugh my head off at your man Howie Morris."

"Howie Morris worked with Sid Caesar," I said. "Maybe you're talking about Don Knotts?"

"That's right," the man said. "Sorry about the mistake."

"Look," I said pleasantly, "I'm in a bit of a bind here. I need to catch up with that yacht over there. Do you think you could give me a lift?"

"Can we ever!" declared the man, shaking his pitcher of martinis. "Marge, better get another glass and some olives—won't the guys back home be surprised when I tell 'em about this!"

He was Ernie. He and Marge were from Walla Walla, Washington, and had rented a powerful outboard for the week they were on Oahu—two huge outboard engines, in fact, at the rear of a spiffy Plexiglas shell that drove through the water like a Cadillac going down the highway. Nothing, however, would persuade Ernie and Marge to set their craft in motion before I had been poured a special martini in a frosted glass from their ice chest. I sensed it would be faster to acquiesce and simply let my cocktail spill subtly into the Great Drink below my feet. Still, the process took nearly five annoying minutes, and by the time they had done their bartender duties, the *Oahu Flower* had disappeared into the horizon, joining an indistinct regalia of other craft that were darting about into the blur of the lowering afternoon sun.

"Don't worry, Steverino—we'll catch her," Ernie assured me. He gunned the two engines and we roared through the waves. My martini, I'm glad to say, spilled quite easily without any conscious attempt on my part. Ernie passed me a pair of binoculars and I scanned the horizon for the *Oahu Flower*. The problem was, there must have been fifty big sailboats in the water and to me, a landlubber of the first degree, they all looked pretty much the same. We were maybe a mile offshore now, far enough from Oahu so that the hotels lining Waikiki had become indistinct. The ocean swells had become larger as we buzzed about the water inspecting the other boats. By the way, it's very difficult to make effective use of binoculars if you're bouncing over the waves.

Finally mine focused on one of the yachts that seemed more familiar than the rest and I actually saw Keoni at the wheel. The *Oahu Flower* was dead in the water, its sails flapping. This seemed odd but I scanned with the binoculars and soon saw what was going on. The *Oahu Flower* had pulled up next to a larger craft, a very fancy cabin cruiser, and Jason and Melanie Patterson were climbing up a ladder from Keoni's boat onto it. As I watched in frustration, Jason and Melanie threw a line loose, the two boats separated, and the cabin cruiser roared away with the Pattersons on its deck.

"Can you catch up with that big cabin cruiser?" I shouted to Ernie over the roar of the outboard engines, passing him the binoculars.

"Hmm," he said, studying the situation. "The *Maui Wowie*—interesting name. But I'm afraid that's one slick boat, Steverino. It's a lot faster than us."

"You can't catch it? Then you'd better drop me off on the *Oahu Flower.*"

"You'll be okay here in the middle of the ocean?"

"Just fine, Ernie," I told him optimistically.

Keoni was surprised to see me, to say the least. And I sensed the surprise was not a pleasant one.

"Steve! What the hell are you doing all the way out here?" he asked as Ernie pulled alongside and I was climbing from one craft to another.

"I was going to ask you the same question, Keoni," I replied, waving good-bye to Ernie and Marge. The couple from Walla Walla raised their martini glasses in our direction in a kind of wet, nautical salute and then roared off in a haze of gasoline fumes and enough noise to frighten the fish for half a mile around.

"Man, I hate people like that!" Keoni said with a sigh. "They have no respect for the sea."

"At least Ernie and Marge aren't killers, as far as I know," I mentioned. "Now, tell me—what were you doing helping Jason and Melanie get away?"

Keoni flashed a thin smile. "Get away? I don't know what you're talking about. I just gave them a ride to their friend's cabin cruiser. There's no crime in that."

"But it's suspicious," I said, "particularly when the Pattersons are fleeing a mountain of bad debts and the rendezvous with the cabin cruiser is set for a mile offshore."

Keoni squinted at Oahu, hazy in the distance. "More like five miles, Steve. And I don't care if it's suspicious or not."

"Keoni, it's time for you to stop playing games and tell me the truth. It's the only thing that can save you."

His thin smile grew broader and turned into a laugh. "Save me!" he cried ironically. "And what about you, Steve? If you think I'm a killer, aren't you a little worried to be alone with me five miles from shore?"

"No," I told him. "Not a bit."

Normally, I think of myself as a truthful person. But I was lying now.

chapter 45

We were drifting, the sails flapping loose, as Keoni began to talk. It hadn't been easy to bring the handsome young actor to this point of candor, but once he began, he surprised me by jumping right to the heart of things.

"Okay, I'll tell you my problem. Someone is blackmailing me," he announced.

I raised a skeptical eyebrow, one of my specialties. "Who?"

"I don't know, naturally. They want a lot of money, fifty thousand dollars, and they want it fast. I could come up with it, maybe, if I sold the *Oahu Flower* and maybe sold my recording studio as well, but I refuse to give in to the bastards, Steve. I don't care if I go down." This seemed like a poor choice of words in the circumstances, but I didn't want to interrupt.

"I did some stupid things when I was a kid—that's what they have on me. You've got to understand what it was like when I was growing up. I lived with my grandma and she could just barely put food on the table. So I worked as soon as anyone would hire me. Odd jobs, you know. None of them paid very well because nobody on our part of the island had a lot of cash to spare. So when I got an offer to work as an assistant groom at a stable full of polo ponies, I jumped at the chance."

"You went to work for Jason Patterson?"

"That's right. He was my Little League coach and he asked me one day if I could help him out. I said sure. So I started going to his house every day after school and all day Saturday and Sunday. I even went when I wasn't being paid. I wanted to be a jockey when I grew up. I even started smoking, hoping it would stunt my growth." Keoni paused, but I remained silent.

"So one day right before a match, Mr. Patterson—that's what I called him then—Mr. Patterson comes and asks me to put some powder in the horses' feed. He said it was a vitamin but I knew what it was. I . . . well, I was doing drugs then, and even selling some, just to my friends. I know what you're going to say, but let me go on. I did what Mr. Patterson told me to but I didn't give quite as much to the horses as I was supposed to. I took what I hadn't used and sold it to this girl in my school who liked to get high."

"Angela Schwartz?" I asked.

He looked at me, startled I should know her name. "That's right. Angie. She was beautiful but pretty wild. She always had enough money to buy my goods, you know, and for me it seemed like an easy way to make a few bucks on the side. I was just so dumb. I knew that the stuff I was giving to the horses was PCP—when people take it, it's a kind of intense psychedelic, you know, but for horses, it just makes them relax. Mr. Patterson was fixing his horses, you understand, to deliberately lose his matches—just like in the script of the show. The stuff he was using was pure and much stronger than anything going around at school. Angie took all of it at one time, and it killed her. They said her heart just stopped beating. It was my fault—I'm not trying to make excuses. But I swear, it hadn't crossed my mind until that moment that I was doing anything so—so dangerous.

"I never went back to the stables. I couldn't face Mr. Patterson. I assumed he'd read about the girl in the paper and put two and two together. I quit selling drugs, quit using them too. It was the best thing that could ever have happened to me. But somebody had to die for me to get my head turned around. I didn't see Jason Patterson again for years, not until I was a big-shot actor and our positions were reversed. Now I was the one with the money and he was the one who was broke. I guess there was a sort of an ugly bond between us though. I knew his secret, that he fixed races. And he knew mine, that I had sold drugs that had killed a girl."

"He's the one blackmailing you?"

Keoni shook his head. "He wouldn't dare. Knowing each other's worst secret, we sort of cancel each other out. I went to him, of course, just to make sure, but I believed him when he denied it. He was totally shocked—it's one of the reasons he's on the run now, afraid that somebody out there knows what he did. Poor guy, he's always wanted to be so posh and respectable. He couldn't stand the humiliation if his polo buddies ever found out what he'd done."

"What about this yacht?"

"I bought it from him. He was desperate for cash, and as a kid I'd always admired the *Oahu Flower*. I guess it was a kind of symbol for me of being rich. I got a real good deal on it and I've been paying it off in installments, three thousand dollars a week—it's what's keeping Jason and Melanie more or less afloat."

"That's a lot of money for you to pay out, Keoni."

He shrugged. "Well, I earn fifteen grand an episode on the show, so it's not beyond my means. I guess I've even enjoyed flaunting my wealth a little in Jason's face."

"And why did you help him bail out just now?"

"Well, that's a little complicated. He phoned me two nights ago, said his gambling debts and all his other debts as well were totally out of hand. There were some Mafia types after him for a bit of a double-cross he pulled—*not* fixing a certain race. So he said he'd decided he and Melanie better disappear, and he asked me to help. He was only asking for a ride out of town, so to speak."

"Who owns the cabin cruiser you took him to?"

"The *Maui Wowie*? Some rich trust-fund hippies he knows, Maya and Jupiter. Maya's father owns half the oil fields in Texas and she's never had much challenge in her life except how to amuse herself. So they thought it would be a temporary cure for boredom to help Jason and Melanie get away."

As Keoni talked, he reset the sail, took hold of the wheel, and we were headed back toward Oahu on a long tack. The wind had come up and the boat was leaning hard to the starboard side. But my mind wasn't on sailing. I was inclined to believe what Keoni was telling me since it fit in with a lot of other things I had suspected or found out. But the blackmail motif troubled me, and I decided to press him to see if his story bent.

"So how did this supposed blackmailer contact you, Keoni?"
I asked. "A cryptic note with the letters cut out from old newspapers? Or was it a disguised voice on the telephone?"

Keoni smiled thinly. "Yeah, a voice on the telephone, actually.
Electronically altered, I think . . . you don't believe me? But as it
happens, I can prove it. When the call came, I was sitting in my
living room next to my answering machine. I pressed the record
button and got the whole thing on tape."

"Very clever of you. But, of course, Keoni, you're an actor—
you could have easily had one of your actor friends make the call.
You even run a recording studio, so you have all the equipment
to disguise a voice."

"But why should I do that?"

"To make it seem like you're one of the victims in this rotten
mess rather than the victimizer. Maybe nobody's blackmailing you,
Keoni—I think you're the blackmailer. I think you're blackmailing
Lance."

"Lance!" he cried. "What are you talking about?"

"Apparently he made some blue movies a long time ago and
you're threatening to expose him if he doesn't pay up."

To my surprise, Keoni laughed. "Pay up! Now, that's really
a hoot! You know, it doesn't surprise me a bit, actually, that Lance
would do anything for a buck—make porno movies, or whatever.
But it would be useless to blackmail him."

"Why's that?"

"Because he's broke. You can't squeeze blood out of a stone."

"What do you mean broke? I've seen his house, his car."

"Well, that's just the problem. He's living way beyond his
means. You know Lance. He has to impress everybody, show how
superior he is to all us common folk. I'm not putting him down,
but the guy has all the usual vices, and then some. Wine, women,
and song—and fast horses and cars as well. I know from Jason
that he has about twenty thousand dollars of gambling debts. So
someone would sure have to be an idiot to try to blackmail him."

I'd been listening with such interest that I hadn't noticed
how hard the wind had begun to blow. There were whitecaps on
the water and we were suddenly riding on swells that were alarmingly high. Keoni hadn't been concentrating on his sailing, but he

seemed to notice the changing conditions about the same time that I did.

"Damn! Man, we'd better get the sails in. I'm afraid I'm going to have to ask you for some help. If you could just go out and pull in the jib, that sail in the very front, I'll hold us on course."

I looked dubiously to where he was pointing. By this time the sailboat was flying along at a definite tilt to starboard, heaving and nose-diving at the same time. I could see that I was going to have trouble just walking out to the end of the prow, let alone doing anything once I got there.

"How about I steer and you bring the sail in?" I shouted over the sound of the wind and the boat slapping against the water.

"I'm sorry, Steve, but it has to be you," Keoni said. "I know this boat. You'll be all right. But if you did fall overboard, I could swing around and pick you up. If I fell in, on the other hand, you'd be sunk in a big way. You probably wouldn't be able to get into the yacht basin, much less come around to get me. You might even capsize . . . look, you got me talking and I wasn't paying attention, and now I really need your help. Just hold on to the lifeline and walk along the port side, over there, the high side. I'm going to turn into the wind. When you get up there, I'll yell and release the sail. You pull it down as fast as you can and tie it. Got that?"

I didn't like the idea, but I made my way out to the forward sail as quickly as I could, which is to say, very slowly and very carefully. Water sprayed over the side every few seconds, and the deck was bucking like a rodeo bronco. When I glanced to starboard, I saw the lifeline—the rope railing, that is—was actually in the water. Not a good sign. The boat was at such a tilt that it looked to me as if we could capsize any second.

When I got to the jib, Keoni yelled, "Ready, Steve?"

"Ready as I'll every be!" I shouted back, and he released the sail, which immediately started flapping wildly in the wind. Before I could get hold of it and start to pull it in, there was a tremendous blow to my left side, and I realized that I was airborne. I hit the water hard and sank straight down.

* * *

When falling into heavy seas it's hard to tell which way is up, so I tried to relax and let myself float to the top rather than attempt to kick toward what looked like the sky—and it worked. I found myself bobbing on the surface like a cork. The good news was that Hawaiian sea waters are warm and buoyant; the bad news was that from the top of a swell I could see the *Oahu Flower* sailing away. I couldn't help feeling a sense of déjà vu. I'd landed in the water off Manhattan Island the year I finally got a chance to play Superman. And then there was the time Cass and I were thrown overboard from a transcontinental luxury liner into the middle of the Atlantic Ocean.

"Come on, turn around, Keoni!" I willed. It was crazy, but the water had cleared my head and suddenly a lot of things had come together in my mind. I was ninety percent certain Keoni was innocent, and maybe eighty percent sure I knew who the real killer was.

"So turn the damn boat around, Keoni, and show me you're innocent!" I said aloud.

It was at that moment that I saw something that riveted my attention—a dorsal fin at about thirty yards off. Anywhere in the world such a sight translates as *shark*. I felt instant terror.

Actually, when I saw the fin I had *two* primary reactions. The one, as I say, was a terrible chilling fear. The other was a wave of deep philosophical disgust at the unfairness at what I assumed was about to happen.

I floated in the water, watching the dorsal fin coming closer and the *Oahu Flower* sail away. It was a moment, certainly, to test one's natural optimism.

chapter 46

Jayne slept alone that night in the huge bed at the Royal Hawaiian Hotel. Being a consummate actress, my wife gave no sign of worry when the operator gave the wake-up call at six A.M. It was to be the very last day of shooting on our episode, "The Ride of Your Life," wrapping up the climactic polo scenes and final denouement of the crime. Jayne ordered a huge stack of pancakes from room service, along with scrambled egg substitutes and a bowl of fruit.

Cass phoned while she was getting dressed. Her smiling facade faltered only briefly as she listened to his news. "Oh, dear!" she cried. "Billy's in the hospital? What in the world happened?" Then, as she listened further, she actually laughed. "Oh, my Lord, what a farce! Well, Billy will probably recover . . . no, you don't say? How extraordinary!"

It wasn't until Cass asked if he could speak to me that it occurred to her that I wasn't just absent at the moment but might be in some sort of trouble. "I thought he might be with you," she said, "although I was worried."

"With me?" Cass said. "I have no idea where he is."

"Do you think we ought to call the police?"

"I don't know," Cass said. "What do you want me to do?"

"Maybe the best thing to do at the moment is nothing," Jayne said. "The limo will be coming in a few minutes to pick me up to take me to the set. Steve knows about our schedule, so maybe he'll just show up there. Maybe he didn't want to call in the middle of the night to wake me."

Jayne rode in the backseat up the Windward Coast. The sky had turned dark and cloudy, the wind was still blowing hard, and it looked as if Oahu might see rain. Finally, the driver arrived at Mokuleia and turned off to the old polo field.

There was a sense of excitement in the air. The parking lot was packed with the cars of all the extras—society people, polo club people, all of them enjoying this opportunity to appear in the crowd scene of a popular TV show. Jayne had never seen so many women in silk, so many men sporting the tropical suits and hats we all imagine will magically transform us into a Robert Redford. Most people in the crowd carried umbrellas, but this did not diminish the festivity of the occasion. The polo ponies were circling the field with their riders. Edgar was setting up an elaborate crane shot, standing in the middle of a group of grips and technicians, barking orders. Danny was pacing nervously, glancing at his watch, most likely wondering how much this extravagant crowd scene was going to cost.

As Jayne stood watching, she saw Cass pull up in Billy's rented Impala. She smiled when she saw Cass open the passenger door and offer a gallant hand to Dottie Konich, the travel agent from Akron, Ohio. Dottie was wearing a Hawaiian-print dress, sported a new suntan, and looked very relaxed and happy by Cass's side.

As Jayne continued to watch, six police cars as well as two dark blue unmarked police vehicles circled the field. From one of the unmarked cars Jason and Melanie Patterson emerged and stood unhappily between two burly cops. From the other unmarked car Jayne saw her loving husband—yours truly—step out, joined by Lieutenant Tony Chen and Keoni.

Yes, I was alive. The fin in the water had turned out to be that of the most friendly dolphin imaginable, not a shark. As for Keoni . . . well, I'm not a guy to spoil a denouement, but I will say that my new friend, the dolphin, even allowed me to rest on his back until the *Oahu Flower* pulled around and picked me up.

Jayne came over and kissed me on the cheek. "What happened?" she asked.

"I'll tell you later."

"Ready for the final scene?"

"Yep."

* * *

Edgar had naturally planned to shoot the final polo match from different angles with three separate camera crews. When everything was ready, the first assistant director got on his bullhorn, told everyone to be quiet and gather around. It was quite a group, the cast and crew of *Hawaiian Wave*. Susan stood next to her friend Elisabeth, both young women looking particularly lovely this morning. Lance was by himself not far from Susan, looking his usual blond, beach-boy self—a perfect television face, I thought as I watched him, as immobile and plastic as a mask. Danny Siderman stood not far from Edgar, talking with his wife, Louise, who towered above him. An odd couple, as we say, but I saw her lean over and whisper something in Danny's ear, probably a funny comment, because he suddenly grinned like a happy little boy. He said something back to Louise that made her laugh in return; I suspected they loved each other in their way.

Keoni moved closer to the camera, his darkly handsome island face set in a frowning pout. A uniformed policeman stood close to his shoulder. I continued to scan the crowd. An imposing gentleman in a voluminous white Nehru shirt caught my eye. It was Bertrand Suuanu looking bigger than life, like some ancient Polynesian king—returned from whatever dark visit he had made to his uncle Davie, the *pakalolo* king who had escaped from prison. There was certainly more to Bertrand than met the eye.

Jason and Melanie, who did not look nearly as aristocratic in comparison, were not far from the second unit camera, still in the company of their husky police escort. Beyond the circle of actors and crew stood the stuntmen and the polo riders with their horses. And farther still, the extras waited in the bleachers for something to happen, talking among themselves. I had heard no one remark on the extraordinary number of uniformed officers guarding the circumference of the polo field. Perhaps everyone assumed that with the number of accidental deaths connected with this episode, the police presence was necessary in some general way. And they were right, of course—it was. I saw Lieutenant Chen standing not far from Cass and Dottie. The lieutenant caught my eye and nodded.

Edgar had raised a bullhorn and was starting to speak.

"Ladies and gentlemen, may I have your attention, please? You may have noticed that William Markham is not among us this morning. He had a small accident last night and, alas, it has been necessary to put him in the hospital."

There was a stir, for this news had taken nearly everybody by surprise. The crew had assumed Billy was simply late coming from his dressing room. Keoni looked at me questioningly. Lance scrutinized the assembly as though Billy must be hiding somewhere, about to pop out and say *boo*. Susan looked at Jayne as if begging her to be gentle. Edgar waited until the attention was focused back his way.

"After considering my options, I've decided to go ahead with the shoot originally scheduled for today. Mack is not a vital character in this scene. With very few changes in dialogue and action, Buddy and Pete can fill in for Mack and bring this story to an appropriate conclusion, I think. Please look carefully at the changes being passed out to you. These apply only to the main characters, of course—those of you from the polo club need not concern yourselves. We're going to start with scene eighty-three . . . places, everybody!"

"Just a minute, Edgar!" I called. "Before we finish the last sequence, I think it best we discuss a matter of two murders."

Edgar turned my way in astonishment.

"I beg your pardon, Mr. Allen. If you are referring to the unfortunate deaths of Mr. Fitzgerald and Mr. Schiller, that is a very sad matter, true—but we cannot delay the filming of an artistic endeavor because of personal matters. Now, places everyone. . . ."

"Hold on!" I said more insistently. "You can shoot this scene after we catch our killer. We'll all be able to concentrate much better on make-believe, I think, after we deal with some urgent real-life problems."

"Steve! Can't we do this afterward?" Danny spoke up, pointing to his watch. "Time is money . . . and do you know how much money it's costing to keep three camera crews waiting, along with all the cast and extras?"

"I know it's expensive, Danny. But in this case, murder takes precedence."

"I'm going to overrule you, Steve. I'm sorry, but I'm the producer of this—"

Lieutenant Chen cleared his throat. "I think we'd better allow Mr. Allen to have his say," he said in a polite but firm manner.

"Nonsense!" said Danny Siderman heatedly.

"It is not nonsense at all," Lieutenant Chen said. "Either you allow Mr. Allen to speak, or I'll drag you all off to jail. Either way, you'll not get to finish filming until this is dealt with."

Danny stared at the lieutenant in disbelief.

"Danny, no need to have a stress attack over this," I told him. "I need only about ten minutes and this whole mystery will be cleared up."

Danny gave me a grateful look—more because of the shortness of time I needed, I think, than the justice I hoped to serve. "Well, if you have to solve a murder, you'd better do it, I guess. But quickly," he said.

chapter 47

All eyes of the cast and crew of *Hawaiian Wave* were upon me . . . except for the murderer, I noticed, who appeared nonchalant and was looking about with unconcern.

"Jayne and I came to Hawaii to help out the son of an old friend who believed someone was stalking him. Fortunately we have gotten to the bottom of that particular mystery, and some other mysteries as well. But it's been like wading through a swamp of old secrets. Not precisely a pleasant holiday."

"Where *is* Billy?" Elisabeth asked.

"Billy had an accident, but he's safe, and he'll be back on the show soon," I assured her. "But let me continue. Jayne and I have been introduced to the world of polo—a very glamorous world, but one in which things aren't always as they appear."

Jason Patterson wisely nodded.

"Then dead bodies began washing up on the Hawaiian waves, Sam Fitzgerald in Hanauma Bay and then Dick Schiller, our script writer, in Waimea Bay. Both appeared to be accidental drownings, though suspicious enough to make me believe a deeper investigation was in order. So we did some digging, and our search led us back to a high school on the *ewa* side of the island and three young boys who grew up together. The more I learned, the more questions I had. It was a complicated case, and I couldn't bring all the loose strands together into a coherent whole. I saw the possibility of motive for murder in the eyes of just about everyone connected with *Hawaiian Wave* at one time or another. But the answer was right in front of me all the time—it was in the script."

The crowd, restless at first, had grown very quiet.

"So let's look at the story of our episode, 'The Ride of Your Life.' Who's the supposedly fictitious killer? Well, I am—in my role as Warren Brent, that is. And why do I commit murder? Because I've been living beyond my means and I'm in desperate need of money. I'm fixing polo matches by drugging my horses with PCP in order to deliberately lose games. I couldn't get away with drugging race horses, say, on the mainland, but on the small island of Oahu no one is looking that closely. Gambling on polo matches is a bigger business than many people might think, but not yet big enough to attract official attention. So for Warren Brent, things are going well until he makes the mistake of hiring a groom who finds out how he is drugging his horses and demands money to keep his mouth shut. Well, our Mr. Brent is a rather desperate human being, and so he kills the young man rather than pay blackmail . . . and he might get away with it too, except our favorite P.I., Mack, finds him out. At least, that's the basic premise of the script we've been filming. We'll call this Script A. However, shortly before his death, Dick Schiller announced that he had some new ideas for the story and wished to make revisions. Edgar is a perfectionist, as we all know, and he convinced Danny that we should go with the revisions. . . . Unfortunately Dick drowned mysteriously before he could deliver the new script."

"That sounds pretty damn suspicious to me," someone nearby muttered. It was the first assistant director, a tall, lanky young man from Los Angeles.

"Very suspicious," I agreed. "It took a bit more digging, but finally we were able to find Dick Schiller's revisions, which he was unable to deliver in person, actually a whole new script—let's call it Script B, though in fact it was written at least a month ago, possibly even before Script A, and it's the story Dick always intended for us to shoot. The differences between the two scripts are vital to understanding our true-life murders. Script B, in fact, starts very much like Script A, but then it goes off in an unusual direction. After Warren Brent—yours truly—murders the black-mailing groom, a second young man is hired to take his place. This young man is a high school student, but he too catches on to what Warren Brent is up to—he starts to siphon off some of

the drug, PCP, which happens to be a foolish recreational drug—
aren't they all—as well as a horse tranquilizer, and starts selling
it at school. In Script B the Brents' daughter, Samantha, ends up
taking an overdose of this nasty stuff at a high school party and
Mack arrives too late to save her. Mack, as well as the audience,
watches her die in a horribly realistic fashion, hand-signaling as
she expires—since she is deaf. A very depressing ending to a
popular TV show, of course, and not one you'd expect to see.

"All this was very puzzling to me. In a commercial format
like *Hawaiian Wave*, you certainly don't expect the heroine to die
and the hero—Mack—to be standing ineffectively to one side,
unable to save her. I couldn't figure out why a writer like Dick
Schiller should want to undermine his reputation by giving us an
ending no one would like, and why he had changed the basic
theme of the show from crooked polo to teenage drug use. As
the art of TV writing goes, this just didn't make sense. Before he
died, Dick kept insisting that this new version would blow a lot
of minds, but personally I couldn't imagine that Danny would
ever allow it even to be filmed. Then my investigation led me to
the past—to Crown High School and the actual tragic death of
a pretty young girl named Angela Schwartz from a drug overdose,
and I began to realize what Dick Schiller had been up to. And
why he was killed."

"My God!" Lance said suddenly. "Keoni was a groom—he
worked for Jason Patterson back when he was in high school. Dick
Schiller told me about this once when he was a little drunk—
Dick and Keoni were at the same school together!"

"That's right, Lance. And Sam Fitzgerald was at Crown High
School too."

Lance seemed shocked. "So Keoni . . . my God, this whole
script really happened, didn't it? Jason Patterson was drugging
his horses to fix polo matches, and Keoni stole some of the PCP
to sell at school!"

I nodded. "Yes, it really happened, I'm afraid."

"And this girl—what did you say her name was? Angela?—
she really died of an overdose of the PCP that Keoni sold her?"

I nodded again.

"And Dick Schiller was planning to expose him with the new script?"

Again I nodded. "Dick had been in love with Angela Schwartz back in high school—an unrequited love, incidentally. Poor Dick wasn't a very balanced individual, not handsome, and she hardly knew he existed. Nevertheless, he carried the shock of Angela's tragic death with him into adulthood and he was yearning for revenge. Script B was close enough to actual fact that he hoped to torture Keoni with it and eventually expose him to the TV public. He had been holding these supposed revisions until the last moment in order to achieve maximum shock value."

"My God, it would absolutely ruin Keoni's career!" Lance said with a shake of his head. "So you're saying that Keoni murdered Dick to keep him quiet? Probably he killed Sam Fitzgerald for the same reason—Keoni needed to get rid of the two people who knew the truth about his past."

This time I shook my head. "No. That's a logical explanation, but it's not the way it happened."

Lance seemed truly shocked now—he was no longer play-acting but sweating, though the day was still cloudy and I don't think he even knew how much he was talking.

Suddenly he laughed. "But the way you've presented this, Steve, Keoni has to be the murderer. He's the only one with a good motive!"

"Nope," I said. "Keoni's *not* the killer—and as a matter of fact, he's extremely sorry for the things he did in the past. You're the killer, Lance."

Lance's mouth opened in a comical portrayal of innocence. "Me, the killer? You're absolutely nuts, Steve! Why in the world would I kill Sam and Dick?"

"Because you were desperate for money, Lance, and they threatened your clever blackmail scheme."

Lance smiled smugly. "Ridiculous! After all, I was the one being blackmailed . . . I was a victim, not a victimizer. I told you about that, remember?"

"You certainly did, but you were simply making it up. You saw that I was making progress with my investigation and it was a clever move to try to throw me off. No one was blackmailing you, Lance."

"You're full of—"

"Shut up a moment, Lance, and listen to me. The way I see it, your problems began when you were first hired as a sidekick for Mack on *Hawaiian Wave*. With your ego and lust for the good life, you wanted the starring role—you wanted to be Mack, not Pete Lambert, the stud with the pedicab business who got only a fraction of the money and the glory. You've always had a grandiose vision of yourself, Lance, and you were living a lifestyle you couldn't begin to support. So you started borrowing from friends, and even gambling, getting yourself in debt to some people who would break your legs if you didn't pay them back on time with the proper interest. You got deeper and deeper in a hole, and then your friend from public television, Dick Schiller, turned up with the answer to your prayers. He had the dirt on Keoni and he told you all about it, what he was up to with his script that was a little too close to life for anybody's comfort. Being a natural predator, you looked at this interesting scenario that had been dropped in your lap, and you figured Keoni would pay anything to keep his past hidden."

The attention of the group turned momentarily toward Keoni. The handsome young actor was standing between two cops with a sad, resigned expression.

"As I said, Dick's idea was to torment Keoni, play cat and mouse with him, and then expose him to the media. But you had a better idea," I went on. "You saw this as a golden opportunity for blackmail, a way to get hold of fifty thousand dollars, pay off your gambling debts, and live the high life to which you felt you had some natural right. Your first problem came when you discovered that Sam Fitzgerald knew about your scheme as well. Sam was a classmate of both Keoni's and Dick's, a friendly ne'er-do-well who happened to show up from the past at just the wrong time for you. My guess is that Sam tried to dissuade you and then threatened to tell Keoni if you didn't give it up. Poor Sam, he wasn't very bright, but I don't think he was evil. Probably Dick told him what you were up to. So you reassured him, you regained his trust. And then you suggested going for a scuba dive in some equipment you had fiddled with. End of Sam Fitzgerald!

"But your problems weren't over. At first you probably imagined that you and Dick could work your separate schemes in tandem—Dick didn't want money, after all, he wanted only revenge. I could see that Dick would most likely approve of your blackmail scheme, since he hated Keoni and this was a way to make Keoni squirm a little more. But Dick was obsessed, completely irrational—not a very good partner in crime. Worst of all, he was impatient. This was a moment he'd been waiting for too long— to destroy the person who had destroyed Angela, the girl he had loved so long ago. So he told you he was going to the media immediately with his story, before you had collected the blackmail money, which hadn't come through as soon as you had anticipated. Dick's premature exposure would have ruined your plan, so you had to stall him. And when he wouldn't be stalled, you had to kill him."

Lance had been sweating, but as I spoke, he seemed to visibly relax. "It's an interesting theory, Steve. But you can't prove a thing, can you? Which is why you're here, shooting off your mouth. But you know what I think? I think I'm going to sue you for libel. Unless you want to settle out of court, of course. I'll accept a million dollars and an apology from you."

It was my turn to smile—a somewhat forced smile, I'll admit.

"Good try, Lance!" I told him. "But as a matter of fact, the police do have proof. You made one mistake. You phoned Keoni to blackmail him, disguising your voice with electronic filters. Unfortunately for you, Keoni was sitting by his answering machine when you called, and he recorded you. We've given the tape to the police lab and they've been able to unscramble it. They have extremely sophisticated equipment for this sort of thing, you know. It took them a number of hours, but they've definitely identified your voice as the blackmailer. They were able to compare the wavelengths themselves to a recording of your voice from the show. Lieutenant Chen tells me it's an absolutely scientific identification, as good as DNA."

Lance's smug smile seemed to freeze in place as he considered this. I held my breath. I was lying, in fact, quite outrageously.

Keoni had indeed given me the tape he had recorded and I had passed it on to the police lab. But after a frustrating night, the police scientist—a nice Japanese woman, Dr. Naguki—informed Lieutenant Chen and me that the tape was clear enough to make only a probable not a positive identification. There was a chance the voice belonged to Lance Brady, but then again, it might not; what we had would certainly not hold up in court.

In short, I was bluffing. There were no wavelengths that we had matched, no scientific certainty at all. Which was why I was performing this charade, though with Lieutenant Chen's blessing. All designed to lead to this moment, hoping that Lance would break.

The half-smile on Lance's face wavered, but then seemed to become more set. "No, I don't think so, Steve," he said slowly. "You can't bluff an old poker player like me!"

I was afraid we had lost him. Probably he saw the very obvious truth, that if we had these so-called foolproof lab results, Lieutenant Chen would have simply arrested him rather than allow me to give a lengthy speech. But Lance wasn't entirely certain—I could see that. He was in a stressful situation, after all, standing there with all our eyes glued upon him, and perhaps he could not calculate with the cold-blooded arrogance that was his norm. He stood indecisively for perhaps thirty seconds, though it seemed longer. And then he broke.

It happened so quickly, we were all taken by surprise. Lance ran and hopped onto the back of one of the polo ponies, catapulting over the rump and landing in the saddle in a move that would have been the envy of any Hollywood stuntman. Before any of us had a chance to react, Lance was galloping off down the field toward the beach.

Cowboy Cass was the first to react. He had been standing with a rope in hand, showing off a little to Dottie—showing her, specifically, a little cowpoke lore, how to tie and hold a lasso. This was fortuitous. Still showing off, Cass did not waste a moment. He jumped onto the back of another polo pony, performing an identical move to the one Lance had just pulled off. And then, as we all watched in astonishment, Cass galloped off in pursuit and in mid-field threw perfectly, lassoing Lance around his waist and pulling him off his horse. Dottie nearly fainted in admiration.

As for the rest of us, we cheered like a rodeo crowd and ran in a group toward where Cass was calmly tying up Lance's feet, treating him like an errant calf.

Lance had completely lost his cool. "I'm going to sue you, you son of a bitch!" he sputtered.

"Smile when you say that," I said, deliberately using Gary Cooper's old line from *The Virginian*.

"I'll sue all of you!"

Lieutenant Chen completed the job that Cass had started, though not with the same élan, slipping handcuffs around Lance's wrists.

"Mr. Brady," he intoned, "you are under arrest for the murders of Sam Fitzgerald and Dick Schiller. . . ."

It was a wild scene to put it mildly. And in the midst of all this action, I happened to notice Edgar Min running about ecstatically with a hand-held camera, capturing almost everything on film.

"I'll use this for our ending!" I heard him cry joyfully to Danny Siderman. "Haven't I always said that life is much better drama than make-believe?"

chapter 48

followed Jayne into the private hospital room in Kailua. Billy Markham was lying on a high-tech bed with his left leg in a cast, hanging in suspension from a bunch of wires. Despite his injury, he was grinning. The room had a fine view of the Koolau mountain range outside his window, but Billy's attention was closer at hand, focused on the young redheaded woman sitting by his side. They were holding hands, and it was really very sweet. She had a pale, freckly face, very pretty and delicate; her red hair was short and boyishly cut, but that was the only thing boyish about her. Now that I had a good look at her, I was surprised I had ever mistaken her for a man. I had seen her before, of course; this was the infamous stalker who had eluded me for the past two weeks. A stalkerette, in fact.

"Uncle Steve, Aunt Jayne, I'd like you to meet Fifi . . . Fiona Patterson," Billy said proudly.

I noticed we had become uncle and aunt again, but under the circumstances, I didn't mind. Fifi rose and gave us each a hug and a somewhat French peck on the cheek.

"I'm so glad to meet you both . . . officially," she said nicely.

"Yes, it is nice. After all our unofficial encounters."

"All the time she was just trying to protect me. She wasn't stalking me at all!" Billy told us happily.

"Jayne's told me all about it," I said.

"It's so horribly dangerous being famous these days. Crazed fans. Paparazzi . . . my God, look what happened to Princess Di! Billy just looked so vulnerable to me," Fiona said. "I had to make certain he was all right."

"I don't feel vulnerable anymore," Billy sighed happily.

It was a relationship made in heaven, goofy enough, but love probably never makes entire sense. Jason Patterson's daughter from his first marriage had fallen in love with Billy Markham from afar. Apparently all her protective instincts had been roused when she discovered that Billy's new episode concerned crooked polo and that her father would be involved in the filming. She knew all about her father, of course—they were not close and she didn't trust him much. All in all, it seemed the sort of situation where a vulnerable boy like Billy could get hurt, and so she had been keeping an eye on him, not stalking him, hoping to protect him from harm. She had done a pretty good job, basically, keeping an eye on things—sometimes a closer eye than Jayne and I and Cass and Lieutenant Chen. She had been the one to send us to Harley's Hangout to find Dick's body; with her constant spying, she had overheard Lance set up a late-night rendezvous at Waimea Bay that she believed to be suspicious, and she had done her best to alert us.

"Did Aunt Jayne tell you how we finally met?" Billy asked.

"Aunt Jayne tells me everything," I assured him.

But being in love, he had to tell it again. "After my father told me that my mother was dying, I felt like such a sissy, you know. Here I was, afraid about everything, terrified about my own personal safety, when my mother was being so incredibly brave.

"I felt like such a coward," he went on mournfully.

"You're not a coward," Fifi assured him. "You're simply wise enough to take proper precautions."

Billy shook his head. "I was a hypochondriac, a real paranoid scaredy-cat. That night, after we all had that drink at the Royal Hawaiian, when my father was there and that firecracker went off at our table—"

"I remember the incident," I assured him.

"Well, I went back to my hotel room afterward and I felt like such a coward moving out of my house just because of a small thing like my mailbox getting blown up. I mean, I hate hotels—"

"Do you?" Fifi interrupted.

Billy shrugged meekly. "I'm always worried about hotel fires, you know. I can't sleep, wondering when the fire alarm is going to go off and if I'll have to jump out of a fifth-floor window. So I was lying there about midnight and I thought to myself, this is ridiculous! It was better to go home, where at least my bedroom was on the ground floor in case I needed to make an emergency exit. I guess you think I'm pretty weird, always thinking about stuff like that. . . ."

"I don't think it's weird at all," Fifi told him. "Whenever I go someplace new, that's always the first thing I do—figure out an escape route in case of a fire or an earthquake."

"Do you really?" Billy asked.

"You bet! I can tell you right now, for instance, the fastest way to get out of this hospital, in case there's a tidal wave, or something."

I rolled my eyes at Jayne as Fifi went on to tell us the nearest emergency exit to Billy's room, and how they should be sure to take the back stairs and not the elevator, because electricity can suddenly go off during unexpected catastrophes. This took a few minutes to work out, how Billy would be able to get downstairs with his broken leg. In order to hurry them up, I volunteered my shoulder for him to hold on to so he might get to the ground floor in case of tsunami, fire, earthquake, or volcanic eruption. Finally, Billy got back to his story.

"So in the middle of the night I just decided to go home. I packed my bag and took a cab back to Waimanalo. It really made me feel better. The cab dropped me off at home and I noticed a bonfire on the beach—just at the end of my property line. Well, I was a little alarmed, you know, particularly since there was a breeze that night and I thought maybe the fire could spread. So I was marching out to the beach in front of my house, but I didn't see Killer—you know, my guard dog. . . ."

"I remember Killer," I assured him.

"Well, Killer was stretched out in a shadow and I tripped over him and landed wrong, on my left knee, which I'd broken badly as a child. It was a stupid accident, I guess, but it sure hurt. I just lay there in agony, knowing I'd broken it again. And then Fifi was there, standing over me, saying I shouldn't move, she'd go and call an ambulance."

"I'd been keeping guard from the beach," she said proudly.

"Normally I knew where Billy was all the time, but I didn't know he had checked into the Royal Hawaiian that night. I thought he must have gone to a party, and this worried me, naturally—accidents can happen at parties. So I thought I'd just stay up and make certain Billy got home safely."

"She got cold though, and made a fire on the beach," Billy added.

"That was dumb of me," she apologized. "You wouldn't have broken your leg if I'd remembered to bring a sweater to wear."

"I'm glad I broke my leg," he gushed, "because I finally met you!"

"Oh, Billy!"

I sensed that Uncle Steve and Aunt Jayne were in the way, so we gladly departed the hospital room.

"She'll be even better than a guard dog," I said as we walked down the hallway. "At least we've cleared up the matter of our mysterious stalker." Cass was waiting for us in the cafeteria. Somehow in all the excitement we had skipped a few meals, so we went through the line. Jayne and I each got the low-cal salad plate; Cass, much braver, tried the spaghetti with meatballs. We took our trays and sat down by a sunny window overlooking a small courtyard garden.

"Well, I guess I understand most of this mystery, but there are still a few loose ends that bother me," Cass said as he tried to wind the loose ends of the spaghetti around his fork. "Like how was Sam Fitzgerald killed? And why?"

"Try a knife," I told him.

"To cut my spaghetti? I had an Italian buddy once who said that was cheating."

"I'm talking about how Sam was killed. Lance has been telling all to Lieutenant Chen. He says Dick Schiller actually was the one who killed Sam—he used a knife to make a very small incision into the rubber air hose to Sam's scuba tanks. The rubber was pretty old so it was hard to spot the cut, but it was big enough to let water in and cause Sam to drown. Dick was afraid Sam was going to spill the beans and tell Keoni what was going on, and spoil the grand moment of revenge Dick had been lusting for most of his adult life. Poor Dick really was crazy—Lance figured he had to get rid of him if his blackmail scheme was ever going to work. And Lance was truly desperate for the money. It turns out he was in debt to some guys who were planning to do serious harm to his kneecaps if he didn't pay up fast. He couldn't take any chances on Dick's craziness getting in the way of his plan to soak Keoni in exchange for keeping quiet about Keoni's past."

"So what's going to happen to Keoni now?"

"Well, that's interesting. Apparently Keoni has set a news conference for later this afternoon and he's planning to confess the entire saga of how he sold drugs in high school and was responsible for a girl's death. He wants to make amends and use his story as an example to other kids to stay off drugs. Danny Siderman has been freaking out, naturally, thinking that *Hawaiian Wave* is all washed up. But when he heard about Keoni's decision to speak about his past rather than try to hide it any longer, I saw the hint of a smile on his face. He seems to think that Americans are a very forgiving people and that Keoni might emerge from this a bigger star than ever. With all the publicity from the murders, he's starting to think that *Hawaiian Wave* is going to have a whole new life."

"But the show can't continue without Lance!" Cass objected.

"Sure it can. That's the main rule about show business, after all—the show must go on. Keoni's part will get bigger to take up some of the slack, and Danny has decided to hire a new actor."

"To play Pete Lambert?"

"No. Pete and his pedicab company will be written out. The new character is Samantha Brent, who will be Mack's personal secretary in the show, as well as assistant sleuth."

"No kidding? And Susan's going to play Samantha?"

"You bet. That girl's career has just taken a major upswing."

"Even with her . . . well, you know. . . ."

"Her handicap? Absolutely. The fact that she's deaf will only make her more interesting to the American public . . . Danny's counting on it. He feels this is just the right time for a handicapped actress to break through, and I think he may be right. Incidentally,

Susan and Keoni are getting married, which makes her success complete, I should say."

Cass opened his mouth in astonishment. "Good Lord! When did this happen?"

"Earlier this morning," Jayne said, very pleased. "Keoni proposed and she accepted. She knows it's going to be a little rough for Keoni in the coming months, after the news of his past comes out, but she plans to stick by him."

"Well, well!" said Cass. "This Hawaii venture hasn't been such a failure after all."

"How about you and Dottie?" Jayne asked, blank-faced.

"Oh, that's been kind of a tropical lark, you know. But Dottie has responsibilities back in Akron, and I guess I'm just an old cowboy bachelor used to my solitary ways."

"I think a good woman might make you very glad to become unsolitary, Cass," Jayne remarked.

Cass blushed a little and managed to change the subject back to crime. "So what about Jason and Melanie Patterson? And what about Bertrand and his uncle Davie and the *pakalolo* farm? And Raymond Markham buying medical marijuana, and yachts sailing to California, and all that?"

"Whoa, Cass! These all turned out to be side issues that have nothing to do with the main crime—the murders of Sam and Dick. But still, I guess we need to take them one at a time," I suggested.

"Okay, then let's start with the Pattersons. How do they fit in?"

"Well, Jason Patterson's a pathetic social climber who set the stage for disaster years ago when he decided to fix polo matches for money. His real name is Gus Patterson, by the way, but he thought Jason sounded more aristocratic. Gus grew up in a working-class family in Chicago, and he arrived in Pearl Harbor in the early seventies as a navy recruit during the Vietnam War. When he got out of the service, he stayed in Hawaii and became fascinated by polo and the very chi-chi world surrounding the sport. That's when he changed his name, hoping to join the crowd. But he never really had enough money to participate. There was a first marriage, resulting in Fifi, but that was a failure, like most things in his life. He won his first polo pony in a poker game and then started fixing matches as a means to finance his social ascendance. A sad character, all in all. Melanie thought he was the real thing when she married him—she thought she had married a rich man, not a phony, and I don't imagine she was very nice to him when she discovered the truth."

"So how did Dick Schiller find out about Jason and Keoni and crooked polo and PCP—all the things he wrote up into his script?"

"Dick knew Keoni back at Crown High School, remember. He knew Keoni was working as a groom for Jason, and that Angela died of an overdose of a horse tranquilizer. Dick was flaky but not stupid. He put two and two together and started looking into Jason. I'm not sure exactly how or when he found out that Jason was fixing matches—maybe it was a wicked guess, or maybe he kept digging up the past until he found some sort of clue. Eventually, he went to Jason and paid him five thousand dollars to act as a 'research adviser' on his script about polo. Jason, of course, accepted the money without blinking an eye. This is what Jason and Dick were doing together when I saw them having dinner at the Surf Room—Dick was still digging into Keoni's past, trying to find more dirt to help feed his lifelong obsession with revenge."

"Good Lord, that couldn't have been a very pleasant meal. Did Jason tell you all this?"

"He told Lieutenant Chen after the coast guard picked up Melanie and him in the *Maui Wowie*. But I was present during the interview."

"So this *Maui Wowie* boat," Cass asked, "was it one of the yachts Bertrand's uncle Davie used to ship marijuana to California?"

"Apparently not, as far as we can tell right now. The boat's owned by a rich hippie couple—left over from the sixties—but they seem to be clean. They raise horses on Maui, which is how Jason knew them, and they thought it was a bit of a lark to help Jason and Melanie escape their creditors. The Pattersons weren't headed to Hong Kong, of course—the phone message I found was deliberately left to throw me off the scent, as well as anyone else who came looking for them. They were headed much closer to home, to Maui, where they hoped to hide out long enough for everything to blow over."

"Will they go to jail?"

"I'm not sure. Their debts are a civil matter, and as for fixing polo matches, it's a little hard to prove in a court of law. Lieutenant Chen is trying to work out some sort of plea bargain where they'll admit to at least some of the charges against them in exchange for a reduced sentence. Whatever happens, don't expect to see them on the polo circuit anytime in the future—for Jason that will be punishment enough, I think."

Cass lowered his voice. "Now, what about Bertrand? Was he involved in his uncle's drug business? . . . I have to admit, I kind of like the guy, and I'm sorry to find out bad things about him."

"It's suspicious, isn't it, the way he disappeared."

Cass sighed. "It sure is, I'm afraid!"

I smiled. "Well, don't worry, Cass. I like Bertrand too, and he's clean as a whistle."

"But didn't he run off to join his uncle Davie when Davie broke out of prison?"

"Yes, he did. But it was to convince his uncle to give himself up and go back to finish his term. He was afraid Davie was going to get killed, you see. Bertrand did a clever job as a go-between, arranging for Davie to give himself up peacefully to Lieutenant Chen . . . and that's pretty much it. Did I leave anything out, Jayne?"

"Lots of things, Steve. But you covered the main items at least. Dear Lieutenant Chen has invited us for dinner tonight at his favorite Chinese restaurant on the island . . . you too, Cass. The lieutenant is very happy with us at the moment. With all his recent success solving crime, he's going to be made a captain!"

"A toast to Captain Chen," I offered, raising my water glass from my plastic cafeteria tray.

"Wait a second! One more question," Cass objected. "What about the final scene of the show at the polo field? Don't you still have to film that?"

"Not at all," said Jayne. "Edgar decided that he could use the hand-held material he got this morning and splice everything together. Danny's thrilled not to go over budget by rescheduling the crowd scene, and Edgar is convinced he's going to win an Emmy."

"Now, that *would* be a crime!" I laughed. And on that note, Cass and Jayne and I clinked water glasses.

On Sunday afternoon we all flew home to relatively peaceful Los Angeles. Jayne and I sat near the window while Cass was across the aisle. I could hear him from time to time, above the drone of the engines, telling the woman sitting next to him all about his recent exploits filming *Hawaiian Wave*. The way he put it, you'd think he was the star of the show.

"Well, back to reality," I said wistfully to Jayne. "No more sunset walks along Waikiki. No more scent of plumeria in the tropical breeze!"

"Are you telling me you're going to miss Oahu?"

"Sure. What do I have waiting for me at home? A book to finish, an appointment with our tax accountant, a big decision to make whether we're going to repaint the house. Work, work, work."

"After murder in Hawaii, it sounds like fun, fun, fun to me," said my wife.

"You know, it does to me too," I admitted.

Just then a flight attendant came down the aisle and leaned over to Jayne. "Mrs. Allen, there's a phone call for you from a Captain Tony Chen. You can take it on the telephone on the back of the seat in front of you."

"Would you do me a favor, dear?" Jayne asked.

"Why, certainly."

"Take a message, please. And tell Captain Chen we've just gone on vacation."

The Berenstains' Baby Book

Also by Stan and Jan Berenstain

How to Teach Your Children about
  God without Actually Scaring
  Them Out of Their Wits
How to Teach Your Children about
  Sex without Making a Complete
  Fool of Yourself
It's All in the Family
It's Still in the Family
Baby Makes Four
Marital Blitz
Lover Boy
Bedside Lover Boy
I Love You Kid, But Oh My Wife
Office Lover Boy
Have a Baby, My Wife Just Had a
  Cigar
What Dr. Freud Didn't Tell You
Flipsville-Squaresville
Mr. Dirty vs. Mrs. Clean
You Could Diet Laughing
Education: Impossible
Never Trust Anyone over 13
Are Parents for Real?
Be Good or I'll Belt Ya

Children's Books

The Big Honey Hunt
The Bike Lesson
The Bears' Picnic
The Bear Scouts
The Bears' Vacation
The Bears' Christmas

Inside Outside Upside Down
Bears on Wheels
Old Hat, New Hat
Bears in the Night
Berenstains' B Book
C is for Clown
He Bear She Bear
The Spooky Old Tree
The Bear Detectives
The Berenstain Bears & The
  Missing Dinosaur Bone
The Bears' Almanac
The Bears' Nature Guide
The Berenstain Bears' Science Fair
The Bears' Activity Book
Papa's Pizza
The Berenstain Bears' Christmas
  Tree
The Berenstain Bears' New Baby
The Berenstain Bears Go to School
The Berenstain Bears Go to the
  Doctor
The Berenstain Bears Visit the
  Dentist
The Berenstain Bears' Moving Day
The Berenstain Bears & the Sitter
The Berenstain Bears Get in a Fight
The Berenstain Bears Go to Camp
The Berenstain Bears & the Messy
  Room
The Berenstain Bears in the Dark
The Berenstain Bears & the Truth

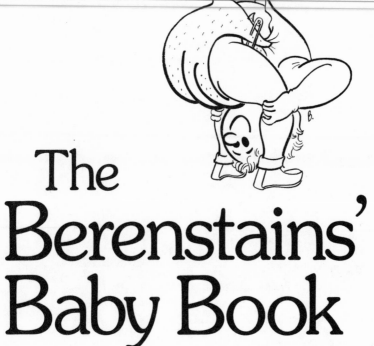

The
Berenstains'
Baby Book

Stan and Jan Berenstain

Arbor House · New York

Library of Congress Catalogue Card Number:
83-70467

ISBN: 0-87795-509-3

Manufactured in the United States of America
10 9 8 7 6 5 4 3 2 1

This book is printed on acid free paper. The paper in
this book meets the guidelines for permanence and
durability of the Committee on Production Guidelines
for Book Longevity of the Council on Library
Resources.

For Leo and Michael

Contents

1
Pregnancy

The most important thing to remember about pregnancy is that it's a perfectly normal condition. At first, you'll hardly know you are pregnant except during those brief and precious periods when something deep within reminds you that momentous changes are taking place.

Your first parental duty is to find a good doctor. Since compatibility between obstetrician and patient is absolutely essential, it is vital that you find an obstetrician who suits your personality and temperament. The following catalog of typical obstetricians may help you in considering your choice.

The Old Family Doctor
Old Doc Beamish has delivered 6,796 babies, including a fair number of his present patients.

The Taskmaster
Some women, lacking confidence in their own resources, prefer a strict disciplinarian.

VIP (Very Important Physician)

Doctor to the international set. Merely to be on Dr. Miklemuch's patient list is a distinction. He has delivered personages of note all over the world, and may, at any minute, be called to attend a movie star, an heiress or a member of royalty—leaving an assistant you've never met to take care of you.

The Woman Obstetrician

Many women feel the female obstetrician, being a woman herself, will have a more sympathetic understanding of the patient's plight.

Before long, you will enter upon a regular obstetrical program. At first, you may find your experiences a little strange—even a bit bizarre.

But as you become adjusted to the routine of regular visits you will come to enjoy the camaraderie of the obstetrician's waiting room.

You may decide to investigate the "natural" childbirth method. This approach is based on the idea that full knowledge of birth as a natural process will banish fear and anxiety . . .

... and since fear and anxiety can be contagious, the husband as well as the wife must be fully indoctrinated.

Even when you reach the extreme late stages, your pregnancy is not a "confinement" in the Victorian sense. Of course, there are some things you'll do well to avoid . . .

. . . certain types of chairs,

. . . certain kinds of cars

MATERNITY EXPRESS

. . . and sudden starts and stops.

While you've been working through the final stages of your blimp impersonation, solicitous friends and relatives have kept your phone ringing off the wall. Your mother-in-law is convinced that the whole process is taking much too long and that your delaying tactics are for the specific purpose of embarrassing her.

Your fancy obstetrician calculated the date on which you are to be become a parent, has circumscribed a four-week period as a general target area and, at its chronological center, pinpointed the natal day. But now that you are well into the *succeeding* four-week period, it becomes clear that, like Truman in '48, you are going to make monkeys out of the experts.

At long last, however, you detect the unmistakable signs and portents and, after a mad dash, you arrive at the hospital sixteen hours early.

A NAME FOR BABY

BOYS

Name	Meaning
Amos	Industrious, serious, dues-paying
Andy	Lazy, silly, non-dues-paying
Anthony	See Antony
Antony	Seeing Cleopatra
Barney	Googly-eyed
Basil	Wrathful, boney
Ben	Short for Benjamin
Benjamin	Long for Ben
Bob	No, I'm Ray
Donald	Loquacious, incomprehensible, web-footed
Egbert	He's your kid, lady
Ernest	Frank
Ethelbert	Scarred for life
Frederick	Corruption of Fredryck
Horatio	Proud of his bridgework
Ken	Enamored of Barbie
Llewellyn	Diminutive of Lllewelllyn (Wellsh)
Orville	Wrighteous
Otto	Reverse spelling of Otto
Owen	In debt
Ron	Hewer of wood, getter of votes
Roswald	He'll hate you
Rudolph	Red-nosed
Siegfried	We dare you
Thomas	Hardy
Wilbur	Flighty

GIRLS

Name	Meaning
Adeline	Sweet
Amy	Little woman (also: Beth, Jo and Meg)
Antoinette	Scatterbrained
Barbie	Hot for Ken
Barbra	Adenoidal
Brunnhilde	Fat
Cloë	Much sought after
Delilah	Snippy
Esmeralda	Wonderful! A baby sister for little Roswald
Evita	Musical
Gail	Windy
Gaiyle	No such name
Isabella	Gullible
Isolde	Very fat
Jane	Mate of Tarzan
Jill	Fetcher of water
Katrina	Chases dirt (Old Dutch)
Mae	Inexcusable spelling of May
Shirley	Friend of Laverne
Susan	Lazy
Susanne	Very lazy
Sylvia	Enigmatic

2

Helpers—and Others

After about seventy-two hours of fitful bed rest and a few hours of gingerly interaction with your issue, you are evicted from the hospital, the tired but trim mother of a superlative little baby. Mother, Father and Baby are now on their own, a proud little family unit— and they should insist on remaining so until they have had a chance to set up their defenses. In nearly all cases it is a fatal mistake to accept offers of help from the maternal grandmother. The paternal grandmother, of course, is absolutely out of the question.

The fact is that there is nothing particularly difficult about caring for a brand-new baby. An infant's daily needs are extremely simple: food, dry clothes, a bath and sleep. The new baby will sleep as much as twenty hours a day, as though instinctively determined to make the most of this antisocial luxury while it's possible. Though the new mother is usually perfectly able to care for her baby, she is under doctor's orders to forego general household duties. As an interim factotum, Daddy is her best bet. The shiny new Daddy is obedient, dedicated, even worshipful, and makes the ideal postnatal auxiliary engine; also, he's had about nine months to wangle a week's leave from his job—two, if he's any kind of operator.

Don't interpret the fact that your newborn may sleep as much as twenty hours a day to mean you will be able to catch up on your reading. It will take you at least that long to contend with your mail, your phone and your doorbell. It seems, dear parent, that you have joined a list. Privy to this list are all the manufacturers, salesmen, entrepreneurs, promoters and con men whose commodities have remotely to do with babies, and it turns out that they are all fanatically interested in your new status as a parent. Every mail brings a slew of letters offering sincerest congratulations and multitudinous marvels designed to take the sting out of parenthood—a whole line of indispensables ranging from bibs to bar rags, a miraculous combination feeding chair/play table/toilet, a charter membership in the Toy-of-the-Month Club and a fascinating brochure on a revolutionary new method of birth control based somehow on the international date line.

You will be reminded that it is not your child's exclusive function to come trailing clouds of glory: about every fifth phone call will be put through by the representative of a wide-awake diaper service soliciting your baby's business. The caller will be a smiley-voiced young lady who seems not to hear your statement to the effect that you are already committed to disposable diapers, and is still in there pitching when you hang up.

Members of the AHNP (the Association for the Harassment of New Parents) are not above using the direct approach. Even before Mommy has lost her hospital legs, there will come a knocking at your chamber door. "How do you do, sir?" (Answering the door is one of Daddy's jobs.) "May I take the liberty of congratulating you on the birth of your new baby? I represent the Dawn Studios, specialists in baby photos. We are prepared to . . ." Members of the AHNP are specifically excepted from protection under the assault laws.

Your duties as secretary, receptionist and switchboard operator will make it difficult for you to get to know your youngster during the day, but don't despair. Baby's nocturnal activities will enable you to get pretty well acquainted during the wee hours.

Your friends and relatives will form a little club of their own, and, unfortunately, to these well-wishers you are obliged to be reasonably polite. The first meeting of the association will be held at your house, preferably in the nursery, and the chief topic for discussion will be the baby's resemblance to one or the other of its parents. Thank them all for the lovely presents, appoint yourself sergeant at arms and adjourn the meeting just as soon as a majority opinion has been reached.

One of the parent's most arduous duties is the protection of the child from doting grandparents. The road to spoiled children is paved with grandparents' good intentions. The situation is particularly dangerous if your baby is the first grandchild, but not until the tenth or so can you afford to ignore the hazard.

The situation is an even more unholy mess if all four grandparents reside in the same city. The visits then become a mad competition between in-laws. Following are listed some of the subversive activities engaged in by grandparents, together with appropriate countermeasures which you should take:

1. The grandparent's first impulse upon seeing the grandchild is to pick him up. It matters not that the child is happy in the crib, coach or playpen. Nor does it matter that it required a supreme effort of stamina, will and native cunning to get him to lie there quietly in the first place. *Up* he's snatched! Then, after a few minutes of knee dandling, Grandpa glances at his watch and discovers that he'd better hurry if he's going to pick up Grandma in time to make the first show. After all, he just

dropped in for a few minutes, and doesn't want to keep you folks. So, putting Baby back where he found him, he bids you adieu; but you don't hear him over the mounting decibels from your infant.

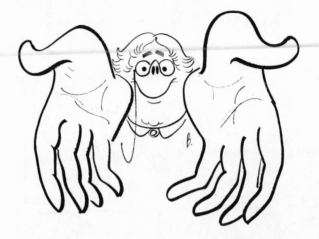

In this matter, as in all dealings with grandparents, *be firm.* Make it perfectly clear that it is *your* baby and is *not* to be picked up without your permission. Hurt feelings may result, but that can't be helped. Remain deaf to the argument that they managed to bring *you* up all right; the only rebuttal to that is unflattering to yourself.

2. Grandparents will feel it is their right to drop in without warning at any time of the day or night. If these impromptu visitations are permitted, you will soon be bordering on gibbering idiocy. Far better to have an early understanding on the subject than to let the pressure mount until you explode. If you are nursing your baby (and this is an excellent reason for doing so), you can modestly insist that Baby dine unattended. Since they are not interested in sleeping infants, that cuts out several more hours of the day which would be convenient for visiting. Point out that their grandchild's regular schedule is what's responsible for the weight gains and general well-being, and if they approve of such good health it follows that they must approve of the schedule. Give them a place on the schedule; if

Experienced
"Oh yeah, Missus, I done all kinds of work—practical nursin', rivetin', hash slingin', mangle operatin' . . ."

The Character
"I'm allergic to cats, dogs, house dust, feather pillows, mohair and chiming clocks. I require prune juice and jasmine tea. About phone calls . . ."

The Perfectionist
"You'll notice I'm wearing what is known as a surgical mask. I have brought with me a supply of these . . ."

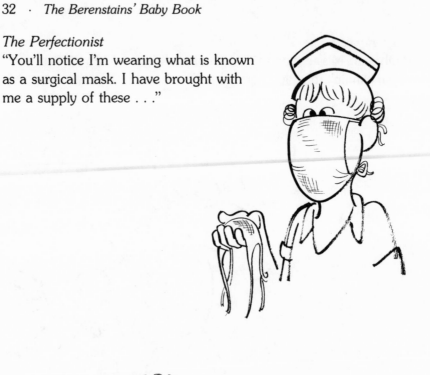

The Queen
"Hey, look. This is the third day this week you got home late!! Cream and sugar, please . . ."

The Surprise Package
"My sister couldn't come . . ."

If you are fortunate enough to find a dependable, nonexorbitant sitter, treasure her, coddle her, ply her with Arpege—*and* keep her name and phone number a dark secret from your less fortunate friends.

3
Feeding Time

"Gesundheit!"

Keep mealtime a pleasant, happy experience to which your child looks forward. Of course, your own enthusiasm for the ritual may be somewhat dimmed owing to the fact that the only food Baby seems to want is what's in the cat's dish under the sink. But don't give in. Though you have your work cut out for you, the task is not impossible. The key to success lies in your own attitude. If each meal is regarded as a contest, the parent will be the loser. It is impossible to reason a child into eating; the trick is to get the food into the baby without using force. Or, at least, without having to resort to a crowbar and a ramrod.

While there are many available generalizations on such feeding-time subjects as weaning, when and how to introduce solid foods, etc., they are not much help in dealing with your particular little General.

Accomplishing such steps as milk from the cup, finger food and utensils is largely a matter of trial and error—and error, and error and error.

You may start milk from the cup when Baby is as young as four or five months . . .

. . . or you may wish to wait until Baby is a little older and has greater lip and tongue control.

But whether you introduce the cup early or late, it's important to follow Baby's lead.

Different children react to solid food in different ways. Yours may be utterly bewildered by the first experience with solid food and reject it completely . . .

. . . or may take to it like a true little omnivore.

Yours will probably fall into the middle category of infants who can take solid food or leave it (taking what they like, of course, and leaving what they do not, even as you and I). You'll learn all those little preferences soon enough.

Your child may, for example, dislike spinach and other "strong" vegetables intensely, whereas the attitude toward cereal and starches may be one of bored intolerance . . .

. . . while at the "high interest" end of the preference pattern, Baby may be wildly enthusiastic about mashed banana or other dessert foods.

But since you have at least a moral obligation to feed a nutritious and balanced diet, you're going to have to find a way to get some of those nonpreferred foods past those locked jaws. Here is an approach that may work wonders.

As you sit down to feed your little impassive resister, pretend you are facing an adult dinner guest whose company you find delightful. Bring into play all the qualities which have won you a reputation as a charming hostess. If your table talk is sufficiently diverting, your child will never notice that the main course is strained liver. Discuss only subjects of mutual interest—the dog's latest trick, the cute little chipmunk that lives out back in Daddy's woodpile or the mole on the end of the nose of the lady next door, a subject that was abruptly opened for discussion in her presence only yesterday.

An important experience like a trip to the zoo can provide enough conversational ammunition to last you a half-dozen meals. Your little raconteur may have to disgorge a few mouthsful of mashed ripe banana in order to roar like a lion or bark like a seal, but the food ingested will substantially outweigh what is splattered on the wall. At subsequent meals Baby can eat beans like a rhino, chicken like a giraffe and noodles like a hippo. When it gets to the point of eating carrots like a two-toed sloth, you had better think up a new ploy.

Even the most pleasant meal will be peppered with mishaps. You must take these in your stride. You wouldn't embarrass an adult guest by showing annoyance when he knocks over his water glass; by the same token, you must ignore the warm milk trickling down your jeans. Continue reading *Little Willy Wombat* as though nothing had happened. So far, Little Willy has been good for seven spoons of baked potato, and may be worth seven more if you don't break the spell.

As Baby comes to feel more at home in the mealtime environment, he or she may develop little mealtime idiosyncrasies. Baby may decide simply that the meal isn't worth eating without a certain special spoon, for example.

But with the increase of neuromuscular control, Baby will develop new eating skills . . .

. . . will become an efficient chewer . . .

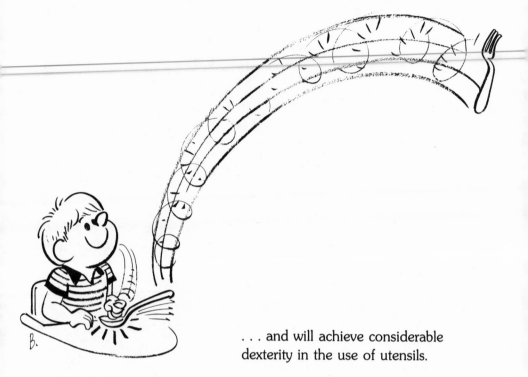

. . . and will achieve considerable dexterity in the use of utensils.

As personality develops, Baby's mealtime mood is bound to vary somewhat from meal to meal. If, however, your offspring's eating behavior seems to be going steadily downhill, it may be necessary to revaluate the mealtime climate. If a change of pace seems called for, Daddy might take over feeding for a while. Everything is a little more fun with Daddy.

The self-assertiveness which evidences itself at about age three often takes the form of balkiness at meals. Here are a few little tricks which may help you through this difficult period.

Letting the child set the table . . .

. . . select the menu . . .

. . . or even help in the actual preparation of food.

You may find that a change of scene may do wonders for a lagging appetite—a luncheon party in his own room for his own toys using his own little table and chairs and cups and saucers, for example. Simply moving the mealtime outdoors may lend just the needed air of excitement.

Or you might ask your youngster's opinion about what might be a "fun" place to have lunch.

As you work with your youngster, his or her feeding "personality" will become readily apparent—and whether Baby turns out to be a "picky" eater, a two-fisted trencherman or something in between really doesn't matter as long as you and your pediatrician are comfortable with his weight-gain pattern and general health.

4
Bathtime

Once home from the hospital, a parent's first big task will be to give the newborn a bath. Though you had been anticipating this operation with considerable apprehension, a demonstration given by that redheaded snip of a nurse—during which she bathed a half-dozen assorted babies without even mussing her bangs—has almost convinced you there is nothing to it.

Having prepared your baby's "bath tray," a pink or blue waterproof affair that usually leaks, check the necessary items once again: boric acid, baby oil, baby cream, baby powder, castile soap, zinc ointment, Vaseline, absorbent cotton, swabs, tissues, comb, brush, nail clippers, safety pins and a strong sedative. Chuck that other stuff out: the gilt-initialed nail buffer (a shower gift which you thought "too cute for words" at the time), the angora powder puff with a silver safety pin for a handle (another shower gift) and the miniature baby bottle filled with infant suntan lotion that squirts out through a miniature nipple (something for which you have only yourself to blame).

First a briefing on the operation of the bathinette. Some woolly-minded relative has probably given you the latest, most deluxe model: "You'll never use all the attachments, but they're nice to have." Well, they're not nice to have. Get rid of them. Strip the thing down until nothing remains but the bath hammock itself. One of the thousand gadgets you will remove is the draining hose. This will leave a hole in the bottom of the tub, which can be plugged with a bit of eraser from the end of a pencil. Although a bucket is needed to bail out the water at the completion of the bath, you have elimi-

nated the daily floods which would be the direct result of using the drainage hose. Some other attachments to be dispensed with are the all-too-collapsible Handi-Gadget Rack, the Handi-Spray (a hose arrangement ideally designed for fighting forest fires) and the handiest item of all—the Handi-Dressing Table, a canvas affair which will turn on you if not disposed of at the outset.

Now that you have seen to it that your equipment is in perfect working condition, partially fill the bath hammock with lukewarm water. Test it with your elbow. If you don't feel anything, it is just right. On the kitchen table to the left of the bathinette, undress Baby and cover the squirming body with a small towel. This serves to muffle screams, too. Swab the eyes, ears and nostrils with boric acid. Except for the face, on which you use water only, soap the baby thoroughly section by section, being especially careful to keep your youngster's soapy hands away from the face. Now lift the small towel, with Baby inside, and dunk the whole business in the bathinette. This will be like dunking a roaring outboard motor in a lily pond. Quickly return bathee to the table. Blot—don't rub—the baby dry; you can attend to yourself later. Sprinkle with baby powder, add diaper and clothes, and wade to the bedroom for a feeding. Suggest to Daddy that he put down that paper and at least clean up the kitchen before you institute divorce proceedings.

As children grow older they enjoy the bath more and more, and instead of crying when you put them in, they shriek indignantly when you take them out. At three months Baby will be flailing and thrashing like a hooked trout. At six months your tot will turn the bath water into a little piece of the English Channel with an excellent impersonation of Gertrude Ederle. At nine months, with the addition of an overall lurching and heaving motion, the bathinette will begin to travel precariously across the room, sloshing as it goes. At this point the contraption has outlived its usefulness. Collapse and store it, provided its last voyage did not reduce it to scrap. It has no trade-in value.

Introducing your nine-month-old to the "big" tub will be just that and nothing more for the first day. Your youngster will have no part

of it. Explaining that "that's where Mommy takes a bath, and Daddy, too," won't change anything. You may try the terribly modern approach of getting undressed and demonstrating *how* Mommy takes a bath in the big tub, but Baby will remain adamant. The kid's probably tired of being pushed around. No sooner had he developed a good steady drag on a bottle of milk than it was replaced with a cup; no sooner had he acquired the ability to sit than he was obliged to stand; and no sooner has he perfected the technique of navigating his bathinette than he is confronted with this large, cold and obviously unwieldy affair.

In the child's own good time, however, even the most stubborn will accept the new outrage. When you call to Daddy to come see his little doll taking a bath in the big tub, be sure to tell him to dress accordingly. Doll, in the meantime, has flung the plastic duck overboard, taken a few seal-like flips, manipulated the drain handle and, incredibly enough, yanked the chrome stopper out by the roots. For succeeding baths, it would be wise to have on hand a variety of seaworthy trinkets, beguiling enough to forestall the complete demolition of the plumbing accessories. Little boats, plastic or tin cups, celluloid fish or frogs (though Baby would be enchanted with the genuine articles), a dipper, a funnel, an ear syringe and a number of small balloons would be a good beginning. For the next few years these things will see the two of you through many a jolly aquacade. And it's obligatory: after all, you want to keep your angel at least within shouting distance of godliness.

5
Bedtime

Putting a really young child to bed is not normally a big problem—a full belly, a warm bed and your reassuring presence will usually do it. But putting an older bundle to bed is one of the severest drains on the wellsprings of intelligent parenthood. If you are to keep bedtime from resulting in the complete breakdown of discipline, you must formulate a plan for abetting the sandman before your child is old enough to see through your transparent schemes. Provided a sound bedtime routine is arrived at early in the game, Baby will have become so conditioned to bedding down by the time he starts feeling his oats that, although your tot's best efforts may drag the process out, they won't quite be able to drag it down.

A Regular Hour
Be just as insistent that your child goes to bed at a regular hour as your child is that you rise at a regular hour. If you are not firm on this point, you may as well turn in your uniform now.

Division of Labor
There is nothing in the Bible that says that putting to bed is woman's sole responsibility. With all that upper-body strength, Daddy is ideally suited for this back-breaking task. The important bedtime ritual usually begins with the nightly repetition of a favored game or activity. Children, being instinctively ritualistic, know intuitively that repetition is central to meaningful ritual . . .

. . . and insist upon perfect
execution of a rigidly
prescribed procedure . . .

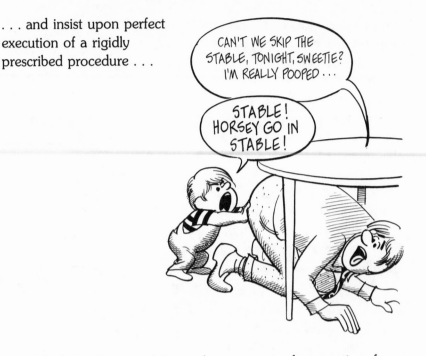

. . . which leads inevitably to the moment of separation from
Mommy . . .

. . . and the crucial act
of going upstairs.

Going Upstairs

Going upstairs represents a symbolic break between the child and
the rest of the family, and can lead to serious separation anxiety if
badly handled.

An exciting piggyback ride can provide a smooth transition.

Evening Bath

The evening bath is of great value in subduing your little valve-in-
head engine. Allow the child enough time to enjoy the evening tub,

but don't allow dawdling. A calm, quiet bath with some favored bath toys is a key event in the bedtime ritual.

After you've managed to get your tiny seal out of the tub and toweled off, allow the child to do the toothbrushing. Do the toothpaste squeezing yourself, of course, and use very little. Letting a small child get a grip on an open tube of toothpaste is sheer madness.

Bedtime Story

With the very young, the bedtime story should be a simple, somno-
lent narrative with no complex overtones. Your child will, almost
immediately upon the installation of bedtime stories as a regular
feature, insist on taking complete charge of programming. The
younger the child, the more likely the feeling that repetition, rather
than variety, is the spice of life. It is not unusual for a child who is
one and a half to insist on "Beantalk" for as many as forty-five nights
in a row. Toward the end of a long run like this, Fee, fi, fo, fum! can
have powerful emetic properties, and it's up to Daddy to keep a stiff
upper digestive tract.

Though dual-purpose weapons are usually unsatisfactory, it is
possible to make a subsidiary use of the bedtime story when the child
begins to develop a moral sense. By this time Daddy will have long
since worn out his stockpile of traditional stories, and found it necessary to write his own stuff. The injection of a little propaganda of a
virtue-rewarded persuasion into these homespun masterpieces may
exert a wholesome influence—until, that is, the little one's critical
faculties also begin to develop and an immunity to sermonizing is
built up. There are a few weeks in between, though, when you can
get in a few homiletic licks.

In all bedtime stories, to the traditional "and they all lived happily
ever after," it would be wise to append the coming of nightfall and
the retirement of all major characters. This may seem a cheap trick,
but it is really only one more legitimate exercise of parental license.
Handled with taste, these sedative codas can achieve the stature of
a minor art form. For example: "And then Aladdin rubbed his lamp
again. When the Jinni appeared, Aladdin said to him: 'Jinni, I am
very tired. I wish you to bring me the finest bed in the whole kingdom.' And the Jinni said: 'O Master, the finest bed in the whole land
belongs to little Ned Nitey, who is this very moment falling asleep
in it. Surely you do not wish to disturb him.' So Aladdin told the Jinni
to get him the second-finest bed in the kingdom, and when it was
done, Aladdin climbed into it and fell fa-a-ast asleep."

If, perchance, you are tempted to play a little fast and loose with some portion of the bedtime ritual . . .

. . . say, by skipping some component of a treasured story . . .

DON'T—you will be dealt with summarily!

Finally your efforts to put the bundle to bed will be rewarded and punctuated by the last act of the bedtime ritual—the goodnight kiss . . . But don't count on it.

Occasionally, the child will feel the need to expand the bedtime ritual—to make it more meaningful—and the sensitive parent recognizes such an occasion and does his best to cooperate.

After which he gets to work on a little bedtime ritual of his own!

PROGRESS REPORT

Since one of the principal propositions of this book is that children need to be dealt with as individuals, it might be instructive to consider the highly varied results obtained in a series of standardized tests administered to a group of randomly chosen children.

Test I—PAPER FOLDING

Examiner demonstrates the folding procedure, offers subject paper, and says, in calm, confident manner, "Here, you try it."

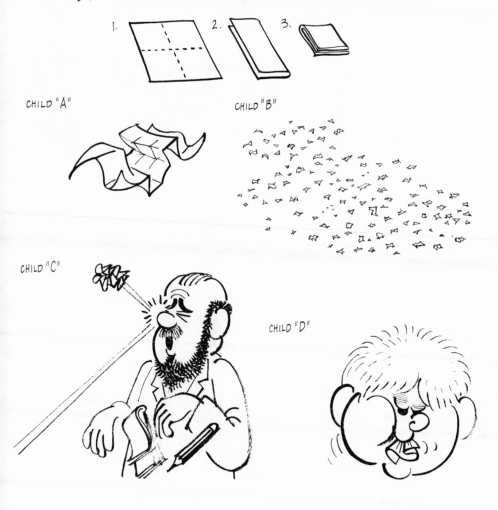

6
Toidy Days

The realization of the ideal of dry pants may completely exhaust your reserves of perseverance and grit, but, like Boulder Dam, it's worth all the effort. For it's a sunny, sunny day when your child achieves complete mastery of recalcitrant plumbing and you are able to bid farewell to diapers forever.

There are many different approaches to the question of when to start toilet training. The best approach in a particular case depends largely upon the individual "trainer." A relaxed parent who is inclined to take things in stride may prefer to wait for the problem to solve itself. Others may wish to begin toilet training early. If Baby is regular, early training may be simply a matter of noting the child's own rhythm and placing baby on the chamber at the same time each day.

On the other hand, a baby may be perfectly healthy and be very irregular.

This may make the toilet-training job a little more difficult, but you will soon learn to *sense* when to put Baby on the chamber—by a particular facial expression . . .

. . . or a favored stance.

Your own attitude toward the bathroom and its function is the key to your success. Throw all modesty out the window. Pocket the key to the bathroom door and keep the door open. Have a warm light glowing within, and toss a cozy mat upon the floor with the word WELCOME imprinted thereon. As soon as Baby is steeped in the jolly atmosphere of the place, and familiar with the role of the toilet in particular, it is time to set up your tot's own little throne.

However you approach the toilet-training problem, you will want to consider a toidy for Baby. There are two toidy alternatives.

You can get Baby a special toilet—it consists of a cabinet and a receptacle, with a seat on top. Besides being low and accessible to Baby, this type of arrangement offers the added convenience of being easily transportable from one part of the house to another.

Or you may prefer getting just the toidy seat. The separate unit with a detachable training seat is recommended. This seat may later be used on the big toilet. It should be equipped with a deflector—seat and deflector being, preferably, all of a piece. This type of seat is the most desirable for boys and girls alike, the point being that, like a Western saddle, it makes dismounting difficult; also, a girl's seat would greatly inconvenience small male guests. To illustrate: a young trainee of our acquaintance was most bewildered when, having been invited to sit on little Debbie's toidy seat on the big toilet, he urinated into the sink opposite.

There is no shortage of practical toidies, of the type described, available in baby furniture departments—and even less of a shortage of highly impractical ones: a ten-inch lifesaver with a Disney Duck quacking at the helm; a spidery affair of blue plastic which collapses into pocket size for convenience when traveling but is not so convenient when it comes to a hurried reconstruction; and the hard-to-resist super-deluxe upholstered leatherette number which plays "Please to put a penny in the old man's hat" when it is sat upon.

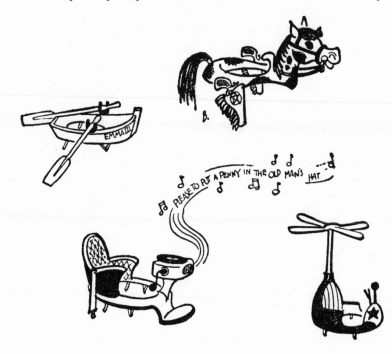

You may begin bowel training anytime after baby is able to sit up strongly. On the day you decide to take the plunge, wait until the time you usually expect a soiled diaper, then strap Baby on the new potty. Never refer to the strap as such, but by all means use it. Don't fasten it on the sly. After placing Baby in the seat, say simply, "I'll buckle your nice blue belt for you." Before those steely fingers begin testing it, stuff them with a banana, a piece of orange or some other intriguing food Baby's allowed to have but is seldom allowed to actually handle (for obvious reasons).

As the youngster sits there kneading a banana or massacring an orange, you must convey what it is that's expected. Your baby is too young to comprehend a long verbal briefing, but is apt to astound you with an ability to grasp the meaning behind a grimace or a grunt. If you are a particularly adept mime, your efforts may be rewarded the very first day. Don't be disappointed, though, if they are not. Actually, you have done well if all you have engendered in your trainee is a grimacing and grunting acceptance of the potty. Eventually, say in about two weeks, Baby may accidentally use the potty for its intended purpose. Offer congratulations. Show that you are impressed. If your enthusiasm is sufficiently contagious, Baby may have another accident in another couple of weeks. After this, Baby may hit the jackpotty three or four days in a row. When Baby has caught on to the extent that there is only one miscalculation in the diaper every two weeks, your virtuoso is ready to take up Bladder Control.

Bladder Control consists of putting the tot on the pot every hour on the hour. It also entails sponging up a puddle every hour on the hour, roughly two minutes after you take the child off the pot.

Stated in its simplest terms, your objective is to get the puddle in the pot. The solution is largely a matter of sticking rigidly to a schedule and constantly keeping a weather eye squinted for signs of precipitation.

Throughout the toilet-training program it is best to maintain a casual manner. When, however, Baby seems to catch on to the idea of the toidy, of course show that you are pleased.

On the other hand, if Baby doesn't immediately understand what is required, assume an attitude of patient understanding.

The time to dispense with the low chair and use the training seat on the big toilet comes when your toddler's legs grow long and sturdy enough to carry Baby, seat and all, into the next room to let you know he is "froo." You may try to strong-arm the underneath clamps into holding the seat to the chair more securely, but Little King Kong will be delighted by the challenge and drag the whole clanking business down the hall to help you see who's at the front door.

When your child graduates to the big toilet, appeal to pride by making it clear that it's a signal honor. It's the big league now, and unless Baby can keep up with the fast company, it'll be back to the minors for further seasoning.

Gradually, as Baby grows and gains confidence, he can be introduced to the big toilet and left pretty much to his own devices.

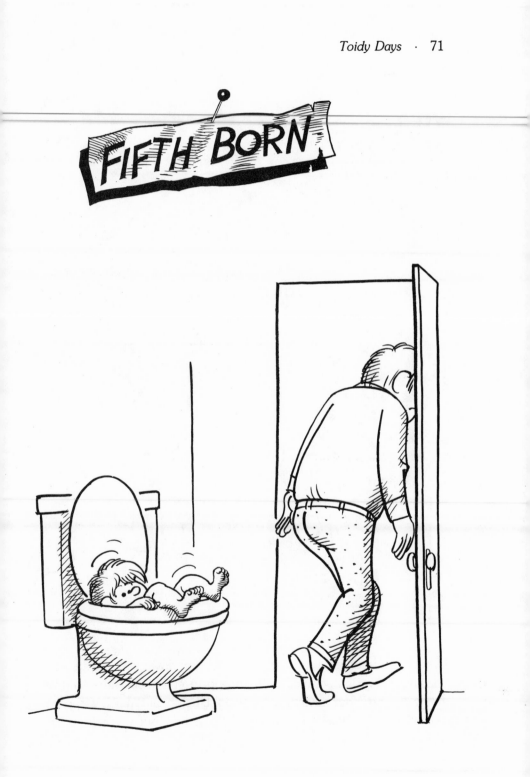

7
Illness

When your youngster shows signs of coming down with a cold, you may as well resign yourself to the proposition that you are going to take a licking. Your advantages in weight, height and reach compare favorably with those Goliath held over David, but you will be so hamstrung by doctor's orders that you are doomed to share the ultimate fate of your fellow Philistine.

You can hardly blame your invalid for setting up a howl as soon as the family physician comes into view. For all the chin-chucking, the doctor is just an extension of a hypodermic syringe to Baby, and the howling isn't likely to cease until Doc is on the way out.

If you hear yourself saying, "It won't hurt, sweetie!" bite your tongue. Always tell as much of the truth as your child can understand —if not out of a fundamental moral imperative, then at least in an effort to establish and maintain the most valuable attribute you have as a parent—your credibility. If you con your three-year-old into believing that the shot won't hurt, why should he or she believe your later claims that marijuana, booze and skipping school will?

Afterwards, you study the page of instructions you took down with one hand while rapidly undressing and dressing your screaming pinwheel with the other. As nearly as can be made out, your scribblings read as follows:

> kpchd inbd untl tmpisnm
> 1 tspnf prcn ev3hrs
> nsdps at bdtm if nc
> plty of lqds.

Don't get panicky. The key to this cryptogram is the telephone. Take a look at the prescription (thank heaven you don't have to read *it*), and note the office hours at the top. Then simply phone the office and review the directions. The good doctor will be expecting your call.

The fly in your healing ointment is the item "kpchd inbd untl tmpisnm," which has been translated to read, "Keep child in bed until temperature is normal." It would help no one to make public the intelligence that even the most expensive pediatricians are unable to carry out this mandate. Yours not to reason why, yours but to make an honest effort to keep your sniffle-machine in bed. The best you can hope for is to render Baby comparatively inactive for a while—say, for six consecutive minutes at a time.

The most effective method for keeping a small child quiet is dishearteningly like the most effective method for getting a small child to do anything he's agin: distraction. It is superfluous to point out that this is more easily said than done. By the time the average child is about two, the average parent has been squeezed dry of the ability to distract. The following list is for the benefit of these mummies and daddies who are beyond thinking up new ways of degrading themselves:

Songs

Dredge your subconscious. Perhaps you'll come up with "The Monkeys Have No Tails in Zamboango," "Way Down in Dear Old Borneo" or "I Can Dance with Everybody but My Wife." Try to recall your old school songs and yells. Properly bowdlerized Army and Navy songs may fascinate the convalescent into plucking at the coverlet for an extra hour.

Stories:

If your repertory is completely exhausted and you are too enfeebled to make up new ones, try scrambling the old ones. "Rumpelstiltskin and the Forty Thieves," "Ali Baba and the Seven Dwarfs" and "Snow White and the Beanstalk" have a certain shock value and may help to keep the invalid idling in neutral for another hour.

Parlor Tricks

Ear wiggling, knuckle cracking, the handkerchief cradle trick, the separating thumb illusion, the Here's-the-church-and-here's-the-steeple-open-the-doors-and-see-all-the-people routine are all sound, if admittedly demented.

"1 tspnf prcn ev3hrs" (one teaspoonful prescription every three hours). This is another catch-as-catch-can imbroglio. Your doctor knows as well as you do that baby simply won't down anything that doesn't taste pretty. As a consequence, you can trust Grimes Drugstore and Candy Kitchen to produce an elixir which will discourage the cold germs without offending their host's discriminating palate. It does not follow, of course, that the patient will permit a dosing without a fuss in any case. It is traditional that Mommy or Daddy join Baby every three hours in a therapeutic toast. Don't resent the spoonfuls of perfumed glue you are called upon to swallow in line of duty. The germs have heard about you, too, and like as not are infiltrating your own esophagus right now.

Decoded, "nsdps at bdtm if nc" reads, "Nose drops at bedtime if necessary." If your offspring is one of the vast majority who greets the sandman with thumb in mouth, you really have no choice but to resort to nose drops. The only alternative to clearing that stuffy little nose is to try to get Baby to shift to stogie-style thumb-sucking, breathing out of the other side of the mouth. Not many children can manage this, so drops are required. Administering them is a two-person job; and since it is of extreme importance that patient and curators get all the sleep they can, no holds are barred.

8

First Toys

Whether you are choosing a toy for a newly arrived bundle whose skills are confined to sucking and flailing, or a four-year-old homemaker who has expressed a fierce desire for a real stove, with a real oven, equipped with an automatic timer and a real pressure cooker suitable for canning, a high degree of critical judgment should be exercised.

When selecting toys for tiny babies, all other considerations must be ignored in favor of this paramount one: the child's safety. Make your decision on the basis of what may be called the toy's "suckability." This leaves out all the furry, cuddly, squeezy, jingly things well-meaning relatives and friends have sent, and, with the exception of those fetus-like rubber dollies and grotesque little plastic fish, practically everything in the toy store, too. There are available, to be sure, a few toys scientifically designed for infants. These are often especially commissioned by progressive toy companies from famous industrial designers and carry a snappy price tag. But for parents of ingenuity, there is a way out. For in any American five-and-ten, the same money will buy a whole battery of toys with superlative suckability ratings, provided, of course, you stay away from the toy counter. The pet department is a good place to start. A dog bone, Saint Bernard size, is an ideal infant's toy. It is made of an excellent grade of rubber, is practically indestructible, eminently washable and costs next to nothing. On your way to the houseware counter to get a set of brightly colored measuring spoons on a ring, stop by the hardware department and pick up the business end of a sink plunger; as Baby gets older, graduate to a larger size. There are literally dozens of blunt, colorful plastic and rubber items for sale in the five-and-ten which make excellent infant's playthings and have the added value of remaining useful after baby has outgrown them. There's no telling when an extra plunger may come in handy.

When your child is about six months old, it's time to start hauling out the stuff that has been arriving in a steady stream since you left the hospital, but which so far wasn't deemed quite suitable. Baby is now ready for the heady pleasures of stuffed animals. These should not be taken down from the closet shelf and presented en masse, but should be produced one at a time and applied when they will do the most good. This stockpile of giant pandas, fuzzy ducks, teddy bears and cuddly bunnies can prove a valuable strategic weapon during spells of colic, sieges of teething and in the breaking of hunger strikes. They should never be offered as a bribe or as a direct reward, but should be used for diversionary purposes.

Even the very young child will develop maniacal passions for certain playthings and will insist on taking a few of these very dearest friends along at bedtime. It's a bit lonesome in there all alone, and it's understandable to want the company of Pluto the dog, Ding-Dong the elephant, Fifi the French poodle, Piggy-Wiggy, Bunny-Bun-Bun and others too revolting to mention. Incredibly enough, Baby is perfectly able to get a good night's sleep in this menagerie. But if you'd rather not have your tot spend the night under conditions as congested as the stadium for a Superbowl game, it's safe to tiptoe in later and thin the ranks a bit. Just be sure you don't tuck in Raggedy Andy and consign Baby to the toy box with Pluto, Ding-Dong, Fi-Fi and the rest.

COMFY OBJECT AT 4 MONTHS

COMFY OBJECTS

Psychological research has shown the importance of the favored toy, or "comfy object." This is the special toy or object with which the child comes to identify, and which is necessary in times of transition, during trips away from home and while falling asleep at night.

A recent survey shows the following preferences for particular comfy objects:

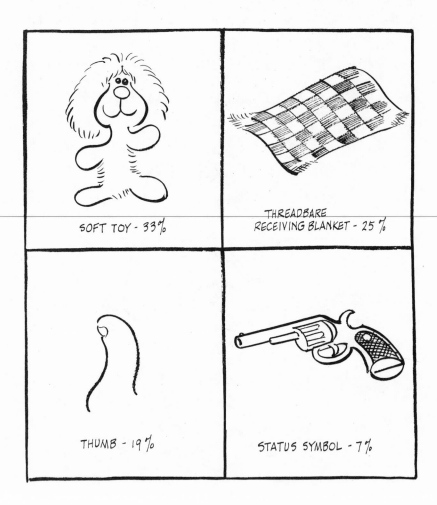

SOFT TOY - 33%

THREADBARE RECEIVING BLANKET - 25%

THUMB - 19%

STATUS SYMBOL - 7%

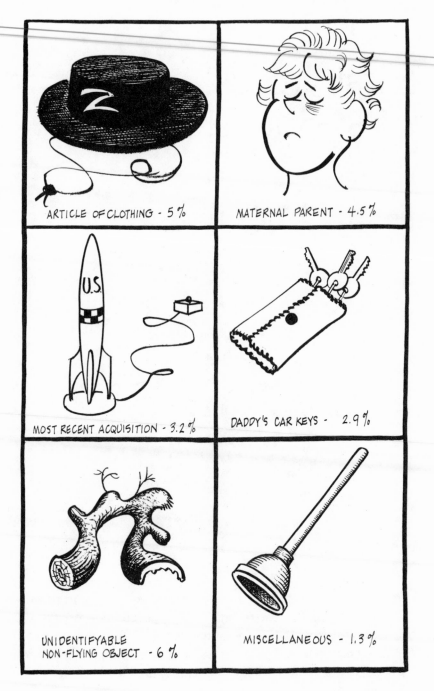

ARTICLE OF CLOTHING - 5%

MATERNAL PARENT - 4.5%

MOST RECENT ACQUISITION - 3.2%

DADDY'S CAR KEYS - 2.9%

UNIDENTIFYABLE
NON-FLYING OBJECT - 6%

MISCELLANEOUS - 1.3%

9

First Words! First Books!

From the day they bring their newborn home, the proud parents' ears are cocked for Baby's first word. The duration of the wait depends largely on the degree of objectivity a parent is prepared to bring to bear on the subject. The father who first hears his infant son pronounce the word "Daddy" as clear as day has disrupted more than one christening.

It takes considerable restraint to keep from interpreting your small one's every gurgle as an addition to a rapidly expanding vocabulary; but to be brutally realistic about it, the very young baby is physically and mentally incapable of genuine speech. This is not to say that a three-month-old cannot say "da-da" or "ma-ma." Many of them do, but it is merely an unconscious reflex, a mechanical mouthing of those particular sounds. They say "ga-ga" and "la-la" with equal conviction.

When your baby is about eight months old, he or she will probably produce that magical first word. For our purposes here, a word is loosely defined as a specific sound with a specific meaning. For some reason, parents generally assume that Baby's first words will be "Ma-ma" and "Da-da." Perhaps they feel it's the least Baby can do to show some appreciation. Well, in most cases, they are sorely disappointed. Their child's first effort might be anything from the simple word "ball" to a garbled version of "Wisteria," the cat's name. Actually, your child's speech will for a long time consist not so much of words, but rather of highly questionable approximations of words. It might be helpful to indicate right now with fearless candor what your fifteen-month-old's vocabulary actually amounts to:

The actual word	Your child's version
ball	bah
shoe	ooh (very high-pitched, with puckered lips)
pillow	baba
umbrella	umbaba
I want	(two swine-like grunts)
toilet paper	bay-*pah!*
what's that?	zat?
water	lala
glass of water	googalala
trolley	baba
baby	bebe
bus	beh
banana	nanna
Grandmom	nanna
airplane	r-r-r-r-r!

There's nothing abnormal about this state of affairs; you'll get the hang of it before long, like African explorers coping with the native dialect. But at this point, a strong word of caution: *Do not indulge in the use of baby talk!* If you succumb to the temptation, which, granted, is great, your punishment will be swift and terrible. You will be saddled with umbaba, bay-*pah* and googalala for years to come. Besides, if you encourage the child by imitation, you are being grossly unfair: a small child is susceptible to flattery, and will treasure the baby talk which has earned such an appreciative audience. Baby will not be able to understand why words and expressions which were once so satisfactory become objectionable to the very people who once found them worth imitating. We're not saying the kid is heading for the psychiatrist's couch, but serious maladjustment can result from more trivial causes. Call a spade a spade, not a pade.

Once a child gets the hang of a particular word, don't be too surprised (or embarrassed) if you hear it used indiscriminately and to excess.

As they tune in to language, children just seem to naturally gravitate to vocabulary we'd rather they didn't acquire. Your first intimation that your little one has been sponging up all your oaths, epithets, asides and chance remarks about in-laws and neighbors can be one of life's most profoundly mortifying experiences. The time and place vary with the child, although invariably both are remarkably well chosen. A one-year-old can do the job as neatly as a two-year-old, making up in succinctness for any feebleness in vocabulary.

For instance, it will dawn on you that from now on you had better watch your words when your one-year-old utters a particular one in a crowded, acoustically perfect bus. What word, we won't say. (Goodness knows *where* your angel picked it up!)

As children grow older, their memories absorb like blotting paper and their sense of timing becomes more acute. Thus, the longer the child waits for just the right moment, the more exquisite the parent's torture is likely to be. Imagine lifting your three-year-old so that he or she can look into the baby carriage at Mrs. Dugan's new twins, and hearing, "Mommy *said* you looked like you were going to have twins."

As with any situation which sees you and your child at odds, you are basically helpless. This is not to say that you can afford to sit back and let poor enough alone, for, as with any situation which sees you and your child at odds, it can get immeasurably worse. The first thing to do is assess the damage. Since it was about two months ago that you made your passing remark about Mrs. Dugan's appearance, you are warned that anything you may have said during that time can be used against you. In other words, little Wotan is well stocked with thunderbolts.

The outlook, though fraught with peril, is not completely hopeless. In a general way you can prepare some defenses against your toddler's loose tongue. List mentally the people you are most likely to have slandered in recent months. List only the worst cases, people against whom you have conducted a running campaign of invective. On these, Baby has a complete dossier of items which won't bear

repeating. Suppose you should suffer a visitation of The Plague—
your pet name for sister-in-law Maxine. See to it that child and aunt
are rigidly segregated. Some ordinarily forbidden treasure, such as
Daddy's college yearbook, can be offered up in a sacrificial sort of
way to distract Baby until the danger is past. Meanwhile, if you keep
the conversation moving, and on a low enough plane, it won't occur
to your guest to play the attentive aunt.

Of course, things can't always be handled so neatly. In most cases
there isn't time for preparation. You'll often have to be able to
manage a sudden and gargantuan sneeze to drown out the offending word or phrase. Sometimes a spontaneous peal of hysterical
laughter is called for, or even a sharp scream. You will have to think
fast to explain these curious demonstrations, but it can be done. If
things get really grim, though, you may simply have to clap your
hand over the little mouth.

An unexpected reprise of a causal verbal indiscretion is bad
enough, but to have your child suddenly volunteer a highly unsuitable idiom can be much worse, especially if your most staid neighbor
is calling to discuss your possible participation in the forthcoming
neighborhood bazaar. To prevent this sort of disaster, the parent
must take an inventory of personal language habits and resolve to
discontinue the use of all profanity. Generally Daddy is the principal
culprit in this respect. He no doubt needs a good bit of toning down,
and Mother will have to be in charge of the project. The battle will
be half won if she can somehow gear the thing to his pocketbook.
This is the procedure to follow:

First, notify him that he must stop using such atrocious language.
He will be astounded, and in all sincerity demand to know, "What
atrocious language?" When he stops stewing, say pleasantly, "All
right, then, if your language is so fit for young ears, perhaps you'll
agree to a little experiment." Whereupon you whip out an agreement
that reads something like this:

> In order to curb our use of objectionable language in the pres-
> ence of our child, we, the undersigned, agree to the following
> schedule of penalties, said penalties to be forfeit to the other
> party to this agreement:

Objectionable slang	10 cents
Anatomical references	25 cents
Profanity (simple)	35 cents
Profanity (compounded)	50 cents
Obscenity	75 cents
Compound profanity and obscenity	One dollar

With his child's welfare at stake, Daddy can hardly refuse to sign the contract. Though he will have embarked on the venture in order to protect his child, it will be a desire to protect his pocketbook that will accomplish the cleanup; he will soon find that he cannot afford the luxury of salty speech. Mother's reward is twofold: she can take pride in a job well done, and she can buy herself a little something with the dimes, quarters, halves and dollars that will inevitably accumulate, iron resolutions notwithstanding.

Conversation within earshot of your youngster, having dwindled to such bland stuff, may be somewhat frustrating. To a certain extent, pig Latin, high school French and the spelling out of words will provide outlets for a little steam. But be careful not to overdo it, or your little eavesdropper is likely to relay to wealthy Uncle Ben the intelligence that you have called him an ompous-pay, *stupide* old s-l-o-b.

Just as they are fascinated by the spoken word, children are fascinated by the written word. The conscientious parent introduces the youngster to books as soon as possible.

The importance of exercising extreme care in choosing the books which your child will read and reread cannot be overemphasized. Lack of intelligent discrimination in this matter can be so discouraging that the child may never come to know the wonderful world of books. Here are some questions to ask yourself about any book you are considering for your child:

1. If the child hits you with it, will it hurt?
2. What will be the effect on the book if the child takes it into the bath and gives it a good scrubbing with Daddy's toothbrush? Finally (and of least importance), what will be the effect on Daddy?

3. If half the pages are ripped out and torn to shreds, will it affect the story line?

4. In the event that the child demands it be read over and over again for as much as an hour, will it produce nausea?

5. Is the volume small enough to be quickly and easily hidden in the event that you *have* been forced to read it over and over again for as much as an hour and it *has* produced nausea?

6. Is the type bold enough to be read through a thin layer of strained squash?

7. Will it fill a specific need? Is it exciting enough to distract the child while you spoon in the cereal, or is it sufficiently soporific to produce sleep after a wild day at the sandbox?

If the answers to these questions seem to be in the book's favor and the cost isn't much more than four or five dollars, it won't do much harm to buy it.

Once you've bought the book, catchily entitled *Cockie-Lockie Bakes Some Cookie-Lookies,* and taken it home, what then? Should you just hand it over and say, "Here's a dollar book I brung ya"?

Definitely not! Hold on to it. It's money in the bank. Keep it under wraps until, in the normal course of events, a crisis arises. Then say, in your most casual manner, "If you don't stop eating the leaves off Mommy's nice philodendron, I won't give you the pretty new book I bought you." If you manage just the proper tone, Baby will stop. Baby might even spit out the latest mouthful. You then have Baby —and philodendron pulp—in the palm of your hand.

Your cherub sits down beside you on the sofa, and you begin to read. *"One bright sunshiny day, Cockie-Lockie got up and said, 'Isn't this a bright sunshiny day! I think I'll bake some cookie-lookies!'"* As you struggle through to the end of the tale, your docile little lamb leaps from the sofa and heads for the playroom. And is back in a flash with a tall stack of all the books stashed away in there. The little darling nestles down beside you, face lit with a happy, anticipatory

smile. There's nothing for it but to take the top book off the pile and begin to read: *"One bright sunshiny day, Bunny-No-Good was hopping down the path. As he hopped, he passed seven naughty dandelions. 'Naughty Dandelions,' he said . . ."*

Later—much later—you go numb and it isn't so bad.

COMFY OBJECT AT 6 MONTHS

PROGRESS REPORT

Test II—BALL THROWING

Examiner demonstrates act of throwing ball, offers subject ball, departs and views behavior from behind one-way viewing glass.

CHILD "C"

CHILD "D"

10
Self-Reliance

The little girl who is provided with simple polo shirts and jumpers will quickly learn to dress herself, while the little doll who is fussed up daily in starched petticoats and frilly pinafores that fasten in the back will have a wretched time of it. Similarly, the boy who is simply and comfortably clothed in T-shirts and boxer pants will be slipping into them "all by hisself" by the time he's four, whereas Little Lord Fauntleroy will rip off those complicated buttons in a rage when his mother heckles him with: "Heavens, darling, try dressing yourself once in a while. A big four-year-old boy like you!"

At two and a half, your tot will probably try to remove socks by grabbing at the piggie end and pulling toward his face. He pulls and pulls. Nothing happens. Eventually his hand slips off and connects with his nose. After this, be sure to slip his socks off his heels for him when he's in the mood to undress himself. Then when he grabs a handful of sock and yanks, he'll get results: there will be a sock in his fist when it connects with his nose.

A few months later he'll catch on to the heel-first gimmick, and then attack the shoe-removing problem. First, he'll tug at the shoe-laces until they are securely knotted; then, after a long, hard pull, he'll clout himself smartly on the forehead when the knotted shoe finally leaves his foot.

In spite of the bumps and bruises on the outside, inwardly your child is bursting with pride. The "I do it myself!" stage has arrived. During this period every day is highlighted by an unaided attempt to perform a new feat. The degree of this daily disaster depends on the parent's ability at sleight of hand. If, between the time of the screeching decision, "I do it myself!" and the actual deed, Mommy is able to sidle into the bathroom, kick the step-up in place, lift the toilet seat and retire to a neutral corner without arousing suspicion, Baby will perform that first unassisted void with relative success.

You may expect your child to do the following things as the desire for independence is asserted:

AT 3 MONTHS YOUR CHILD . . .

. . . recognizes and responds to a human face . . .

. . . fixes gaze on near object . . .

. . . smiles in response to friendly overtures.

AT 6 MONTHS YOUR CHILD . . .

. . . may recognize Daddy . . .

. . . may cut the first tooth.

AT 9 MONTHS YOUR CHILD . . .

. . . may evidence an irrepressible urge to pull himself up to his feet.

Initial failure will just strengthen his resolve to try again . . .

. . . and, if need be, again . . .

. . . until he succeeds.

AT 12 MONTHS YOUR CHILD . . .

. . . makes tentative overtures to adults . . .

. . . may feed himself mashed potatoes—with his hands.

AT 18 MONTHS YOUR CHILD . . .

. . . loves to perform little errands . . .

. . . is enthusiastic about "clean up" activities.

AT 20 MONTHS YOUR CHILD . . .

. . . begins to feel a burgeoning sense of possession and property.

It's *his* pussy cat . . .

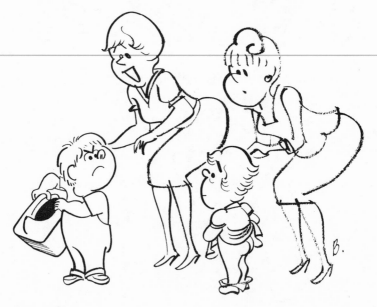

. . . *his* toidy.

AT 24 MONTHS YOUR CHILD . . .

. . . has much greater manual control than heretofore, and can—turn
pages . . .

. . . manage faucets . . .

. . . use scissors.

AT 36 MONTHS YOUR CHILD . . .

begins to have strong feelings of independence which are expressed in a fierce need to "do it myself." The child

. . . insists on tying his own shoes . . .

. . . squeezes his own toothpaste . . .

. . . is willing to undertake the job of undressing himself.

AT 4 YEARS YOUR CHILD . . .

. . . can dress himself—provided the complete attire consists of a cowboy hat and Daddy's slippers.

AT 5 TO 6 YEARS YOUR CHILD . . .

. . . can do everything which up to now he *thought* he was doing "all by myself."

PROGRESS REPORT

Test III—FORM BOARD

Examiner demonstrates Form Board, disassembles it, offers it to subject and says, encouragingly, "Here, you try it."

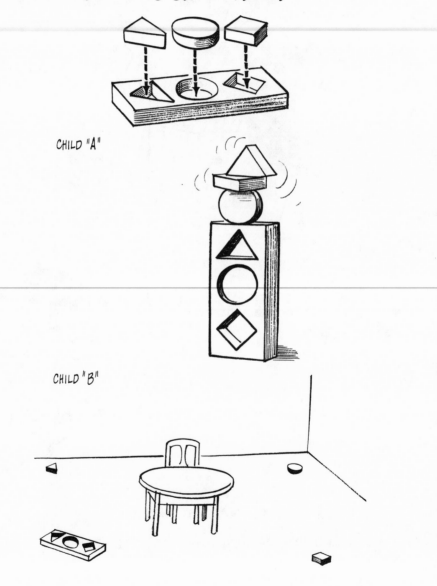

CHILD "A"

CHILD "B"

CHILD "C"

CHILD "D"

11

First Games

As a parent, you have an obligation to spend as much time as possible at play with your child. The sense of security, the self-confidence, the mental and physical exercise and the development of group spirit which these play sessions will encourage in your offspring are vastly important contributions to the child's general well-being.

Herewith some suggested games and activities for parents and kiddies:

1. Bom-Bom-*Bootz!*: You can begin playing this with your child as soon as the soft spot in the skull, just above the forehead, closes. Do not indulge in this game after your child reaches the age of two. There are reliable records of parents having suffered serious concussions from playing Bom-Bom-*Bootz* with overage youngsters. Queensberry rules: the parent crouches on the floor facing the child. (For parents, all games entail physical hardships.) In unison they cry, "Bom-Bom-*Bootz*!" and crash their foreheads together. Baby is delighted,

screams with hysterical laughter. Parent accepts two aspirins proffered by mate, who is scheduled to play the winner.

2. Peekaboo: This game is very popular with children between the ages of one and one and a half. It has the advantage of requiring no special equipment or talent, and the disadvantage of being utterly inane. To play, the parent must crouch down behind a chair or sofa on which Baby stands facing the back. Parent leaps up, grimaces wildly, and shouts, *"Peeka-boo!"* Baby is delighted, screams with hysterical laughter. This routine is repeated until booee's knees give out or until booer falls exhausted to the broadloom.

3. Round-and-Round: This game occurs spontaneously to the children a few minutes after they learn to walk, and remains a

popular after-dinner activity until they are old enough to know better. It is fiendishly simple, consisting merely of both parent and child standing in the middle of a room and revolving, at first slowly, then more and more rapidly until the speed of an oriental dervish is achieved. Baby is delighted, screams with hysterical laughter. This is continued until, in the case of the parent, an overwhelming nausea sets in. Children seem to be able to keep it up indefinitely, but of course they smoke and drink less and get more sleep and eat next to nothing for dinner. That this is your little one's idea of fun, however, is pretty dismaying. Still, if Baby elects to play Round-and-Round, there's nothing for it but to pocket your editorial opinion and make like a pinwheel.

4. Hide-and-Seek: In your efforts to educate your small bundle of muscle to less homicidal forms of recreation, you mention Hide-and-Seek, a game remembered fondly by most parents. With great persuasiveness the rules of the game and its peculiar charms are described. No sale. Hide-and-Seek just isn't exciting and Baby expresses not the slightest interest in it—that is, not until a little later in the evening when the word "bedtime" is mentioned. Then little Houdini stages a disappearing act that needs only a flash of fire and a smell of sulphur to complete the effect. Finally, having searched high and low, you find the missing person—low—absorbing dust under Daddy's desk in the study. To your stern injunctions to come out of there and behave, you get a righteous protest: "I only playin' Hide-'n'-Seek!"

5. Horsey: This is a fine old traditional diversion which helps father and child get to know each other real well. It helps Dad to get better acquainted with himself, too, in that he is reintroduced to muscles with which he hasn't been on flexing terms for more than a decade. Pop's part in the game is brutally elementary: he pretends he's a horse. For his little playmate, the illusion is perfect, whatever private misgivings Horsey may entertain. With a bone-jarring leap the steed is mounted. "Giddap!" In an effort to coax more speed out of the sluggish nag, our rider digs sharp little heels into Horsey's tender flanks.

Horsey whinnies

in pain and gallops off around the coffee table. Baby is d. & screams with h. l. If these rodeos are allowed to become regular inclusions on the evening's agenda, Daddy's impersonations are apt to degenerate from prancing palomino to sway-backed, spavined glue bait.

There are other, and more bone-crushing, entertainments, but it is not the purpose of this book to be exhaustive. Your child will take care of that.

Until the toddler or, more accurately, "totterer," is about four years old, play periods with other youngsters will require adult supervision. Whether actual presence on the scene is necessary depends on the individuals at play, but being at all times within earshot and easy bounding distance is mandatory.

Let us look in on a simple game of building blocks. Leo—age two and a half—is strenuously erecting a wobbly column of blocks,

repeatedly intoning, "Dis is a big daddy hippo house wif a hippo pool in the back"; Debbie—age two—is squatting nearby with a block in each hand, sucking them alternately; and Carol—age three —is winging anything she can get her hands on at the cat under the crib.

Even as you enter the room unnoticed, a simple nonmalicious act of one child sets off a chain reaction of such blinding speed that you are unable to arrest it or even minimize its effects. Leo, having exhausted his supply of blocks, "borrows" one of Debbie's. Debbie hangs on for dear life, and bops him on the head with the block in her other hand, lodging a strong protest all the while. Carol, taking advantage of the fracas, wades into Leo's precarious hippo house, and the shattering crash diverts Leo's attack from Debbie. Possibly you will catch Leo in time to save Carol from a vicious frontal assault, but the ensuing tears, fury, hurt feelings and wounded pride are what require your major attention.

The two visitors are by now screaming, "I want my mommy!" and since the last thing you want is for their mothers to discover them in adversity under your roof, your first move is to the cupboard for lemon candies. With an uneasy truce thus won, philosophize with them. It is very important that however you preach the lesson to be learned from the incident, no one should be blamed for it. If it was anyone's fault, it was yours. Had you been on hand to direct Leo's attention to the unused blocks in the corner, he wouldn't have grabbed Debbie's. What you must do is take each in turn and point out what he or she did that made the others cry, and if possible, coax an apology from each. A box of unmedicated Band-Aids will effect a bit of magic at this point. When each has a patch over a real or imaginary bump, the misfortunes of war will be forgotten, and equanimity restored—at least, until someone decides to play with the only ball in the room alone.

The very small child doesn't care a fig about how nice it is to "share." If his Daddy gives him a ball, it's *his*. Everything in his room is *his*. Anything *anyone* has *ever* handed him is *his*. From the time he was an infant, no other person ever touched his personal treasures, for reasons of hygiene. By the same token, he wasn't permitted to handle other babies' toys. He was constantly being told, "No! No! That's Davey's rattle. Here's *your* rattle"; "No! No! That's Stevey's book. Here's *your* book!"

It's hardly surprising, then, that when confronted by an interloper, he guards his possessions with a ferocity that would do credit to a mountain lion. Before Debbie has a chance to wriggle out of her snowsuit, Leo gathers up an enormous number of things in his arms,

sits on as many others as he can, and exclaims: "Dis is mine! Don't you touch it! You can't have my bear! You can't have my duck! You can't have my cat! You can't have my Humpty Dumpty! Dis is *mine* toys!" A good way to resolve this dilemma is to demonstrate how profitable sharing can be. You should say, in a loud, judicial voice, "Well, now, it doesn't look like Debbie's going to have much fun sitting around doing nothing, so if Leo doesn't want her to play with his things, I'd be very happy to let her play with something of mine." As you hand Debbie your change purse with a couple of pennies in it, you say to bug-eyed Leo: "Now, Leo, don't you touch it! It's for Debbie to play with." Leo will then noisily abandon his loot, and his jaw will jut forward, signaling an impending cloudburst. Just as his lower lip begins to quiver, suggest, "Maybe Debbie will let you play with it, though, if you let her play with some of your nice toys." Debbie doesn't give a hoot about the purse (she's got one of her own at home full of quarters), but she would like to get her hands on Leo's bear, duck, cat and Humpty Dumpty, and yank their eyes out.

Many a tug of war in the sandbox with a shovel or bucket serving as the bone of contention can be avoided by simply outfitting your child's sandbox with several identical shovels and buckets. If you and your child are visiting at the poorly appointed sandbox of a neighbor, don't allow the other child's parent to force the youngster to give up possessions to a "guest." Insist on returning home for a supplementary shovel or two. As a matter of fact, when you and your child visit other homes where there are children, make it a practice to take along a few of your child's prize toys. Then when confronted with the don't-touch-mine toys routine of another youngster, your child will be in an excellent bargaining position.

Even under the best conditions, life among the tots is turbulent. So don't worry too much if your youngster's social life seems a succession of brawls—as long as the kid wins a fair share. After all, is the history of civilization any more civilized?

COMFY OBJECT AT 12 MONTHS

12
Quiz Biz

You have found, no doubt, that your child is a very hard quiz-master. There is no opportunity to choose a congenial category. You get no sly hints. You don't even get rewarded with a box of the sponsor's product and a thank-you for a grand try when you flub one. The questions run the gamut from the ridiculous ("Daddy, are we rich?") to the sublime ("Daddy, what does God look like?").

You probably manage to rise to the occasion with the ridiculous or the sublime ones, but how about all those questions in between?

Let's take one of these questions—"What is a scallop?" is a pretty average kind of question—and try it on for size. Here are some answers to the question "What is a scallop." Choose one.

    a. "Well . . . they're just scallops, that's all."
    b. "They're seafood."

c. "I don't know."

d. "I don't know, but let's look it up."

If you choose answer *a,* you lose a turn. This is no answer at all, and no self-respecting fiver would let it go at that. If you choose *b,* go back three spaces. You could hardly expect any reasonably bright five-year-old to be satisfied with *b.*

No cigar, either, if your choice is *c.* The parent who offers answer *c* may be on firm moral ground, but is giving up too early in the game. "I don't know" is straightforward and honest once or twice, but if fed a steady diet of answer *c* your kid may decide that you are a couple of dunces, a conclusion most kids don't arrive at until they're at least seven. And if you don't think you are likely to be stumped often enough for it to make any difference, tell us, do *you* know what a scallop looks like before it is plucked from the sea and deep-fat fried into its little brown jacket of bread crumbs?

Which leaves *d.* If *d* is your choice, go to the head of the class. "I don't know, but let's look it up" is your best bet for a number of reasons. Your child will be provided with authoritative answers, will develop confidence in you as an information bureau and won't be so likely to consult with corner cronies when some really delicate question crops up. And besides, you find out some of the damnedest things "looking it up." Did you know, for instance, that the common beaming scallop has a row of tiny eyes around the edge of its shell? These eyes are dark, iridescent blue in color, and glow with a lovely fluorescence. So the next time your relentless quiz-master asks you a toughie, look right back into those lovely fluorescent blue eyes and say: "I don't know, but let's look it up. After we've looked it up, let's all take a nice short nap."

Now, it may be perfectly all right to answer a simple question like why the leaves turn all pretty colors in the fall with a song and dance about Jack Frost skittering about on the North Wind sloshing paint in all directions, but the question of where babies come from and, ultimately, how they got there in the first place deserves an answer of a little more substance. This bit of inquisitiveness is not just the venting of a stray curiosity; the general subject will intrigue your child until Social Security sets in, so you may as well start giving out the word—and some of the words—right now. To the "Why's," resist the temptation to fall back on that last resort, the mechanical and desperate and all-embracing answer, "Because." That's cowardly.

Since stammering, stuttering and rolling your eyes are, at the very least, undignified, it would be well to anticipate some of the more obvious questions so that you can deal with them with at least a modicum of dignity and coherence. The first inquiries into the mysteries of life will come along between the ages of three and four. Just as it is important to avoid a cock-and-bull story which must eventually end in a blind alley, it is important, at least at this point, to avoid any luridly graphic explanations depicting the ripe ovum being pursued up and down mysterious passageways by hordes of darting spermatozoa. Don't let yourself be panicked into exhaustive lectures replete with references to fallopian tubes and complicated further by sweeping tangential references to the birds, the bees and the petunias. After all, all the kid asked was, "Mommy, where do babies come from?"

The answer is very simple: "They grow inside their mommies." Don't bother holding your breath for the next question, because, honest, your child doesn't know you've been backed into a corner.

It's okay if babies grow inside their mommies. The kid just wanted to know. True, there may be a few related questions: "Where do babies grow inside their mommies?" Answer, "Right here." "Is there a baby growing inside of you right now?" Answer, "I don't think so." The kid'll be too busy digesting the material already at hand to proceed to the next point.

These bits of information may rattle about in your tot's uncrowded cranium for weeks before it dawns that there are some loose ends lying around. If your child is the sort that takes things personally, the next question may be, "Did I grow inside of you?" Having no alternative, you answer affirmatively. "How did I get out?" It is becoming clear that Baby is warming up to the subject and is prepared to lay down a barrage worthy of an Inquisitor-General.

"How did I get out, Mommy?"

"Dr. Carter helped you."

"How did I fit inside?"

"Oh, you were very, very little."

"Was I real teeny-weeny?"

"You were real teeny-weeny."

"Like a little froggy?"

"Well, uh, no. As a matter of fact, you were just a seed, and—

"Like a orange seed?"

"Well, uh—"

"Tangerine seed?"

"Well—"

"Grape seed?"

"W—"

"Watermelon!"

"Please! You'll simply have to stop interrupting if you want me to tell you things. Now, I can understand that you'd like to know how big you were . . . Well . . . Do you remember the geranium seeds you planted in the spring? Well, you were even smaller than that."

"But I growed."

"Yes, you growed. Grew."

"How did I fit after I growed?"

"Grew, dear. Oh, there was room."

"Like my room?"

"Not that kind of room—"

"With wallpaper?"

"Dear, you're interru—"

"And windows?"

"Please!"

"And curtains?"

"Sweety, I just had the grandest idea. How would you like a great big piece of graham-cracker pie?"

And so it will go: Questions and answers and great gobs of graham-cracker pie.

With panel discussions about impotence, the G spot and transvestite rights, and news breaks about rape and mass murder just a channel hop away from Big Bird and Mr. Rogers, it is all but inevitable that you are going to be called upon to answer some other very challenging questions.

You can, to a certain extent, postpone the inevitable by rigorously limiting your child's TV viewing to suitable programming. Channel-hopping can be eliminated by the simple (but expensive) expedient of procuring one of the newer knobless sets and retaining strict control of the "space command" device. But no matter what you do, it follows as surely as the morning after the night before, that as our society binges on even greater openness and freedom of information, parents are going to have to deal with questions that older generations of parents never even asked, much less had to answer.

It is usually possible to frame an appropriate answer on any subject about which a child has managed to frame a question. Keep your answer simple and brief. Sample question and answer: "Mommy, what's test tube babies?" "Well, sweetie, you know how usually babies grow inside the mommy's belly (we *presume* you've already gotten *that* out of the way). Well, some mommies can't get babies started, so scientists and doctors have figured out a way to get the baby started outside the mommy's belly, then put it in afterward."

If the issue in question is a highly controversial one, it may be useful to suggest that different people have different ideas on the subject. If your child wants to know what you think, by all means state your case. Remember, though, that a young child is really not equipped to deal with the emotional head of steam a parent may have built up over the years. Which is to say: Just because you are a nut on a particular subject—dogs running loose, Richard Nixon, zoysia grass—is no reason to saddle your child with your preoccupations.

Sometimes, because of the press of other business or a potentially awkward situation involving other people, it is necessary, even advisable, to postpone the answer to an important question. This is acceptable to most children provided you have a good track record of honoring rain checks. And with really tough questions, a brief postponement offers the advantage of giving you a chance to figure out just what the heck you're going to say.

COMFY OBJECT AT 18 MONTHS

13

Junior Viewers

Ignoring the TV problem is tantamount to consigning your sprout to the intellectual scrap heap. If you are not prepared to deal with it at the outset, you can expect to be superseded in your child's consciousness by the business end of a cathode-ray tube.

While it is true that unlimited viewing by tots results in something like shortening of the medulla oblongata, it does not follow that they should be denied completely the use of the set. The wisest course to follow with your youngster is some sort of rigid supervision. For a child of two or three, a half hour a day is plenty. Some more sedentary small fry can take more, other volatile types not that much. Strict adherence to whatever time limitation seems best for your child is the prime element in your campaign to prevent your pupa from emerging from the cocoon as a witless moth interested in nothing more glowing than the nearest television screen.

Even aside from the important future considerations, this spoon-

feeding is of utmost importance. Today's child does not take tele-
viewing lightly. Children concentrate on the screen with trancelike
intensity. This half hour of transfixion can use up as much energy
and imagination as all the rest of a child's day's activities combined.
In order to enforce the time limit, it may be expedient to circulate
some fiction to the effect that there just isn't any more to be seen.
You can switch on an empty channel or two if proof is demanded.
In the face of such a convincing demonstration, your child will
probably accept your story and be satisfied to acknowledge the
incident with a short crying fit and let it go at that. This sort of
fabrication may have to be repeated every day for a couple of weeks,
but sooner or later your budding viewer will become conditioned to
the idea that there is etiquette surrounding Television, just as there
is attending Mealtime (sigh of despair), Getting Dressed (groan of
anguish) and Bedtime (sob).

During the time your tot's watching TV, attention to such a small
detail as the type of chair to be used can contribute to happy viewing.
A strong rocking chair is recommended because it affords the child
a means of getting rid of the tension that accumulates during the half
hour. But even though a child is able to rock off some of the steam,
you can expect a volcanic explosion when the fog lifts.

Every child has an individual way of releasing this TV tension. In
one case that has come to our attention, the child, a little girl, springs
from her hassock and, using the oval braided rug as an indoor track,
emulates an Olympic runner. As she tears around the edge of the

rug, she whoops like a terrified crane. We advised a rocker in this case, and it seems to have cut down on the whooping. Another child, a boy, would drag his TV rocker into the kitchen, where his parents were sneaking supper, and throw it at his daddy. In this case we prescribed a hassock, and Daddy no longer eats all hunched up. There's no telling what your little cherub may work out. Don't be surprised if the kid simply walks up to you and punches you in the nose.

Once a child shows a real interest in TV it is very easy to fall into the habit of using the set as a sitter. Parents who are conscientious in every other way will often take television on as a kind of built-in sitter without ever considering its qualifications for the job. The quickest way to convince yourself that TV is a bad risk as a sitter is to watch what passes for children's entertainment during a normal week or even for a few days. The difficulty is not that there are no

good children's shows. There are some, though for every really good one there are a dozen mediocre ones and three or four really atrocious ones. The difficulty is simply that a two-year-old is not ready to watch *any* television alone. It is important for the new viewer to have a constant viewing companion, and you are elected. As a youngster's TV guide, it will be up to you to make meaningful what the child can use, and to prevent him or her from being disturbed or confused by what cannot or should not be used. For example: your toddler is watching an excellent network children's show. At the half hour, the host tells the kiddies not to go away, he'll be back in a minute. The nature of TV is such that there's no telling what the local station is going to do with that minute. Your little viewer might see anything from a "public service" spot advocating safe driving, which depicts a ghastly automobile accident, to a commercial for a downtown movie house, which attempts to lure the public away from TV by showing a clip of the current attraction's high spot—two hulking brutes fighting with bullwhips.

Another of your responsibilities as TV guide is to prepare your child for life in the advertising age. With the ad industry directing heavy fire via television, your tot urgently needs to know how and when to duck.

Children who watch too much television and whose viewing is unsupervised often develop a tendency to see the real world in terms of the twelve- or seventeen- or twenty-four-inch screen. The little boy who, upon being told that Uncle Ned died, asked who shot him, wasn't kidding. Neither are the tots who think that people just naturally bash hell out of each other all the time; or that for every reasonably decent law-abiding citizen there are a couple of dozen crooks; that a lion, a tiger, a gorilla, or all three, are just as likely to be lurking around the next corner as not; that, next to squirting stuff under your arms, the most important human activity is drinking beer.

It's true, of course, that small children have always managed to pick up some pretty silly ideas, but until television came along they had to work at it. They had to dig their misapprehensions out of nursery rhymes, fairy tales, magazines, comics and the movies. With

television, all they have to do is sit there. TV is just about the perfect factory for mass-producing crazy mixed-up kids. But you must see to it that, in your case, it doesn't. You've got to train your child to evaluate what's on TV and you must stand by to supply the right frames of reference.

On the other hand, it won't do to turn your tot into a full-fledged agencyphobe—the kid may grow up to be the president of BBD&O, and you wouldn't want to plant the seeds of a deep neurosis. Here are some suggestions for putting a child wise without creating a complete cynic:

1. Explain the whole idea of commercials to your child. Don't be bitter about it. Just explain that they are things put on television by people who want to sell things.

2. Unless a commercial is really objectionable, you should avoid a point-blank attack. The indirect approach is better. Such remarks as, "Do you want to go to the bathroom during this commercial, or do you want to wait until the next one?" and, "Oh, goodie, a commercial! Now we can go get our milk and cookies," will convey the idea.

3. When your child refuses to use the brand of toothpaste you yourself have been using for the last ten years, averring: "You hafta get Mickey Mouse toothpaste! Mickey Mouse toothpaste is the best!" you might say, "Have you *ever* noticed that on commercials almost everybody says their thing is the best?" Pause. "Well, what that usually means is that they *think* theirs is the best."

The next time somebody tries to tell *your* tot that theirs is the best, you may have the satisfaction of overhearing the response "You jus' *fink* yours is the best!"

4. It is a mistake to give the impression that all TV advertising claims are false or excessive. However, a graphic demonstration that this is sometimes true may provide your child with just the right amount of sales resistance. Suppose, for instance, your youngster has an unreasonable dislike of a certain type of dessert product. Suppose, further, that Uncle Jolly, a favorite TV personality, has announced that this stuff is not only utterly delicious but that it tastes like ice cream, and your child, not recognizing it, has been after you to get some.

This is a perfect setup. Get some with all haste, and serve it, perhaps with some such comment as, "Here's that delicious dessert that tastes just like ice cream that Uncle Jolly is always talking about." Tiny Tot is delighted and piles into it with gusto. But one taste and disillusionment descends. Soon your babe

disconsolately raises spoonsful of the stuff and lets them plop back into the dessert dish. Check the impulse to say, "I told you so." Offer, instead, a nice dish of ice cream.

5. Give credit where credit is due. There are many commercials on television that are worthwhile. If you find a commercial especially interesting or amusing, say so, and encourage your child to do the same.

The animated cartoon has been, almost since the advent of television, the backbone of children's programming. It's not unusual for a three-year-old to watch forty or fifty of the things every week. This is not only too much TV, it is the wrong kind of TV.

Generally speaking, the animated cartoons which are shown on television are very poor material for children under five. In expressing this viewpoint we are no doubt laying ourselves open to a charge of "hogwash." A likely scoff might run: "That stuff never hurt me when I was a kid. Used to see four or five of them every Saturday at the movies." Our answer is that it is one thing to see four or five of them a week at age eight, but quite another to absorb forty or fifty a week at age three. At eight, a child has begun to have a pretty good grip on reality, and is able to recognize the crazy clichés of animated cartoons for the nonsense they are. But the three-year-old is struggling to gain some kind of understanding of the world, and is likely to sponge up any idea he or she can get hold of. A child may want to know what a boat is, for instance. The animated-cartoon definition of a boat is very simple: Boat: a thing that sinks.

We aren't suggesting that a few cartoons will qualify a child for a paragraph in some future edition of Krafft-Ebing or will produce a morbid fear of boats, airplanes, autos, bushes and empty houses. What we are saying is that too many of the wrong kind of cartoons early can seriously handicap a child in the struggle to adjust to the world.

You can prevent your three-year-old from being put off stride by cartoons by educating him or her to see them for what they are. To begin with, as we have said, the fewer seen, the better. You should

view TV with your child, and straighten things out as required. When Krazy Kat's rowboat sinks (Krazy Kat's rowboat *always* sinks), explain in a simple way that in real life boats don't sink. Don't complicate matters by saying that boats don't *often* sink or that they *hardly ever* sink. A three-year-old can absorb either the idea that boats do sink or that they don't. It's much healthier at this stage that the child believe the latter. When Krazy is subsequently pursued by a huge and ferocious shark (Krazy is *always* pursued by a huge and ferocious

shark), remind your child of the real shark you both saw at the aquarium. Because these were a couple of very unimpressive little sand sharks, they can serve as a perfect object lesson.

Bear in mind that it is not your object to spoil the fun. All you need do is establish that Krazy Kat has nothing to do with real life. It would be a healthy thing, too, if your tot were to understand just what animated cartoons are; that is, a great many drawings shown in rapid sequence so as to give an illusion of motion—just as later, when he or she begins watching adventure shows, it will be important to explain the whole concept of actors, sound effects and trick photography.

Demonstrating the principle of the animated cartoon to your three-year-old is as easy as drawing six dots. In fact, that's precisely how it's done—by drawing six dots. Take any magazine. It should be a fairly thick one with some body to it. Open it at random. In the white margin at the top of the right-hand page, about two inches from the right-hand edge, make a black dot. On the next page, a little to the right of where you placed the first dot, place another dot. Repeat this operation until you've got six dots on six succeeding pages, each one a little to the right of the preceding dot. Now, all you have to do is flip the pages. Of course, the dot appears to move. Your child, of course, is delighted; but what is more important, he or she is also enlightened. If you really want to astound your audience, you might refine the demonstration a bit by drawing a wavy line on each of six pages—to represent water. Then go back and draw a little sailboat—a simple triangle will do—on each wave line. Flip the pages, and eureka! the sailboat moves.

Once it's clear that a particular show runs to brutality and violence, declare it out of bounds. Such shows run pretty much to form, and you should be able to evaluate them from a mercifully small sampling. Two or three carefully selected half-hour adventure shows per week are a fair quota for your junior viewer. You ought to watch these shows with your child. When things get tense, mention that you both understand that the bad guy sneaking up on the Solo Ranger is really an actor playing a part. Be careful, though, about making any such comments about the Solo Ranger himself. A brief statement to the effect that of course nothing bad is going to happen to the hero because then there wouldn't be any more shows is about as far as you may go. Remember, you're not there to take the fun out of things but to offer reassurance when the situation gets tense, and to soften the violence in which even the most housebroken of the kiddie adventure shows abound.

Refrain, then, from commenting derisively every time the hero shoots more than six shots from his six-shooter without reloading. That would be carping. You are, however, well within your responsibilities if you explain that the inevitable wild brawls are largely illusory. An extremely graphic demonstration can be produced simply by turning off the sound during one of the fiercer combats. The mighty blows which appear to land so resoundingly are actually misses, and without the powerful suggestion of the sound track, the pretence becomes obvious even to a devoted, bug-eyed little fan. You needn't feel guilty about disabusing your tot of the idea that the good guys and the bad guys are practically killing one another, for, like the lady in the Thurber cartoon, sooner or later we are *all* disenchanted.

The question suggests itself that if TV is such a troublemaker, why let your child watch it at all? Unless you are of the small, embattled group that continues to hold out against television, the question pretty much answers itself. If you've got one of the things in the house—and it's about a hundred to one that you have—you child is going to look at it. And a good thing. For, with all its faults, television has tremendous educational value.

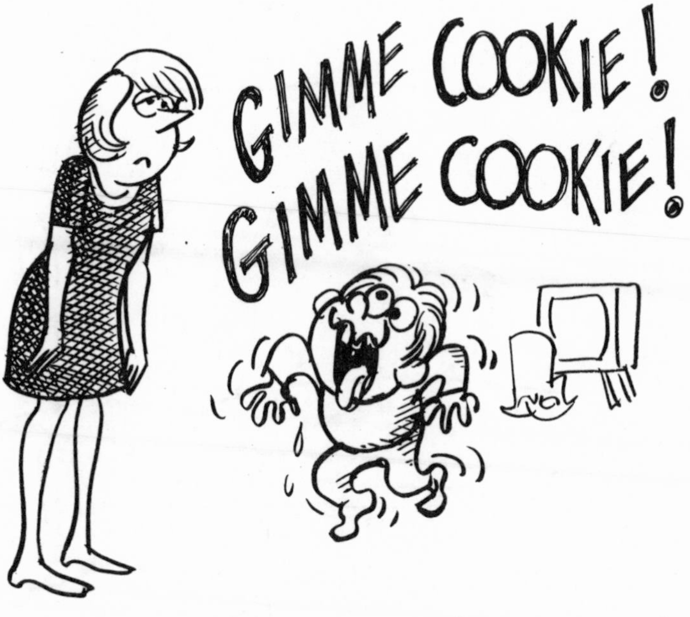
GIMME COOKIE!
GIMME COOKIE!

PROGRESS REPORT

Test IV—DRAWING

Examiner offers subject a piece of paper and a crayon and asks child to draw a picture of a man.

CHILD "A"

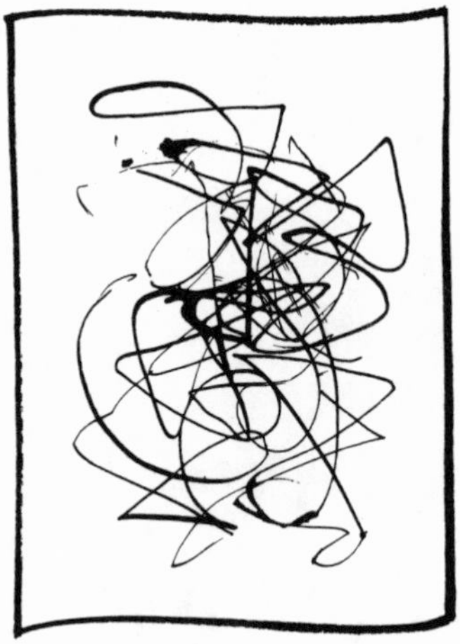

CHILD "B"

CHILD "C"

CHILD "D"

14
Maintaining Discipline

As your child scrambles through the daily routine, it is inevitable that all that insatiable curiosity will occasionally move down the path of nonproductive behavior. Nonproductive behavior may be defined as acts which have the effect of reducing perfectly good, useful objects to worthless scrap.

Consider how the amount of trash you put out each week has increased as your little wrecking contractor has grown. If these negative tendencies are allowed to flourish unchecked, you may find some day that your entire house has been put out with the trash.

Your whole future may depend on your adherence to a few simple rules *today*. If, already, the neighbors have begun to avoid you on the street, think what it will be like day after tomorrow.

Lay Down the Law
A set of enforceable laws is as necessary to the proper conduct of your home as it is to that of your government. The laws can be very

simple. For instance, "Don't throw the ashtray." As the child probes this ruling for loopholes, it will occur to your little lawyer that you haven't said anything about not *dropping* the ashtray. You must be on the watch for this sort of technical hairsplitting. Before the child can put the thought into action, another law must be shoved into the breach: "Don't *drop* the ashtray." When it's clear that this latest legislation is poorly written and open to considerable interpretive analysis, it proves necessary to draft a third bill which supersedes the two previous ones: "Don't touch the ashtray, or I'll knock your little block off!"

Be Alert for Trouble

There are, of course, certain obvious telltale storm signals which are easily spotted, such as the strident screams of a little girl being snatched baldheaded, the sharp report of a ceramic lamp base

exploding or the enraged roar of an innocent passerby who has been drenched with the hose. In these cases, the parent can arrive quickly at the scene of the crime, sift the evidence and dispense justice.

There are, however, many less obvious portents that can easily escape the notice of the inexperienced parent. Beware the sudden silence in the playroom. Your child is up to something. Spontaneous statements like: "Leo love Mommy. Mommy love Leo?" should be regarded with suspicion. If you notice him quietly reading a book for which he has previously displayed nothing but contempt, listen for the sound of running water. And if you should be advised, "You don't have to buy me a birthday present this year, Mommy," lock him in his room and search the house from top to bottom.

Don't Give In

Never let your child get his own way by means of a temper tantrum. When a tantrum occurs, calmly but firmly remove the child's shoes and put your noisemaker in the crib. Leave the room and close the door. In an hour or two, when the child realizes it is getting no response, the racket will taper off to a hoarse wail. And finally, silence. Waiting out the calm after the storm is universally agreed to be one of the most harrowing experiences of parenthood. Many parents make the mistake of worrying about what the neighbors will think, and after only five or ten minutes of anxious listening, during which they convince themselves that the child has snapped one or more vital blood vessels, they are apt to rush headlong into the room with lollipops and apologies. For these unhappy creatures temper tantrums are daily occurrences and lollipops become a supply problem.

Crime and Punishment

We disagree with Mr. Shaw's dictum that one should never strike a child except in anger. Striking your child, even though the great majority of us do it occasionally, always represents some form of parental failure. As for striking a child in anger, this represents a double failure: failure to control the child and failure to control yourself—a much more serious lapse.

The appropriate punishment for your small miscreant's small misdeeds is prompt, appropriate deprivation of privileges, accompanied by unmistakable expressions of disapproval—even anger if the crime is sufficiently grave.

Truth and/or Consequences

Another of the parent's most important responsibilities is the teaching of the difference between right and wrong. Since none of us always does the right thing, we often find it expedient to cover our deviations from perfection with deviations from truth. Obviously, this is a vicious circle, but it is so firmly superimposed on the family group that we must learn how to live with it.

Here are two simple rules which, although not very golden, can help keep things under control:

1. Don't lie to your child unless it is absolutely necessary.
2. Don't get caught at it.

What constitutes necessity in this matter is something the individual parent must rationalize personally. The child's health and welfare are good criteria. The child's *and* the parents' health and welfare are better ones. There will come Sunday mornings when you will be able to earn yourself an extra hour of sleep simply by convincing your rooster that it *isn't* daytime yet. It may even be expedient to suggest that it's the *moon* that's beaming through the curtains. If you get away with it, it's a lie well spent. Unquestionably it's for the child's own good. With that extra hour of sleep, you'll be able to give a more brilliant reading, later on, of Mickey Mouse, Peanuts and Hagar.

The proper cultivation of some of your child's most important habits will rest squarely on a foundation of lies to the effect that that's what Daddy did when *he* was a little boy: "When Daddy was a little boy, he brushed his teeth three times every day." (Daddy has a complete upper and lower bridge to attest to the fact that his mother often discovered spiderwebs on his toothbrush.) "Daddy always took his vitamins without a fuss. That's why he's so big and strong." (When Daddy was a little boy, vitamins hadn't been invented, and the closest he ever got to his cod liver oil was the time he licked what

he thought was the molasses spoon. As a consequence, Daddy *isn't* very strong, though come to think of it, he *is* getting bigger every day.) "Daddy never left his things lying around when he was finished with them." (Daddy still doesn't put his toys away.)

Even if you are scrupulously careful with your strategic use of the fib as an aid in the rearing of your child, your little Portia will eventually find it is a two-edged weapon and use it against you. You won't have to provide an opportunity to learn the technique by imitation; it occurs to children spontaneously. How you behave in the face of your child's first big fat lie will have a lot to do with the future of wholesale deception in your home.

In many cases the parent forces the child to tell the lie in the first place by insisting on a formal confession of guilt when faced with such irrefutable evidence that a confession is superfluous. If you roar at a three-year-old, "Did you do that?" it won't occur to the tot standing there in front of the marked-up wall holding a red crayon that the question is rather a rhetorical one. He or she will simply weigh the possible answers, and likely decide that "No" is the best bet. If you demand to know who, then, did the foul deed, the child will profess complete bafflement. If you then suggest through gritted teeth that he or she reconsider the plea, your tot is apt, having gotten into the swing of the thing, to come up with a diabolically ingenious whopper.

Resist, therefore, the impulse to undertake the role of prosecuting attorney in cross-examination. When a situation arises that might tempt your child to depart from the truth, don't force the issue. Assume, don't question, the child's guilt. Any normal kid is perfectly capable of thinking up that first lie without any encouragement from you.

Until your child reaches the age of four or so, it will be pretty easy to hear the testimony and deduce the truth. This is likely to create the false but fortunate impression that you are omniscient, reducing considerably your child's inclination to fib. When the time comes for your youngster to rocket out into the world on a tricycle and begin comparing notes with colleagues, however, your feet of clay are in imminent danger of discovery. Not only that, but having whittled you down to size, the child's next step will be to exploit this new knowledge in an intuitive search for your Achilles' heel.

Before you have suffered a complete loss of prestige, however, you can and should embark on a new program calculated to save face all around. This consists of explaining the nice distinction between "lying" and "pretending." It's all right, you say, to "pretend" up to a point—so long as you both know that's all it is; but if the child tries to make the story stick, the game falls flat and you won't have any. If you play your cards right, you'll find that things will go more or less smoothly. Your youngster tells you a palpable untruth; there follows a stimulating battle of wits as stylized as a Chinese drama; then you say, "Okay, now tell me what *really* happened at Debbie's house this afternoon." Chances are you'll get the straight dope. And that's all there is to it—except to phone Debbie's mother and assure her that she is welcome to use your Mixmaster while hers is being repaired.

15

First Outings

Eventually your child will become sufficiently aware that there is a big wonderful world out there, so there is nothing for it but to screw up your courage and undertake some outings.

Perhaps the most important thing to remember in dealing with children is that no two of them are alike. Advice and handy-dandy rules (like these) are useful only if you adapt them to the needs of your particular child. There *are* children who are so sturdily (or insensitively) constituted that they need very little preparation for anything—and there are those at the other extreme who need a scenario at every turn of the road. But most kids fall into that middle range that includes most of us—individuals who would like to have

149

some idea just what the heck is going to happen next. A little sensible preventative orientation can not only save you and your child a certain amount of upset, but may even head off a few galloping traumas at the pass.

This raises the issue of doing whatever it is you have to do to make your little charge presentable.

If your special problem is a little boy, you are probably wondering what to do about his hair, and—with justice—dreading the ordeal. Except for the rare little numbskull who will stand for anything, the first haircut will be sorely needed long before he will accept the ministrations of a professional barber.

Cutting Baby's hair is just a shade easier than bathing a tomcat. You will need help, all the help you can get. Can the man next door dance a jig? Have him in. Can the mailman make a noise remarkably like a cannon by clicking his tongue against the roof of his mouth? Urge Officer Callahan to come sample your latest culinary triumph. Of course, if Daddy is the only entertainment you can get, you'll have to make do.

The workman being no better than his tools, you should obtain the best pair of scissors you can find. If these happen to be snaggle-toothed affairs which have to be screwed together every three snips, well, chin up: there's no turning back now.

Some other things it might be good to have on hand are: an unlimited supply of ice cubes, a large box of lollipops, piles of old newspaper, a bunch of old ladies' hats (preferably the kind with a lot of net and ostrich feathers), some large paper bags, two ripe bananas, a box of corn flakes and a big pile of assorted kitchen utensils, old jewelry, sewing scraps and bits of string.

The idea is for Daddy to fascinate him while Mommy cuts his hair. The cutting job requires a surgeon's steady hand, the nerves of a steeplejack and inhuman patience. The haircutter must anticipate the subject's every move. Beginning at the back, working around each side, then pruning the front, each snip should be made with an eye to the total effect.

Daddy's job, on the other hand, requires only tremendous endurance and a boundless imagination. Any gymnastic or juggling ability he may have is definitely to the good. An important aspect of Daddy's end of the job is pacing; like a prizefighter, he must conserve his strength so he can go the distance. He should begin with easy things like putting on funny hats, and save the hard stuff, like tripping and falling heavily against the china closet, till last.

Daddy must be acutely sensitive to the demands of his audience. Interest must not be allowed to wane even momentarily. Suppose, for instance, Daddy has hit on the happy device of tearing newspapers into long shreds and letting them float gently to the floor. If, after a bit of this, a certain restiveness is observed, Daddy must vary his routine. Instead of dropping the streamers to the floor, he might begin to eat them, producing with each swallow an intriguing noise like that made by plucking a loose guitar string. The little fellow will soon be chuckling happily again as his mother chops away with desperate concentration.

As you can see, the haircutting problem is one of formidable proportions. There are no simple directions on the package. It is a difficult task, but not a thankless one. For, as you crouch wearily amidst the debris, a wonderful sight may be described through the settling haze of hair. It's your son—and he looks like a *real boy*!

If you're the parent of a girl, of course, you probably don't have to cope with the haircut problem. But before you start gloating, consider this: all the haircuts from now through puberty won't add up to the cost of one wedding.

In any case, now that the child is presentable, it's time to go somewhere.

TRIP TO THE ZOO

On any given sunny Sunday it occurs simultaneously to thousands of parents that the time is ripe for that first trip to the zoo. Blinded by their own brilliance, these ill-fated people fail to see the projected jaunt as anything but unalloyed delight. In their exhilaration they do not realize that the beauties of the zoological garden flourish in quicksand.

For our purposes, the zoo may be likened to a golf course. Each is scientifically laid out so as to test to the full a person's skill and endurance. With each there is a series of tests: in golf there are eighteen holes; in zoo-going there are the dozens of exhibits. Also similarly, the field of activity in each is generously laced with traps and hazards—sand and water on the one hand and refreshment stands selling peanuts, popcorn, Cracker-Jack, hot dogs, soda pop, souvenirs and gas-filled balloons on the other. For the tyro the two enterprises even share the same aftereffects: general exhaustion, blistered feet, extremely sore legs from having walked great distances and a sense of frustration—the result of having fallen far short of a lofty goal.

You won't learn here how to break a hundred, but the following material may help you in your determination to see that the first trip to the zoo results in an accord between your child and the beasts of the jungle, the wood and the plain.

The Elephant House

Parents are often bewildered when their little one emits a piercing howl at the first sight of an elephant. "That's strange," Mommy says

to Daddy. "The little woolly blue elephant that cousin Ethel gave him has always been one of his favorite toys." The only strange thing about it is that Mommy and Daddy should be so obtuse as to expect Baby to see any similarity between the little woolly blue toy and this great gray monster. It's of no use to tell him not to be afraid; that's not why he's crying. He's bawling because he feels horribly, utterly betrayed. Since it was received about a year ago, the little blue puff has been universally referred to as an elephant. Now, after having been told over and over that he was going to see a real live elephant at the zoo, here he is confronted with this ugly, outsized imposter. It's enough to put anybody off stride.

The Lion House

Oliver Goldsmith, poet, playwright, essayist and naturalist, in his work *Animated Nature,* 1825 edition, has this to say about lions: ". . . though he usually feeds on fresh provision, his urine is insupportable." Don't be embarrassed if, as you enter the crowded lion house, your two-year-old loudly paraphrases and corroborates Mr. Goldsmith. It is merely the first of many candid observations your child will make during the afternoon, so you might as well be calm about it. If your child is one of the many whose first sight of the King of Beasts is greeted with less than bubbling enthusiasm, let it go at that and be on your way. Do not under any circumstances sweep the tot from the stroller in order to supply a better look at the terror of the veldt. Don't bother to explain that the lion is a sweet old thing

who simply *loves* little children; this will just confirm all the worst fears. Saunter down to the other end of the building to see some of the smaller members of the cat family. A black panther sleeping at the rear of a cage is a good beginning; or if you want to play it absolutely safe, locate the tabby that is kept about the place to keep down the mice.

The Reptile House

Your zoo will doubtless boast a prize collection of slithery snakes, crawly lizards and warty crocodiles. It is important, as you conduct your child through the reptile house, to avoid making any remarks which might betray your own unhealthy fear of slithery snakes, crawly lizards and warty crocodiles. You don't want your child saddled with such a shamefully medieval attitude, so be sure to smile sweetly at every revolting thing you see, remarking brightly through gritted teeth on how *pretty* the markings are. After you're outside, you can get off by yourself and have a good "Ugh!"

The Monkey House

Having conceded at the outset that Daddy looks like the Barbary ape and Mommy like the sooty mangabey, there is fun for the entire family here. You can have a fine time spotting in-laws while your offspring attempts to analyze the strange appeal of the Barbary ape and the sooty mangabey; but be prepared to pull up stakes and go at the first indication that the dear little simians intend to help the tot's analysis along with a practical demonstration. This uninhibited expression of a vernal impulse will assuredly give rise to observations from your youngster surpassing in candor anything he or she has said so far all day or is likely to say for months to come. If this happens, you have only two courses of action open to you, neither of them enviable: either pretending not to hear and keeping mum or else launching then and there into an indoctrination lecture that will be a source of interest not only to your offspring but to an entire audience of several dozen highly amused onlookers.

The Small-Mammal House
With its teeming population of raccoons, beavers, skunks, possums and woodchucks, the small-mammal house is an ideal place for your young zoologist. These very animals are the heroes of virtually all children's books and records, so no child will have much difficulty recognizing them; but even in this paradise things can go amiss. On one occasion a mink-coated young mother pointed to the little mink at which her three-year-old daughter was marveling and informed her, "It took 278 of those little things to make this coat." The kid cried off and on for eighteen years until her old man bought her a mink coat of her own.

But it is growing late, and so, our little naturalist stuffed full of peanuts, popcorn, Cracker-Jack, hot dogs and soda pop, our expedition heads home, while a gas-filled balloon, having come loose from its mooring on a small thumb, continues its loudly lamented ascent slowly toward the golden heavens.

TRIP TO THE RESTAURANT

You have taken your small child "out to eat." The hostess seems to recognize you as she inquires, "How many?" Making a quick count, you answer in a voice that seems hardly your own, "Three." As you are conducted to a far corner table, it all comes back to you—the hostess, the quick count. . . . The same compulsion which causes the criminal to return to the scene of the crime has drawn you to the very restaurant which was the site of your previous experiment in eating out with Baby. Recollections flood in on you hideously—the shattered high chair, the hurtling saltcellar, the sea of spilt milk. . . . Somehow you are seated. The hostess scurries away as a waitress approaches. Before you can say her nay she adds to the already abundantly set table three brimming glasses of ice water. A shout sticks in your throat like a giant oyster cracker as Baby grabs a corner of the tablecloth and whisks it off the table. There is an avalanche of silverware, a tidal wave of ice water, and sugar cubes are flung across the mystic bowl of night.

—Dream, common in parents of small children.

The best advice on the subject of taking small children "out to eat" is not to; but if you are one of the vast majority unable to get it through your head that eating out is just another of life's little pleasures that was automatically crossed off the list when you took on parenthood, you may be interested in some suggestions for making the best of a bad situation.

1. Never take a hungry child to a restaurant. Blunt the appetite with milk and cookies before you leave the house. This will serve a double purpose: the child is far less likely to be irritable and, having already got milk into your tot, you can afford to be generous about ginger ale while you're waiting for the food to come. Then, of course, there is the added advantage that your wee one will have the opportunity for leg-stretching during your consequential trips to the rest room.

2. Choose a nearby restaurant. A long drive improves no one's humor, least of all a hungry child's. So don't try out that wonderful place forty miles up the pike that Bill and Cora have been raving about. Save it for some night when you've invested in a sitter.

3. Order something for your youngster that is ready to serve. A meatball in the hand is worth two lamb chops queued up in the kitchen.

4. Never stand in line for a meal. Since your child's reaction to the whole business of eating is at best one of bored toleration, the notion of standing in line to be permitted to sit down to a meal is likely to seem so utterly outrageous that he or she may run amok.

5. Keep it gay. If you are relaxed and pleasant, chances are your youngster will at least make a stab at following your example. By the same token, if your gay smile begins to wear thin as things drag on, your child will sense your impatience and sour on the whole operation. And don't count on the Muzak to drown out the protests.

One last bit of advice: If the waitress is empowered to ask if you'll have something to drink, by all means have something. A Scotch on the rocks will raise your feeling-no-pain threshold just enough so that the spilled tomato juice won't feel quite so icky as it drizzles down your leg. Even if you have to drive and it has been truly said of you that "one" puts you on your ear, order it anyway, for the next hour or so is going to be, at best, a sobering experience.

TRIP TO THE MOVIES

Your local Cinema 4 (four theaters, lots of waiting—especially for the rare film that's reasonably appropriate for kids) is a confusing, chaotic place with a vast parking lot usually accessed from a major highway notorious for drag races and jackknifed tractor trailers. So far not so good—not for you and certainly not for your three-to-four-year-old.

Now, consider the theater experience itself. You go into a long, dimly lit room with a mixed bag of imperfect strangers, some bent on fun, some bent on mischief, some just bent. *Then the lights go out and it's pitch dark.* It's enough to scare the living cement out of any self-respecting youngster. Remember, this is the kid who won't even consider going to sleep without a night-light.

Perish forbid you should be so foolhardy as to arrive *after* the lights are out. Finding a seat in a crowded darkened theater is a traumatic experience when you are on your own, but with a small terrified child on your hip—your child will quite sensibly insist on being carried after one look at the situation—it's the sort of shin-kicking, instep-crunching experience that nightmares are made of and could, at the very least, get you lynched.

Now consider the choice of film. There is not a single classic children's film that does not include material that is virtually certain to scare hell out of your three-to-four-year-old—not *Snow White,* not *Pinnochio,* not *Bambi,* not *Dumbo,* not *ET,* not etc. Oh, come on, you say. Those are great films, and to deprive children of them would be almost criminal! Who's depriving?

Are we proposing that you desist taking your tot to these great films? Not at all. We know perfectly well that you can't wait to see them again yourself. (We couldn't—we've seen *Snow White* eleven times. Our favorite part is during the dwarfs' dance when Sneezy blows Dopey to the rafters with a giant ah-choo.)

We are suggesting delay, not deprivation. Why not wait until your child is six, seven or eight to deal with the really terrifying witch in *Snow White,* the Pleasure Island sequence in *Pinnochio* (shades of Kafka!), the death of Bambi's father, the bad guys after ET or the tragic separation of Dumbo from his mother? What we propose, simply and humbly, are some preventative measures, along with

some suggestions about how to cope if and when things threaten to get out of hand.

1. Prepare your child for the experience. The fact that a movie house is dark is taken for granted by adults. But it could come as a disconcerting shock to an unsuspecting tot.

2. While there's no need to impose a total silence rule, point out that while the movie experience bears some similarity to the TV experience, there are differences, and that out of respect for the other patrons your child should keep a zippered lip at least some of the time . . .

3. —except when it's open to receive popcorn, M&Ms (at *ET,* of course, Reese's Pieces are *de rigueur*) or such other comestibles that you have chosen to keep your child quiet. Jujubes are especially good as they tend to gum up the mouth and inhibit speech.

4. Do not sit close to the screen. The witch in *Snow White* is scary enough from way back; up close, she's instant nightmares.

5. If your child wants to watch the movie with ears covered and face buried in your bosom during the scary parts, by all

means allow it. It's a nice close feeling. Under no circumstances should you mock, tease or call your child scaredy-cat. If you do, there's got to be a special place for you in the Inferno.

6. If at some point your child asserts that it's time to go home, give the proposition serious consideration. It may prove the better part of valor.

TRIP TO THE MALL

Shopping malls are second only to airports in the inordinacy of the amount of walking they require for the accomplishment of what would seem to be a simple purpose—entering an aircraft in the one case, buying provender in the other. A collapsible stroller, therefore, is very much in order, at least until your youngster absolutely insists on negotiating solo. Shopping with an infant or very small child is not much better or worse an experience than doing anything in public with an infant or very small child. It usually consists of accepting the applause of the crowds for having produced such a darling chin-chuckable little child while hoping you can get the whole miserable thing over with before the little darling gets sopping enough to just float away.

When your child reaches tothood and develops an independent mind and will, different sorts of problems present themselves. Here are some of the most frequent ones along with some ideas on how they might be dealt with.

Galloping Gimmies at the Toy Store

Malls are rife with marvelous toy stores featuring fabulous displays of precisely the toys your little gimme artist has been nagging you for since Santa forgot to bring them last Christmas. It is important and necessary that you establish, as early as possible, a workable set of rules for dealing with toy-lust in the marketplace. Fortunately, most children are capable of understanding the general idea of limits—the idea that for a variety of reasons none of us—not your child, not you, not even Daddy—can have everything we want when we want it. There are limits relating to money ("Mommy just doesn't have enough money, sweetheart, to buy you that forty-nine dollar 'Wide

World of Monsters' playset."), limits based on age-appropriateness ("... and besides, you're much too young, sweetie, for 'Wide World of Monsters'—the parts are so little they might get stuck in your little throat."), limits arising out of considerations of taste ("... not to mention the fact that I wouldn't consider having the disgusting things in my house!"), and finally, limits based on the exhaustion of patience

("...and if you don't stop that damn whimpering, I'm going to knock your little block clear into the parking lot!").

A reasonable and workable compromise could involve letting your tot buy some inexpensive toy or book during these grueling treks to the mall. The prospect of such a goodie will do wonders for your child's humor and tractability.

The Getting Lost Syndrome

Children vary considerably in their ability to get lost. Some kids can get lost on their way to the bathroom in their own house, while others can maintain a sense of direction and location in a vasty mall. Here are some thoughts on dealing with the great middle ground of youngsters who are capable of getting lost but don't necessarily make a habit of it, along with some ideas and techniques that may save you a few trips to the mall's lost-child station:

1. Some article of very brightly colored clothing—day-glo isn't very chic, but it sure is visible—will not only help keep your tot within eyeshot in a crowded mall, but also has a certain panache.

MOTHERS
OF LOST CHILDREN
REPORT HERE

2. Most children have a tendency to be trailers. The reason for this is that walking behind Mommy allows the child to keep her in view. The trouble with this is that small children are very easily distracted and, since most mommies' legs look pretty much alike, the child is likely to resume following the wrong pair after even a brief distraction.

In an uncrowded situation, you might give your child the responsibility of "leading the way"—then *you* keep your *child* in view.

In crowded mall situations, it is necessary either to hang on to your child or have your child hang on to you. Or, if that is impossible because your arms are filled with the day's plunder, just sort of dribble the kid ahead of you like a soccer ball.

3. Most children who wander off in shopping situations do so out of sheer boredom while Mommy is selecting or trying on merchandise. A simple ploy here is to promote involvement in the experience, perhaps by appointing your youngster guardian of some small purchase. Children are fiercely possessive— yours may put Cerberus to shame guarding your panty hose purchase.

The Pet Store Hazard

The most hazardous hazard at the mall is the pet store—guaranteed to be jam-packed with adorable little animals just waiting to fall in love with your child at first sight. Avoid it as the plague. If you do not, your home will become a landlocked ark filled with animals (and animal problems) of every kind. Of course, if you already have a large dog, a couple of cats, some gerbils, some fish and a parakeet, by all means drop by the pet store. It might be diverting to see some animals you don't have to clean up after for a change.

SUPERMARKET SAFARI

As a general rule, kiddies under three should be cart-ridden. The one-year-old who is permitted to explore the supermarket on foot will quickly find the way to the low bins of the vegetable counter to see eye to eye with the potatoes. Unless yours is in serious need of minerals, too many unwashed spuds may have an undesirable effect on a child's metabolic balance. Similarly, the unchauffered two-year-old will lose no time in discovering the cookie counter. As a result, you will kill the better part of your shopping session by having to restack its entire contents.

When your child is old enough, he or she should be allowed to help. Definite assignments—one at a time—are in order. Unless briefed in this fashion, the acquisitive four-year-old may be responsible for fifteen or twenty unspecified items turning up among your groceries at the checker's stall. At this point, you either pay your money and take your goods, or you ignore the line piling up behind you and take time out to eliminate such choice surprises as a half-dozen giant rat traps, a quart of pine jelly soap, one hundred yards of plastic clothesline and a half-gallon jar of brandied persimmons.

To sum up: the very best rule to follow with regard to visiting the marts of trade with your youngster in tow is—Don't.

COMFY OBJECT AT 24 MONTHS

16
Creativity

A child reaching the age of two begins to feel the urge to create. Catching this creative instinct at the time of its first stirrings and channeling it intelligently will contribute greatly toward keeping your family ship on an even keel. You may assume that the time for channeling has arrived when your youngster encompasses some grand inventive scheme by wreaking havoc on a useful, even treasured, household object. Entering the living room to see what that odd noise is, you discover your wee one standing on the stair landing, violently belaboring the newel post with a prized needlepoint sofa cushion. It has come open at one corner, and tiny white feathers fill the air. Beaming, your tot announces, "Look, Mommy, I making *snow*!"

An ideal creative toy for the two-year-old is a good supply of modeling clay. The clay available at most toy stores is put up in sets of colored strips. Before you present it to your two-year-old, however, you must mash all those lovely bright strips together until you have a uniform gray glob. The purpose of this preliminary kneading is to save your little sculptor the frustrating experience of having all the pretty colors neutralize right before those stricken eyes. Otherwise, as little Rodin begins to roll out a snake and the colors merge into a dull gray, "It pupposed to be a *green* nake!" the whimper will

come, the eyes welling with tears. So it's much simpler to begin with a big unesthetic lump. Such a lump contains the makings of approximately thirty-two snakes of varying sizes and family relationships. When the tiny artist has manufactured a big granddaddy snake all of ten feet long and dragged the giant reptile clear into the kitchen via the living room and dining room to allow you the privilege of first gander, it's time to allow some branching out into other media for a while.

When your young Picasso is able to identify a particular scribble with a particular image in the mind's eye, he or she has a perfect right to announce the creation of a picture. It may be just a slight variation of the scribble your child has been producing for months, but if now you are proudly informed that it represents a kangaroo skipping rope in a snowstorm, take the kid's word for it.

When your minor master deigns to show one of these masterpieces, regard it attentively. If the title of the work is not volunteered, it's perfectly good form to ask what the picture is supposed to be. Perhaps upon being told it's a picture of a "whole bunch of giraffes eating the tops off the trees," you are able to detect some element of the picture which seems to bear this out. At which point you might play a long shot and say, "Oh, yes, I see their big long necks." If it pays off, fine. But if the artist straightens up to his or her full

twenty-seven inches and says in a hurt, indignant tone: "No! That's their *teefs*! Their necks is over *here*!" beat a fast apologetic retreat and keep the incident in mind when next you are tempted to leap to a naive conclusion.

Resist, as well, the temptation to offer the artist constructive criticism. Your particular artist simply cannot use it. Another pitfall to avoid in your role of patron of the arts is flattery. If you are indiscriminately and excessively enthusiastic, you may find yourself written off as a well-meaning but soft-headed old party whose comments are hardly worth soliciting.

It is important that the tools which you place at your child's disposal keep pace with need. The mother who tries to play safe by restricting her child to pencil and bridge pad when the creative urge requires more soul-stirring things is just asking for trouble. Little Michelangelo may emerge from the bedroom at some small hour and turn an expensive papered room into a private Sistine Chapel. Not having paints, the budding artist will have to make do with what's around the house, and may discover that mustard, catchup and plum jam are excellent paint substitutes. They come in handsome decorator colors and have sufficient covering power to require only one coat. No brush or roller needed; you just smear it on with your hands.

After your child works through pencils, crayons and chalk and slate, it may be time to bestow the accolade of paints and brushes. The paints could be some reasonably yielding set of "hard" colors in a paintbox. (Test the color with a moistened finger. If no color comes off, ask to see something else.) Another excellent solution, if you are willing to risk opaque liquid water color in jars (variously called tempera, gouache or show-card color), is to buy some basic colors and pour out just enough for one session. An ordinary muffin tin makes an excellent receptacle.

A good place to shop for brushes is the paint counter of the five-and-ten. It is usually stocked with a variety of low-priced round ferrule brushes. These are inexpensive and will bear up almost as well under your small fry's swab-the-deck technique as quality brushes costing many times more.

Here are a couple of tricks that will help keep your painter in paper at no expense and with little trouble. Select the three or four pages from each issue of the daily newspaper that carry no large ads or pictures—the want-ad, classified and editorial pages, for instance. Stash these away daily and you'll be ready when your youngster goes on a painting spree. At the beginning of a painting career a child is not likely to resent the fact that the paper is less than pristine. Then, too, newspaper is wonderfully absorbent, facilitating a swoop-down and sop-up operation if the muse of painting is in imminent danger of death by drowning.

If you are a bag saver (and who isn't?), you are in an excellent position when the young master's willingness to paint on old newspapers shreds to resentment. Simply smooth out a large brown paper bag, and cut the bottom off. Slit it down one side and open it out flat. You will have provided a surprisingly large piece of heavy-duty drawing paper. If you are a big saver worthy of the name you should be set for some time to come.

PROGRESS REPORT

Test V—EXAMINING A BOOK

The examiner offers the subject the book and suggests that the subject look at it.

CHILD "A"

CHILD "B"

CHILD "C"

CHILD "D"

17

Day Care

Some things about the experience of parenthood haven't changed very much—the miracle of tiny fingers and toes hasn't changed at all, the fretful bane of colic and the angst of teething have been preserved intact.

But some things do change—rapidly and radically. In the past twenty years, the number of working mothers in the population has grown from 17 percent to 50 percent. This enormous change raises many issues, not the least of which is the matter of child care. What, years ago, was generally a judgment call—will nursery school be good for little Jill or Johnny, is he or she too young, is there a shortage of kids in the neighborhood, etc.—has become for many parents as urgent a necessity as food and shelter.

Indeed, finding adequate child care so you can keep on working has a considerable bearing on whether you will be able to *afford* food and shelter in this perpetually inflationary society.

If you are part of the minority that still has the option of choosing whether to use day care or not, you should start by considering your own particular situation.

Nursery schools do serve a vitally important function. They afford the child, who might not otherwise have it, an opportunity to play and work in the company of a reasonably representative cross section of kids. *How* representative is, of course, a question for the parent to look into when selecting a school. It's not just a matter of the child's day-to-day fun. A four-year-old *needs* the company of children of similar age.

If your neighborhood has an abundance of prekindergarteners and enough play space to accommodate their burgeoning activities, there's no need to send your youngster to nursery school. The parent

who sends a child to nursery school simply as a matter of course is not giving the kid a fair shake. If circumstances are such that a child can develop happily and healthily at home, then, generally speaking, the child is better off there.

Too many three- and even two-year-olds are sent to nursery school simply because a baby has arrived on the scene. The parents of these tots may pay abundant lip service to the idea that it is important for children to have brothers and sisters, but in practice they follow a policy of rigid segregation. "How is Jackie getting along with his new baby sister?" Jackie's mother is asked.

"Oh, just beautifully!" she gushes, adding: "Jackie's in nursery school from nine till three-thirty. Then he watches TV from three-thirty 'til supper, then after supper the baby goes to bed. Oh, yes, it's working out beautifully. There's just one trouble. He keeps trying to get at her in the morning before he goes to school. But even that's no real problem. His daddy's still home at that time, so there are two of us to watch him."

That the four-year-old is not entirely ready for school is argued by the fact that the weight of professional experience indicates that five is the age at which kindergarten becomes feasible. At five, children start liking the feeling of being part of a group. They enjoy learning songs together. Buttons and bows come within their ken. And nineteen out of twenty five-year-olds are good bets to make it to the bathroom every time.

All the disadvantages, both inherent and extrinsic, to the contrary notwithstanding, if your child doesn't have playmates of the same age and if your neighborhood is uncongenial, nursery school can contribute much toward development. Just as there are situations in

which nursery school is obviously not needed, under other combinations of circumstances nursery school may be the *only* answer.

Which brings us back to the majority of parents in this country. Here are some of the factors to be considered when choosing a day-care facility. As with so many of the problems and concerns of parenthood, common sense is much more important than special knowledge.

Visit the Facility While It's in Session
One big reason for starting your nursery-school shopping early is to be able to visit the school while it's in session. Call or write the schools you are considering, explaining that you may wish to enroll your child next September and that you'd like to pay a visit. Headmasters usually prefer to take the parent of prospective enrollees on a nice quiet after-hours guided tour of the "plant" with much attention paid to equipment, feeding facilities and the like. Make it clear that you want to see the school in action.

If management would prefer a cozy chat in the administrator's office after the evidence has all gone home, regard the establishment with suspicion.

Observe the nature of the interaction between the kids and the care-giving staff. Do the kids generally appear to like the "teachers"? Is there plenty of unforced cuddling and comforting of the kids who seem to want it and need it, and a respectful "hands off" policy for kids who prefer to interact in other ways—like beating the teacher at chess, for example?

Don't expect to find a nursery school where seldom is heard a discouraging word and calmness and quietude reign. There is no

such. Four-year-olds have a natural flair for anarchy, and there are bound to be altercations. What you want to find out is how they are handled. What does the teacher do when Eugene walks up to Sally and smashes her over the head with a bucket of sand? Does she make it damn clear that we just don't do things like that in this school, or does she put her arm around the little monster and say sweetly: "Now, Eugene, Sally doesn't want to play that game now. I'll tell you what! Suppose you come in and help me put out the soup for lunch." If sweet talk seems to be the order of the day rather than just desserts, you'd better ask yourself how your youngster is going to fit into the picture. Will he understand that Eugene behaves atrociously because he "suffers from feelings of insecurity," and that the school is "helping him with his problem by giving him the feeling that he is loved?" He will not! What he will understand is that the way to get to help with the soup is to smash Sally over the head with a bucket of sand. Beware of the sort of school that prides itself on being able to do wonders with "difficult children." All too frequently the wonders are performed to the detriment of the kids whose parents have led—or dragged—them more or less in the ways of righteousness.

Don't Believe Everything You Read

It has been said that every business is a people business. In no area is this more to the point than in the matter of choosing a day-care facility. The quality and quantity of personnel is much more important than the latest word in plant and equipment. It's people who care for children—not stainless steel mini-kitchens and mint collections of Fisher-Price preschool toys. It takes a tremendous amount of teacher power to operate a nursery class of four-year-olds. For example, for the conscientious nursery-school teacher the rigors of winter are stupefying. From the first frost to the first robin the kids come to school accoutred in a collection of boots, galoshes, snowpants, leggings, storm coats, parkas and ponchos fit for, at the very least, an expedition to one of the poles. It is practically impossible for one teacher to get twenty or so four-year-olds out of and back into the correct clothes. It's a brute of a job for two or three teachers.

Much more difficult to assess than the quantity of supervision at a nursery school is the quality. You can find out about teacher *quantity* simply by asking, but it's not that easy to determine teacher *quality*. It's true that the school catalog provides a background on each member of the faculty—schooling, experience and so on—but unless you have an almost professional knowledge of the field such credentials won't tell you much. For example, the dossier on Miss Hilary Flute might read: "Miss Flute, who has taught our nursery class of four-year-olds for the past two years, comes to us from four years of teaching at the Beaver Valley Suburban Day School in Chillicothe, Ohio. She earned her degrees at Pestalozzi State Teachers' College." Chances are this history indicates eight to ten years of the soundest kind of training and experience, but, on the other hand, what's to prevent Pestalozzi State from having been a hotbed of wildly progressive educational theory and Beaver Valley Suburban Day from having been the kind of place where the teachers stand around discussing abnormal child psychology while the kiddies pistol whip each other with the six-shooters they brought in for "Show and Tell"? If the catalog poop sheet is only the sketchiest kind of guide (it *does* tell you if the ink is dry on the teachers' certificates), how *can* you tell about the teachers at a given school? You'll just have to patch together a working opinion from what you see at the school. You should, for instance, get a distinct impression that the teachers are in control of the children.

Seek First-Hand-Experience Recommendations from Parents You Know and Trust

When seeking good child care—or a good gynecologist, acupuncturist or divorce lawyer, for that matter—there is no substitute for the recommendations of fellow-sufferers who have been there. You can talk to people who have sent theirs to the particular school. It's one of those rare legitimate occasions for taking it upon yourself to bother perfect strangers. After this systematic program of spying, prying, probing and snooping, you should be able to come up with a reasonably well-informed guess as to which school your child should attend come next semester. An added advantage to planning things far in advance is that you'll have the whole summer to figure out how you're going to scrape up the tuition.

Does the Space and Operational Format of the Facility Allow for a Flexible, Interactive Schedule?

Day care works best when children are permitted to move in and out of various types of activities as their individual needs and attention spans require—perhaps quiet puzzle play for a while, then maybe a quick dip into the maelstrom of action play, then perhaps a little role-playing in Doll Corner.

Of course, there is a need for an overall schedule involving such events as opening class, mealtime, nap time, snack time, story hour, etc., but it is the substructure created by the individual child that gives that sense of autonomy that even the youngest toddler needs.

The Mayhem Factor

During your visit to a prospective day care center, make a rough count of cuts, bruises, black eyes and broken limbs in the school

population. If the count is impressive, ask questions. If answers are not forthcoming, or run to glib commentaries on the issue of over-protectiveness, be forewarned.

Not that a school population that looks like the Wild Bunch is *necessarily* disqualifying. If your youngster is of a type more likely to give than to receive, you may figure *c'est la guerre* and sign up.

Now that it's all settled, you can get down to the business of worrying about how your toddler is going to take to the whole idea. You can even lie awake a few nights as the first day of school approaches if you tend to do that sort of thing. But *don't*, by word, deed or facial expression, communicate your concern to your child. A four-year-old who is "ready" for school will take to it like the proverbial duck. The school will probably tell you how they want the first day "handled." With four-year-olds attending school for the first time, most schools like to have the parent come and stay until the child makes it clear that it's all right to go home. This knowledge is communicated in various ways. Your child may surprise you by sending you packing almost immediately with a big kiss good-bye and a "See you later!" But don't be disturbed if the child wants you to hang around for a while and seems to prefer a sub rosa departure with him or her looking the other way while you sneak out.

Occasionally a child who really is ready for nursery school will make more of a production of letting Mommy or Daddy go home than seems appropriate. We don't mean the pitiful ones who are palmed off onto the school by derelict parents. These children have a legitimate beef against school or any other medium of their parents' delinquency, and are going to show their resentment one way or another. We refer to the child, who for reasons probably not even the child knows, wants you to come to school the *second* day, too. Don't get panicky if your child is one of these. Play along for a while. When it turns out that you're the only parent still hanging around, your youngster is apt to realize how silly you look standing there and give you your walking papers. Probably your tot will ride a school bus, and it's a big help toward getting things off to a good start if you see to it that he or she rides the bus to school the first day. A nice ride on the school bus is the pleasantest kind of initiation into the group, and the sooner your child identifies with the class, the easier will be the transition to school life. However, you should be at the school to meet the bus.

If your child goes off to nursery school with a good guard up and comes home rent and spent, it shouldn't take you long to figure out that he is not "making out" at school. On the other hand, if he or

she zooms off each morning with the zest of a soldier of fortune taking off for a Central American revolution and returns with the air of conquering hero, it's a simple deduction that he or she is "making out" just fine. Chances are, however, that your child represents neither of these extremes but, instead, goes to school more or less willingly and returns more or less in one piece.

While you may be able to garner a few bare facts by point-blank questioning—"We play with blocks"; "One of the toilets is stopped up"; "The bus driver has a red hat"—you will probably find out little or nothing about how your adventurer is "making out." In fact, he or she may seem puzzled and resentful at all the questioning, and clam up completely. It's not surprising that a child should react this way. In the first place, for four years your tot has been building an image of you as a remarkable person—omnipotent, omnipresent and omniscient—and here you are twitching like an idiot, slavering over such irrelevancies as the color of the bus driver's hat. Another reason for resentment may be that your child very likely doesn't know *how* to tell you what happened at school today. The relating of one's experiences is a skill in which the average four-year-old has had little or no practice. The technique of getting a small child to "open up" involves three elements. The first, aimed at perpetuating the myth of your omniscience, calls for the use of simple guesswork. The next two, the Leading Question and the Loaded Question, are designed to overcome the witness's limited ability to tell you what you want to know. Do not, in the first instance, try to convince a child that you have full and complete knowledge of all school experiences; just try to give the idea that you have a pretty good idea of what goes on and that you need all this information merely to fill in the details and the proper names. You might begin by guessing the names of classmates. Simply by sticking to some such common names as John, James, William, Mary, Anne and so on, you're bound to come up with a few bull's-eyes—as many as five or six, with any luck at all. Since that's probably more than your child can remember, he or she will be impressed and pleased with your performance, and won't see any significance in the fact that you *didn't* guess Vernona, Charlene, Stephanie and Kevin. You don't have to stop with name guessing. You can press your advantage by coyly wagering, "I'll bet there's a girl in your class who cries a lot."

"Hey, there is! There really is! Her name is Patty."

"And I'll bet there's a class meanie, too."

"How did *you* know? That's mostly why Patty cries. Because Peter hits her with the xylophone stick."

"And a class comedian—you know, someone that's always doing silly stuff?"

"Yeah, that's Howard. He always pours a cup of water on peoples' heads when they're taking a nap at rest time."

Now you have enough bits and scraps of intelligence to piece together the kind of Leading and Loaded Questions which your four-year-old will be unable to resist answering.

"When Peter hits *you* with the xylophone stick, do *you* cry?"

"Course not! I bop him with my tambourine!"

"When Howard pours water on *your* head at rest time, does it wake you up?"

"Well, the first day it did, but not anymore, because now before rest time I get a mouthful of water and don't swallow it, and then when Howard comes around I squirt him. That's what *all* the kids do."

Try not to be alarmed at what you may find out goes on behind the dotted swiss curtain. The important thing is not that Rhythm

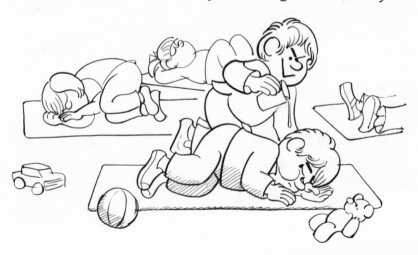

Class is really a "bop" session, or that rest time is actually a continual water fight. The important thing is that your child does seem to be "making out."

COMFY OBJECT AT 40 MONTHS

18

Reasonably Good Housekeeping

The child who is encouraged to enter the mainstream of family life has a much better chance of realizing his or her potential than one who is not. But isn't encouraging a normally obstreperous youngster to "enter the mainstream of family life" likely to result in spotted rugs, marked-up baseboards, marred table tops and broken crockery? The answer, of course, is yes. But rugs can be cleaned, baseboards repainted, table tops revarnished and crockery replaced, while the damage to a youngster as a result of being made to feel

like a second-class member of the household may be irreparable. Or, to put it another way, it's far better to fulfill your responsibilities as a parent and let the house go to pot a little than to "keep things nice" and let your kid go to pot a lot.

Your job, then, is to keep the family home in reasonably good order, convincing Junior all the while that it's *his* castle, too. Some suggestions on the subject are offered in the following five-year guide to reasonably good housekeeping.

THE FIRST YEAR: THE FLOOR'S THE THING

During the hands-and-knees period, a child is necessarily floored. It's a mistake to try to protect your floor by restricting crawling activities to a couple of stain-proof rooms like the nursery and the kitchen. Your offspring should be given pretty much the crawl of the house. It you have a rug or rugs you're going to make a big fuss about when the inevitable happens, either convince yourself that they're only rugs, or take them up for the duration. No rug is worth giving a kid a complex over. Generally speaking, though, it's not so much a question of protecting the floor from Baby as it is a question of protecting Baby from the floor.

Your little crawler will do well enough on wood floors provided you watch out for splinters. Rugs, of course, are great for crawling,

as are asphalt, linoleum and plastic tile. One type of floor covering that is notably unsuitable for crawling is rush matting. If you don't believe us, just bare your knees and try crawling around on some for a while yourself.

It need hardly be said that Baby should be kept away from wiring. It should also go without saying that your floor must be kept clean enough to eat off, for Baby undoubtedly will—anything he or she can lift.

THE SECOND YEAR: CLEARING THE DECKS

About now, things begin to get really interesting. Baby, age one, has begun to walk, and it's clear that you are going to have to make some changes. Quick, better get those plants off that low table! And that lamp, put it up on the bookcase! Hurry, the kid's going after the milk glass! . . . But hold on a minute. This is turning into a shut-the-door-they're-coming-in-the-window affair. The situation calls for something better in the way of a solution than racing Baby to the milk glass. It's time for something like an agonizing reappraisal.

Are you really sold on your present decor? Aren't you a little sick of Cozy Cottage Colonial? And don't you think those wonderfully stark Shaker rooms that appeared in Architectural Digest last month were stunning? Well, even if you don't think so, you're probably beginning to get the idea. With your toddler up and about, you're going to have to clear the decks for action. Pretend that simplicity is the thing this year. Sell yourself on stark. Look what the Japanese can do with a hunk of bamboo and a few sheets of rice paper. Pretty

soon you won't be able to stand your pepper-mill lamp with its chintz-ruffed gingham shade. Fie, you will say, on your butter-churn umbrella stand. Milk glass you will eschew. Now, hurry, before you lose your nerve; gather up all these precious items and put them in a safe place. Of course, it's all just a maneuver. Down deep you love all your Cozy Cottage Colonial things as dearly as ever. You needn't feel the least bit guilty about relegating them to the attic. It's just a temporary measure. Our plan calls for their gradual reintroduction into the decor a few months hence.

Not only will your child have calmed down considerably by then, but he or she will have had an opportunity to learn to put that newfound walking ability to all sorts of wonderful uses—operating the pull-toy duck that says *quack* and the push-toy hen that says *cluck,* carrying armloads of toys around the house, jumping off the rug onto the floor, and just plain strutting—in short, much too busy to notice that the pepper-mill lamp has been sneaked back onto the drum table and that the butter-churn umbrella stand once again occupies its proud position by the door. As for that milk glass, it's probably a good idea to let it collect dust in the attic a little longer.

THE THIRD YEAR: TOY TROUBLE,
OR STUMBLING BLOCKS

During the third year the problem of toys begins to assume major proportions. The basic difficulty is easily pinpointed. A two-and-a-half-year-old is much better adapted to the job of dumping the contents of the toy box than a thirty-two-and-a-half-year-old Mommy is to the job of gathering them up and jamming them back into it. Pinpointing the solution to the problem, however, is not quite so easy. Getting sore won't help. The only way a child can find the yellow space gun is to dump the toy box and kick around through the rubble until it turns up. You certainly wouldn't want him to jeopardize that tender little gun hand by putting it into the toy box! There's not much point in getting sore at Daddy either, even though hardly a week passes that he doesn't add to the confusion with some new product of the toymaker's art.

You may as well face it: the tremendous accumulation of toys that is proving so prejudicial to reasonably good housekeeping isn't anybody's fault. It is just another result of "progress." Progress, never a simple thing to deal with, is especially diabolic in this case. But one thing is obvious—you're going to have to do *something.*

A good first step is to get rid of that big catchall toy box. It may have been a good idea back in the days when the baby's toy collection consisted of a half-dozen cuddly animals and a few rattles. It was really very handy, in an emergency, to be able to grab everything up and stuff it into the capacious toy box before the company arrived. But those days are long gone. It's been a good year since that capacious toy box held even half of the toys, the remaining half having been seeking its own level in such places as the bottom of the closet and beneath the junior bed.

Having put the old toy box out to pasture and dragged everything out of the closet and out from under the bed, you are faced with quite a pile. (Perhaps the toy box can be put out to pasture quite literally. With a coat of outside enamel, it may be just dandy to stand beside the sandbox as a wintering place for sand toys.)

Your general objective should be to give everything a sort of place. We say "sort of place" because there is an astronomical

number of items to store, and a strictly limited number of places in which to store them. Even if you were to cram your child's entire wardrobe into one drawer, that would still give you just a half-dozen or so empty drawers. Now cram the entire wardrobe into one drawer. Next, break the toys into as many groupings as you have empty drawers. All plastic Indians, cowboys, horses, cows and so on might make up one group; blocks, logs, bricks and so on, another; everything with wheels, another; musical instruments, another; and so forth. But since toys don't classify as neatly as flora and fauna, you're bound to end up with some arbitrary combinations. Don't let that worry you. The wind-up toys won't mind doubling up with the puzzles, nor will the yo-yos object to being thrown in with the educational toys. Then assign each group to a drawer. Drawers, of course, are most practical for much of the stuff that has to be stored, but any odd nooks, niches or crannies you can make available will certainly be useful, too. They're fine for stuffed animals. Your youngster might, in fact, object strenuously if you were to try to shut up that great and good friend Monkey in some stuffy old drawer.

The next thing to tackle is getting your child into the habit of putting things away. The worst mistake you can make at this point is to approach the subject head on. It's not fair to expect a two-and-a-half-year-old to do the job out of a sense of responsibility. Your objective should be simply to get the child used to the activity of putting things away. One fine day, after the new system has been in effect long enough that the child has become thoroughly familiar with it, you suffer a simulated lapse of memory.

"My goodness," you allow in your best casual tone, "I forget where these blocks go . . ."

"In here!" your child shrieks gleefully, scooping them up and putting them in the proper drawer—delighted with being the authority on where things go. "Not in dere!" he or she screams happily when you make "a mistake" and put a rhinoceros in the block drawer.

"My goodness!" you say, "how can you remember where all these things go? Now let me see, where do these sailboats go?"

"Here! Let me put 'em. You'll put 'em all wrong."

When your tot tires of playing the expert, you can enlarge your program to include a series of races and contests. A three-year-old can get pretty excited over such challenges as, "Let's see who can put away more bricks," and, "Can you put away all your crayons by the time Mommy finishes vacuuming the hall?" And if you conduct these dodges artfully enough, your child won't know till it's too late that it was all part of a devilish plot to train him or her to pick up the mess.

THE FOURTH YEAR:
THE HANDWRITING ON THE WOODWORK

There are some things you've just got to accept. For example, you may as well just accept the fact that your offspring is going to knock over about as much milk as he or she swallows, and compose your notes to the milkman accordingly. There's no use making your three-to-four-year-old cry over spilt milk. Though a good cry after a particularly wet day in the milk shed may do *you* a world of good.

In some areas, you have a choice. The crumb question, for instance, can be answered either way. It follows as the morning after the night before that if your child is at liberty to munch anywhere there is going to be a trail of crumbs from basement to attic. You can diminish the problem by avoiding such crumbly stuff as short-bread cookies, providing instead some such close-knit between-meal fare as pretzels, but you're still going to have to keep the vacuum handy even so. On the other hand, you don't *have* to put up with the crumbs at all. You can simply lay down a rule that all eating is to take place at the table. Bear in mind, though, that you are in somewhat the same position as the character in the fairy tale who was granted a quota of three wishes. Similarly, three rules is approximately your quota, so you'd better make each one count. If "No eating away from the table" is the sort of rule you can really put your heart into, by all means adopt it. But if it does not strike a really responsive chord, skip it and save the slot for a more important prohibition.

There are some kinds of behavior, however, that are entirely unacceptable, and must be sternly dealt with. It is usually during the fourth year that most children try their little hands at impromptu mural decoration. When you first discover the handwriting on the woodwork, your impulse, quite naturally, is to find the culprit and whale away. But would the punishment fit the crime? A review of what probably happened may help you decide. Let's see, now. Little Angelica was watching "Captain Wallabey," and The Captain was explaining about rectangles. He showed how a rectangle was like a long square, and how you could draw a whole picture using just rectangles, with a rectangle house and a rectangle sun and rectangle tree. Pretty interesting stuff. But as he eases into the commercial: *"Oh,* look! What have we here! *Yes!* It's a box! A box of *Flakies*! And what *sha-ape* is the box? . . . That-a-at's right! It's a *rec-tangle . . ."* Little Angelica eases out from in front of the set and rolls over near the sofa. What's that under the sofa? A crayon. An *orange* crayon! She thinks that if she had a piece of paper she'd draw a rectangle. There's paper in her room. But the nice white baseboard is right there by the tip of the crayon, and if she moves the crayon just *that* much . . . What you have on your hands, it would seem, is not a "crime" at all, but a normal, experimentally minded three-and-a-half-year-old with a healthy resistance to sneaky commercials. But, you may protest, isn't a three-and-a-half-year-old *old* enough to know better than to write on the wood-

work? No, not at all. There are very few things in life that any of us "know" simply by virtue of having reached a certain age. The child is, however, old enough to be *taught* better than to write on the woodwork.

Of course, he or she has to learn that it's wrong to deface the household. But it's even more important that a child learn *why* it's wrong. If you can begin to give a real understanding of what it means to be a member of the household, the life expectancy of the old homestead may be appreciably extended. You can't expect to get very far toward accomplishing this goal unless you address your little miscreant in terms he or she can understand.

Parents have often been warned not to "talk down" to their child. Presenting new ideas in terms a child is most likely to understand is not "talking down." It's just common sense. An utterly irrelevant explanation of why it's not a good idea to write on the woodwork in terms of how hard all those nice builders had to work to build our nice house for us is likely to mean a lot more to a child than an utterly relevant one on the same subject in terms of how hard *Daddy* had to work to make enough money to *pay* all those nice builders. An explanation in terms of some immediate experience is likely to be especially effective. "Remember a couple of days ago when we painted your steam shovel and dump truck?" He nods enthusiastically. "Well, suppose somebody came along and put crayon marks all over the nice new paint. How would you like that?"

He glowers ferociously. "I'd sock him!" he states with heat.

"Well, you might not. You might just want to explain to him that you're not supposed to write on toys. And then he'd want to help you clean them up!"

"I'd get a big stick and sock him over the head!"

"Now, here's some cleanser, and here's a rag for you and a rag for me."

"I'd—I'd push him in the mud!"

"There! That's fine! Now it's all bright and clean again. Say, where are you going?"

"I gotta go out and look at my steam shovel and dump truck."

THE FIFTH YEAR: THE BIG PICKUP

Baby has finally made kindergarten, and you have your long-awaited opportunity for a really full-dress expedition into the breeding ground of most of your housekeeping troubles—Baby's bedroom. Up to now you have been restricted to the risky business of a commando raid every now and then—a quick dash into the room while your tot was out bike riding, an armful of tangled toys grabbed from under the bed, and a quick dash to the cellar, where they were thrust into the utility closet with the booty of previous raids. You recall with a chill that dreadful time he or she came home unexpectedly from Debby's and caught you red-handed. But you're through with all that. The kid's a mile away at kindergarten, and won't be home till the school bus arrives.

As you stand there with your mop and your broom and your big wire trash burner, looking slowly around your child's room, you feel, for a minute, as Pip in *Great Expectations* must have felt when he first entered Miss Havisham's sitting room. An icy draft of panic stabs through you. You want to run. We'll board it up, you think wildly, and start over from scratch in the guest room! But the awful

feeling passes and you come to your senses. It's not so bad, you think, recalling that you've already made a start. The many and varied collections were prime difficulties, and some weeks ago you convinced your offspring that the professional thing to do was to *catalog* them. With your help the stone collection, the feather collection, the bottle-top collection, the tooth collection, shell collection, Dixie-lid collection and *all* the other collections were transferred from the ragtag assortment of boxes which had housed them to a set of kitchen cannisters which you contributed to the project. You think with a sense of profound relief that never again will you wonder what's in that old Whitman's Sampler box, and idly lift the lid to find six grubby, grisly cicada shells staring eyelessly up at you.

When attacking a problem as far gone as a child's room, it's important to treat the causes rather than symptoms. The dust, the

cobwebs and the general disorder are all symptoms. The cause of the trouble is that there is just about twice as much stuff in the room as there should be. The solution is plain. Half the stuff must go. But eliminating half of your child's goods willy-nilly is certainly not the answer. The trick is to perform the feat in such a way that the child never feels victimized. This is not the impossible stunt it may seem. The secret to bringing it off is the fact that a child hardly, if ever, uses half the things in the room. It is simply a matter, then, of clearing out the half that is hardly, if ever, used. There are three techniques which are basic to the task. These are Thinning, Platooning and Stashing.

"Thinning" involves the permanent withdrawal of an item from circulation. This has nothing to do with the elimination of broken toys, torn books and the like, but refers specifically to items that are as good as the day they were received from Uncle Ned, Aunt Ellen and Cousin John. Generally speaking, toys that are considered more trouble than they are worth are good candidates for thinning.

After double-checking to see that you have not thinned anything that the youngster is likely to miss, stow your haul in the top of the storage closet. Next to the tree lights is a good place. Then it will

automatically turn up when you need presents for Uncle Ned's, Aunt Ellen's and Cousin John's kids.

"Platooning" is the short-term withdrawal of groups of toys on a circulating basis. For example, your child has about seven dozen records in the collection. Since he or she is interested in only about a dozen at a time, you may as well get the remaining six dozen out of the way. As the records in play begin to tire, they can be taken out and a fresh platoon sent in.

In addition to being useful in cleaning out the room, platooning is helpful in other ways. It is a great help, in times of crisis—during a seige of measles, for example—to be able to trot out great numbers of toys which your child has all but forgotten. Almost any type of toy can be platooned. It's just a question of what you can get away with.

"Stashing" involves the storing of items that are unsuitable, owing to your tot's tender age, until he or she is old enough at least to read the directions.

Gigantic construction kits containing everything you need to make an authentic scale model of the *U.S.S. Missouri* are eminently stash-able. So are magic sets, puzzle sets, electrical toys, microscope outfits, chemistry sets and giant 1,000-piece fun-for-the-whole-family jigsaw puzzles. The duration of the stashing period varies with the item. The Mighty Mo construction kit can be brought out just as soon as Junior is old enough to understand that it must not be taken into the tub when Daddy finally gets it finished, while that 1,000-piece jigsaw puzzle, on the other hand, should be stashed practically indefinitely.

But you can't expect to bring order out of chaos in one morning. You'd better start tapering off; that school bus will be pulling up at any minute now.

RECORDS

NATAL AND POSTNATAL DATA

Method of conveyance to hospital _____

If cab, describe circumstances (how long it took to arrive, cab driver's conversation, etc.) _____
_____

If auto, describe circumstances (how many test runs hubby made, what difficulties starting, how many wrong turns) _____
_____

Where was obstetrician at time of delivery?
(check one):

      Florida   Mexico   Lake Placid
      Gaspé   Paris   The 19th Hole

Did obstetrician's substitute make it to hospital in time? _____

Weight gain during pregnancy _____
Birthweight of baby _____
Cost of new wardrobe _____

Amount of hospital and obstetrical bills _____
(Divide by birthweight to determine cost per pound _____)

Write brief account of delivery experience _____
_____
_____

(attach additional sheets if necessary)

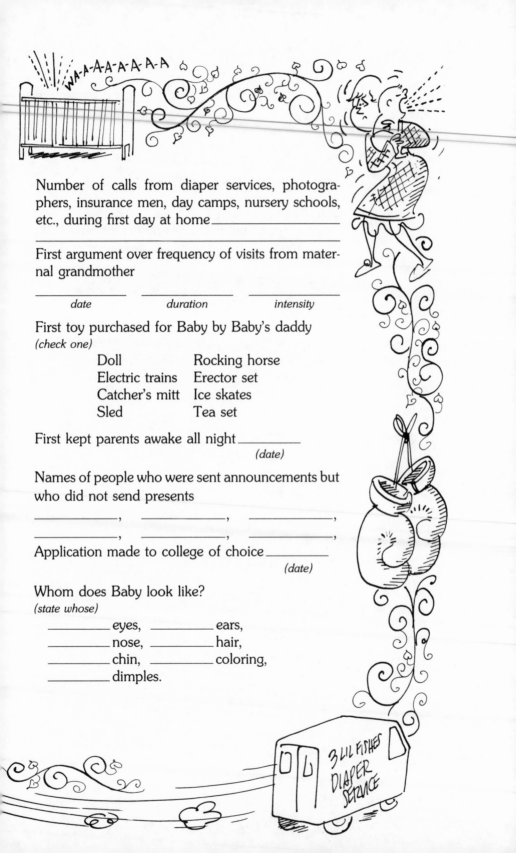

Number of calls from diaper services, photographers, insurance men, day camps, nursery schools, etc., during first day at home_____

_____

First argument over frequency of visits from maternal grandmother

_____   _____   _____
   date   *duration*   *intensity*

First toy purchased for Baby by Baby's daddy
(check one)

Doll	Rocking horse
Electric trains	Erector set
Catcher's mitt	Ice skates
Sled	Tea set

First kept parents awake all night_____
                                    (date)

Names of people who were sent announcements but who did not send presents

_____, _____, _____,

_____, _____, _____,

Application made to college of choice_____
                                      (date)

Whom does Baby look like?
(state whose)

_____ eyes, _____ ears,
_____ nose, _____ hair,
_____ chin, _____ coloring,
_____ dimples.

FIRST EIGHTEEN MONTHS

Baby began to crawl at _____ months.
Describe crawling method (standard crawl, belly drag, crab crawl or other) _____

Baby's special tastes in food (check as many as you like)

Thousand-leggers	Burnt	Rubber bands
Wood shavings	matches	Cigarette butts
Parakeet	Dust devils	Philodendron
feathers	Dog hair	shoots

Baby began to walk at _____ months.
Describe mode of walking (waddle, strut, lurch, ramble, amble, clamber, saunter or other) _____

Was administered first spanking at _____ months.

First disappeared from yard at _____ months.
Was missing for _____ hours _____ minutes.
Was found in own home under _____ bed.
                                    (state whose)

Found by _____
                (if police, give badge number)

Smashed first priceless heirloom at _____ months.

Diaper service discontinued at _____ months.

Was administered second spanking at _____ months.

Diaper service resumed at _____ months.

First locked self in bathroom at _____ months. How freed (emergency squad, door removed from hinges, unlocked door himself or other) _____

Number of snapshots taken of Baby first six months *(circle nearest approximate figure)*
100   200   300   400   500   1,000   2,000

Number of snapshots taken of Baby second six months *(circle nearest approximate figure)*
16   13   7   3   0

Brought home first dead animal at _____ months.

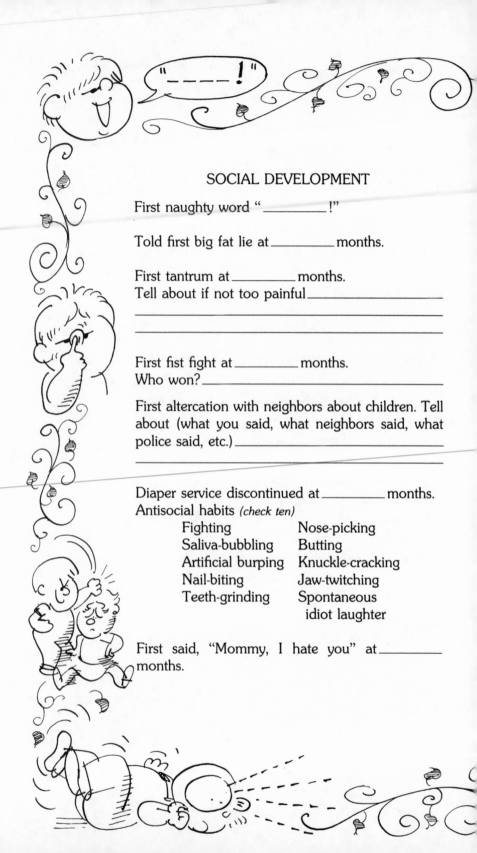

SOCIAL DEVELOPMENT

First naughty word "_____!"

Told first big fat lie at _____ months.

First tantrum at _____ months.
Tell about if not too painful _____
_____
_____

First fist fight at _____ months.
Who won? _____

First altercation with neighbors about children. Tell about (what you said, what neighbors said, what police said, etc.) _____
_____

Diaper service discontinued at _____ months.
Antisocial habits *(check ten)*

Fighting	Nose-picking
Saliva-bubbling	Butting
Artificial burping	Knuckle-cracking
Nail-biting	Jaw-twitching
Teeth-grinding	Spontaneous idiot laughter

First said, "Mommy, I hate you" at _____ months.

Punched first sitter at _____ months.

Diaper service resumed at _____ months.

First birthday party
(circle word or phrase that most nearly characterizes party)

        Fiasco   Total failure
        Never again Calamity
        Washout   Nobody was
        Holocaust   actually killed
        Disaster

First said, "Hello, stupid" to perfect stranger at _____ _____ months.

Favorite insults

_____, _____, _____,
_____, _____, _____,

First cheated at a game at _____ months.

Brought home first awful joke at _____ months.
Give tag line_____

Decided that "BM" was the funniest word in the language at _____ months.